CW00369515

THE EMBALMER'S BOOK OF RECIPES

ANN LINGARD

Tom — with best wishes

Ann

December 2008.

Indepenpress

Copyright © Ann Lingard 2009

All rights reserved

No part of this publication may be reproduced,
stored in a retrieval system, or transmitted
in any form or by any means, without
the prior permission in writing of the publisher,
nor be otherwise circulated in any form of binding or cover
other than that in which it is published and without a similar
condition including this condition being imposed on the
subsequent purchaser.

First published in Great Britain by Indepenpress

ISBN 978-1-906710-17-0

Printed and bound in the UK
by Cpod Trowbridge, Wiltshire.

Indepenpress Publishing Ltd
25 Eastern Place
Brighton
BN2 1GJ

A catalogue record of this book is available from
the British Library

Cover design by Jacqueline Abromeit

Artificial eye, photographed
by Rosamond Wolff Purcell:
from *Finders, Keepers* (1992) – see Acknowledgements.

About the Author

Formerly a scientist living and working in Glasgow, Ann Lingard changed career to become a writer and broadcaster. She and her husband now run a their own company, Plumbland Consulting, from their small-holding in Cumbria. As well as writing fiction and non-fiction, Ann works to bring scientists, writers and artists together – she is also the founder of *SciTalk*, www.scitalk.org.uk, the free resource for fiction-writers.

Her works of fiction include:

Figure in a Landscape
The Fiddler's Leg
Floating Stones
Seaside Pleasures

Further information can be found on her websites, www.annlingard.com
and www.plumblandconsulting.co.uk

What they said about *Seaside Pleasures*:

'A very fine piece of writing that, uniquely among modern novels, makes real use of science rather than wearing science on its sleeve ... a true two-culture achievement.'

Matt Ridley

'Immensely readable and extremely clever, *Seaside Pleasures* is a remarkable novel... the blend of past and present, fact and fiction is both curious and compelling.'

Ann Thwaite

'A clever balance ... that blurs the boundaries between fact and fiction.'

Oxford Times

'A big book with a MIND behind it.'   Jane Gardam

'Ann Lingard has written a thoughtful, compelling story ... a very human account. The book is a rockpool in itself, concealing seaside secrets as well as pleasures deep beneath the surface.'

North Devon Journal

See www.annlingard.com

ACKNOWLEDGMENTS

There were many photographs, paintings and specimens which inspired me during the course of researching and writing this book: images and videos of several of them can be seen on my website, www.annlingard.com — and I am very grateful to the people and organisations who so generously granted me permission to use them.

The Wellcome Trust kindly awarded me a History of Medicine grant to allow me to research the paintings and works of the Dutch anatomists in Amsterdam and Leiden, the Hunter collections in London and Glasgow, and the writings of Ruysch and others in the Bodleian Library, Oxford, and the Wellcome History of Medicine Library in London.

I am also extremely grateful
to Dr Wil van der Knaap, friend and former colleague, and a wise and funny adviser, chauffeur, guide and interpreter during my trip to the Netherlands; to taxidermists Dick Hendry, formerly of XZ Resources, Glasgow, for very helpful discussions and providing a fund of ideas, and George Jamieson, at Cramond Tower, Edinburgh, and Clive Scott in Hawick, for allowing me to watch them at work and wander around their workshops, and for their tolerance, good humour and readiness to pass on information and anecdotes in response to my questions - I take full responsibility for any errors about the practice of taxidermy; to Adam Day, auctioneer at Mitchell's mart in Cockermouth, who was deeply involved in the 2001 foot-and-mouth crisis in Cumbria - I have drawn heavily on his moving and horrific diary of that time, *To Bid Them Farewell*

(2004, Hayloft Press) and any errors I have made about sheep husbandry are entirely mine; to Professor Emerita, Dr Antonie Luyendijk-Elshout, for her kind and informative letters and for sending me reprints of her own scholarly work on Frederik Ruysch; to Professor Hal Cook, Director of the Wellcome Trust Centre for the History of Medicine, University College London, for sending me a draft of a chapter (*Time's Bodies: crafting the preparation and preservation of naturalia'*, now published in his book *Matters of Exchange* – see Bibliography) and for generously allowing me to quote de Bils' embalming recipe in Chapter 16; to Professor Ian Stewart at Warwick University for suggesting that 'my mathematician' should work on quasicrystals, and for sending me a 'simple' guide to the topic; and to Dr Uwe Grimm at the Open University for his interest, and for sorting me out with titles and themes and background on the applications of quasicrystal research; to Dr Ian Porteous of the Department of Mathematical Science, University of Liverpool, for showing me around the department and giving me some ideas on 'what mathematicians talk about'; and to Dr Simon Rutherford, for coming up with the name 'Octocalliope' in the course of discussions about the materials from which the artwork should be made.

Ian Stewart and Simon Rutherford are both Contributors to the national resource for fiction-writers, *SciTalk*, www.scitalk.org.uk .

My thanks, too, to Rachel Lackie for dreaming up the name for Louisa Mason's terrier.

Finally, I am deeply indebted to friend and former colleague Dr Tom Shakespeare, for not being scathing when I explained I wanted to write about an achondroplasic, and for reading a draft manuscript – and for putting me in touch with Sandy Marshall, formerly of the Restricted Growth Association, and Jo Hookway (whose father, I was later delighted to discover, was a well-known mathematical physicist) and Margaret Milne. Both Jo and Margaret welcomed me into their homes and were open and straightforward in talking about achondroplasia, and Jo also read and commented on the draft manuscript. I cannot thank them sufficiently.

ONE

John tugged at his eyebrow and his large, square face crumpled in concentration. He held the telephone tightly against his ear, and nodded as he listened.

'Aye. Aye… Fluke's bad round here, right enough. Aye. It's a wet land, that's for sure, it disnae drain well.'

He glanced at Madeleine and, seeing that she was listening, looked quickly away.

'Aye… That would be fine. Next Tuesday then. Aye. You'll come to the house, I'll be waiting for you.' It was a statement, and he replaced the telephone in its cradle on the wall.

Someone was coming to the farmhouse. She waited for him to tell her; he still spoke to her, she supposed from habit.

He was a big man, in his mid-thirties, but as he stood awkwardly in the doorway, she wondered how she had missed noticing that he had grown haggard, and she felt helpless because there was nothing she could do.

'Some doctor, from the university. Says she's doing a survey—'

'*She?*'

'Aye. A lady doctor. She's doing a survey or something into liver-fluke, she wants to come and look for herself. She's after getting the snails.'

He had been going into the scullery to put on his boots when the telephone rang, and he stood there in his socks; there was a hole in the toe and she could see the yellowed rind of his toenail.

It reminded her: 'Is your thumb still sore?'

1

He blinked and was still for a moment, then he looked at his left thumb, and held it out towards her. The nail was black and purple, the skin around it suffused and straining, taut with the pressure.

'Aye, my thumb is still sore,' he said gently.

She reached out and touched it, the rough, hardened skin, but he withdrew his hand and she saw how his face went blank as though he was drawing a shutter down.

'A doctor coming,' Madeleine said. 'Next week. I'd better start and make the house nice, then.'

'Aye.'

After John had gone out into the yard Madeleine stood by the sink, staring out of the window. The white cockerel was courting the hens, and Madeleine laughed to herself at his ridiculous side-stepping, and the way he dragged his wing, trailing a cloak for his queen of the moment. Why did he think that made him seem desirable? The hen ignored him, staring dreamily into the distance as she scratched the ground, then stepped back a pace or two to interrogate her scratchmarks.

The petals of the African violet on the windowsill were velvet-blue, and Madeleine lifted the pot and tenderly plucked off a discoloured leaf. Condensation from shirts drying on the pulley had pooled at the bottom of the window and mould had scribbled the hems of the orange curtains. The kitchen was warm and humid, 'like the rainforest', Madeleine imagined to herself (was that where African violets grew?); but the world outside lacked warmth or colour and the wind's pale blade sliced the grey air.

The air, or perhaps it was the ground, pulsed with the revving of the tractor as John shunted it to and fro in the yard. She wondered what he was doing, then remembered that he had mentioned something about pallets, stacking pallets, and although she could only see the top of the red cab above the drystone wall, she imagined the prongs of the forklift, spearing the wooden trays exactly between their bars, carrying them like plates of vol-au-vents extended to guests at a Christmas party.

Her attention was caught by something that flickered in the wall and she re-focussed her eyes, hoping for a recurrence and that it was no illusion but was real. Years ago the flickering had begun: tiny rectangles and triangles, ever-shifting patterns of black and white at the periphery of her vision, a kaleidoscope without colour that gradually encroached, creeping inwards until the real world was obliterated for an hour by a changing world of her mind's own making. Ten, twelve years ago, a time when she had been unafraid to visit a doctor: 'Visual migraine', he had pronounced and, in naming it, had dispelled her fear of the unknown. 'Nothing you can do about it, it'll come and go.'

But this time the flickering had been a mouse. It reappeared, running delicately between the stones like a child gymnast upon the *barre*; stopped to sniff the air, nose pointing, tail curled across faded yellow lichen, then disappeared as quickly as it had come.

'Maddie! Mad!'

John stood by the side-gate, waving to attract her attention. He had put on his old green overalls as a concession to the cold, but the top buttons were undone as though to point out that this was not mid-winter, merely an unseasonal spell of cold in April. 'Blackthorn winter,' he called it.

Madeleine opened the back door.

'Maddie, can you come and give a hand?'

She looked back into the kitchen, undecided, not wanting to leave the security of the house.

'Please, Maddie – it's the lambs.'

Whenever he spoke to her his voice was calm and reasonable: she loved his voice, she wanted to catch his words and clutch them to her. But now there was a sharpness to it and she glanced at him quickly.

'They'll die if we don't do something.'

The roughness of his fear and sadness frightened her, and she nodded.

'I'll get my coat.'

He needed her to help him, to carry bales. They built small shelters of pallets and straw, in the open barn, in corners of the yard, and even in the garden. Madeleine's frozen fingers were nipped by baler twine as she carried the rustling straw and her old tartan coat bristled with the hollow stalks but she helped, uncomplaining and frightened by John's haste.

The blackthorn hedges bore white flowers, a smirr of snowflakes on black pencilled twigs, but up in the field there was no colour except shades of grey, the sky merging with the sodden land. Her slithering footsteps left muddy trails, and lambs lay huddled and quiet while their mothers nosed at the scanty grass and the biting wind scoured the landscape.

The ewes cantered for the open gate, their fleeces juddering, and lambs panicked bleating after them so that the lane to the farm was filled with the roaring of sheep, and they packed the yard with a panting, steaming mass of uncertainty. It took Madeleine and John more than an hour to sort them out and reunite lambs separated from their mothers, and soon the barn and every shelter was full. Then there was water to be carried, and troughs to be moved, while the wind drove stinging sleet into every corner.

John brought her an armful of packed-tight hay.

'You take this to the ones in the garden,' he said, and Madeleine knew he didn't want her to see how little hay remained in the barn.

The grass was not growing and soon the hay would run out, the silage was gone and the feed bills had been unpaid so long that there could be no more credit. The ewes were undernourished, and orphan lambs lay down and did not rise again, but died because there was no milk-powder. Madeleine carried the hay to the ewe and wished she could take the twin lambs inside into the rainforest warmth of the kitchen, away from this unforgiving Ayrshire landscape.

But they still had eggs. When John came in for his tea she fried eggs and bread on the Aga, turning her head to feel the comforting heat on the left side of her face, and watching surreptitiously as he washed and dried his hands.

'If only the sun would shine…' she said.

'It will take more than that.'

His hair was thick and fair, and the stubble on his chin glinted gold. She liked that, and would also have liked him to grow a beard, but she didn't tell him so. There was no longer a mirror in the bathroom, because one day a few years ago she had unscrewed it from the wall and taken it down, later telling him that it had broken. He had nodded and after that he had shaved by feel, but more recently he had often allowed the stubble to grow for two or three days.

She pushed aside the unpaid bills and uncompleted forms that littered the table, and sat down opposite him.

'What shall we do?' she asked, feeling the hopelessness begin to rise inside her again.

'We'll manage somehow, don't be afraid, Maddie. Perhaps the doctor from the university will pay us, perhaps we can charge her for gathering the snails.'

'Tenpence each. We'll make our fortunes.' She laughed bitterly and, resisting the urge to pluck at her face, knowing how it disturbed and perhaps revolted her husband, shifted on the chair to sit on her hands, leaving her food untouched.

'We should sell up.'

'Don't talk like that, Mad, you know it's no use. Where would we go? What would we live on? The ewes'll get by somehow, we'll all get by.'

'You'd be better off without me, you'd find something if you were on your own.' In her squirming agitation, her hand was released and of its own accord it leapt to the corner of her mouth and began pulling and massaging the growth.

The look he gave her was such a mixture of despair and alienation that she couldn't stay any longer at the table, but jumped up and ran to the door (uncaring that her knife clattered to the floor and that she had trampled the fallen teatowel) and escaped to the safety of the chair in the dimmest corner of the sitting-room.

And so began another of those phases of dark hopelessness when day and night were scarcely distinguishable and she longed even for the precise definitions of a visual migraine to impose some certainty upon disorder. She was barely aware that John came and went, occasionally bringing her a mug of tea, coming and going through the house. When she wondered, she assumed he was with the sheep, out on the farm; once or twice, smelling hot fat, she thought he might be cooking.

Then there was a time when he stood before her and said, '*Maddie.*'

She raised her head, but didn't meet his eyes.

'Maddie, please. The lady doctor is coming this morning.'

'A doctor?' She was confused. 'But I don't need a doctor.'

'The university doctor – the liver-fluke woman. Do you think you can tidy yourself – will you tidy the kitchen? She may want a mug of tea.'

'I don't want to see her.'

'No.' He was trying to be gentle with her. 'No, you don't have to see her if you don't want. But the place looks bad, it needs tidied. Please, Maddie, we must make a good impression, it may be she can help.'

Gradually his words penetrated the fog that was in her brain, and began to make sense, and after some time she pushed herself out of the chair, feeling the aching stiffness in her legs. What could the snail woman do? Madeleine couldn't even begin to puzzle out an answer, but washed herself and changed her clothes, and then she set to in the kitchen. It was still early, barely seven o'clock; the gate and wall were rimed with frost and above the hill the sky was a cold, pale blue. Lambs bleated, and the ewe in the garden shelter stood up and stamped her foot as the black-and-white farm cat approached too close.

The African violet was limp from neglect and Madeleine gently dripped water onto the soil beneath its leaves, then began to wash the accumulated mugs and dirty dishes and the frying pan that was opaque with congealed fat. In a haze of incomprehension she put away cutlery, and swept mud-flakes, sinuous as flattened snakes, from the brown lino. She made a neat pile of the unopened envelopes and bills, and squared the short row of cookbooks and manuals on the dresser.

Soon a red car drew up to the gate and John came out from the yard; he was wearing his old tweed jacket over a patterned pullover and, courtly, he held the car door open for the driver. The woman had short brown hair, and was sensibly dressed in waterproof jacket, jeans and boots. She shook hands, and Madeleine watched as she introduced John to a sulky-looking girl in her twenties who came round from the passenger side. The girl had dark wavy hair that was escaping from a shapeless black woollen hat, and she didn't smile; but the woman had a pleasant face.

In sudden panic Madeleine filled the kettle and placed it on the hob: the teapot and cups and milk were already waiting on the table. She snatched another quick glance out of the window, ready to flee into the bedroom, but the snail collectors had picked up their rucksacks and John was starting to lead them off along the lane. The snail-doctor stopped briefly and looked back, staring at the kitchen window as though she sensed Madeleine's watching presence. She waved then turned away.

For a long while Madeleine stood irresolutely by the sink, gazing out unseeingly at the world. Then, after warming her red tartan jacket and old grey socks on the battered chrome hob-cover, she pulled on her boots and went outside. Although the air in the valley was frigid and still, the sun was already starting to touch the top of the field behind the farm, and the high pasture glowed startlingly green. The ewe in the strawbale shelter snickered softly to her lambs and they ran to her, butting her udder with their heads so that her rump lifted in the air; the shelter and scanty hay were caked with their droppings.

Madeleine untied the wooden pallets and dragged them apart.

'Come on,' she said. 'Come with me.'

With a long stick in her hand she slowly walked the ewe and her offspring out of the garden, and along the lane. She didn't hurry, merely allowed the ewe to feel the pressure of her presence, so that the sheep zigzagged calmly in front of her, the lambs jostling and darting at their mother's flanks. She moved so slowly that the ewe waited patiently in the lane while she opened the field gate.

'In you go,' she said, and was sure she felt the ewe's profound sense of liberation as it galloped off across the frosted grass then stopped to graze.

Liquid notes poured earthwards from an unseen lark, and Madeleine leaned on the gate, squinting at the sky, her mind emptied.

Some time later she heard quiet voices and, unobtrusive as a shy vixen, she slid into the field and behind the hedge. There was a strange pleading note in John's voice and with a dull shock she realised he must be speaking about her.

'If you could just look at her, doctor... I don't know any more what to do.'

'Mr Tregwithen, I'm not that sort of a doctor, I'm not a medical doctor.'

'She's just lost heart. The hopelessness has infected her, and made her ill.'

'Perhaps then it's in her mind.' The woman's voice was gentle. Madeleine wondered whether the sulky girl was listening too.

'No, no! There's nothing wrong with her mind, she's not mad. You'll see it for yourself, if she'll let you look at her.'

Their voices were closer, the other side of the hedge, and Madeleine pressed against the vegetation, hiding yet wanting to observe the speakers too.

The woman was walking next to John, looking at the ground as she spoke, but when she drew level with Madeleine's hiding place, she paused and looked up. Her eyes met Madeleine's through the hedge and she seemed completely unsurprised.

'I think your wife is just here,' she said to John. 'Hallo, Mrs Tregwithen.'

'*Maddie*? Mad?'

The girl, hearing his words, laughed a sudden high-pitched sound.

'Is that you? What are you doing there?' John hurried to the gate.

'I brought the ewe.'

She stood away from the hedge and saw how the visitors stared at her, how the doctor's face froze before she glanced away, and how the girl stared unashamedly.

'Did you find the snails?'

Madeleine was calm. She had not looked at her own face for a very long time, but she could imagine what they saw: the growth at the corner of her mouth, like the gnarled bark formed by a tree around an alien wire; a crumpled lava-flow, petrified, but not grey – the colour of damsons, of thickened jam brought to a rolling boil.

'No, your husband was just showing us where to look, we're going back to fetch the collecting equipment.'

Maddie looked away, towards the steeply-sloping field, and saw that sunlight was sweeping down across the land. Silver-tipped leaves darkened, and began to drip gold droplets; scarlet fire hung shimmering from thorns; the sunlit grass glistened with moisture and the lambs skipped across silver shadows cast by trees. The hedgerows steamed.

Suddenly the girl laughed again, and pointed.

'Look at the sparrows!'

Madeleine looked, and saw two sparrows arguing on a branch; steam drifted upwards around them but they were oblivious, quarrelling and shouting with fluttering wings.

'It's a sparrow sauna,' the girl said, with a sly glance.

Madeleine noticed how the doctor glanced again at her face with compassion in her eyes, but she didn't care.

Steam almost hid the sparrows from view, and she began to laugh.

'A sparrow sauna. Yes!'

She caught the girl's eye, and they began to giggle together helplessly, at the absurdity of everything, and when she looked at John, his face so shone with hope that she was dazzled and had to look away.

Two

Lisa held her breath and tried to hear whether Suzanna was still in the room. She was sure her sister would be sitting on the bed, waiting for her to cry or scream.

'Suzie?'

There was no sound.

'Suzie. Let me out.'

She managed to turn her head so that her mouth was near the faint line of light along the edge of the lid. Suzie had said she was not to call out, so she tried to speak softly.

'Suzie, let me out, I want to do a wee-wee.'

Silence.

'I need a poo. I'll do a poo in my knickers. I want to get *out*.'

Silence.

The trunk smelt of Lego blocks and wooden jigsaws. Mummy said the trunk had belonged to Grandpa when he was in the war. It was made of wood with bent wooden bands that held it all together, and there were two big brass locks that you had to push into holes and you opened them by pushing round knobs with keyholes in them, but that was very hard. The trunk was covered in cloth that was falling apart, you could scratch at a corner and pull the threads. Mummy said the cloth had been green because Grandpa was in the army and that was the colour of the army, but she had painted it blue to go in Suzie's and Lisa's bedroom. There were blue covers with red and yellow hearts on their beds and the trunk was the same colour. Hearts were red because there was red blood in them and Suzie had told her the yellow hearts were the ones that had wee inside. When you drank your juice it turned into wee and went into the yellow heart. When you ate your food it turned into poo and there was a big brown heart inside you too. Wee was all right but the poo-heart was horrible and smelly.

Lisa's hands were clasped against her chest because Suzanna had told her to lie on her side but she could still move them, and she wriggled to get more comfortable then felt around the head-end of the trunk to check if Suzie had left any of the toys inside. She touched a piece of paper in one corner. It was part of the lining of the trunk and she pulled it so that a little piece came away. She brought it near to her face and it smelt dry and powdery; it was a comforting smell and she rubbed the paper against her cheek.

Suzie had said she was going to go away and use the telephone. Lisa said she didn't know who to phone, but Suzie said yes, she did, and anyway she could read and she could look up the number in the big yellow book. But Lisa thought she was still in the bedroom, just keeping quiet. Perhaps she was lying on her bed reading. *Or perhaps she's looking in my cupboard and playing with my secrets?* – the tiny red-and-green plastic car found in the park, the shell that Ben at playgroup had given her and said it was made of pearl.

'Suzie?'

Still no reply.

She'd liked Ben and wished he was in her class at school but he had gone to a different school. Granny had said Ben was a mongol and she was sorry for his mum because he'd be nothing but trouble, thank goodness at least Lisa wasn't like that. Lisa didn't know why Granny said that, because Ben was nice and smiley. Judy's daddy came to school every day and he brought their dog, a big brown and black dog with floppy ears, and when Mummy had asked what sort of dog, he had said it was a mongol and something about Heinz tomato soup.

Lisa didn't much like the dog, it was too big and not at all smiley. Not like Little Puppy who lay on her pillow, who was red and cuddly and had a black woolly nose and smile. She wished Little Puppy was in here with her.

'Removals,' Suzie had said. 'I'll look up removals. There are lots and lots of them, and the men come and take things away in a big lorry if you ask them to.'

Suzie was not very nice to her a lot of the time. When Suzie's friends came round to play, she made Lisa go away into the kitchen, or if Mummy was down in the shop, she sometimes made such a fuss that Mummy had to keep Lisa with her. But Lisa liked the shop, it wasn't too busy and people didn't tread on her, and it smelt nice. Sally, who helped Mummy in the shop, gave her little broken bits of flowers, and the pretty paper and bits of ribbon, so she could make her own posies. One time she asked a lady if she would buy the posy she had made, and the lady laughed and took it and gave her 20p.

'You're training her early, then,' she'd said to Mummy, but Mummy went a bit red and said, 'Oh no, she wants to go to college and be a teacher like her Dad, don't you, love?' And Lisa had said yes because it would make Mummy happy and it would be nice to be a teacher and know a lot. But she wasn't sure she wanted to do what Daddy did. Most of all she'd like to be famous and important so that Suzie would be proud of her and would say, 'You know Lisa Wallace that was on TV last night? She's my sister and she's really famous and very rich.'

It was getting warm in the trunk and Lisa began to feel a little bit afraid. What was that noise? There was something rustling. Her feet didn't reach the end of the trunk and suddenly she was sure that there was something in there with her. Should she try to feel it with her toes? No, what if it moved? It might try to run up her legs. It might bite her. No, there was nothing there, it couldn't have got in, there wasn't a hole. It might have squeezed in through the crack where the lid came down. It could change its shape, go all flat and creep in then make itself into a furry ball and run around.

'*Go away*!' She lashed out with her foot but she didn't hit it, it was hiding in a corner. She felt very hot. For a moment she couldn't breathe, she was panting.

She couldn't help it. She shrieked. 'Suzie! Let me out, it's trying to eat me!'

If Suzie had phoned the removal men perhaps they would just be coming to the door, and Mummy would see them and want to know why they were there. They'd come upstairs and Mummy would let her out and say there had been a mistake.

'Mummy!' she cried out, no longer frightened what Suzie would say. Suzie wasn't there. 'Mummy, Mummy!'

But what if Mummy wanted them to take her away, too? What if she thought it was a clever idea of Suzie's?

There'd been that time when her back had hurt and Mummy and Daddy had taken her to the doctor, and they'd all looked at her back and talked about her as though she wasn't there. Then a nurse had given her some toys to play with in the next room but the door was open and she'd heard Daddy ask how tall she'd get and other things, and Mummy had started crying and sniffing, and said they could never understand how it had happened, and there was so much to learn.

And they came home and had juice and biscuit and Daddy had laughed and said, 'The doctor says there's nothing to stop you being a rocket scientist, Lisa. But you'll just have to build little rockets.'

He had kept on saying that for several days, and Mummy had even told Sally, who had said, 'Lisa's going to be a rocket scientist, aren't you, Lisa?', which was why she had remembered the words. Rocket scientist. And Daddy had said that if she was, she'd have to show him what to do, because Daddy made things with metal too. He fixed things that got broken, he had

14

a workshop in the garden and a helmet and a gun that made blue flames, and that was what he was a teacher of at the college. He'd help her make rockets. They'd help each other.

She wished Daddy was here now.

And suddenly Lisa hated being in the trunk and was really, really scared, and she began to shout. 'Mummy, Mummy! *Mummeeee*! Mummy, come and get me out. Mummy, let me out, I'm scared.'

Soon she couldn't even call because her nose was blocked and she couldn't wipe it, and her face was hot and wet.

'Mummy!'

The sobs shook her, she couldn't breathe, she whispered 'Mummy' over and over again. And then she was so tired she thought she would go to sleep, so she curled up as much as she could and put her head on her arm and went to sleep because she didn't like being awake any more.

Mummy came running into the room, her footsteps were heavy and her voice was high and and loud.

'What have you done? How long has she been in there? You *stupid* little girl.'

Mummy was banging at the lock-things, trying to get them open, and calling, 'Lisa. Sweetheart. Lisa, are you all right? I'll get you out. O my god. Lisa.'

Lisa lay still and quiet because Suzie was there too and would be cross. Then the lid of the trunk was opened and she opened her eyes and Mummy was crying and cuddling her and pulling her up and kissing her and wiping her eyes and nose. And everything was lovely and Mummy loved her and didn't want to give her away, and Suzie didn't say anything at all.

They all went into the kitchen, and Lisa sat on Mummy's knee and her legs stuck out straight, but Mummy held her round her middle and rocked her.

And then Lisa remembered and was worried. 'Did you send the removal men away?'

'What? What are you talking about?'

Mummy turned Lisa's face towards her so that the yellow paintbrush she'd made of her hair and with which she was stroking her face was tugged from her hand and hurt her scalp. Suzie got down off her chair and started to go out of the kitchen.

'Suzie told the removal men to come and take me away. She said they took away things you didn't want any more.'

Mummy sat very still, holding Lisa's hand, and just stared at Suzie.

'Did you tell Lisa that? Suzanna?'

Suzie shook her head and didn't speak. But then she said, 'But I don't want her because she's little and ugly and she can't do lots of things. And she makes me feel embarrassed when my friends are here. They call her a dwarf.'

'But I *can* do things. I'm going to be a famous rocket scientist and I'll be rich and look after you,' Lisa said. 'And you mustn't call me a dwarf. It's rude.'

She snuggled against Mummy and stuck her tongue out at Suzie, and felt very safe.

'Oh Suzie. Come here.'

Mummy held out her hand and Suzie wiggled her shoulders and shook her head, but then she came and Mummy held them both in a hug, and was very still, and Lisa was happy but a little bit afraid.

THREE

The envelope stated: *'To the young lady who lives in the basement flat'*. Ruth Kowslowski opened it and unfolded the single sheet of paper, on which a poem was written in black ink. The letters sloped elegantly and evenly to the right.

To *"The Girl-with-the-sky-in-her-hair"*

Your red hair
Reaches out
And entwines the blue sky,
Wraps it in shining fingers
And pulls it down
Around your head,
Like a blue silk shawl.
You are a celestial pillar,
Rapt in beautiful, fierce anger;
And even the cat
Is cowed.

There was no signature. She read it again, and then saw herself leaning on the railings, high above the lane. He had seen her and seen her anger, and his image of her transcended reality. She felt beautiful. A celestial pillar: he magnified, even deified her. He captured her with his words.

But minute writing at the bottom of the page stated, 'What you need is a Tom.' Was his name Tom? Was this a proposition? A declaration of love, or of intent? The man was old, he had thin grey hair and his skin was pale, and grainy in the folds. The poem suddenly held threat, and she shuddered, and did not want to open the lumpy black sack to which the envelope had been taped. She poked at the bag then smoothed it against the hard outlines of the object within – and she grinned as she ripped the bag open.

The basement flat which Ruth shared with Jay was at the end of a yellow sandstone terrace that curved around the top of a hill overlooking Glasgow's West End, in an area of tall multi-occupancy houses with multiple doorbells. The flat was small and badly-converted, but because it shared only its ceiling and one wall with neighbours, Jay felt sufficiently insulated to play music loudly without causing offence. The neighbours in their terrace and in the one that ran at right-angles apparently disagreed, but since most of the noise occurred in the afternoon, Ruth did not feel too troubled. Also, Jay had a particularly charming boyish smile which counteracted the dripping bloodied teeth of the dragon tattooed on his arm when he explained that this was his job, he was a DJ, and why didn't they come along to the club he was playing tonight, he could definitely get them in free. Ruth's hours of work were irregular too because she worked shifts as a Health Care Assistant (or an 'Auxiliary' as her mother had still insisted on calling it, making Ruth think of war-torn canvas and women tearing sheets for bandages) at two of the local hospitals.

Jay was revolted by some of the stories she recounted, but she had become more and more interested in the workings of the human body and how they could go so horribly wrong. The English degree which she had dropped after two years seemed increasingly irrelevant, and her former university on the crowded southern coast of England could have been on a different continent, not just a different country. She was fascinated by X-rays and photographs of scans and the 'naming of parts'. Some of the patients were quite knowledgeable about their own conditions, they had print-outs from the internet, and were delighted to tell her their intimate and gruesome stories. A few of the nurses would explain things if they had the time, but Ruth soon found that it was much more fun to pester the medical students, who trailed round the wards with the consultants. A couple of them became her friends and one afternoon, when Ruth should have been sleeping and the students should have been revising for an exam, the three girls lay and chatted in the autumn sun outside the back door of the flat. Music blasted intermittently from the open window as Jay mixed tracks for his next gig.

'I hate drum 'n bass. And where's the sun gone?' Lizzie sat up and shivered. 'Is there any wine left?'

Ruth, lying on her back on the thin grass with her arm across her face in the hope that this would keep her nose from turning pink, merely mumbled but Isobel, who had collapsed with her face on an opened file, reached out for the bottle. She tipped it and swore.

'No, you've drunk it all. I hate you! My boobs are squashed and my bum's too big and I hate medicine and want to be a fighter-pilot. Aaaaargh.'

Ruth sat up and looked at her. 'You can't be a fighter-pilot, you'd never fit behind the wheel. Or joy-stick or whatever it's called. Sounds a bit dodgy to me. Go and get some water. If you want a drink.' Then she leapt to her feet and screamed, 'Oh, fuck *off*.'

Lizzie and Isobel watched in astonishment as she ran towards the bottom of the sloping garden, waving her arms and shrieking.

'S'okay. Just a cat.' Jay stuck his head out of the window and grinned. 'Probably crapping on the nasties. It drives her wild.'

'Yeah. Scary.'

Lizzie stood up and looked around. 'Nasties?'

'The yellow things by the railings.'

Nasturtiums straggled unconvincingly across the dusty soil

at the bottom of the garden. Ruth was leaning over the metal railings, chucking stones down into the lane below, and she was still fizzing with anger when she turned round.

'Nearly got the little bugger. It was that filthy orange one, it was scent-marking the post.' She thumped one of the two posts from which the washing-line, decorated with mildewed clothes-pegs, was suspended. 'They just take over. They think our gardens are here for their convenience. And people encourage them by leaving out food. Come and look at this.' She caught at her hair and held it back with one hand, as she pointed down below the railings. 'Just look at all that food.'

Lizzie tiptoed, barefoot and wincing, across the unkempt lawn. 'Good grief! What sort of nutter puts all that stuff out?'

The lane, sunk down behind the terraces and bounded by high stone walls, had once been neatly surfaced with setts, but the stones had long since been displaced and broken by lorries and an endless sequence of men with road-drills, spades and inappropriate tarmac. Wooden doors, many of them broken or propped open, gave access from mostly-grimy gardens, and next to one of them, amongst the dustbins and litter-drifts was a collection of saucers and bowls and opened tins.

'A cat-lover. An old man.'

'Yeugh. Think of the rats. You'll get bubonic plague and Weil's disease and – tapeworms? Is it tapeworms, Iso? Toxo-something. Oh shit, I'm supposed to know all that stuff,' she wailed.

Later that evening, after everyone had left, Ruth washed her black tights and went outside to hang them on the line. Two cats were facing each other in the lane, singing; an unearthly noise that sometimes frightened her in the night. She hated the cats' casual acceptance that any patch of sunlight was theirs; that the dustbins and shrubs were parish boundaries to be marked with pungent stink; that the garden soil had been provided for their convenience. She hated the way they clawed open the garbage sacks then sat, heads tilted, chewing on stringy offal or kitchen towel soaked in miscellaneous juices. She loathed the small gangs that paced with twitching tails and glared at the opposition; she spied on them as they hunted for newly-parked cars, searched out the warmest engine, and stamped their feet in triumph on the bonnet. She hated them. She rapped on the window or opened the back door and threw things.

One time she had hurled a shoe at a tabby with such force that the missile had dropped over the railings out of sight. She had hopped across the garden, but had hesitated at the top of the steps because an old man had been in the lane. He had come out of the peeling garden-door that belonged to a house with sixteen doorbells at the front. She had seen him before and knew he often put out bowls of food; once or twice he had even nodded to her. On this occasion he had held out a bowl and called in a strangely high, thin voice.

'Pusss-puss-puss. Here, puss! Puuusss-puss-puss-pusssss.'

Cats had appeared from everywhere: lifting their heads, arching their backs and stretching, they had leapt off resting-places and bounded towards the call. The man's feet had been hidden by the multicoloured snarl of fur as he had set down the meat. After he had left, she had gone down to the lane to fetch her shoe, treading cautiously on the slimy steps; the fat tabby – smilingly undeterred – had peered down at her from the wall and purred.

Now, as she hung out her tights, she saw the man again. Again he called, and again the cats appeared from nowhere. But this time he did not set down the bowl of food. He held it high and out of reach, and pushed the cats aside with his foot so that one, and only one, could receive the gift. He walked backwards, encouraging the brown Burmese to follow him, enticing it into his garden. The graceful animal stepped daintily out of sight and the green door closed.

Six months later, on a fine morning in early Spring, Ruth stopped at the supermarket on her way back from a night-shift. Her clothes were sweaty and her hair smelt of the geriatric ward on which she had been working, and after buying milk and fruit she decided she would sit for a while in the park. The trees were still bare but the lawns were awash with crocuses, blue and white snouts pushing out from the earth, their open mouths revealing throats as yellow as baby blackbirds'. She chose a bench in the sun and sat with eyes closed, head turned upwards towards the warmth. After a while a judder indicated that someone had joined her on the seat, and she opened her eyes a crack to see who it was, irritated that she wasn't to be allowed to sit on her own. The old man seemed familiar and she looked again. She was almost sure that he was the cat-man from the lane, but he wore a tweed jacket and cap, and was even older than she had thought.

It was very annoying, the way he fidgeted and muttered, and she was on the point of moving when he said, 'Excuse me. I wonder if you could help. What is the name of the spice that one obtains from crocuses? Or croci, I wonder if that is more correct?'

'Oh, I'm sorry... I don't—'

'You see, I've forgotten. Wretched memory, how it begins to fail one, when one is reaching mature, shall we say, years.' His voice was surprisingly gentle, self-deprecating. 'The spice resides in the stamens – those are the yellow rods inside that produce the female gametes.'

'Yes, I know what stamens are.' Ruth was a little offended although she was not sure about 'female gametes'. 'It's saffron.'

'Ah yes. Saffron. I am forced to wonder who had the idea that the stamens of croci would impart such a subtle and *expensive* taste to rice and cake.'

'Are you thinking of collecting some saffron yourself?' Ruth was intrigued.

'Oh no, not at all. I merely needed to collect the word. I am most grateful.'

He turned to watch a squirrel that had been pottering and sniffing amongst the flowers. His lips were moving and sometimes his hands twitched. The squirrel reared on its hind legs and looked around, then dropped onto all fours and scuttled towards a tree; arms stretched sideways, tail erect and quivering, it leapt up the trunk like a speeding leech. The man made a little sound of pleasure and his sallow face brightened for a moment.

'Did you see that? That's what I find so hard to capture. The skeleton itself must flow, and loop, and turn.' He was trying to explain with his mottled bony hands. 'But the words must flesh it out – they must disguise the structure. That is what I cannot get right.'

Ruth wondered briefly if the old man suffered from some sort of dementia, yet he seemed quite lucid.

'I am not explaining myself well, you haven't understood, have you?' He looked at her fleetingly. 'Please listen:

Sinuous snake-shape slithering

Through *saffron* –

– you see, that's why I needed your help –

Through saffron.

Furry fluffball,

Grey among blue goblets,

Uncoiling and stretching

Its bristling, prickling

Whiskered tail...

No, that is rather clumsy. I shall have to work a little harder.'

'Yes. I do see. I think.' Ruth was not sure whether to be impressed or wary of the old man's pretension. 'Have you made poems for other animals? How about a cheetah? Or an ordinary cat? You're fond of cats, aren't you?'

She was now sure he was the cat-man.

'Fond of cats? No, I am not fond of cats. There is no fondness in them, they do not reciprocate – they can only take. Good heavens, look at the time!' He had jumped up without looking at his watch. 'I must be going. Goodbye. It has been pleasant talking to you.'

He scurried away, holding himself stiffly, his legs slightly bowed. As though he had wet himself, Ruth thought, then realised that the hours on the ward had had a bad effect on the way she viewed the world, and that it was time she went back to the flat for a shower and sleep. Jay should be there, sleeping too.

A few days later she saw the cat-man again. She had chased a ginger cat down the garden and it had bundled itself together and leapt over the railings, hurling itself at the wall on the far side of the lane. Scrabbling desperately, it pulled itself up to the top and sat there, panting and furious. Ruth burst out laughing, and then realised that the man was below her in the lane. He held a carrier-bag that hung heavily although the wind rattled rubbish amongst the weeds.

'No, I am not fond of them,' he said loudly. 'Nor, it seems, are you.'

'It was... *defaecating* on my flowerbed.'

The old man continued staring up at her, wordlessly, until she became uneasy and turned away.

Ruth carried the letter and the black bag into the flat, and read the poem again, then pulled the bag fully open and stared into the cat's unblinking eyes. His back was arched, his ginger hair bristled stiffly around his neck and his legs, fixed firmly to the stand, were stiff and straight. She expected him to raise his tail and spray the cupboards, marking the kitchen as his territory. Every part of his body signalled, 'Keep off!'

The ginger tom had been captured, and recaptured. And she reflected that she too had been immortalised – petrified like Lot's wife – by the old man's words.

The following week she bought a small fossil fish in the Museum gift shop and wrapped it in blue metallic foil. The bones of the fish had been compressed and preserved by the hardening sediment, and were finely drawn as though by an engineer's pen. She walked down the road to the house with sixteen doorbells, and her feet crunched as she went up the front steps.

Thoughtfully, she pushed aside the small, crushed shoulder-blade with her shoe, then looked at the rows of bells. She had no idea which bell was his, so she rang one at the bottom of a row.

A woman appeared by the partly-open bay window next to the steps. 'Wha' d'ye want, hen?'

'Sorry to bother you. I was looking for the old man who feeds the cats. Which bell is his?'

'He's no' here, hen, he's flitted.'

'Do you know where he went?'

'No, he just flit in the night, he didnae tell anyone. He must've been a few drops short of a dram – can ye guess what he left behind?'

'No,' Ruth shook her head. But she had a very good idea.

'Cats! The place was full o' stuffed cats! If yous after findin' yer cat it's likely in his room, hen, do ye want tae come in and see?'

Ruth laughed and shook her head. 'No, I don't like cats.'

As she walked back up the hill she wondered if there was a stuffed squirrel, too; and if there was, how the old taxidermist would have fleshed out its skeleton. Although, thinking about that shoulder blade, perhaps there wasn't a skeleton inside. Possibly someone at the Museum could tell her how it was done.

FOUR

'Beer? Capuccino?'

The young man held the laden tray above Lisa's head as he waited, coolly polite, for space to be cleared on the wooden table. Lisa thought about that weight above her head, the four half-litre glasses of lager, the heat of the coffee, and she hastily pushed the postcards into a pile. They were all aerial views of tulip-fields; some were striped like the rough canvas of a deck-chair, narrow bands of red, orange, green and yellow; in others, the patterns were more intricate arrangements of rectangles and trapezoids, bounded by the dark curving ribbons of canals.

Kees spoke to the waiter in Dutch, but he shrugged. 'I'm from Oz, mate. I only work here.'

Everyone around the table laughed and Stefan asked, 'Whereabouts? I was over in Melbourne for a couple of weeks last year.'

'Small world! I'm from Adelaide but my sister and her kids've just moved to Melbourne.' The waiter's indifference vanished and he became quite animated. 'Where're you all from then? You here sight-seeing?'

'Oh, we're from all over – the UK, Germany, Switzerland, Czech Republic, anywhere that people can string a few numbers together. Kees here is our local boy,' Stefan nodded at Kees who, despite his wild hair and denim jacket, was nearing forty, 'and I work in Brussels. We're here for a conference.'

'Numbers? You're mathematicians or something, then, are you? I thought you'd just come from a convention of postcard collectors.'

26

'We're into patterns,' Lisa said, and the waiter stepped back as he looked down at her, perhaps realising that he had been encroaching on her space. 'That's why the conference is out at Leeuwenhook.'

'Right.' He clearly could not think of anything to say. Perhaps he did not know that Leeuwenhook was in the middle of the bulb-fields.

'Tesselations, patterning in different dimensions – filling spaces,' one of the other men added, not very helpfully. 'And what do you do when you are back home?'

'I'm a clinical psychologist. Taking a year or two out to do some highly sophisticated research on the mind of the European alcoholic,' he grinned as he sorted out change from the leather bag that was strapped around his waist. 'Cheers, mate!'

He wove away between the packed tables, picked up a paper napkin that had blown onto the ground, kicked out at a scrounging pigeon, then stopped to take an order from a Japanese couple.

'Australian bars are all staffed by Brits, and British bars by Australians,' Peter said.

'I thought it was all Poles these days. But I hear that British academics are being head-hunted by Australia.'

'Do they want applied mathematicians? I'd go like a shot.' Peter was a postdoctoral researcher in the same department as Lisa in Liverpool and had told her that he needed to make some useful contacts at this conference because his funding had less than a year to run. He had been assiduously networking, and was clearly hoping that Stefan Greatorex might be able to offer him a job in Brussels, but Lisa privately felt that Peter was not as good as he liked to make out.

Stefan, on the other hand, was quietly impressive. Stocky, dressed in open-necked white shirt and jacket, with thick dark hair and public-schoolboy-casual good looks, his appearance seemed at odds with his attitude. Lisa had already noticed that he listened carefully when others were talking to him, and was generous with helpful suggestions. The postgraduate students probably felt comfortable because he did not attempt to crush them with negative criticism or the importance of his own ideas. He was a physicist rather than a mathematician, but the borders of his research overlapped with hers. Perhaps she could persuade him to give a seminar in her department next time he was in England.

She looked for her glass of wine, but the waiter had placed it out of reach amongst the postcards and folders of conference abstracts that were stacked on the table. She touched the arm of the Czech professor next to her, who was talking rapidly to her German neighbour while scrawling diagrams on a paper napkin.

'"Bistro maths". Douglas Adams.' Lisa smiled at the professor. 'I'm sorry to interrupt, but could you pass me that glass of wine?'

The woman looked at her in surprise for a moment, dragging herself back to the Café Waag from the stratosphere of theory. Her face was hard and bony, her hair improbably black, her eye-shadow forget-me-not blue, but her smile was very sweet.

'Of course. Your wine. I am sorry I was not seeing...'

Lisa smiled back. 'It's okay, Australians all have long arms. By the way, did you know that the incidence of broken arm bones in gibbons is nearly thirty per cent?'

Stefan Greatorex must have overheard for he burst out laughing. 'I'm sure that's the jungle equivalent of an urban myth. And anyway, gibbons aren't marsupials. Sorry, Sonja, we've broken your train of thought.'

'It is all right. I think it was already perhaps an express train out of control, I am glad you have stopped it, like the – what are they? The things in a station.' Sonja held out her arms, hands vertically upwards, fingers splayed. 'Boof! Like that.'

'Buffers?'

'Perhaps. Buffers.'

'An old buffer – like Kees,' Peter suggested.

'What? What does that mean?' The Dutchman leaned forward, grinning beneath his moustache. 'I am not so very old. But I am very, very wise.'

The conversation became more general and light-hearted, and after a while several members of the group decided they would go off to do some shopping and sight-seeing.

'Are you coming, Lisa?' Peter asked.

'No. I'm happy to sit here a bit longer and watch people. Or perhaps I'll go and find the bus, if anyone else is ready to go back.'

The turrets of De Waag cast complex shadows and the bricks of the square glowed warm ochre in the sun, but the air was cool. Despite the chill, Easter had brought tourists and conferences to Amsterdam, and the pavements and trams were sufficiently crowded to make Lisa feel uneasy. The road around the square was busy with cars and the cyclists wove unheedingly amongst them. A companion would be an asset. She shifted on her chair, easing her calves against the ridges of woven cane.

'I am in need of another beer, Lisa, so I shall stay,' Kees said. He had taken a plastic pouch of tobacco out of the breast-pocket of his denim jacket, and he concentrated on rolling a very thin cigarette. 'And this man here looks thirsty, too.'

'Yes, another beer would be good,' Stefan agreed, lifting a hand in farewell as the others left. 'And since I come to Amsterdam fairly often I'm afraid the novelty of wandering around the city wore off a long time ago.'

'Ah. I hope I can show you something special when we have had our drink. Very relevant. Very near. You will not have far to walk. Even your little legs will manage, Lisa.' Kees slid the cigarette paper along his tongue to seal it and grinned at her.

The men moved the extra table and chairs out of the way so that the three of them could sit comfortably together, and this time the waiter was a little more careful with the positioning of their drinks.

'So, a Dutchman who works in Geneva and a Brit who works in Brussels – you are British, aren't you, Stefan, even with a name like that? You make me feel very parochial.'

'Were you born in Liverpool, then, Lisa – have you always stayed in the one place?' Stefan asked.

'No, I've travelled really widely,' Lisa laughed. 'I was born in Bakewell, in the Peak District. That's in Derbyshire, towards the North-East of England,' she added for Kees' benefit. 'And I was a student in Manchester, then did my PhD there too. But how did you come to end up in Brussels?'

'I married a Belgian. We met at a party in Stratford, she was front-of-house at the theatre, and I was working on my doctorate at Warwick at the time. She was keen to go back to Belgium, and I'm reasonably fluent at speaking French because my mother was from Strasbourg. My mother just happened to like the name Stefan, incidentally, even though it's slightly incongruous coupled with Greatorex. I was fortunate – I suppose I was in the right place at the right time, you know how these things can happen – one of the Free University's spin-off companies was looking for someone with my expertise, limited though it is, and my wife – as she was then – was able to get a job with the European Commission. Since then I have moved jobs a couple of times, shifting more and more towards the field of quasicrystal research.'

'But you have stayed in Brussels?' Kees asked.

'Yes. My daughters still live there, with their mother.' Stefan dabbled the bottom of his glass in a pool of spilt beer. 'I'd like to get back to the UK really, but I wouldn't be able to see the girls so often.'

'Children take away a person's energy and emotion. I think they should be outlawed, except that we would die out as a species. Although I am not sure that my girlfriend, woman-friend, I am not sure how you call her, agrees. I suppose you do not have any children, Lisa.'

Stefan glanced at Kees quickly, clearly embarrassed. Lisa had become used to Kees' blunt manner in the short time that she had known him, and even found that she enjoyed it, but his statement nevertheless surprised her.

'Well, no. But then again, I haven't yet found a suitable father. Though I'm probably getting too set in my ways to be a mother.'

'You are too special, too rare. And too clever! All men will be too frightened. Except for Dr Greatorex here and I, who are both very brave men. And I wish now to show you this special thing as a present. But I will first see whether it is possible.' He crushed out his cigarette and surprised her by reaching forward to touch her hand, stroking her fingers with a curious expression on his face, and then stood up and made his way towards the dark interior of the café.

The intimacy of that sudden gesture shocked Lisa; for a few seconds she held her breath and and hoped that her face was not as red as it felt. She turned on her seat so that she could look out on the Nieuwmarkt. It had once been a market place and De Waag had been a weighing-station, but both now dealt only in people: business people, office workers, families with trailing teenagers, retired couples, young people with backpacks – their paths criss-crossed, some straight, some meandering, some stationary or sessile. There were people sitting on café chairs, people propped against railings, or perched on the edge of the canal; people reading maps or newspapers, or talking to each other, themselves, or mobile phones; or staring, eyes glazed, into a drug-induced parallel universe. A blind man, marching with white cane and confidence, was ambushed, mid-calf, by a baby-buggy pushed by a chattering, oblivious girl. A tanned woman, white-suited, caught him as he cried out and teetered, and scolded the girl loudly in Dutch. Their small drama attracted attention, and

Lisa relaxed, turning back to the table. She caught sight of Kees coming out of the café, still talking to someone who stood in the doorway, and then he came towards them, smiling broadly.

'Are you ready? Drink up, Stefan. We can go.'

He was full of pride and good humour, and Stefan gulped down his beer and stood up.

'Right. Lead on.'

He hesitated for a moment, as though wondering whether to pull out Lisa's chair for her, but she had already slipped down and gathered up her bag and coat.

'We have to walk a very long way. Just to the other side of this building.' Kees pointed to the right of the red-brick bulk of De Waag.

Slowly, waiting for Lisa without appearing to do so, he led them round the corner to an archway surrounding a pair of red-painted wooden doors; panelled, studded, and grilled, they were forbidding but he pressed the polished doorbell that gleamed above Lisa's head. The wind swirled sweet-wrappers and a bedraggled feather around her feet, and she shivered and felt unwelcome. The door remained closed and no-one came. Kees rang the bell again and there was a rattling and scraping as the door was pulled open, and a young man with a yellowish complexion, wearing baggy trousers and a polo-shirt, stood on the threshold.

At once Kees began explaining his mission in Dutch, and for a while the young man looked unconvinced. He stared at Lisa and Stefan and appeared not to be listening, but then something caught his attention and he laughed, a single guttural bark, and asked a question. When Kees replied, he nodded, and stood aside to let them into the tiny vestibule, then shut and bolted the door and pushed past them to the stairs.

Stefan raised his eyebrows in query and gestured for Lisa to precede him, but she shook her head. 'I'll follow you – wherever it is we're going.'

The narrow spiral stairway was steep, the steps tall, and she was soon breathless and struggling. From a landing, doors opened into offices that were equipped with computers and bright with modern light, contrasting incongruously with the ancient stones. The men waited for her to catch up. There were more stairs and then their guide opened a wooden door and she followed the others into a high octagonal room that was panelled in wood, its high domed ceiling embossed with coloured shields. The room was empty apart from a few piles of books and papers, and the space startled her.

'How extraordinary.' Stefan stood in the centre and looked around. 'What was it used for, Kees?'

'Something to do with the old Guild of doctors, no – surgeons. And it has been other things too. This man, he is called Theo and works in the library downstairs. He will tell us if I ask him. But this is not what I brought you to see. We must follow him.'

Theo led them between wooden pillars into a sort of meeting room where gold and ruby light filtered through coloured panes of glass and glowed on the polished floor. The rich colour lit their faces and clothes as they hurried after their guide, and Lisa would have liked to stop for a moment and hold it in her hands. But Theo walked over to a small wooden door and pushed it open. 'We must go in here.' He gestured for them to go ahead.

Kees grinned at Lisa. 'Go in. You will love this.'

There were chairs and a table, but although the furniture almost filled the space it was of no significance for the character of the narrow room was described by its walls: arches, niches, and circular and square frames were set within the plaster.

'Just look at these pillars! It seems impossible you could do this with bricks.' Stefan ran his hand up one of the helical curves that framed an alcove.

'This one seems to disappear back into the wall – and yet it's completely flat.' Lisa reached up to touch the surface of a complex *trompe l'oeil* pattern that gave an impression of perspective. 'This is unbelievable!' She hurried from one pattern to another, laughing in her amazement. 'Kees, why are they here?'

'These are the rooms of the bricklayers' guild. They used them to show off their skills.'

Lisa stroked one of the panels, feeling the contrast between warm brick and cold marble insets, and revelling in the complicated pattern that completely filled the frame.

'You really are a genius,' she said to Kees, genuinely delighted. 'This is just perfect, isn't it, Stefan?'

'You see, the bricks are special, they are very small.'

'Small but perfectly formed,' Stefan said, and then hit his forehead with his hand and looked embarrassed. 'Ach! Sorry.'

'It's okay.' Lisa touched his elbow and laughed at him. 'You'll end up not being able to speak at all if you try to watch your words. And I certainly don't take offence or even notice unless you over-react. Like that.'

Stefan grinned ruefully. 'Point taken. A blow below the belt,' and he ducked away quickly, bumping against their reluctant guide.

Theo grunted, then spoke to Lisa. 'Do you have a camera? You can make a photograph for your research. I will make a photo of you in front of it also.' He was unsmiling and she felt his chilliness, but she smiled pleasantly at him and searched in her bag for her camera.

'Thank you. Though the room is so small I'm not sure a photo would give the best impression.'

She showed him how to work the camera and stood in front of one of the panels while the others squeezed themselves against the further wall. The flash, as always, startled her and she could imagine clearly what it had captured: Dr Lisa Wallace with her long blonde hair, dome-headed, an achondroplasic, small and imperfectly formed, against a backdrop of miniaturised perfection.

FIVE

The skin was soft and damp, as flexible as a fine suede glove. Ruth's face was so close to it that the faint smell of white spirit made her nose prickle. She slowly rolled the face back over the skull, pushing the lips with a blunt-ended seeker, pinning them in place; now concentrating on the eyelids, smoothing the short red fur around them to align the fibres. The polyurethane form was light in her hand but solid, mimicking neither the delicate postorbital arches nor the fragile interlocking plates of real bone. Carefully, carefully, carefully. She said the words to herself inside her head, repeating the familiar calming mantra, coaxing the skin that had been turned inside-out like the inverted finger of a glove. Now the ears had been revealed and the muzzle that was emerging was recognisably that of a squirrel. She was calm, focussed entirely on her work, already thinking ahead to how she would position the limbs. The furry scrap of skin, seemingly too insubstantial to fit a whole animal, flopped on the workbench as she turned the head to face her then readjusted its right eyelids and perked up the tufted ears.

She straightened up and took off her glasses, staring out of the window to refocus her eyes. Two woodpigeons were flapping clumsily in the ash tree, advertising their attempts at copulation. Ungainly, unattractive birds, she thought; mating in birds always seemed so incompetent. Blinking, she put her glasses on again, picked up one of the pieces of wire that she had already cut and straightened, bent it to make an elbow, and quickly wrapped it with tow. The soft brown fibres wadded the wire and she pulled thread from a reel, bound it tightly round the tow, shaping muscles; sliced the thread neatly with a scalpel; built up the upper arm and paw, checked the arm's diameter against that of the skin. A right hook? An upper-cut? She wasn't sure of the boxing terminology. South paw, a boxer who led with his left.

She remembered how the squirrel's limbs had been positioned when George had brought it to her, and smiled. It had been rigid, its legs outstretched and straightened like a gliding flying-fox, and George had stood at the door of the workshop and held it out with one hand, grinning so broadly that his smooth and ruddy face was creased and his eyes almost hidden.

'Bet you'll never guess how this one died.'

'A red! Oh, what a shame.' She had taken it from him but could see no sign of a wound. 'Where did you get it?'

'I was drilling over at Dawsons'. You know that field down at the bottom where the electric goes through? The yows were on the turnips a few weeks back?'

Ruth had frowned, trying to think where he meant.

'You must know it, there's trees, wild cherries they are, and a couple of they electric poles in the field with a square box, transformer or summat on them. Right near the edge? I have to go careful round that, give it a bit of a wide berth, like.'

'Right.' She had nodded, not really knowing where he meant, but deciding it was not important.

'I could see there was something there in the grass at the bottom of the poles, thought it was a dead bird, kestrel or something. But it was this.' He had jerked his head at the squirrel and started to laugh.

'"Danger of death", it says. There's one of they yellow signs with a black zig-zag. "Keep off!"' George's face had become even redder and great gouts of laughter had bubbled out of him. Just watching him had made Ruth giggle too.

'Poor la'al bugger! Probably climbed up to read what it said.'

'More likely it couldn't read. Look at the poor little thing, stiff as a board.'

'*Fsss*! A thousand volts.' George had staggered around, arms outstretched, head back, so that Ruth had feared he would fall backwards down the stairs. 'Dead!'

She snorted gently with amusement as she eased the tip of the bent wire into the inverted paw. George and his tractor had been doing contract work around the farm for several years, and Ruth thought Madeleine was lucky to have found him. He was a likeable, reliable lad, tall and well-built and in his early twenties, though he acted like a daft young lad a lot of the time. Probably because he likes to make us women laugh, she thought.

The red squirrel was in perfect condition, unlike some of the greys that had been shot in the cull. Poor la'al bugger indeed. The reds were so precious. There was too much tow in the upper arm, she would have to take the wire out and re-wind it.

She stopped what she was doing and breathed out slowly, clutching again at the calmness that had threatened to slip away. The tow was as soft and brown as musk-ox hair, and she buried her fingers in the tow-bag for a few moments to feel the mammalian warmth. She pushed aside the forceps and the pliers, and yet again examined the photographs of the boxing-match, trying to visualise exactly how she would position the squirrel's left arm. Then the excitement at what she was about to create spread through her like a warm wave and she patiently set to work again, becoming oblivious to the familiar sounds of the barn and the fussing chickens in the yard below.

Some time later a clattering roar, abruptly shut off, startled her and she glanced at the clock. Midday already! George must have finished for the morning. She had been working on the squirrel since just after eight, and now all its limbs were wired and shaped, and the tail would curl gracefully up its back. The mannekin for the torso, which she had moulded from wood wool and string, lay ready on the bench, and she hoped that George would leave her in peace so she could complete the final step before beginning to sew together the belly skin.

The dogs were barking and she heard him shout at them to be quiet, but then his feet were pounding up the wooden stairs. As usual he stopped outside the workshop door then knocked softly and opened the door just enough to peer through the gap.

'Hiya, Ruth. Sorry, did I startle you? Is it okay if I come in?'

She smiled and sighed. 'Hi, George.'

'Hell, it's like an oven in here.'

He bounded in like an exuberant Springer spaniel, smelling of slurry. Despite the chilly April day he was wearing only a tee-shirt over his jeans; Ruth had the fan-heater going, and a pullover under her navy boiler-suit.

'Hey, it's "Red and Dead". Can I see him?'

'Careful! No, don't touch – look at the state of your hands.'

He clasped them behind his back and grinned.

'Stand still and don't talk, I need to concentrate. I'm just about to attach the limbs to the body, then you'll get a better idea.' She slid her hand under the skin, and the head and legs drooped stiffly around her palm. But George had just noticed the photograph of the boxers that was clamped upright in the vice.

'Aw, I thought you were going to make him into a footballer. Carlisle United, you have to do that.'

'But you know I can't, it has to be a Victorian or Edwardian sport.' She stopped and pinched her lips with her fingers for a moment. 'When did soccer start? I don't know. Anyway, this is to be a boxer.'

'Who's he going to fight, then? You'll never get another red.'

'He has to fight a grey, of course. Actually, this one will be on the defensive, and his opponent will be very much on the attack. *Bam*!' She pushed out her right fist, straight-armed, and added, rather primly, 'As in nature, the grey is the aggressor.'

'Aye. Well. But footie'd be more exciting. He could've just scored a goal – like this.' He whipped the back of his tee-shirt up onto his head, raised his arms and careered around the workshop shouting, 'Yeah! Yeah!'

The uneven boards of the hayloft shuddered and Ruth's workbench rocked, but as she snatched at the rolling reel of thread she saw how pale his back and stomach were in contrast to the muscled tan of his arms.

'You're getting a beer-belly,' she said. 'Go away and leave me in peace.'

'George?' The shout came from down below in the yard.

'Uh-oh. There's the boss shouting.'

'*George*! Where've you got to, wretched lad?'

Madeleine Tregwithen drove across the yard, wishing, yet again, that the '*clunk*'-ing from the front right wheel would disappear. The Land Rover was feeling its age, and she knew that she would never be able to afford to replace it herself. Perhaps there was some sort of grant, there were grants – and paperwork – for everything these days, if you could manage to figure it out. She stopped outside the feed-store and then dragged a sack of mixed corn from the rear of the vehicle, heaved it onto her shoulder, grunting slightly, and carried it in to one of the bins. A Wellsummer hen squawked in fright and ran for the door with yellow-legged stride.

Madeleine was a large woman who, once fleshy, had lost weight in recent years. She had somewhat stern and bony features, her lips were thin, her nose narrow and sharp, and her cheeks were marked by deep grooves that ran down towards the corners of her mouth. She did not often smile, although she was frequently and privately amused, but when she did, the side of her mouth that was surrounded by a purplish growth remained immobile as though she had had a stroke. She had become strong from necessity and although she was in her late fifties, she intended to remain that way. As she hoisted the second sack she wondered if Ruth was watching from upstairs, and her eyes glimmered briefly with amusement. What name would Ruth give her now?

'Madeleine is a name that goes with shady hats and slacks,' Ruth had once said. 'Definitely "slacks", beige with a sharp crease down the front, not trousers. A trug over your arm, a little garden fork in your hand. And kneeling-pads!'

Beige slacks: trousers for an easy and delicate life. She replaced the lid on the corn-bin and picked up three brown eggs that had been secreted inside the grass-box of a rusting mower. Damned hen, why couldn't she lay in the hen-house like the others? The uneasiness that had been with her since midday returned and she surprised herself with the thought that it would be good to talk to Ruth. She hesitated to disturb her, but in the dozen or so years that Ruth had rented the hay-loft (and to Madeleine it still remained the hayloft and not a studio), a quiet and trusting friendship had evolved between them.

Yet she paused at the foot of the stairs, dithering uncharacteristically, remembering how, earlier in the day, she had shouted to George to come and get his dinner, and he had pounded downstairs like a young bullock. Young bullocks let out onto the Spring grass, galloping across a field, heads down, legs kicking, careless: 'Wee stirkies', Daniel had called them. A spasm of sadness had caught at her heart, but had mercifully been replaced with irritation as George had emerged, stamping his hooves and bellowing, 'Sorry, boss!' into the yard.

'There's some broth for you. And hurry up. Had you forgotten that I need to go to town?'

'Sorry, boss.' George had grinned, not sorry at all.

'Did you fix that silage-feeder in the top field?'

'Aye. When the yows'd let me get to it, they're that desperate for the silage. Bunch o' hop-heads.' He had held onto the door-frame and lifted his feet in turn, inspecting the soles of his boots for mud. 'They're clean.'

'Not clean enough. You'll need to take them off.'

Propping a foot on the rustic pot that contained a mis-shapen conifer, he had bent to unlace his boot and shouted after her into the kitchen.

'Talking of druggies. Did you hear about Elaine Nicholson's grandson? Police caught him with a load o' cannabis on Saturday night. Said he must be dealing with that amount. Daft la'al bugger! She'll no' be so pleased to see his name in the paper this time.'

Madeleine had stirred the soup before replying. It was a good thick soup, with the last of the leeks, the ones that were going soft at the end of winter.

'What was his name in for last time, then?' she had asked eventually.

George had padded in from the back kitchen, the toes of his thick grey socks flapping like beached flat-fish, and had washed his hands at the sink.

'Use the sink in the back-kitchen, why can't you?' Madeleine had realised that she had sounded more than usually brusque but hearing Elaine's name, so soon after being reminded of Daniel, had startled her.

'Sorry, I forgot.' George had glanced at her, clearly surprised. 'Broth smells good. Football or something like that. He was in the school team.'

In town she had bought the local newspaper and had scanned it quickly, but the small article ('Drugs bust in city centre') did not name Daniel's grandson, merely mentioned that the boy was aged fourteen.

Now she slowly climbed the stairs to the hayloft and knocked at the door before opening it.

'Are you too busy to have a cup of tea? I'm about to put the kettle on.'

Ruth stared at Madeleine rather blankly. Her glasses lay on the pad of file paper in front of her, and her hair had partly escaped, or been pulled from, the elasticated band that held it back. It stuck out in wiry coils around her face.

She sighed and blinked, then nodded. 'I could certainly do with a break.'

'I'm not interrupting? Are you writing one of your articles, for that blog or whatever it's called?'

'I was just jotting down a few ideas.'

'What's this one going to be about?'

'Dressed animals, I think, since I'm working on the squirrel at the moment. Walter Potter's "Kittens' Tea-party", Plouquet's pine marten teaching maths to rabbits – that sort of thing. They were hugely fashionable in Victorian times. But I'm not sure I've got enough information here, the book I want is at home.' She stood up, yawning and stretching. 'Come in and look at the squirrel, I'm quite pleased with him.'

Madeleine sniffed as she entered. 'What's that? Paint? You ought to open the window, these chemicals can't be good for you.' She looked around the studio, amazed, as always, that so much equipment should be needed to stuff a few dead animals.

'I was painting around his eyes. I don't notice the smell after a while.'

The squirrel was propped on a temporary stand next to the microwave oven, and Ruth picked it up and brought it over to the window. With one leg stretched forward and the other bent back, one arm thrown upwards, the squirrel was clearly on the point of being felled by a massive body-blow; its torso curved around the punch and its eyes bulged.

Madeleine exhaled sharply in surprise. 'It's like a frame from a film. You've just frozen the action for a split-second. It's perfect, Ruth. It makes me hurt to look at him.'

'Yes. He's done for, isn't he? Poor fellow. I kept feeling very apologetic that I was doing this to him. He deserves better.' She stroked the red squirrel's head as she laid the animal on the table. 'But I'm afraid his opponent is much stronger. Now I've got to get hold of unbleached linen from somewhere – you don't have any, do you, stashed away in a chest in the attic?' She stretched her arms above her head and twisted her body from side to side. 'Do you need some milk? There's some here that needs using up.'

'What an inviting offer,' Madeleine said drily. 'I expect I can manage to run to fresh milk. Come on down. Why do you need linen? Not that I have any.'

Ruth followed her downstairs. 'For sewing the breeks. I'm not yet sure how I'm going to make the gloves. Shall I bring these eggs?'

As they passed the kennel, the two border collies, who had been waiting expectantly, rushed at the wire. Ruth walked over to greet them and at once Beth, the young bitch, rolled submissively onto her back, tail waving gently.

'She's useless,' Madeleine said. 'I'd hoped she'd have learnt a few tricks from Gip, but she's still useless in the field. And I could really do with another good dog right now, with the lambing due to start in less than a month. We'll be bringing the ewes down to the in-bye land in a week or so.'

'Lambing. Now that's something to look forward to.'

The two women exchanged looks and Ruth followed Madeleine into the house.

Thick-walled and slate-roofed, the house had staved off the harsh Cumbrian winters for at least three centuries. Its kitchen was the room that Ruth knew best: a low-ceilinged room, one window looking out towards the yard, the other onto a small garden. The cream-painted walls were glossy and uneven, the solid floor covered by vinyl with imitation yellow-patterned tiles. Each side of the sink were worktops covered with cream Formica, and the table and stick-back chairs were of some dark-stained wood. An oak settle with a vertebra-bruising back stood against the wall that led into the hall. Probably nobody had ever sat on the settle and even if they had wanted to, it would be impossible now because three wire trays, each containing a pile of letters, bills, and leaflets advertising farming initiatives and veterinary products, were lined up side by side along the seat.

Every time she entered the kitchen, Ruth was pleased by the incongruity of the cushions and curtains. Once, early in her tenancy of the studio but when she had become less inhibited by Madeleine's seeming coolness, she had picked up a cushion from a chair and stroked the patterns with her finger. Such colours! Dark teal, bright yellow, carmine and madder brown: the names were familiar to her from her artists' colour book.

'Where did you get this material? It's... so unusual.'

'Out of place?' Madeleine had looked at her sharply. 'Doesn't fit in? John's niece bought it. It's Finnish. She bought it in some posh store in London when they came over from South Africa. She made up the curtains too, while she was here. Thought it would brighten up her auntie's old-fashioned kitchen.' Her eyes had glimmered briefly.

'You didn't mind?'

'I needed new cushions. She was being thoughtful. They're different.'

Now, as she pulled out a chair, Ruth saw that the material was wearing thin and she wondered if Madeleine would ever replace it. She picked up the local paper that was lying on the table, and glanced at the headlines with not much interest. Madeleine brought over a plate with a couple of rock buns and buttered slices of malt loaf.

'Look at page four,' she said quietly. 'Down at the bottom right there's a bit about a lad caught with drugs.' She waited while Ruth turned the pages and found the piece. 'It doesn't say who it was – but George said he'd heard it was Rick. Elaine's grandson.'

Ruth looked up at her.

'It would never have happened if they'd been able to stay on the farm.'

'Madeleine, you don't know that. He's a teenager, and boys his age don't hang around on the farm all the time under the supposedly good influence of their parents.' Not that Abigail sets much of an example, she thought privately.

'And grandparents. Grandfather.'

'Oh no. You can't start blaming yourself for this. That would be truly ridiculous, even self-indulgent,' Ruth risked. 'And anyway, the paper doesn't give any details, so we shouldn't make premature judgements. There may well be a reasonable explanation.'

Madeleine did not reply, but placed the metal tea-pot with its knitted red cosy on a mat on the table. She sat down heavily, still frowning.

'It's daft, I know. But something reminded me of Daniel earlier, and then there was this... the two things together...'

Ruth did not know how to set the older woman's mind at rest; the age gap was perhaps too great, there were nearly thirty years between them, and neither woman was good at communicating personal feelings. Suddenly she stood up and unbuttoned the top half of her boiler-suit, and pulled it down. She reached into the back pocket of her jeans.

'This may amuse you,' she said, although she was not amused by it herself.

She unfolded a warm and slightly bent sheet of paper on which was printed a photograph, and handed it to Madeleine.

'That's me, when I was a student. And Stefan. We were at university together and he was reading physics. He works in Brussels now.'

'Switch the light on, will you, so I can have a proper look.'

The fluorescent tube above the sink flickered and then its harsh white light lit the print-out, accentuating the colours: Ruth's short red hair, her skin pale against her green bikini and the tanned arms of the stocky young man against whom she leaned. Both were laughing at the camera; Stefan's arms were clasped around her, and their sandy legs were intertwined.

45

'He looks nice.'

'Yes. He was. But I met Jay and went off to Glasgow instead. Stefan's married with two children. He married a Belgian.'

'So why are you looking at the photo now?'

'He wrote me an email a few days ago, because he'd been searching for something on the internet a while back and he'd come across my name – and it led him to my blog. He read some of my essays.'

'And the photo?'

'He sent that as an attachment too. He said he had been looking through his files and that was the only one he could find, and that we had probably both changed a lot since then.'

'Happily married, is he?' Madeleine's voice and face were expressionless.

Ruth looked at her sharply. 'He was interested in the article, and wondered what else I was doing these days. That's all.'

Madeleine folded the paper and passed it back. 'I might just have one or two old linen napkins somewhere. I'll have a look when we've had our tea.'

Six

Kissing Babies:

Ruth Kowslowski's blog

A broadsheet photograph, front page, shows the politician, jowly, slightly sweaty, holding up the baby. We cannot tell the sex of the child because only its face is visible, encircled by white fake-fur, but its arms are rigidly extended, and its wide-open eyes are fixed on the politician's bushy eyebrows. The child's mouth, frozen by the photographer's flash, is half-open and perhaps bellowing in fear.

In 1697, Czar Peter the Great kissed a baby in the house of Frederik Ruysch, Praelector in Anatomy of the Amsterdam Surgeon's Guild. Ruysch's baby, pink and open-eyed, lay peacefully amongst embroidered cloths, and did not emit a sound.

'The very idea that all children want to be cuddled by a complete stranger I find amazing': a comment in 1996 by a member of the Royal Family. She's right, of course, and she has never aspired to be a People's Princess. It *is* amazing. And they probably don't.

So why do mothers hold out their babies? What is the purpose of the kiss? To test the politician's humanity, to check that he (for it is usually a 'he') has the country's future at heart even though it may just have been presented to him in all its noisome grubbiness? Is the imprint of the moist lips a transient lucky charm that protects against recession, redundancy and further reductions in public transport? Or will the baby grow up indoctrinated with the much-recounted story, so that in the pub on a Friday night he/she says, 'Hey, you know Bloggs? That famous (Conservative, Labour or even Lib Dem) bloke? He kissed me when I was little and it really changed my life – I started to grow up!'?

Peter the Great had different reasons. The baby that he kissed was not just resting in its cradle but was long dead, embalmed and displayed as a specimen in Ruysch's *Wunderkammer*. The story was put about by Dr Ruysch's maid that the Czar of all the Russias believed the baby was alive, because its skin was soft and blooming, as delicate as the plums that Ruysch's daughters painted in still-life. Another servant disagreed: the Czar had attempted to breathe Life into the not-living. Peter was Tall – 6 foot 7 inches – as well as Great, but despite his height he could certainly see that the baby was not alive. He had already spent days examining Ruysch's Cabinets and talking with the skilful anatomist and embalmer (*Konstenaar*, artist, that was what Ruysch sometimes called himself), a man he still referred to twenty years later as his 'teacher'. Peter kissed the child in recognition of Ruysch's skill, for the child was lifelike, in both its colour and form. Its eyes were open, fringed with lashes, and stared unblinkingly at the Czar. The glass eyes gave the child the appearance and power of life. Perhaps that kiss was also elicited by pity as well as wonder at the baby's innocence and beauty. Who now can tell? But the story of Peter's apparent gullibility has been preserved for more than three hundred years.

Papin implies that even Death – who thought he had got his hands on the child – is forced to think otherwise by Ruysch's artistry: *Mortuus, arte tua, Ruyschi,/ Vivit, docet, infans,/ Elinguis loquitur; Mors timet ipsa sibi. (Through thy art, O Ruysch, a dead infant lives and teaches and, though speechless, still speaks. Even Death itself is afraid.)*

The recipe for Ruysch's preservative fluid, his *liquor balsamicus*, was a closely-guarded secret, but was based on alcohol, probably brandy from Nantes, mixed with herbs, pepper and oil of turpentine. Balsam or balm, embalming, *balsemen*, all refer to aromatic substances and their uses, as ointments and unguents. In 1717, Peter the Great came back to Amsterdam for a second visit, and bought Ruysch's entire collection and had it transported to his own *Kunstkammer* in St Petersburg. A rumour was put about that the sailors drank the brandy from half the vials, but this surely wasn't true for the Czar would certainly have had the sailors put to death. One might say it was a missed opportunity for the Czar, for what delightful retribution it would have been to display their skeletons and pickled body parts: *'Hand of a light-fingered thief', 'Liver of a drunk who drank embalming fluid', 'Sea-legs of a sailor'.*

Nevertheless, the alcoholic preparations continued to present a temptation for a couple of centuries to come for it is said that even in the twentieth century a janitor in the Anatomy Department at Leiden was caught drinking from a preparation made by Ruysch's contemporary, Albinus.

The embraced baby looked good, it even smelt good (oil of lavender was included in the *liquor*), but it was the pinkness of its flesh, the inference of warmth, that made it seem alive. And there, literally, lay another secret recipe. For Ruysch was not merely an expert embalmer, he was the most successful of the 17th-century anatomists who were learning the topography of the body's multiple, ramifying vessels through the art of injecting them with colourful preservatives. Swammerdam injected mercury into blood vessels, using a special syringe invented by Reinier de Graaf; by 1667 he and van Hoorne were able to fill the blood vessels of the uterus with a mixture of warmed red wax and tallow. Ruysch studied Swammerdam's technique and refined the recipe, probably including resin and coloured essential oils (only Peter the Great's court physician was let into the secret). Anastomosing blood vessels and lymphatics were revealed like delicate coloured lace.

Rachel Ruysch, creator of exquisite paintings of flowers and insects, their painted texture so detailed as to be almost tactile, sat lace-making – not knitting – while her father severed the heads or arms or legs of injected and embalmed babies. She made lace-trimmed batiste sleeves and lacy collars, which were wrapped ('prettily and naturally', according to her father) around sewn-up stumps and wounds; a tiny pink arm holds out a thread from which dangles a preserved eye; another arm, clothed in a pretty sleeve, reaches out to clasp an enlarged bladder. Babies in tiny coffins were dressed in lace garments and adorned with flowers and beads. In the Boerhaave Museum, Leiden, and amongst the remnants of Czar Peter's collection in St Petersburg are the jars that contain embalmed foetuses, naked except for their beads. Beads adorn their necks, their waists, ankles, elbows, wrists or knees, in single, doubled or tripled strands of blue and white and sometimes green. Did Rachel thread these too? What is their significance? We may never know, but they are un-Dutch, primitive. Did Rachel, in her teens, help her father as he fixed a foetus' sitting posture and tied the necklace around its neck? Did she want to kiss and hug the sweetly adorned, reanimated form?

In 1685, when Rachel is 22 years old, Michiel van Musschen paints her, the subject of *An Allegorical portrait of an Artist*. He is twice her age, and arranges the thick rope of her hair across her bare shoulder. She is beautiful and serene, her skin is clear and soft. Van Musschen compares her to Minerva, the patroness of Art, and he paints a baby-faced cherub flying down to place a laurel wreath upon her dark curls. Rachel would like to play with the black-and-white spaniel that scampers around the table, but she must sit still for she is dignified, intelligent, an object to be desired.

Not so her brother, Hendrik. His portrait is that of a young boy, a still embryonic doctor and anatomist. In 1683 Jan van Neck paints *The Anatomy Lesson of Dr Frederik Ruysch*, illustrating members of the Surgeons' Guild. They examine the placenta of the well-preserved body of an over-large but newborn baby. The baby is pink, apparently merely sleeping although Ruysch has opened up his abdomen. The tracery of placental blood mimics the lace cravats of the surgeons, and the umbilical cord is a gilded rope. Hendrik, at that time aged twenty, is shown as a boy and holds a baby's skeleton.

So many babies! Where do they all come from? 'Where *do* they all belong?'

Rachel and her husband, the portrait painter and lace-merchant Juriaen Pool, were to have ten children. We do not know if any of their babies died. But would she and Juriaen have asked her father to embalm them, so they might live forever? We would like to think it was unlikely, but we cannot tell. Ruysch's babies were not for entertainment or even to be used as specimens for teaching anatomy, they were artworks – and moralistic in tone. They were symbols of *Vanitas mundi,* the pointlessness of pleasure – 'we're doomed, we're going to die!' (Ruysch himself died in 1731, at the great age of 93, but it isn't recorded whether his longevity was due to inhalation of *liquor balsamicus* fumes.) They were not regarded at that time with horror or disgust. Death was everywhere, a daily occurrence, it was God's Will (a Calvinistic God, at that) so we would do well to remember the transience of our lives on earth, and the ultimate irrelevance of earthly objects. Ruysch's babies were all perfect, and perfectly virtuous and innocent.

He certainly had access to large numbers of both normal, and teratologically abnormal, foetuses. In 1668 he was entrusted with the training of Amsterdam's midwives. Ten years later he was appointed as 'doctor to the court', which allowed him to take possession of all the dead babies found in the harbour. It was a period of history when birth rates and mortality rates were high, for many reasons. Today we are scarcely replacing ourselves, the rate of reproduction is less than 2 in Britain, even less in Italy, the country of babies and extended families; unwanted babies need no longer be conceived.

But unwanted babies will always find their way into the world, and be abandoned. A thin wail, a choking cry, comes from a telephone kiosk, a doorstep, a black bin-bag or a handbag on Paddington station. In Hamburg there is a 'postbox' where a desperate mother can lift the flap and leave her baby on a warm and comfortable bed, no questions asked, no identification necessary. (Is there a warning – as with 'Low Bridges', 'Max width, max height' – to prevent over-large parcels being posted?) The newly-delivered baby is lifted from the bed, kind hands stroke her silky hair and touch the pulsing fontanelle. Does she understand that comforting kiss, that it signifies Life?

Ruysch's babies mock the frailty of their parents, who gave them brief life. A foetal hand, its severed wrist hidden by a lacy cuff, plays ball with a '*segmentum humani testiculi*'; in another jar, the lace-capped leg of a baby rudely kicks a prostitute's syphilitic skull.

Seven

Ruth stood as though paralysed, the vacuum-cleaner lifeless at her heels. Notebooks, papers and files, paperbacks of the Russian novelists that she was re-reading unmethodically, balls of twine, a chunky Icelandic pullover, and a purple vest top with a needle and thread stuck into it. Too many things. She decided almost at once to abandon the attempt to tidy up. Stefan might be here within a couple of hours. After all these years.

It was only a week since he had emailed that he was due to give a seminar in Liverpool and yesterday he had telephoned her. They had spoken to each other. He sounded very English, exaggeratedly so: perhaps living abroad had done that. He was intending to visit the Lake District with a friend, and he wanted to come and see her. No, he had been more circumspect, he 'had wondered if there was any chance' et cetera; apologetic and conditional, as though he had almost hoped she would say it was 'out of the question, bugger off back to Belgium and leave me alone'. Perhaps she should have. What was the point of meeting again? A long-ago lover, just the first of several. She hadn't even bothered to enquire why he wanted to see her. She wished he had stuck with looking at her website.

The small window of the sitting-room rationed external heat and light as though they were unsustainable, and Ruth thumped it with a book, then forced it open in the hope that some warmer air would enter. The scent of the honeysuckle that was gradually burying the fence drifted in and she inhaled and then let her breath out slowly as she looked around the room.

Why bother? she said out loud. I don't have to impress Stefan. Or his friend. A mathematician from Liverpool, a Dr Lisa Wallace. Well.

She dragged the vacuum-cleaner back to its hiding-place under the stairs and went through to the kitchen. The extension had been added fifty years ago and was flat-roofed and leaky, cold in the winter and too warm in the summer, but although it shared a wall with the adjoining house, it was bright with the light from uncurtained windows. Ruth picked up her cereal-bowl and mug from the table and dumped them in the sink, then stared thoughtfully into the garden. She might have to give Stefan and his friend some sort of lunch. Stepping over the chicken wire stapled across the bottom of the open doorway, she went out into the long strip of garden. The over-fed, half-blind cat from next door lay in a coagulation of grey fur on top of the henhouse, and she lobbed a stone high in the air so that it fell with a clatter onto the corrugated-iron roof of the shed. With a wail of fright, the cat leapt down off the henhouse and crashed into the metal water-pot, so that a curtain of water drenched its fur.

'*Yesss*!' Ruth raised clenched fists in triumph. Three times out of five; the cat never learnt.

Two of the brown hens were dust-bathing, half-opened wings, half-closed eyes, wriggling their bodies deeper into the earth. They had pushed aside the netting that covered the young lettuces and one end of the row was trampled and pecked.

There were only two eggs in the henhouse; a poor return, she thought, two eggs from six hens, who were eating their way through fresh lettuce and sacks of pellets and mixed corn. The hens were from the local battery farm, sold off for pennies at the end of a year. The first time Ruth had bought some, several years previously, the woman had carried them out, three birds hanging silently head-down from each hand, and put them in the cardboard box. Not until Ruth had opened the box at home had she seen their scrawny naked necks, their raw red bottoms and how they lifted their feet in discomfort. They had huddled together, staring up at the henhouse roof, waiting for the sky to fall in, and for a week had not ventured through the open door. But then they had discovered freedom and an atavistic urge to scratch in the earth and peck and preen, and they had re-fledged and grown fat and glossy. As the days had lengthened into Spring, they carried on laying every day, and Ruth scarcely knew what to do with the eggs because Madeleine had good layers too. But then, as now, the clock had started running down and the internal quota of eggs had been used up – and she would have to end their briefly happy lives. George had shown her how to do it, the quick tug and twist, and now she could do it too.

Egg and lettuce sandwiches. If that wasn't sufficient, there was some cheese. Probably.

What had she and Stefan worn in the late eighties? Was that when she wore long dresses and army boots? Or brightly-coloured indie skirts and off-the-shoulder jumpers and long scarves? She was mildly surprised that she could not remember how she or Stefan had dressed as students, and realised that she had no preconceptions about how he might look now. She wandered back into the kitchen and wiped the eggs with the dishcloth. Cupping her hands together, she sluiced cold water over her face, then pulled off the elastic band around her hair and raked her hair free with her fingers. The red wiry curls sprung up around her head and shoulders. She caught sight of her imperfect reflection in the window and felt as though she was looking at herself for the first time in months, and was suddenly taken aback by the realisation that she was in her early-thirties and probably too old to have unkempt long hair. For a moment she imagined herself taking the kitchen scissors and shearing the unruly mass at the level of her chin;

she made scissors of her index and middle finger and caught a hank between them. Yes, she could do it now, why not? But of course she wouldn't.

The phone started ringing in the sitting room and she knew it would be Stefan, saying that he and Lisa were lost.

'You're not far away.' She gave him directions through the nearby lanes. 'There's a barn in a field down on your left. Two hundred metres beyond that there's a white house on your right with two front gates. I live in the left-hand side. Park on the road behind my van, there's not much traffic. See you soon.'

'Lisa' was a lean, tanned name, fine-boned and efficient. The words of the Christopher Logue poem came into Ruth's head: 'Lithe girl, brown girl', accentuated by the jeering notes of the saxophone. She went to the laptop that was on the table in a corner of the sitting-room and, finding Stefan's first email message, opened the attachment and looked at the photograph again. Her first lover, her first love.

'Hi, are you Polish?' she had asked him. It had been the end of her first year and she had just finished her last exam and was celebrating on the lawn outside the student union bar. 'I'm Ruth Kowslowski and my Dad was Polish. Perhaps we're related.'

He was good-looking in the photograph, but that dated back to student days, and now he was probably flabby and balding. She wished that he was not coming to visit.

'There's the barn, down there. What a view! Imagine living here.' Bassenthwaite Lake glittered in the distance, and sunlight and shadow moved slowly across the flanks of Skiddaw, the colours and patterns on the great hill changing constantly. Elder flowers were creamy soup-plates in the hedges and newly-shorn sheep were uneasily white.

'You're nervous, aren't you?' Lisa changed gear and glanced at Stefan. He was fidgeting with his watch and had pushed himself more upright in the passenger seat. 'My driving is impeccable so that can't be the reason. I'm still not sure that I should have come with you, you know. I shall be the proverbial gooseberry.'

'Oh, I need you. I keep telling you that. You are to be my insurance policy.' He smiled at her briefly. 'If I ask whether you need to get back, you must say yes, and we can escape.'

'It's nice to feel useful. But what if you want to stay, after all?'

'I haven't exactly thought that through.' His smile was more genuine now. 'Well, we're here. The left half, she said. This seems a strange house to find in the back of beyond.'

'It was probably built by the local Victorian squire to house his horny-handed sons of toil. And has now been gentrified.' She drew up behind a muddy red van, glancing through the garden gates as she did so. 'Although perhaps by only fifty per cent.'

The garden on the right was paved and gravelled, with a raised rockery and a few tubs of plants but Ruth's garden was a rectangular box of vegetation, the contents spilling over its edges in search of light. Lisa let Stefan walk ahead of her to the door and as he ducked beneath the honeysuckle a starburst of bees and flies exploded around his head. The slate path was slippery with wormcasts and leaves and the house's walls were streaked with green. Goosegrass, boot-strapping upwards, caught at Lisa's sleeve.

'Tennyson was clearly colour-blind,' she muttered as she tried to remove the prickly strands.

'What?' Stefan glanced round at her, almost irritably.

He really is nervous, she thought, and added aloud, 'Nature *green* in tooth and claw. But don't worry about it.' She smiled at him. 'I know I don't really know you well enough to offer advice, but take a deep breath then smile before you knock at the door.'

She would have liked to take his hand at that moment, to grip it and say something meaningless such as 'everything will be fine', but of course that was out of the question. His hands, resting on his thighs, had distracted her in the car; the fingers were long and fine-boned with perfectly-trimmed short nails. They looked almost too perfect, like his clothes – beige fleece jacket placed carefully on the back seat, deep red cotton shirt and dark green trousers, worn with brown leather shoes, not trainers. Yet he did not seem to be a vain man, he was too diffident and unassuming. She could not work him out, but she was afraid that he would find this Ruth to be a very different person from the student he had known all those years ago.

'You are quite right, Dr Wallace.' He breathed in and out a couple of times then bared his teeth at her in a rictus of terror just as Ruth opened the door.

'I heard you arrive—' she was saying but then stopped dead.

'Sorry, we should have warned you that a madman and a person of restricted growth were about to appear on your doorstep,' Lisa said, and started to giggle. 'Oh dear, that was such a bad introduction. Would you like to shut the door and we'll start again?'

'No. No, that's okay.' Ruth and Stefan were staring at each other, unsmiling, then Stefan held out his hand.

'Ruth.'

She took it and he leant forward and kissed her briefly on each cheek. For a moment they seemed unable to let go and Lisa suddenly wanted to trot away back down the path.

'Ruth, this is my colleague, Lisa Wallace. She's the one who invited me over to the UK to visit her department.'

Ruth looked down at Lisa from the step and attempted a welcoming smile though she was clearly overwhelmed.

'Hallo. Come in. It's nice to meet you.'

She squeezed against the wall so that they could pass and then knocked Lisa's head with her elbow as she tried to reach over her to shut the door. Mutual embarrassment and, on Lisa's part, pain, followed briefly, and then somehow the three of them managed to find their way into the living room where Ruth, by now flustered and with red patches on her cheeks, suggested they sit down while she made some coffee. Lisa quickly assessed the big squashy armchairs, each of which was covered with colourful but threadbare throws that might have been Indian bedspreads, and chose the wooden chair by the table. Stefan was left with no option and was engulfed by an armchair as though by a hungry amoeba. For a few moments they both sat in silence, listening to the clattering in the kitchen.

'I think I'd prefer a glass of cold water,' Lisa said. 'Why don't you go through into the kitchen and ask her? I'm quite happy to sit here for a while.'

Stefan nodded. 'Good idea. Thanks.'

Lisa sat quietly and looked around. The room was clearly two small rooms that had been knocked together, and the door that would have led in from the corridor was blocked by a bookcase. From the rear window she could just glimpse the side of an extension, presumably the kitchen, and a low hut at the bottom of the back garden. Around her was a jumble of pebbles, bones, papers, feathers, a couple of stuffed mice on a wooden stand, an empty glass dome, piles of books, and discs and tape cassettes, many without their identifying cases, many of them dusty. Perhaps taxidermists, by their nature, never threw anything away. Old bills and their torn envelopes lay on the table, newspapers and logs were stacked next to the ash-filled grate but, despite the sagging wiring of the wall-mounted lamps and the electric cables weaving out of a three-way adapter plugged into an ancient socket, the laptop computer on the table was a smart recent model and the print-outs and books next to it were neatly tagged with yellow 'post-it' notes.

She could hear Ruth and Stefan talking, in the hesitant manner of almost-strangers. She could not hear their words, merely the music of their conversation: Stefan's warm tones, the way his sentences grew longer and wove amongst the silences between Ruth's increasingly abbreviated and staccato questions and replies. Lisa knew they were the same age, but Ruth had not kept herself in trim the way Stefan had, her stomach was flabby above the waistband of her faded jeans and the green V-neck top did not improve her figure. Why had she not bothered to dress up or at least wear something more flattering? I bothered, she thought, with a hint of self-righteousness, looking down at the long skirt that she had made herself out of fine Liberty cotton, a pattern of subtle-coloured minute flowers. Lisa wondered whether Ruth was making a point or if she really was oblivious or even uncaring about her appearance. Presumably Ruth and Stefan had once thought they were similar, 'kindred spirits', but now they seemed so different, not just in terms of their exterior shells, but in the patterns of their lives. She wondered if they would find points of contact.

They were taking a long time, had they forgotten her? That familiar feeling of exclusion which she usually managed to quash, often by muttering words aloud to herself such as 'self-indulgence' and 'self-pity', wormed its way into her mind, and she slid down from the chair and wandered around the room, examining the various artefacts. A framed photograph on a bookshelf attracted her attention. At first she could not understand the subject and she stood back, to re-focus. Then the dark spiky shapes resolved themselves into the stiff legs of cattle, pointing skywards through the smoke and flames, like smoking shattered architecture in the aftermath of a blitz. It was a copy of a famous photograph taken during the epidemic of foot-and-mouth disease in 2001. In the foreground an overlooked lamb, alive but motherless, stared through the fence towards the flames. The loneliness of that small creature next to the horror of the massacre had briefly gripped the nation.

Lisa shuddered, not only because of the chilly room. She walked out into the narrow hall that was made even narrower by waterproofs hanging from hooks, boots, and a couple of boxes of dog-eared wildlife magazines that looked as though they had come from a car-boot sale. She could see Stefan in the kitchen, leaning back against a cupboard and holding a cereal packet in his hands, watching with great concentration as Ruth filled mugs with boiling water. He glanced round quickly.

'Lisa. Sorry, we got involved in one of those "and where did you go then?" conversations. Oh, I forgot. Ruth, I was supposed to tell you Lisa wanted water not coffee.'

'No, no, if you've made coffee that's fine. Sorry, I didn't mean to interrupt. "Coco pops"! I haven't eaten them in years. Is that your lunch, Stefan?'

'Hah. No, I'm discovering Ruth's secret indulgences. Delicious – take a handful and remind yourself of that uniquely artificial taste.'

'The secrets of the single woman. I have a few of those, too, which I'm sure I wouldn't want discovered.'

'Skeletons in the cupboard.'

Ruth closed her eyes and sighed exaggeratedly. 'That joke is so over-used. There's a glass over there, Stefan. Fill it from the tap – the water's all right to drink, we're on the mains.'

'I was looking at that photo of the funeral pyre in your living room,' Lisa said as she took the cold glass. 'Were you very badly affected here? I guess this whole area must have been very tightly restricted.'

Lisa had noted that Ruth's earlier red patches of embarrassment had faded to an attractive pink flush, but now it suddenly seemed as though a plug had been pulled and the blood had drained away.

'It was terrible. We don't talk about it,' she said curtly. 'Some people will probably never recover.'

Stefan looked from one to the other, questioningly.

'Foot-and-mouth disease. It hit Cumbria especially hard.' Lisa explained. 'Sorry, Ruth. That was tactless of me to bring it up.'

'Of course we heard about it in Belgium. But not realising at that time that I knew anyone in Cumbria, it all seemed rather remote. A British disease. Mad cows and Englishmen go out in the midday sun, and so on.'

Stefan smiled, trying to smooth away the tension, looking very hard at Ruth. Lisa suddenly had the distinct impression that he wanted to seize Ruth and kiss her, and she felt so embarrassed that she had to look away.

Ruth tipped the seat forward to let Stefan climb out. They had travelled in Lisa's car rather than her van, and she had navigated them to the pub for lunch, and now to Madeleine's farm. Conversation had become easier in the pub, and she had found herself suggesting that Stefan and Lisa might like to visit her workshop.

'Have you got time? Or do you have to drive back to Liverpool?' She noticed that Lisa, sitting, did not appear to be so very short.

'Oh, I'm just the chauffeur, I fit in with our foreign visitor's busy schedule.' Lisa put down her knife and fork and looked at Stefan, waiting for his reply, but he carefully folded his paper napkin, avoiding eye contact with either of the women.

'I don't think we need to rush back, do we, Lisa? We had even wondered about staying in the area, perhaps finding a bed and breakfast. What do you think? How are you feeling?'

Rather surprised, Ruth guessed, but she liked the way in which Lisa calmly said, 'I'm fine. And a night in the country would probably do me good. Perhaps you could suggest somewhere for us to stay, Ruth.'

'Madeleine Tregwithen does bed and breakfast. I rent the studio in her barn. If you like the look of the place, we can ask her if she has any vacancies. But there are lots of other places if she's fully booked.'

Ruth wondered if the farmhouse would present any physical problems for Lisa. She had been noticing the small ways in which Lisa coped with her disability. Sure, she had had all her life to get used to dealing with the persistent minor difficulties of living in a world designed for taller people, but she did so entirely naturally and without fuss.

'My dad made the extensions,' she had said, when she saw Ruth looking at the raised foot pedals in the car. 'He's a welder and he's always enjoyed making things for me, he treats it as a challenge. I have a special grab for picking items off supermarket shelves. As long as they're not too heavy – I've had the occasional tin fall on my head, or broken jar on the floor.'

The two women had smiled at each other and Ruth was filled with curiosity about this small woman – she was not much more than four feet high – who lectured to students and researched an esoteric branch of mathematics. Ruth had never previously heard the words 'quasicrystal' or 'aperiodic order' until she sat eating her pie and chips in the pub. Lisa and Stefan had attempted to explain it to her and she understood, or thought she understood, about crystals – there were some on the table, salt and sugar, and melting ice. Some of the chemicals she bought were in crystalline form, and diamonds were crystals of carbon.

'Basically, they are solids made of vast numbers of sub-microscopic building-blocks – atoms and molecules – arranged in endless repetition.'

'And they're self-organising! It's almost miraculous when you think about it,' Lisa had enthused. 'Solids are created that are inherently symmetrical – and do you know, there are as many as two hundred and thirty possible classes of symmetry? I still find that amazing. And yet the symmetries of quasicrystals are completely different again.'

'I don't understand about the symmetry,' Ruth had said.

'Crystal lattices have what's called pure periodic symmetry in three dimensions – when people look at crystals using X-rays, the X-rays are diffracted to form patterns of light spots and dark. Each crystal type has its own characteristic lattice. But then in the early 'eighties, everything suddenly became very confusing because materials were found that showed X-ray - like point diffraction patterns, but which were definitely not crystals. And they weren't amorphous solids, either. So they became known as quasi-crystals. Their symmetries were quite different, and ordered in different ways, they didn't fit into the two hundred and thirty symmetries that Lisa just mentioned. A whole new branch of crystallography came into being.'

'Raising all kinds of exciting new questions in maths and physics. Stefan works on the more physical side–' Lisa grinned at him '–and my research is into the maths of aperiodic order. Crystals fill space with periodic symmetry, but quasicrystals fill spaces in entirely different ways, and in more than the usual three dimensions.'

'I think it's safe to say that I can't get my head around more than four dimensions, quite literally. It makes my brain hurt, it falls into the same category as trying to imagine what's beyond the edges of the universe,' Ruth had said, somewhat drily.

But when she discovered that Stefan and Lisa had met in Amsterdam she was on safer territory, and at Lisa's mention of De Waag her voice rose in surprise.

'But that's where the Surgeons' Guild had its headquarters in Ruysch's time. It housed the big anatomy theatre which figures in de Keyser's famous painting of Dr Sebastien Egberts' anatomy lesson. Did you go to the city museum? The anatomy lesson series are fascinating, there's Rembrandt's paintings of Nicolaes Tulp and the one of Joan Deyman's lesson – you must know that one? Where he's opening up the skull. And van Neck's and Backer's painting of Ruysch's lessons... They follow on logically from the other guild paintings, all those men in black looking out at the viewer...'

Stefan interrupted. 'Sorry, Ruth. We were complete philistines, we just sat in the sun and drank beer.'

'But you succeeded in getting into De Waag! I tried but I

didn't know who to ask. Somebody told me Ruysch's coat of arms was on the ceiling. But of course you wouldn't even have thought to look. If only I'd known you were going there I could have pointed you in the direction of all manner of—' She stopped, realising she was becoming too emphatic. 'Sorry.'

'It's true, there were painted shields inside the ceiling of the dome.' Lisa seemed amused at Ruth's sudden flow of words. 'Who is Ruysch?'

'Stefan should know, I mention him in that essay you said you'd read, Stefan. He was an anatomist and embalmer.'

'Er... something unpleasant to do with pickled eyes?' Stefan was clearly guessing, but Ruth was suddenly distracted by the sight of Lisa's hand. The three middle fingers wrapped around the wine-glass were of almost equal length. She stared at them, seeing the shape of the bones as though X-rayed.

'Trident fingers, a characteristic of achons,' Lisa saw the direction of her attention. 'Give me a helmet and a Union flag and I could stand in for Britannia. I'd be interested to read some of your essays, I can look at them online, right?'

The switch in subject confused Ruth and she struggled for a moment. Essays. She was about to say that she would give her the web address when the implications of some of the content hit her.

'*No*! No. You wouldn't like them. No. Sorry.'

'Oh. Right.' Lisa's face crumpled in a wry smile as she raised her eyebrows. 'I'll take your word for it. And I'll assume you don't want reprints of any of my papers either. Though my collaborative work on diffraction and deformed model sets is said to be fairly cutting-edge. Dr Greatorex here thinks so anyway, and he's a man to be reckoned with.'

Now, as Ruth held open the car door and Stefan uncoiled himself from the small space in the back and stepped out into the yard, Ruth felt his heat and smelt the beer on his breath. For a moment their bodies were so close that she could almost feel them pressed together. She had tried to ignore how he had kept staring at her for the past few hours, as though he could not quite believe what he was seeing and feeling. Was it love or lust? How trite if he should 'fall in love' again. But she didn't care. She caught Stefan's eye, and they both knew the urge was inescapable.

Eight

Madeleine touched Lisa's arm and pointed silently. The barn owl beat slowly along the margin of the field, circled and came back again; rhythmic, unhurried, its moth-wings catching the low golden light. A lamb, startled, ran bleating to its mother, burrowing to find the comfort of her udder, its tail wagging. The owl hawked to and fro, then, unsatisfied, flapped over the hedge and out of sight. Neither of the women spoke and Madeleine's throat was tight with gratitude. To the North, the Solway Firth was a band of pale mercury, and beyond it the Scottish hills were layered in hazy pink and gold.

Earlier, the ewes had cantered across to the Land Rover in expectation of food, but now they had dispersed and were determinedly grazing, one or other occasionally raising her head to bleat half-heartedly for her lambs. Eight lambs had formed a gang and raced from one corner of the field to a rise and back again; leaping, flinging their rear legs sideways, butting heads and then pausing to make further plans. They never failed to amuse Madeleine and soon the glimmer in her eyes translated itself to open laughter, and the two women laughed out loud together.

Madeleine struggled to understand the emotion that filled her, she was so unused to this feeling of deep contentment that made her eyes prick with tears. She felt such peace and a sense of belonging. At her age to feel like this!

Then she spluttered with laughter. 'Long in the tooth! I was just thinking about myself. But where *does* that saying come from? Not from sheep-farmers, that's for sure – ewes' teeth wear down, poor old things.' Then, conscious that Lisa was looking across at her, she stroked her left cheek; out of habit, unaware, her hand hiding the purple scar.

'Rabbits? Guinea-pigs? I have a mental picture of ancient Mandarins with long wispy beard, toothless but with enormous curling finger-nails. But you're not old. How old are you anyway – late fifties? And how many women your age could lead your sort of life? Running a farm on your own.'

Madeleine thought for a moment. 'I'm fifty-eight. And I don't run it entirely on my own. George helps out – you've not met George, he's a good lad at heart. He helps with the lambing and does all the contract-work. And there are plenty of people willing to give advice.'

'I can imagine that.'

'I had a lot to learn. When John got ill I realised how little I knew, really. Before that happened he'd taken over more and more of the running—' The familiar cold fear welled up within her and she wiped it away, smoothing her palms on her skirt and crumpling its plain blue cotton with her hands. 'There was so much to re-learn. It was easier when I switched to mules – though I've bought a few Herdwicks again since I re-stocked. We had Herdwicks before, we had more land on the Fells then but I sold it after John died. They've a mind of their own, Herdwicks, and I've always liked them for that. You'll know which are the Herdwicks amongst this lot, of course?'

'Oh of course! They must be the ones with the intelligent faces rather than looking like asses. Go on, then, show me – and explain about mules. I thought the point about mules was that they're sterile, so they don't sound as though they would be much use for producing lambs. Or even foals. Stop teasing me, you know quite well that I'm completely lost.'

'These mules are Scottish blackface crosses. We had the pure blackfaces in Ayrshire but these mules are good, they've mostly produced twins this year. They didn't need too much help, either. The Herdwicks are the grey stocky ones with white faces, theirs are the all-black lambs. At the moment. They'll change. That's another thing I like about them, the way the lambs' faces turn white. I asked Ruth why that was but she didn't know.'

'Interesting. I wonder if Ruth and Stefan are enjoying the sunset? Though I don't suppose they've even noticed it.' Lisa grinned at her. 'It's a relief to have a break from them and all those surging hormones. Thank you, Madeleine.' She breathed in deeply then sighed. 'And this is a most perfect place. Thank you for bringing me here.'

They sat quietly and watched as the hazy horizon caught and squeezed the sun, spraying deep red colour high up into the cirrus clouds, spilling it over the flat surface of the distant sea. Windows of houses and moving cars on the Solway plain flashed crimson, and the tops of the hills behind the field briefly leapt into relief, then flattened into grey.

Madeleine drove the Land Rover back across the field, opening and closing the gates herself. As she drove home through the narrow lanes she tried to recapture the inner stillness that she had felt earlier, but any mention of her farming life with John always created a mental disturbance that was hard to dispel. Ayrshire, with its wind-swept rolling farmland, lay to the North-West, towards the sunset but hidden by the Galloway hills. She and John had been happy there in the beginning, but later the farm had become a focus of their despair. And that despair had divided them; they had tried to ignore it and to start a new life in England. They had sold the Scottish farm and what remained of the stock, and had bought this smaller farm on less productive land. John had said he'd always wanted Herdwicks, he wanted hill sheep and to keep them on the hills. He hadn't liked the Highlands and had felt that Cumbria was a safer alternative. He'd learnt to talk of yows and tips and 'twinters'. He had gradually excluded her from the day-to-day work, he had run the farm himself, doing all the dipping and the dykeing, getting help with the silaging, and had bought in hay. In return, she had run the house and managed the garden; she had seen to it that there was food on the table and clean shirts in the cupboard. They had met at meal-times, they had even shared the same bed; but there was a barrier between them, an emptiness. He blamed her; she had sunk into blame-worthiness.

'*Ouf!*' Lisa, who had been gripping the sides of the seat tightly, grunted as the Land Rover hit a particularly bad pot-hole. 'And I thought city roads were bad! My spine has been concertina-ed, I'll go home even shorter. How many sheep did you say you had?'

'Sorry.' Madeleine dragged her mind back to the present. 'I'll slow down. About fifty ewes, and around eighty lambs. They kept us busy at lambing time and then there were three to bottle-feed. But I like lambing, I always have, even the difficult ones. Even in the wee small hours.'

'You're out here in the field in the night? In the rain and snow?'

Madeleine laughed. 'Good grief, no. We bring the ewes down to the farm and bring them in at night to keep an eye on them. We need to be able to pen them if there's a problem or if they won't take to the lamb. A couple of years ago we had real trouble. I'd borrowed a Texel tup, a big brute he was, good conformation, but the lambs were just too big for the ewes. What a struggle we had to get them out. A fair number went wrong, we lost quite a few. But as I said, we did a lot better this year. And I like being out in the barn at night. I take a thermos of tea and the radio, and often Ruth comes to help. And George and I take turns in the daytime, or he calls me if he needs another pair of hands.'

'Ruth helps?' Lisa was clearly surprised.

'Did you think she just dealt with dead things? She used to be a nurse when she was in Glasgow. But of course Stefan probably didn't know that either, so why should you? She's not afraid of a bit of gory work, and she's had to pull out a good few lambs in her time. She knows what to do. You might not think it but she can be good company. Quiet, mind. But we get on well enough. You two didn't exactly hit it off, did you?' She glanced at Lisa then wrenched the steering wheel as the vehicle wandered close to the verge.

'No.' Lisa pursed her lips and frowned. 'No, we didn't, really. I think she was rather overcome at meeting Stefan and my being there added to her confusion. Sometimes people find it hard to know how to deal with me. I think she and I would get on better under other circumstances.'

'You were saying Stefan might come back to work in England.'

'I really hope so. He'd be an enormous asset to our department. I'm referring to his skills, naturally, not just to his looks.'

'Of course you are!'

'But I have a feeling, after today, that his decision might depend less on the academic standing of the department than on how he and Ruth get on. Not very professional, of course, but very understandable.'

How does one 'deal with' an achondroplasic? Madeleine wondered. The word echoed in her head: she had not heard it before this afternoon, and she mouthed it silently, 'ay-chon-dro-*play*-sick', as she turned into the yard. Stefan treated Lisa as he would – did – any other person, herself included. With none of that skittering away of the eyes, or surreptitious staring, or enforced joviality. In the same way that Daniel had treated herself, with the normal amount of respect and disrespect that one accords a friend. Such people were rare and to be treasured.

She drove up to the mounting block at the side of the yard and braked.

'There we are. Madam, your horse awaits.'

Lisa laughed; she had been delighted with this solution to climbing into the Land Rover and now she opened the door and stepped out onto the pitted red sandstone step. 'Perfect.'

As they walked across to the house she said, 'I'm so glad I'm staying here, instead of driving back down the motorway and into the city. And it's still light at, what, nearly eleven o'clock. Will you have a nightcap with me, Madeleine? I have my emergency bottle of brandy in my bag.'

'Thanks, no. I'll never get up in the morning if I do, and I need to be out at six to check the sheep. But let me bring you some fresh milk for a cup of tea to have with your brandy. And you won't be needing to breakfast early, will you?'

Neither of them expressed any opinion as to whether Stefan would require breakfast too.

Madeleine was unable to sleep. She heard Stefan return just before midnight and come quietly up the stairs. He had the twin-bedded room next to hers and the floorboards creaked; she could imagine him cursing as they signalled his return. But he had returned, and that made her wonder. She also wondered why Lisa had preferred the room with the double bed. She had taken Lisa a little jug of milk and her practised eye had noted that the small bowl of pot pourri was missing from the top of the chest of drawers. Doubtless Lisa had put it a drawer, she didn't seem like the sort of guest who'd pop it in her bag. The mirror was too high on the wall. What if she couldn't reach the slider for the shower-head? Did she have to take special medicine? Did achondroplasics get ill? 'A-chons'. Lisa had abbreviated it. Like acorns. From little acorns do big oak trees grow. That had been another of Daniel's sayings. But not in poor Lisa's case. She was not 'poor' Lisa, though, she was a Dr Wallace who did not hide in a corner despite... despite the fact that her strange body was much more visible than an ugly purple growth.

Madeleine threw the bedclothes back and sat up, wafting her nightdress to cool herself, then lifting her long greying hair away from her hot neck. The room was thick with unstirred air and she got out of bed to stand by the window; stars shone steadily in the stillness and there were soft sounds of birds stirring in their sleep. Nearly one o'clock: in another couple of hours it would be light, and the wren would open its beak to bellow its deafening dawn song beneath the bedroom window. A voice out of all proportion to its size: what did a tiny wren know about anything?

She was confused by the mixture of curiosity and gratitude and, she had to admit, cold appraisal that Lisa had aroused in her. She had never met a dwarf before, though she had seen a dwarf man once, walking along the street with a strange rolling gait. They were oddities, misfits, unnatural. They used to be displayed in freak shows, didn't they, with the Bearded Woman, the Fat Man and the Siamese Twins? And perhaps the Woman with a Purple Fungus on her face.

Lisa was not afraid to display herself: she gave public talks, she stood on a stage in front of people and they all looked at her. She was brave although she had insisted she wasn't. To be brave you have to be conscious of something to be overcome.

'I don't think of myself as an achondroplasic,' she had told Madeleine. 'It doesn't define me to myself. I am *me*, the external appearance is incidental. I know that might be hard to understand, but I can't see myself. I don't see my flat nose and large skull and short limbs. I only remember them when I have to make my clothes or buy new shoes. "I think therefore I am". And I'm here inside my head.' She had tapped her domed skull.

But Madeleine, frightened of the Freak Show, had always hidden.

She moaned now, a tiny aching noise, and sat down on the bed, covering her face, recalling the horror of the darkness that followed the flickering light; the black-and-white kaleidoscope that turned to black, when she would sink into the pit where time was frozen and she was dead; and the eventual struggling out, a dull re-birth. Hiding, and hidden away, she had wasted so much of her married life because she hadn't known that she had the strength within her to resist. She knew now, because Daniel had shown her, and the black days would never be allowed to return. Had Lisa Wallace always known her own strengths?

She and Lisa had eaten dinner together in the kitchen. Earlier, in the afternoon, Ruth had brought her visitors across to ask about accommodation and Madeleine had shown them the rooms and made a pot of tea. There had been the question of where they would eat dinner, and much debate, which Lisa had resolved with sudden asperity, insisting she was tired and would drive out to find herself some fish and chips and then go to bed and read.

'I've a better idea, Dr Wallace. There are lamb chops in the freezer,' Madeleine had said, to her own surprise. 'I don't normally do dinner unless guests have booked ahead, but I've got to cook for myself so it's no trouble to cook for one more, if you don't mind taking it as it comes. You can eat in the dining room and read, if you like – or you're very welcome to sit here with me. Whatever suits you.'

It had surprised her that Dr Wallace wanted to eat with her, and she had worried about the height of the seat and arrangement of the table, so that she had been awkward at first and unable to think what to say. But then she had remembered that Ruth had given her a bottle of red wine some weeks previously and, because she was unused to alcohol, a half-glass had inspired her conversation.

Lisa had been interested in the farm and the business of farming, admitting that she was a 'townie' who knew little about the countryside.

'Do you have any children?' she had asked. 'I read that the children of farming families were all deserting the land because they think the life is too hard and uneconomic.'

'No, I don't – and it's certainly true they're all quitting. Who can blame them?' But then – and she didn't know whether it was the small amount of wine she had drunk or because even then she felt an affinity with Lisa – she had blurted out, 'What if my children had looked like this? If they'd had to go through life with everyone staring and making remarks, and—' She had suddenly realised what she was, in effect, saying. 'I'm stupid, I shouldn't have said that. It's so much worse for you. My—' She had slapped at her cheek. 'This is so small in comparison.' She had gathered up plates and pushed her chair back, distressed by her selfishness.

'It's not trivial at all. Don't reproach yourself, Madeleine. But surely your birthmark, or whatever it is, isn't heritable?'

Madeleine shook her head. 'I don't know. It wasn't so bad early on...' She had carried the plates over to the sink, and with her back turned, asked, 'If you had children, would they be like you? Do you mind my asking?'

'No, I don't mind, it's something that always puzzles other people. My child wouldn't necessarily be like me if my partner was average height. There's a fifty per cent chance the child would be average, too. I sometimes try to imagine what it would be like to have a child who would outgrow me.'

'*Could* you have a normal baby? Would it be physically possible?' Madeleine had glanced at Lisa shyly.

'Ah, the bluntness of a stock farmer!' Lisa had grinned, apparently unfazed. 'Yes. Provided my back stood the strain. Of course, if I married another achon, then there's a seventy-five per cent chance our children would be achons, too – and if one inherited a double dose of the gene, then that would be very serious, potentially fatal. But I don't want to marry someone like myself.'

Madeleine had wanted to ask about that too; her head had buzzed with questions. 'But I suppose that at least one of your parents is, well, like you?'

'No. I was a complete surprise to them. I'm a mutant! Actually, as you might imagine, I came as a shock to them.

Ultrasound scans weren't such a refined diagnostic tool at that time. But my parents are down-to-earth types and were very supportive after they got used to the idea, especially my father. They're amazing, really. They've always treated me as normally as possible, and they were determined right from the start that I should learn to do as much as I could for myself.'

'You were lucky. Do you have brothers or sisters?'

'A sister. Normal, married, two normal children. She believes she makes up for my deficiencies. We're not very good friends, unfortunately.' Lisa had shrugged, and Madeleine had felt the hurt that lay beneath that shrug.

They had sat in silence for a while, before deciding to drive up to look at the lambs. There had been a warmth between them, and Madeleine felt she had never talked to anyone like that before.

NINE
Copper Kettles:
Ruth Kowslowski's blog

On July 5th 1893 an Exhibition of 'A Collection of Hunterian Relics' opened at the Royal College of Surgeons, in London. Not the relics of Dr William Hunter, FRS and President of the Royal Academy, but of his younger brother, John, the naturalist and surgeon, born in Lanarkshire in 1729, who died, very suddenly, in London on October 16th 1793.

Amongst the interesting items on display is a *'Copper, in which the Irish Giant, Charles Byrne, who was exhibited in London as O'Brien the Irish Giant, was boiled.'* The copper was lent by Professor Chiene, of Edinburgh. The catalogue has a further explanatory note: *'This copper was in Hunter's house in Earl's Court and was sold there in 1866 when the house was pulled down. On the death of Byrne in 1783, Hunter obtained his body and macerated it in this copper... The skeleton of Byrne is in the College Museum.'* As indeed it is, to this day.

As for poor Hunter's sudden death, there is also exhibited the *'Sofa on which John Hunter died. Whilst speaking at a meeting of the Board of Governors at St George's Hospital on October 16th 1793, Hunter was contradicted by one of his colleagues. He immediately left off his speech and in an excited state, hurried to an adjoining room; where he fell into the arms of Dr Robertson and almost immediately expired.'* Fortunately for him, his body was not macerated in the copper, but was placed in a vault at St Martin's in the Fields. Of which, more later.

The College Museum has an engraving of Sir Joshua

Reynolds' portrait of Hunter, and Byrne is thus twice immortalised for, in the top right corner of the portrait and behind Hunter's head are the lower portions of two gigantic femora and their two feet – the legs of that most famous Tall Man who, from the angle of his skeletal feet, must be standing on tip-toe, perhaps to increase his height even more. Byrne may be the tallest man on display, but his legs are not the longest: that dubious honour goes to the 'Kentucky Giant', 7 feet 6 inches tall but with the longest femora of any known giant skeleton. His personal history is not known, only that his skeleton was 'acquired in 1877' by Joseph Leidy for fifty dollars, and is now exhibited at Philadelphia's Mütter Museum.

John Hunter has a square, kindly, thoughtful face and his forehead is broad and tall beneath his curly reddish hair. He doesn't look like a giant-killer.

To be fair, it seems that poor Charles Byrne, aged 22, height 7 feet 7 inches, drank himself to death. The story of Byrne is well-known, much has been written about him, both fact and fiction. He was born on the Derry/Tyrone border in 1761 and, because those were times when the exhibition of 'freaks' was commonplace, Jack Vance, from a neighbouring village, persuaded him that he could get rich if he toured the shows and fairgrounds: a sideshow attraction. On April 11th 1782, Byrne and Vance (self-important as the Giant's Agent) reached London and on April 24th an advertisement proclaimed: *Irish Giant. To be seen this and every day this week, in his large elegant room, at the cane shop, next door to late Cox's Museum, Spring Gardens.'* Admission was half-a-crown. By the late autumn, the public was jaded, the novelty had worn off, the price had dropped and the Giant O'Brien had moved twice, to rooms no longer so large and elegant. A year after his arrival in London, he was robbed outside a pub – of £700, presumably his entire worldly wealth which, for some reason, he was carrying in his pocket.

Despair, too much alcohol, and ill-health – Charles Byrne knew he was dying and somehow he also learnt that the anatomist John Hunter was very keen to obtain a giant's skeleton. Byrne didn't want his bones to be boiled, he didn't want to be exhibited any more, alive or dead. He gave instructions that after his death his body should be watched day and night until a large lead coffin had been built. His body was to be placed in it and it should be carried (how many tonnes would a giant lead coffin weigh?) out to sea and sunk. A newspaper reported after the event that *Byrne's body was shipped on board a vessel in the river last night... to be sunk in 20 fathom water: the body-hunters... have provided a pair of diving bells, with which they flatter themselves they shall be able to weigh hulk gigantic from its watery grave.'*

No diving bell was needed. Hunter, having sent his assistant Howison as spy, bribed the men whom Byrne had employed to sink him. Fifty pounds, one hundred pounds, the price escalated. Five hundred pounds was later reported as the sum involved. Byrne's body was removed and carried by hackney coach then Hunter's carriage to Earl's Court where, since Hunter feared that his body-snatching would be discovered, Byrne's body was 'quickly cut to pieces and the flesh separated by boiling'.

'*I lately got a tall man,*' Hunter wrote to Sir Joseph Banks.

Presumably John Hunter and Howison (not to be confused with William Hunter's assistant, William Hewson) boiled and re-assembled the skeleton themselves. Ten years earlier William Hunter had fallen out with Hewson, for Hewson 'had employ'd a Man to pick Bones out of the Tubs and fit up a Skeleton for him, without Leave'. Benjamin Franklin was called in to settle the dispute (poor Benjamin was often called in for this purpose). Although Hewson was highly skilled at injecting lymphatics and preparing specimens, he was eventually dismissed – and disinherited.

In Shepherd's 1840 engraving of the College Museum, Charles Byrne's skeleton with its smiling skull towers over the other exhibits from the top of a mahogany case. A photograph taken in 1852 shows him prominently displayed. And so he remains, in the twenty-first century, and we think of him kindly and with sympathy. Perhaps finally he has been able to smile at the thought that his story as well as his bones (and a portrait of his *feet*) are still preserved and admired nearly two hundred and fifty years later.

Bourgeois was a footman, or at any rate he was employed in 1717 to stand on the footboard of Peter the Great's carriage. The Czar and his Czarina had found him at the Calais Fair, a giant exhibit at 2.27 metres high. Later, when Bourgeois saw the Czar's Kunstkammer, he would surely guess where his bones would find their final resting-place. In 1724 his dead body was boiled in a copper kettle, and his skeleton reassembled. 'An old head on a young body'? Unfortunately the opposite is true, for his skull was destroyed in a fire in 1747 and the replacement skull was elevated to a higher position than it had occupied in life.

Did the Czar visit Calais before or after Amsterdam? In 1717 he paid a second visit to his 'same old teacher', the Dutch anatomist and embalmer Dr Frederik Ruysch. Imagine Bourgeois accompanying his new master on a tour of Ruysch's museum, ducking beneath the low dark beams, secretly shuddering at the skeletons and animals. Czar Peter so admired Ruysch's collection that he asked his own physician, the Scot Robert Erskine, to buy it – for 30,000 Dutch guilders, an enormous sum. The specimens were future companions for Bourgeois in St Petersburg.

A fire is lit and a little maid hurries to and fro with jugs of water to fill the copper; she heats the water so she may wash and scrub the clothes. But in John Hunter's house, the copper was used for boiling bodies from which to extract bones. Hunter's copper was lent to the Exhibition of Hunterian Relics by a Scottish professor, and Frank Buckland, Esquire, son of Dean Buckland of Islip, Oxfordshire, lent a chair. The chair bore a brass plate with the following inscription: *This Chair is made from the bedstead of John Hunter...* 'Buckland had been given the bedstead by 'Professor Owen, FRS., etc, who wrote "... it is the frame of the bedstead in which John Hunter lay when brought from St George's Hospital".'

What a tangled network of old boys' ties! Owen, of dinosaurs and founder of the Natural History Museum, the devious Owen, a curator of the Hunterian Collection – and Frank Buckland, naturalist, collector, taxidermist, expert on fish and fisheries, and a kindly, well-liked man.

Nearly one hundred years after the giant Byrne's death, in May 1871, Buckland was visited by 'a strange party from the other side of the Atlantic': Miss Swan the giantess (7 feet 6 inches) and Captain Martin van Buren Bates, 'about as tall', and both aged 24 years old. Bates was 'a splendid-looking fellow, very unlike pictures of the giant in the "fe fa fum; I smell the blood of an Englishman" legend.' Not only was Bates splendid, but he and Miss Swan apparently made a splendid couple too. 'I make bold to say that Miss Swan is the most agreeable, good-looking giantess that I have ever met,' Buckland wrote. 'She is ladylike in manners and address and would be a most agreeable neighbour at a dinner-party.' He had the opportunity to test this three years later, when he entertained the splendid couple at dinner in honour of their marriage.

Giants came to Britain from all around the world: Chinese, American, Irish and French. Buckland dined with 'the Chinese Giant', Chang Woo Gow. Buckland himself was the cause of a 'breach of discipline' in his regiment, a spreading roar of laughter one Sunday in 1862, when he appeared on church parade in the company of 'Brice the French Giant and a dwarf then exhibiting in London.' Brice, like the skeletal Byrne, was apparently 7 feet 7 inches tall, and a well-proportioned and amiable man. A frequent visitor to Buckland's house, he gave him a pair of his shoes and a cast of his hand as mementoes. There is a story that 'A lady dwarf was one day invited to meet him, but with untoward results; the good-natured giant took her up, as a little girl, on his knee, causing an explosion of indignation. "I am nineteen," she cried, "and to treat me like a baby!" It was long before her ruffled dignity could be appeased.'

Such a mixture of dwarves and giants was a potent image: alive or dead. Charles Byrne's skeleton dwarfed that of Caroline Crachami, 'the Sicilian Fairy', as they posed together in Hunter's Museum. The Kentucky Giant in Philadelphia's Mütter Museum cannot, as a matter of principle, be identified, but beside him is the skeleton of poor Mary Ashbury, a dwarf forced into prostitution who died in childbirth. The skull of her poor dead infant is held on her hip. Some might argue that such specimens were displayed for the instruction of aspiring surgeons, but comparative anatomy surely requires the placing of a third skeleton, a person of normal stature.

John Hunter's dead body, of normal stature, was not macerated in a copper, but was placed in the vaults of St Martin's in the Fields. In 1859 Frank Buckland determined to find the body of his hero, 'the greatest of Englishmen', and spent two weeks searching through the vaults. *'The stink awful,'* he wrote in his diary. Then on February 22nd he 'found the coffin of John Hunter. At work all the morning and about three in the afternoon found it, the bottom coffin of the last tier but one. It is in excellent condition, and the letters on the brass plate as perfect as the day they were engraved. "John Hunter Esq., died October 16th, 1793, aged 64".' On February 23rd, Buckland went down into the vaults again with Professor Owen: 'I wish I could have made a sketch of him, with his hand on the coffin, looking thoughtfully at it; it would have made an excellent subject.' Buckland was very ill for several days after this rummaging in the foetid air, but he was well enough to attend the re-interment of Hunter's coffin (and presumably therefore of Hunter's bones) at Westminster Abbey in late March.

The photograph that he took of the coffin was presented to the Royal College of Surgeons and displayed in the Hunterian Relics Exhibition, on a stand in the middle of the Library: the furniture and the Copper were placed along the North wall. Giant O'Brien smiled inscrutably in the hall downstairs.

TEN

'I was straightening his bedclothes and something fell on the floor. It was a wee black thing like one of those cylindrical liquorice allsorts, you know the sort? "What's this?" I said. And he had a look and then he started roaring with laughter and shouting, "It's a toe! It's one of me blasted toes!" And he was showing it round, like this—' Ruth held an imaginary object between thumb and forefinger and waved her arm '– like a kid at primary school trying to attract attention. He wasn't a bit upset, he pulled up the sheet to look at his foot and all he could say was, "See where it came from? Good riddance to it, hen – three down and two to go!" He was laughing and spluttering and he was so happy that I couldn't stop laughing either – you should have seen us! I was bent double, holding onto the bed.' She started laughing again at the memory, remembering that glorious moment of black humour. 'We were making a terrible racket and the duty nurse got very cross with me. "Unprofessional" and so on.'

Stefan's eyebrows were raised and he was half-laughing himself, disbelieving. 'Did he honestly not mind? And anyway, I thought nursing staff were supposed to dispense sympathy, not roll around helplessly laughing.'

Ruth looked at him for a moment, and saw that he really had not understood.

'The last thing he needed was rote sympathy. He *wanted* to laugh. He'd been lying in that bed for a couple of weeks, and his toes were gangrenous and stinking – he was a diabetic. A couple of them had already been amputated, and that had hurt. He just wanted to be rid of the others and to go home. There's nothing worse than being in one of those wards, surrounded by old, sick people. He was old but he wasn't sick, and he said his toes hardly seemed to belong to him any more. He couldn't feel them and in any case they were at the far end of his body – see.'

She nodded at Stefan's feet. She was lying next to him on the shore, leaning back against a boulder, and his legs were stretched out, his shoes incongruously urbane against the fine gravel. He had his arm around her shoulders, his fingers playing with her hair, so that he had to lean away from her to see her face. She glanced at him quickly, noting that he must have shaved at Madeleine's, noting the pores in his chin and cheeks and the fine wrinkles where he narrowed his eyes. Too often during dinner she had looked up to see Stefan staring at her. It was a mannerism that had at first flattered her, that he was apparently so entranced, but soon she began to feel awkward and conscious of every defect in her complexion and her clothes. Where had he learnt to do this? Did he do it with other women, under the impression that it charmed them? She wriggled her shoulders and stretched, fingers linked.

He removed his arm and picked up a pebble and lobbed it into the water.

'That photo I sent you,– I still really cannot believe that we are here, together again and sitting on a beach, admittedly a lake-shore, after all those years. It seems almost incredible that we have found each other again.'

'You found me,' Ruth pointed out. 'And we're very different now.'

'Does that matter?'

'Why "matter"? Our difference doesn't impinge on global politics or global warming, it's irrelevant. Of course it doesn't *matter* in any sense of the word.'

Stefan grunted and she could see that although he was clearly trying not to laugh, his eyes were shining.

'Why are you so amused at that?'

'I suppose I was attempting to broach the topic of compatibility, whether opposites attract – or even whether diversity is to be applauded. But let's abandon that line of research very quickly, before you launch an annihilating salvo and leave me for dead. Toes and all. I'm impressed, though, by your robust attitude to death and decay. There was no suggestion of that when I knew you before.'

'There was no need, I hadn't been exposed to anything that needed a robust attitude, as you call it. Our characters were hardly formed then, Stefan, were they? Students just play at life. We had a good time. Life hadn't really tested us. Either of us.'

'That was not how it seemed when you told me it was over, and went off with that guitarist, or whatever he pretended to be, to Glasgow. You dropped out and disappeared, and it took a very long time for me to come to terms with that.'

'You found your wife. You've got two daughters. And you seem to have a successful career and to enjoy your work, you're internationally known – and in demand, apparently.'

'My wife divorced me.'

'Ah. So, having tracked me down and discovered that I'm single, you have some romantic notion that your first love has merely been waiting for you to stagger back along the track, older but wiser, into her arms, and your life will be complete?'

She could not help taunting him. His calm, rational conversation had begun to irritate her, so that she wanted to prick him and rouse him. She had lusted after him this morning, she had schemed ways of being alone with him, of having sex. And now he merely bored her. She gathered up a handful of pebbles and stood up suddenly, intending to throw them in the water. Small waves sighed on the sand.

'Don't, Ruth.' He stood up too and caught her elbow. She forced herself to look at him and was embarrassed to see that his eyes were wet. 'We're too old to play silly games. Let us try to enjoy each other's company for the next hour or so, then you can drive me back to the farm, and Lisa and I will leave tomorrow after breakfast and leave you in peace.'

He put his hands on her shoulders and pulled her towards him, holding her so that her cheek was pressed against his hair. Ruth, feeling guilty, encircled his waist with her arms and dropped the pebbles behind him. They held each other awkwardly, Ruth balanced on her toes, and then suddenly everything seemed simple and they were pressing against each other, and their mouths and tongues met. Hands fumbled with buttons and zips and bare-chested, bare-breasted, they squirmed together for maximum contact. There was nothing diffident about Stefan now, as he tugged at one of her nipples and pushed his other hand down inside her jeans, fingers pressing, seeking entry.

Ruth's back arched against him, the shuddering was beginning, her skin was so sensitive it prickled. She grabbed his wrist. 'I want *you* inside me. Quick!'

He muttered that he'd got a condom from the gents' at the hotel, and struggled to extract it from his pocket.

'Oh *fuck*!' Ruth gasped, and pushed him away, trying to pull the front of her shirt together. 'There's a couple coming — with a dog. Don't look, just do yourself up, quickly.'

A few seconds later, a golden retriever ambled over with smiling face, its tail waving gently like a banner, and sniffed at Stefan's leg.

'Ben, come here!' The man's voice was sharp and Ben, with an apologetic backward glance at Stefan, trotted after him. The couple nodded, 'Evening,' and Ruth heard the woman whisper something as they walked down to the water.

'I've shrivelled away with fright, I wasn't sure what the dog was after.' Stefan spluttered.

'Well, at least they didn't see your bare bollocks twinkling in the sunset. I think we'd better go back home. Sorry.'

A line of gulls flew silently overhead with slow wingbeats,

heading towards the sea, and scurrying waders trilled on the shore. The sky was pink and silver in the late evening light, but the path through the trees now seemed dark and full of obstacles, and Stefan held her hand, his fingers intertwined with hers, as they walked silently back to the van.

'Perhaps it would be better if you dropped me at Madeleine's,' Stefan said. He was watching her again, still holding her hand, but now she had the courage to look him in the eye.

'Yes, perhaps it would. I'm sorry this hasn't been quite what you wanted, or at least, what I think you wanted. That you came all this way and—'

'And what did you think I wanted, Ruth? Why did you allow me to come to see you? Surely you didn't think it was because I was interested in taxidermy, fascinatingly complex though it is. Very nearly a science in its own right, or at least a pseudoscience. You could have put me off, or even been completely frank and told me to stay away. There must have been something you wanted too.'

Ruth was chilled by the change: his voice was cold and flat, his eyes so unsmiling. She had grown unused to explaining or even examining her motives in great detail, and now she looked away, trying to think what would be best to reply. Cotton-grass rippled like spindrift on the distant marsh.

'I don't think my reasoning was very profound, Stefan,' she eventually said. 'It isn't, usually. I was curious to see what you had become. And when I first saw you at the door, still looking so – *good,* and the way you looked at me... I had the feeling you had come back to, well, claim me, in some way. And I wanted you to make love to me. But I didn't want you to love me. I don't love you. But look—' She knew her face was scarlet, she had to stop talking, to catch her breath. 'No, wait! I want to say – it might have been easier if you had come on your own. *Why* did you bring Lisa? She's been a complication, I don't understand why she had to come with you. Or did you so desperately need a driver that anyone—'

She stopped, aware of what she had been about to say. 'No, no. I didn't mean that. You're making me confused, please stop *staring* at me like that, I can't stand it.'

'I think you were about to say that anyone would do, even a dwarf. Or perhaps you think I brought Lisa along as a contrast to make me look even better, a perfect and sexy specimen of manhood. Or perhaps I hoped to impress you with my egalitarian and broad-minded attitude to my fellow humans. Is that what you think, Ruth?'

'You know it's not.' She sighed, suddenly feeling tired and empty. 'Fellow human, singular, in any case. One swallow doesn't make a summer. You should have brought a pregnant black lesbian and a deaf-mute as well.' Unexpectedly, a bubble of laughter burst inside her head. 'And a dog.'

She tugged her hand free and walked round to open the driver's door.

'A dog?'

'Not a cat. I'm not keen on cats.' She reached over and unlocked the passenger door, then waited while Stefan climbed in. 'It was a mistake coming down here to the lake, wasn't it? We should have stayed in the bar.'

'Mmm.'

He looked at her briefly and non-committally, then clipped in his seat-belt and stared silently ahead.

Dusk was creeping across the fell-sides, and mist filled the bowl of the valley below. Scattered lights indicated normal life in farms and houses. The van's headlights trapped a hare, which loped ahead for twenty metres, big as a labrador, and never deviating until it reached an open gate. On a steep uphill corner the engine spluttered, twice, then gargled and died.

Why did this have to happen now?

'It's out of petrol. Don't worry—' Ruth was already undoing her seat-belt. 'There's a can in the back.'

She opened the rear door and tugged the red can from

amongst the cardboard boxes and spare wheel and carrier bags.

'Oh fuck,' she whispered it this time. 'Oh no, oh fuck.' The can was light and empty. She had meant to re-fill it a month ago, after the last time. She shook it, hoping to feel even the faintest sloshing wave.

'Do you want a hand?' Stefan had turned to look into the back of the van. 'I suppose you must get used to this, living where you do.'

'I seem to have forgotten to fill the can.'

She replaced it and shut the door, quietly; she patted the roof of the van, then closed her eyes and breathed in and out, very slowly.

'It's not very far to the farm, and Madeleine will have some. We can walk. I'm sorry.'

Stefan climbed out and looked at her across the roof. 'How fortunate that it's a fine evening. But you can't leave the van here on the corner. We passed a gate not far back. I'll walk down and guide you if you can run it back.'

He was being so reasonable that Ruth felt the need to be defensive and muttered, 'I'm not usually so incompetent.'

But steering the dead van in reverse, zig-zagging and braking without the help of the engine, trying to understand Stefan's signals in the mirror, made her palms and forehead sticky with embarrassment. The rear bumper banged into the stone gatepost and she yanked the handbrake on, no longer caring that the van was sticking out at an angle.

'Nice bit of parking.' Stefan, damn him, was completely impassive. 'Red warning triangle?'

'I haven't got one.' She rummaged in her jeans' pocket to find a handkerchief, but found instead an elastic band and pulled her hair back into a ponytail. Her eyes felt hot and her nose was prickling. 'Let's go.'

'Ruth.'

'Don't be nice to me or I'll cry.'

'Ruth.' His voice was so puzzled and pleading that she could not bear it, but shook her head and strode away.

They walked fast, with little breath remaining for commenting on the bats that flittered beneath the trees and about their heads. A car came towards them but did not stop. Ewes and lambs dozing behind a wall leapt to their feet and galloped away in fright. A vehicle came grinding up the lane behind them and as they stood to one side, flashed its lights and hooted.

'George! It's George's pick-up.' Ruth waved with relief and rushed to speak to him.

'I saw your van. Is it brock?' He beamed up at her, his arm resting on the open window.

'Ran out of petrol. Have you got a can in the back, George?'

'Nah, this runs on diesel. But the Boss'll have some. Can you both squeeze in, then? Or you can sit in the back if you don't fancy cuddling up between us, like.'

'We'll manage.' She couldn't help grinning back at him, such was the relief. 'Stefan, this is George who helps Madeleine. Stefan's a friend of mine from student days. He's staying at Whitefoot with a friend.'

'Oh aye. Where're you from then?' he asked, as Stefan squeezed onto the front seat next to Ruth.

'Brussels – Belgium. But I'm working in Liverpool for a few weeks.'

'Liverpool. My brother Ken lives in Wigan, that's close, isn't it? He moved down there after foot-and-mouth, after we gave up the farm, like. Said he couldn't stand the country, glad to get away. Dunno how he stands the smells down there, Wigan stinks worse than a slurry pit. He's a slater, though, works for one o' they big firms, so he's not short of a quid, eh. Says he works all hours, going to make his fortune and live in Monte Carlo.'

'And lose it again at the gaming tables. I don't remember him working that hard when he lived here. He never did come to fix Madeleine's roof, she had to find someone else.'

'So your family got out of farming, did they, George?' Stefan sat forward to look across at him. 'That must have been a tough decision.'

'Nah, it weren't too bad for us.' George glanced at him as he changed down for a corner. 'My dad and uncle farmed together and my dad always said it was a tie. He weren't that keen on sheep, anyhow, said they just lived to die – people see them in the fields looking like all they do is eat and lie around cudding, and they have no idea how the daft buggers like to get theysels stuck, specially the lambs. Always getting into trouble. You should ask Madeleine, she'd give you an earful about lambs. So he was pleased, sort of, when they came to take them away. He's gone into landscape gardening now, out there with his strimmer and getting nice cups of tea. We still live in the farmhouse, mind, but we sold off the land.'

'But you stayed in farming, yourself?'

'I always did contract work. Tractor's mine and I've got more work these days than there's hours in the day.'

'George did contract work during foot-and-mouth, too, didn't you, George?' Ruth squeezed her elbows into her sides, trying to make space.

'Aye. Someone had to. I hated it, mind, but someone had to. There was six weeks when I couldn't go home. My skin was falling off with the disinfectant. People in the cities didn't know that, Stefan. Along here, along this road where it's flat, there was mats with disinfectant – everyone had to drive over them. Same outside every farm, troughs outside shops for your feet. Everything stank of disinfectant – and the smoke. Stink of burning woolly jumpers and roasting meat, day after day. Made you sick.'

'That was the photo in your house, Ruth, wasn't it, that Lisa asked about? But you didn't want to discuss it.'

'I still don't. But since it's my fault for bringing up the subject, let me tell you what I saw. There's a concrete bridge over the main road, leading to a farm. One morning I drove down the main road. It was a fine Spring morning, blue sky, tops of the fells clear, and there were ewes and very young lambs in the field on one side. A typically serene picture-postcard Lakeland scene. Except that there was a police car sitting up on the bridge and driving up behind it was a green tractor with a forklift scoop at the front. George's tractor. Staithes' farm, wasn't it, George? – we've talked about this before.'

George nodded silently.

'When I came back, less than two hours later, there was also a lorry on the bridge, and two more cars, and men in overalls. I didn't want to look because... You have to understand, Stefan, whenever we saw those groups of lorries and police cars... they symbolised the destruction. There weren't any ewes or lambs in the field any more. The road goes up a hill at that point so that the bridge is silhouetted against the sky. And then I saw George drive his tractor onto it, up to the lorry, and the scoop tipped. And all I could see was a *lump* of dead sheep, flopping out in a tangle of heads and legs, thudding down into the lorry. A tangled lump. They would still have been *warm*.'

Ruth's throat constricted and she jabbed her fingernails into her thighs, in pain and anger. Stefan thought she had a robust attitude to death, did he? I have to get rid of him, send him away, she thought, before he finds out. But he had to understand the importance of what she was trying to tell him, to hear the thud of the sheep.

'You tell him, George – about those sheep.'

'What you've said is already bad enough, Ruth. I can't imagine what it was like for you too, George.'

'Not too good. Several times a week, like.' George was not in the habit of expressing his own feelings. 'Those sheep weren't even infected. Voluntary cull, so-called. Ministry phoned Staithes and told them they were coming in the morning, same time as they phoned me. Jason's wife's never been right since, poor woman. And the kid was heart-broken about the dog.'

'They killed the uninfected ones to stop the disease spreading, on the principle of a cordon sanitaire, didn't they?'

'More than a million in Cumbria. Cattle, sheep. Even tried it on with the horses, silly buggers, till someone reminded them it was cloven hoofs. Fields were empty. Cleaned out.'

'Of course we heard about it on the news, and it was shocking, but it was abstract, filtered by the media. But now I have been here—' Stefan paused, apparently trying to imagine the reality '—and seen all the animals in the fields, and the small farms, then heard about it from someone like you, George, I can—'

'It wasn't just the animals, it was the farmers and their families, like. You can re-stock, but...'

'So you can see why we don't like talking about it, Stefan,' Ruth said.

By now they were driving up the lane to the farm.

'Madeleine's upstairs, there's a light in her bedroom. Do you know where she keeps the spare petrol, George? I'm hoping you're going to drive me back to the van, by the way, after we've dropped off Stefan.'

ELEVEN

The bar of sunlight moves slowly across the wall, its edges fuzzy and flickering, filtered by the branches of a municipal tree; it is a summer pattern, and already its passage is sinking towards autumn, when the roofs of the terrace opposite will block the sun until the Spring. Lisa sits in the bay window in the Little Chair that is a relic of her childhood: it is low and armless, with a short seat, of the kind known as a 'nursing chair'. A glass of white wine is on the wooden floor beside her, and the room is plain and white and silent.

Her father had seen the chair in a second-hand furniture warehouse and had brought it home for her. At first she had loved it, but in her teens and student days she had avoided it because it seemed to symbolise her difference. During her postgraduate years, though, when she had needed to escape the pressure of the department and the city and had come home, to the place where she was loved, her Little Chair had become very precious to her. She would lean against its soft, lumpy back and tell her parents edited versions of her life in Manchester. Sometimes she would try to explain the meaning and reality of the abstruse mathematics she was working on, but her mother would look at her with that familiar mixture of worry and incomprehension and say she was just going to make a pot of tea.

Lisa would press her cheek against the Little Chair's back, holding her breath to avoid the faint, sharp smell of cheap pot pourri that drifted upwards from the shop below. Later, when she moved to Liverpool and bought her flat, she brought the chair across and had it re-upholstered and covered in rough creamy material that smells like hessian.

Little Chair maintains the link between her parents and her new independence, and the feel of it against her back and thighs is like the memory of her mother's comforting lap.

She never sits in it when she has visitors, but only when, as now, the latent urge to classify and integrate or partition the fragments of her daily life becomes overt and irresistible. Her mind becomes saturated with images that are graphical in their simplicity: conversations, the interactions between herself and others, small events and their outcomes, are clearly defined as radiating or sinuous lines, or blocks and segments of colour. She has learnt that this is her means of sorting out confusion; she must take the time to examine each image carefully and fit it into the complex pattern.

Is the mental visualisation of patterns and images a cause or an effect of her academic research? She isn't sure. But she is sure that she has inherited her mathematical ability from her father.

That conversation, last year, is a simple three-bar histogram in grey. She was in his workshop in the garden, watching as he machined a lump of grey steel, turning it into a thick-walled cylinder. A squealing descant of pared metal occasionally rose above the solid low hum of the lathe. Glittering spirals fell onto the floor and she bent down to pick up several, as she had always done since she was a child.

'Dolls' hair.' Her Dad smiled at her through his visor. 'Wasn't that what you used it for?'

'Pigs' tails, sometimes. But yes, dolls' hair, very curly and wiry. And it didn't remain stuck on for very long, did it? Mum was always grumbling about the bits scattered over the flat.' She smiled back at him as she stretched and released the coils. 'All that waste. I wish I could think how to use swarf at work, to demonstrate something abstract.'

He lifted his visor, then released the cylinder from the chuck and brought it across to the work-bench in the middle of the floor and held it out to her.

'What's it going to be?' Lisa asked, stroking the warm polished surface.

'I'm going to drill a hole and put a twenty-thou screwthread in – then there's a little widget to be made to screw in and – you don't really want to know, pet, do you? You're just humouring your Dad.'

She laughed. 'You know that's not true, I've always liked coming out here to watch you.'

'Aye, many's the time you'd come out here to escape from your sister. I often wondered if you'd have gone into something more practical like this if you'd been a bit bigger. But there we are – now Suzie's the practical one, with all her cookery classes, and you're the airy-fairy one. There's no telling, pet, is there?' And he asked, as so often before, 'And where do you get all that mathematics from, that's what I always want to know?'

She had often wondered, too, but standing there in the workshop, she had suddenly seen the answer and had laughed at its obviousness. 'Why, from you! Think about what you've just been doing – you think and work in three dimensions, you can see in your mind how these complicated structures fit together. What I do is only a few degrees different from what you do, Dad, except that what I do is mostly invisible and can't be put into practice. But you can spin a surface in two dimensions and turn it into three. Just like that! I have to figure it all out with equations.'

We both deal in the beauty of shapes, she had thought later. We both construct real and imagined dimensions. I should have told him that.

Three grey blocks, stepwise from small to large; her father, the workbench, and her. Was she represented by the one at the lower end of the scale, or by the greatest? She had been amused by the revelatory insight that the answer depended upon whichever taxonomic method she chose to select.

Why does she remember that incident today? Is there a connection with the discussion she had this morning with her research student? He gave his final seminar at lunchtime, and she spent a couple of hours with him beforehand, running through his presentation and guessing at the types of questions that might be fired at him from the floor. She searches the images in her mind and simultaneously notes how the bar of sunlight has captured the pale-green orchid, and printed its spare clean lines on the white wall behind. No, the images associated with the maths are spiky arrows of different lengths radiating from a point. Perhaps it has something to do with Stefan because he sent her an email today from Brussels. But she rejects that connection too, although she will return to it; the anticipation is pleasurable and she keeps that image safe. The connection with Stefan is indirect for she is now aware of an image she failed to examine earlier, probably because it made her feel uneasy. Pale spheres that relate, as yet indefinably, to Ruth Kowslowski in Cumbria. She searches the events of that weekend more than a month ago, seeking the details of the visit to Ruth's studio.

She and Stefan were both curious to see Ruth's workshop, possibly for different reasons. Her own reason was simple, that she knew nothing about taxidermy or how a taxidermist worked. She had a vague idea that there would be bones and skins and sacks of stuffing, and perhaps a stag's head and a stiffly posed bird or two; she expected a faint smell of decay and mothballs, like the clothes rail in one of the less-frequented charity shops. But the workshop was an ordered workplace, the many unidentifiable objects within it apparently arranged with a logic that linked tools and artistry with business practice.

It was a long room, a hayloft, its low beams at forehead-height wrapped warningly with scarlet padding. The contrast with the small rooms filled with miscellaneous clutter that she had seen at Ruth's home perturbed her and she walked (without needing to duck) down to the far end of the room to examine the prepared specimens on stands and in glass cases, which Ruth said were uncommissioned and for sale. There was office space at this end, with a filing cabinet and printer, a thick book marked 'Records', and a pile of paint-spattered picture encyclopedias and guides to animals and birds.

Lisa wandered around, looking at the assortment of machines – a drill, an air compressor, and something that looked like a small and very greasy circular saw – and the dusty packets of borax, salt and a sandy stuff that was labelled 'chinchilla dust', a box of feathers, cartons full of syringes and disposable gloves, packets of pins and rolls of string, all manner of coloured plastic boxes with all manner of strange tools, bags of wire wool and plaster and fibreglass filler, paper towels, plastic containers of formalin and tanning oil and washing-up liquid. There were several glass-stoppered bottles too, filled with yellowing fluids, 'Citrus aurantium' and 'Oil of Lavender', that looked as though they had been salvaged from an old-fashioned Chemist's shop.

She was intrigued, she wanted to know what everything was for, but she had the feeling that this might be the wrong moment for her to ask questions. Photographs and postcard reproductions of paintings of animals were taped to the side of the filing cabinet and she stopped her wandering to look at them, so that she could covertly observe Ruth and Stefan.

They were standing close together by a table in front of the window, Ruth watching as Stefan slowly looked around, shaking his head.

'I find this so difficult to associate with you,' Stefan was saying. 'The last time I knew you, you were always carrying piles of paperbacks or files – on the rare occasions when you decided you ought to work, or at least to fool your tutors into thinking that you were a dedicated disciple of English literature. How did you get here, Ruth?'

'The same way as you ended up getting excited about anally-constricted graphics. We both followed our noses.' Ruth gurgled with laughter. 'In a manner of speaking. It's not difficult.' Her hair, loosely scooped up and caught by a green plastic comb, formed an unfocussed halo, softening the edges of her broad pale face, so that she seemed younger and more susceptible. But it seemed to Lisa that her acerbic comments and edgy teasing were those of a woman who perceived and wanted to maintain a position of strength.

Lisa focuses on that memory of Ruth's face. Is that the origin of the sphere? She tries to locate the reason for her related unease, trying to avoid the memory of the powerful attraction that was already a nearly-visible adhesive between Stefan and Ruth. No, there are many spheres, many *faces*. And now she thinks she knows, that the spheres are to be found in Ruth's house.

She had needed to go to the toilet, and Ruth took her to the bottom of the stairs and pointed out the door. The bathroom was as she had expected, not too clean, faint lines of mould between the wall-tiles, and the toilet bowl in need of bleach. The cistern, a high old-fashioned one, had a chain from which the hand pull had vanished: but there was a lid to the toilet so she managed. She guessed that Ruth's bedroom was at the other end of the landing, facing the front, for the bed in the other room that she had passed – she could not resist peeping in – was heaped with books and spare bedclothes and an assortment of taxidermal specimens and toys. At the foot of the bed was a fierce but balding ginger cat and, next to it, a low display cabinet or perhaps a converted wooden chest, for its top was a sheet of glass. She stepped quickly into the room to look in and saw a collection of large dolls, most of them dressed in white dresses and frilly bows, their long dark hair plaited and be-ribboned or hidden by lacy bonnets that framed their placid faces. They were not dolls for playing with, but rather dolls to admire, if you liked that sort of thing, and Lisa didn't; the few dolls she had owned were malleable and mis-shapen, and mostly lacking hair.

Now she knows where the image of the spheres comes from and, searching for the connection with that conversation with her father, she assumes the link is dolls and their metal 'hair'. She laughs to herself and presses her shoulder-blades against the back of Little Chair, and immediately, because she believes she has solved the problem, the real explanation presents itself. She had been right to focus on Ruth, but the image relates instead to her studio and the postcards on the filing cabinet. It was there that Lisa had seen a photograph of a box of eyeballs, white and glistening human eyeballs, that she had hoped were made of glass. But she had not asked, even when Ruth showed her and Stefan the packets of animals' eyes, plastic and glass, pupils of different sizes, shapes and colours, that she used for deer and owls and snipe.

'It's so important to get the eyes and the eyelids right,' Ruth said. 'Particularly for pets, because their character comes out in their eyes, and that's what the owners remember, not so much the shape of the body. I hate doing pets, especially if the owner wants me to re-create them as lying down and relaxed. There's nothing else to concentrate on, the face is everything, and it's far too easy to get the expression wrong. Usually if someone asks me to prepare a dog or cat, I tell them to put the body in the freezer for a couple of months and not to rush into having it prepared unless they're sure. They mostly change their minds during that time. Probably get sick of pushing it around to get at the peas and ice-cream. The best preparations are the action ones, like that trail hound over there, Bracken. I'm waiting for his owner to collect him.'

The dog had leapt an invisible obstacle and was landing on his forepaws, his tail erect and caught mid-wag, his ears flying.

'He looks as though his owner has just whistled for him,' Stefan said. 'I can see what you mean about the eyes, too.'

'He's laughing, isn't he? It's clever the way you've made him look so happy.' Lisa was very impressed. 'I had no idea that taxidermy involved such artistry and was, well, so humane.'

Ruth glanced at her and frowned. 'The way he died wasn't very humane. It was a bizarre accident – he'd almost finished the trail and was back in the valley, when he ran round the corner of a wall and caught himself on a metal spike. It punctured his lung. Poor lad.' She stroked the dog's head lightly with the back of her fingers. 'Jack brought him straight over that afternoon. Tears pouring down his face. Told me how he'd gone to look for him and the dog had died in his arms, almost as though he was waiting for Jack before he could go. Jack said he'd just sat there with the dog, thinking he might as well die too. The dog was his best mate.'

Ruth bent down to fiddle with Bracken's stand and Lisa saw that her eyes were shining with tears.

Lisa thinks she now understands why Ruth, and perhaps Ruth's studio, is associated with sadness and pale spheres, and she concentrates for a few moments on fitting the memory into place in the intricate pattern that is stored in her head.

She has a pressing need to think about Stefan's message, but first she must think about the forehead and the finger. 'Voorhoofd' and 'Vinger'. She reaches down and picks up the printed email, which is a mixture of Stefan's letter to her and forwarded correspondence between himself and Kees. Stefan had asked Kees if he could find time to return to De Waag and try to gain access for a second time and, if possible, take a photograph (for a friend who was researching the work of the anatomists and their guild) of the painted shield of Ruysch at the centre of the dome. Kees had clearly treated this as a challenge and a pleasure, and it was his latest response, a jumble of irrelevant and irreverent information – as well as a photograph of Ruysch's crest – that Stefan had forwarded to Lisa.

'I hope it will amuse you to discover what insights into the Human Condition we missed in our more mundane search for bricks and mortar,' Stefan had added.

There had been an important lesson, Kees wrote, inscribed just above head height on the sides of the octagon, in Dutch, and in Latin for those who could not speak the local tongue. But since his friend Stefan was an uneducated Brit and could speak only English and French, he had decided to be kind and had translated the inscription into words that Stefan (and his perhaps mythical friend) would understand.

Lisa imagines herself standing beside Kees, trying to read the inscription, and how he would perhaps joke about the height of heads, and she finds she misses him. She tries to pronounce the Dutch words, with their hinted-at meanings:

'*Hoorder, neem u ter harte, en, terwijl gij gaat langs de verschillende dingen van het leven, wees ervan overtuigd, dat ook in het nietigste de Godheid...*'

But she cannot guess the sounds of the consonants, and skips to Kees' translation.

'Listener, take this to heart, and, as thou goest along the different things of life, be convinced that also in the tiniest thing the Deity is still concealed. Those who, in their lifetimes, did harm as evil-doers, become useful after their death, and health derives its advancement from death itself. The dead body gives instruction, though it be dumb, and its parts though being dead advise us not to die in the same way viz as criminals. Forehead, finger, kidney, tongue, head, lung, brain, bones, hands give to you, the living, a warning example.'

'*Voorhoofd, vinger, nier, tong, hoofd, long, hersens, beenderen, handen.*' A warning: she works through the sentence to identify the word, '*Voorbeeld*'. She recalls how Kees had touched her fingers, and she spreads the fingers of her right hand and looks at them, remembering very clearly the strange tingle that Kees' own fingers triggered. She picks up her wine-glass from the floor and raises it to him before she drinks.

Then she drinks another private toast, 'To Stefan – and to funding.' Because Stefan has written to her to say he has finally decided to come to Liverpool to work on a joint project with one of her colleagues in the Physics department, if they can raise the money. Although the tone of his message is restrained, she thinks she knows him well enough to sense that he feels positive and happy, and Lisa wonders if his decision is tied up with Ruth Kowslowski.

She is disconcerted to realise that all the patterns and events through which she has been sorting this afternoon have strands linking them with Ruth.

There remains, as a relic of that Sunday when she and Stefan had driven away from Madeleine's farm, an image of a dark red spiral swirling inside a black box. She wonders if the box represents the car, but she still is not sure.

They breakfasted in the guests' dining-room, sitting on flat chintzy cushions that were tied to the hard chairs. Despite its being midsummer, rain clattered against the window, and it was obvious that sight-seeing would not be part of the day's programme.

'Have you made plans to meet up with Ruth again?' Lisa asked.

Stefan was trying to spread hard butter on his toast and muttering crossly to himself. There was a dark haze of stubble on his chin, and his skin looked crumpled and faded.

'Hold the toast upside down over your coffee,' Lisa suggested. 'The steam will melt the butter, which protects the toast from softening. I'm the only person who will see your lapse of good manners.'

He raised his eyebrows at her but nevertheless tested her idea, grinning when the butter oozed satisfyingly under the knife, then cut the buttered toast into thin slices.

'Soldiers. And in answer to your question – no. We have agreed to go our separate ways, or to be absolutely precise Ruth has indicated that she has no need to become reacquainted with me, and that I should therefore return whence I came.'

He turned the now-empty egg-shell over and bashed it with a spoon until it broke, then pushed it down inside the egg-cup.

'Oh dear.' Lisa ducked her head and pulled a wry face. 'Sounds as though your evening was not a huge success. No, no, don't tell me anything about it. So – do you want to sit in a carpark somewhere and empathise with the mist and drizzle, or shall we go home? To Liverpool, I mean.'

'Ach! Yes, I suppose so. I apologise, Lisa, for messing up your weekend. You have been extraordinarily patient and accommodating, and you have driven us around, and put yourself out enormously. I really am very grateful. I suspect it hasn't been very enjoyable for you, either.'

Lisa spooned home-made blackberry jam out of an earthenware pot, and inhaled the sweet sharp memory of autumn while she thought how to reply. There were layers upon layers to interrogate, too many impressions to mention.

Finally, she restricted herself to saying, 'It's been very instructive, Stefan. It's not often that one learns how to stuff a dog. And Madeleine has been educating me about sheep. Don't worry, for me it's been a good weekend.'

Madeleine is a congruence of purples, and satisfyingly discordant clashes of oranges and red. Madeleine is warm colour, not shape.

After breakfast, Madeleine gave Lisa fresh eggs to take home, and Lisa told her that she would come back again.

'Maybe I'll be seeing you again, Stefan?' Madeleine asked, as she saw them to the car.

He answered evasively, 'Perhaps I'll bring my daughters over for a holiday sometime. You live in such a beautiful place.'

As they drove slowly through winding valleys beneath

hidden hills, Lisa asked him about his daughters, partly to penetrate the tiredness and defeat that seemed to have washed over him. Hesitantly at first, then with growing warmth, he began to talk about them, in his careful, slightly outdated English: how he saw them at weekends, and sometimes after school, but that they were already beginning to lead a busy social life.

'I am concerned that soon they will not have any time for me,' he said. 'They are both very attractive. Annette, she is twelve, the younger one, has straight blonde hair, which of course makes her an object of attention.'

'Like me,' Lisa grinned at him. 'Gentlemen prefer blondes. It's a given.'

'Yes, of course like you, Lisa. It is the red-haired women we men must beware of! Marie, my ex-wife, is blonde as well, unfortunately, and she has shown her own preference for another gentleman. My – our – elder daughter, Sabine, is as *formidable–*' he gave it the French pronunciation '–as her mother, and has phoned me several times since I've been in the UK to tell me how much she dislikes Antoine, and desires me to come home and make her mother see sense. She is angry with me for not being more forceful, I think she would like me to ride up on a white charger, or better still, in a jeep with a Kalashnikov under my arm, and reclaim my lawful, once-wedded wife, so that we could all be one happy family again.'

'Assuming you did such a thing – I'm not recommending the gun, by the way, just a firecracker or two – would Marie be impressed by the show of strength and fall willingly into your arms?'

'She would think it so out of character that she would probably think I was mentally deranged. I am afraid that was always one of her complaints about me.'

'Oh?'

'That I was too compliant.' Stefan gave a short sigh, and studied the map on his knees. 'We should be at Rydal Water soon, where the Wordsworths lived, and where Coleridge should have lived too, if he hadn't abandoned his wife for such long periods.'

'It struck me that Ruth was, if not formidable, rather *intense*,' Lisa said, unwilling to let the subject drop. 'Was she very different from how you remembered her?'

'In some ways, yes, but in other ways she is the same. She has built up protective barriers, though, and I wish—' He sighed again, almost a groan. 'Lisa, I still love her. Can you believe that? I have never forgotten her, and when I saw her name on that website last year I had this ridiculous idea that she might not have forgotten me. Actually, it was worse than that, because I held the fantasy that she might still love me. But I didn't even know if she was single when I got back in touch.'

'I had the impression,' Lisa said carefully, conscious that he was looking at her as she spoke, 'that when she first saw you on the doorstep, there was still a real attraction there. But you've since learnt otherwise. I'm sorry.'

'She was fairly unequivocal.'

'So perhaps you're no longer thinking of Liverpool as your next place of work?'

'Perhaps not. I don't know. I'm not sure what is best to do at present.'

Two forceful women, Lisa thought; and a man who was not easily stirred to anger or masterly decisiveness, but was probably too easily dominated and put down. That was what made him a good listener, and what kept him from moving into the academic élite; it was what made him human.

He was looking out of the window at the fields and she sensed his unhappiness and loss of confidence. She wanted to see his expression but she needed to concentrate on driving. There was too much traffic on the narrow road; tourist coaches and delivery lorries meeting on corners, their wing-mirrors touching like antennae; camper-vans; and elderly men in caps driving slowly so their wives could see the view. Look! she wanted to say to him, Ruth doesn't matter. Look at the grasses and plants creeping through the hedges, look how prolific and colourful they are! Look at the great horse-chestnuts splaying five-fingered leaves to catch the midsummer light! The exuberance of the countryside astounded her.

The next village advertised a teashop.

'I need a wee, and a cup of coffee. Let's have a break. You can buy a postcard for Annette with sheep on it, just to give her a daughter's pleasure in deriding your juvenile choice.'

As she locked the car she said casually, 'I'm curious about Ruth's so-called essays. It doesn't seem to fit with life in a backwater, somehow. Why was she so certain I wouldn't like them, incidentally?'

'Oh.' Stefan looked embarrassed. 'I asked her about that because I was puzzled too. Apparently she has written about giants and also about dwarves – forgive me – in the context of early anatomy collections. She was rather anxious that you should not look at her blogs, she felt very awkward about the subject-matter, on your behalf.'

A print-out of one of Ruth's essays, as yet unread, lies on the floor. The shaft of sunlight has moved on, and now the living room looks inward at itself. Lisa has identified the patterns and colours of events and conversations and has fitted them into a complex lattice, weaving them into places where they sit easily, each compartmentalised into its own Voronoï cell, separate but abutting the edges of others, linked where the links should be made. The images are safe, they are out of reach of Suzie, and there is simplicity also in their arrangement, simplicity like a chink of light, the opening of a trunk.

TWELVE

When John Tregwithen bought Whitefoot Farm, it had been nearly three times the acreage, extending up and over the nearby Fells. The hill ground was rough, a mixture of rock and bog, heather and bracken and – where the sheep had failed to find them – low clumps of blaeberry, but the in-bye and lower pastures were sheltered and often lush. Fifty-odd Herdwick ewes had come with the land because they were hefted to Whitefoot's fell-land and knew it as their territory. Each crop of lambs had learnt that this was the land where they belonged and those that had been kept for breeding had passed on the information.

As the months passed, Madeleine too knew that this was the place where she wanted to stay. This western fringe was in many ways similar to the part of Cornwall where she had grown up, with its coast and moorland, the small fields and deep lanes and, perhaps even more dominant, that feeling of a rural culture that marched to a slower drumbeat and the tunes of a decade or more before. Although she was more conspicuous, she felt less exposed, perhaps because there were more places to hide. The other farm had been too open and wind-swept, and wind was associated in her mind with unhappiness and misfortune.

'If the wind changes your face will stay like that!' That had been one of her mother's sayings. Don't dare pull a face at me, my girl, because your tongue will be forever stuck out, your eyes screwed up, your nose a wrinkled blob.

It was the fault of the wind, for it had not changed; the

south-westerly gales had continued for day after day, blasting the low Ayrshire hills with salt, tearing down branches and lifting outhouse roofs, sending the sheep into wild-eyed huddles. The small purple birthmark beside her mouth had begun to swell like the crumpled billows of an eiderdown, growing unchecked until a day when the wind swung round and frigid air dropped into the country from the North, and the growth had been fixed in place.

'Go to the doctor,' John had urged, 'Perhaps they can cut it off or give you some tablets or something. Go on, Maddie, don't be scared.'

But although she was afraid of what she saw in the mirror, she was even more afraid of asking for a medical opinion. She knew she was tainted, and she didn't want to hear any talk of disease, or to be discussed and treated as casually as John treated a sick ewe.

The growth was not huge but it lacked discretion and Madeleine guessed that it now described her. 'Which one is Mrs Tregwithen?' 'The one with the purple... you know... on her face, poor creature.'

'Mad, I'll come with you. Make an appointment, go on.' At first John had looked at it, had examined it closely and with his fingers. 'Why's it growing? What started it?'

She had got into the habit of turning her face when she talked or positioning herself so he could only see her 'good side.' She put her hand in front of her mouth when she spoke, or pretended to rub her nose.

'They use radiotherapy to stop cancer cells growing, don't they? Perhaps they can do the same for that, X-rays or whatever.'

She just shook her head or changed the subject and all the time self-disgust was growing within her.

Occasionally, early in her marriage, she had persuaded herself that John had married her out of pity. But he had never minded about her birthmark; once, in that relaxed moment after making love, when he had eased himself off his elbows and fallen back onto his side of the bed, he had turned his head on the pillow to look at her, and had said it made her special. He was not demonstrative in his affection for her, but she thought she loved him for his stoicism and strength, the manner in which he got on and did whatever needed doing, without comment, whether it was mending the tractor or worming the ewes or washing his hands before his dinner. She sliced potatoes for chips and watched him at the sink, how he scrubbed at his nails with wordless concentration, rubbing his forearms with the thick green block of soap until the dark hairs were hidden in a froth of white. She was tall, but he was taller and broad, 'a tower of strength', another of her mother's sayings.

She scarcely remembered her birthmark, the 'port-wine stain' as her mother had preferred to call it. (When had they ever drunk port wine?) But when those southwesterly gales blasted the exposed pastures and the port-wine reinvented itself as dark, ripe grapes, her growing disfigurement claimed all her attention so that she could visualise herself without even looking in the mirror and, worst of all, most frighteningly, she could see that John was trying to hide his own revulsion. If he could not stand to look at her, if he was finding it hard to sit opposite her at mealtimes, how could she herself live with what she had become? So she slipped gradually into the shadows, occupying herself with household matters and helping with the stock only when John asked her. Her precious *National Geographic* magazines absorbed her more and more; until the blackthorn winter when the farm had failed.

'For Sale by Auction'. Notices on roadside hedges, nailed to leaning wooden stakes; notices in the local paper.

Why should anyone else want to buy the land that had defeated them? John asked Madeleine bitterly after the valuer had left. Why should anyone want to buy a small dank house through which misery wafted like pale wraiths? she did not ask him in return. And what had encouraged him to believe that Cumbria would be better?

Instead she tried to talk to him about the larks that hung flickering beneath the clouds and poured out their waterfalls of song, and the mornings when the gossamer-coated fields had shimmered like silk saris spread out to dry. Hesitantly, she talked about the smell of dried grass and the steady thumping of the baler as it spat out packages of hay; the chatter and '*squeeeeeze*' of swallows as they sat on ledges in the barns, and the conversation of geese high overhead in autumn.

John put down his mug of coffee and aligned it carefully with the top of the auctioneer's contract. She could not see his face but waited as he rubbed and squeezed his forehead, and she saw how he wiped a tear from the side of his nose with his little finger.

'Maddie.' That was all he said and he walked out into the yard, and away from her.

The hysterical shrieking of the hens roused her from where she still sat at the table. Uncomprehending of how the time had passed, she hurried to the door and saw a sparrow-hawk sitting on the wall, ripping the feathers from a blue-tit held beneath its claws; the hens, their heads tilted and their red combs flapping, were goggle-eyed with shock.

'Sorry,' she said, to all the birds. 'Someone's got to feed you and look after you, haven't they? Sorry about the delay.'

'He didn't come back for two days,' she told Daniel. 'Two days! He took the car, but I never asked him where he went, and he didn't tell me. I fed the hens and saw to the sheep, and we acted as though nothing had happened. And it's too late to ask now – nor do I want to find out. It was all so long ago.'

'It's like the hole in the middle of a Polo. I'd want to know, Maddie, I wouldn't be able to stand not knowing. I was knocked out once in my twenties, fell off my motorbike, and I can't remember anything about the accident, why it happened

– nothing. For years I kept picking away at it, trying to remember. But the doctor said I'd never know, the memory hadn't had time to get stored. Drives me crackers!' he grinned at her.

'Older and wiser now, aren't you, Danny.'

'Aye well, Maddie, fifty is certainly older. You're nearly there yourself. But we're both daft as brushes, and daft won't be the word people will use if they find out about us. It'll be a lot less kind.'

'It's not just "people", Danny.'

'No, lass.'

He shifted his arm behind her neck and pulled her closer to him on the rear seat, so that she rested her head in the hollow of his shoulder. The windows were misted on the inside and the four-by-four occasionally shook when it was punched by a fist of wind. Madeleine shivered and put her hand inside Daniel's jacket, burrowing her fingers into the warmth of his pullover. He lifted his free hand and stroked her hair, and although at first the silence between them hummed with words that neither had ever dared to say, happiness soon wrapped her like a blanket and her mind emptied itself of anxiety.

After a while, Daniel wiped the window with his sleeve; patches of sunlight dashed across the moorland, painting the ground purple and yellow as they passed, catching sheep or perhaps boulders in pencil-beams of light.

'Look at the ravens!' Madeleine leant across and cleared a larger space. The two birds soared upwards and, folding their wings, tumbled and spun in unison, before recapturing the wind and sailing side by side in perfect synchrony. Swooping and spinning, or lifted on motionless wings, they used and teased the wind.

'The kids at school go crazy in the playground when it's windy, it really fires them up. I can see why,' Danny said softly.

Madeleine's heart lurched at the unspoken reminder of his

wife: Elaine was the head teacher's secretary at the primary school.

'Hey, Maddie. It's no good pretending we're like those birds and can escape.' He pulled her awkwardly against his chest, his arms supporting her weight, breath warm on the back of her neck.

'I never have. Even if John... You have Elaine, and the boys. No.' Danny smelt of waxed jacket and warm skin, and an inseparable combination of smells that were associated with the land.

'*This* is escape,' she managed to say. She wanted to tell him more but she didn't know how to talk about her feelings.

'Seems to me that John hasn't ever properly looked at what's around him.' He nodded towards the window. 'Out there. The way you see things, that's what I've always liked about you. He doesn't see what's in his own home, either.'

'Well, it's obvious why he doesn't properly look at me, isn't it?' she said tartly.

'It's not the wrapping that's important, though, is it? Come on, I don't have to keep telling you, Maddie. Just keep remembering that.'

'You're a kind man, Daniel Nicholson.'

He just shook his head.

'I have to get back,' Madeleine eventually said. 'He'll be needing me. And you've to do the milking.'

'Aye.' Danny's face was leathery and brown and creases almost hid his eyes when he smiled. He was not smiling now though, and she was surprised anew at his eyes' blueness when he peered carefully at her face; the eyes of a pampered film-star, she had once told him, not a farmer. 'But you don't need him any more, lass, do you? You've found that out. You'll manage very well – when the time comes.'

She had told Danny that she had 'seen to' the animals that day when the startled hens had dragged her back from her fugue, but she could never admit to him how she had scurried around that Ayrshire farm in panic during John's absence, so out of touch had she become. The detail was in any case irrelevant. It would not be long now, John was fading by the month. Yes, she would manage, she thought, as she drove home along the rocky track across the moor and away from the boundary between the farms.

'There's a dead ewe in the ghyll, looks as though she's been dead a few days. The crows have been at her so it was hard to tell, but she got stuck, I reckon.'

She stood in the doorway and spoke to John's back, raising her voice above the sound of the television. He was sitting in the big armchair and she could see his scalp shining beneath his thinning hair. Two bars glowed orange on the electric heater, and the room was stuffy and over-heated.

'I wrote down her tag so you can enter it in the records.'

'Aye.'

She waited to see if he would comment on her long absence, but after a pause he said, 'That girl came, she rang the bell but I didn't go.'

'What girl? Do you mean Ruth – the one that's renting the hayloft?'

She waited again, and saw that he was nodding.

'Oh well. She'll probably call again. She's just moved into that place at Sandacre, the half that's been empty since Joe Sowerby died. Seems his family don't want to sell so she's having to rent that too.'

John did not reply so Madeleine went upstairs to change. She looked into his bedroom, tidied his bed and, picking up a pullover from the floor, tried to recall what he was wearing now. Perhaps he had meant to put this on, and that was why he was feeling cold. She would take it down to him and save on electricity. Thank goodness she had thought to have a separate meter installed in the barn, but she hoped she had set the rent at the right level. No point worrying yet, though, they would just have to see how things worked out.

In her own bedroom she took off her green corduroy jacket and then her blouse and flecked tweed skirt. Her stomach was pale and fleshy but her arms and neck were still firm, and tanned, and she saw how the flabbiness had vanished over the past year. There was a time when she would have struggled to carry a sack of feed but now she could tip a tup onto his backside and heave a bale of hay without a second thought. Very feminine, quite the Miss Cumbria, she thought. 'I love meeting chickens and I want to travel to marts.' The corners of her mouth lifted as she straightened her bra over her full breasts and then pulled on a long-sleeved tee-shirt that advertised a veterinary product, before dragging on the trousers that she wore around the farm.

She took the comb out of her hair and shook her head so that her hair fell down to her shoulders, then bent down to look in the mirror as she brushed it, seeing the silvery threads glinting amongst the brown. John's hair had turned grey very quickly, but Danny's hair was as dark and straight and stiff as a terrier's. Her eyes crinkled again as she thought of Danny, but she wasn't a silly teenager with time to waste on girlish day-dreams, so she scooped up her hair into the comb again, pulled on a cardigan, picked up John's pullover and went downstairs.

The bleating and bellowing of hundreds of Herdwicks bounced between the concrete floor and the roof of the mart, mingling with the clanging of metal gates and the shouts of the stewards and, from outside, the cacophony of lorries and pick-ups and pressure hoses. The smell of sheep and urine was so strong you could almost taste it, Madeleine thought, but – once she had managed the awkward business of reversing the trailer up to the gate and unloading her own animals – she always enjoyed the organised chaos of the October mart. She had left John to watch where their ewes and gimmer lambs would be penned while she found a space for the trailer in the crowded park, and now she saw him standing with a couple of his friends. Everywhere men stood in groups, feet or elbows propped on railings, hands in pockets or gesturing with their sticks, the predominant brown-ness of flat caps, tweed jackets and polished shoes adding emphasis to the day on which to show off one's sheep.

'Madeleine!'

She looked round and saw one of the few other women present pushing through the ringside crowd towards her.

'Madeleine. Are you all right then? I was just asking after you the other day – I saw Danny Nicholson, and he was saying he'd been over to give you a hand now and again. John's here, is he?'

'He's keeping an eye on the yows. Danny's a good neighbour, right enough. How's your boy doing at university, then? Enjoying life in the big city?'

'Oh, you know, drinking too much and not doing any work, you know how they are at that age.'

Madeleine nodded, sympathising with the woman's obvious attempt to laugh off her anxiety, and glad that she didn't have children to worry about as well.

'How do, Missus Tregwithen. Thought I saw John earlier. Are you selling or buying today?'

A burly florid man who bred pedigree sheep and made a large amount of money from his tups squeezed in next to her, and for a while they watched as sheep were decanted into and out of the ring at a speed that sent them slithering on the sawdust, and the auctioneer rattled off the prices and banged his hammer with hardly time to breathe.

Madeleine calculated that she probably had time to get a cup of tea, but the queue in the cafe moved so slowly that by the time she returned she could see that the Whitefoot ewes had moved up the queue and were a mere three pens away from the ring – and that John was still with them. She had made an effort to dress tidily, so she could be ready to go into the ring if required, but her palms were sweaty at the thought of having to be on show. The owner of the ten ewes currently under the hammer was standing nonchalantly in the ring, chatting to one of the handlers as though he had not the slightest care what price his animals, which were currently skittering around his legs, would fetch. Sale over, he ducked out, and in a few minutes it was Whitefoot's turn.

John tottered into the ring, leaning on his stick. His free arm jerked and fluttered and there was such a look of concentration on his face that Madeleine's throat tightened. He polished his shoes himself, she wanted to say; he's having a good day. Time seemed to slow from its previous hectic pace. The auctioneer waited while the Whitefoot ewes walked in sedately, and the handlers barely moved their arms to keep them circling. John stood twitching and unsmiling in the ring, the focus of human attention, and his ewes were an irrelevance. But when bidding started it seemed that someone was keen to buy the Whitefoot Herdwicks because the price began to creep up. Madeleine had been covertly looking out for Danny, and now she suddenly caught sight of him, standing close by the ring. She was astonished to see that he was bidding. He barely twitched a finger but he kept the price climbing, before he shook his head, just once, and dropped out. He turned away, while the bidding continued briefly and gave the briefest of glances towards where she sat, before grabbing the elbow of a friend and leading him to one side for a chat.

The ewes cantered out of one gate and simultaneously the next batch exploded in through the other, shoulder to shoulder, like a wall of grey water released from a breaking dam. The wave caught John above his knees and his stick went flying. There was a mutter and gasp of horror from the watchers, but one of the handlers managed to grab his arm and steady him, then helped him from the ring. As Madeleine placed her cup under the seat and made her way down to the pens to find him, two or three of her acquaintances nodded and she could see the sympathy and shock on their faces.

But she slipped past the whisperers, and as she walked between the rows of pens, one of the green-coated handlers stopped sorting sheep and came over to the rail. He looked around to make sure no-one would hear.

'I'm that sorry about Mr Tregwithen, it's hard to see a big man like that brought so low.'

'Thanks, Andy. We're managing.'

'Aye. Nice yows. Danny got you a good price, at least.' And he patted her arm.

THIRTEEN

The telephone rang and Lisa pulled her chair along the desk to reach it.

'Dr Wallace? Your sister and her children are here and are going up to the tea-room to wait for you.'

Damn. Was it that time already? Lisa glanced at the wall clock in disbelief.

'Thanks, Jane. Tell them I'll be along in a few minutes.' She put the telephone down and puckered her face at her research student who was working at the computer. 'Ashraf, I have to go. Duty calls in the shape of my nephew and niece. Sorry.'

Ashraf nodded, still staring at the screen, then hit 'return'. A diagram began to appear, line by line, speeding up, and Lisa scooted herself back quickly to look. For a moment, it seemed that the outline would form the shape that the equations had predicted, and she gripped Ashraf's arm.

'Come on, come on, come on,' he whispered, then, 'Oh shit.'

Lisa released his arm and exhaled sharply in exasperation. 'No. What are we doing wrong? Scroll back... no, earlier than that. There, look.'

They began to work their way through the sequence together, altering a single parameter in the fifth equation, and Ashraf ran the sequence again. Again there was the tense wait as the outline began to form – and again the end-result was not what was expected.

'The time!' Ashraf grimaced, the corners of his mouth turned down. 'Look at the time, Lisa. Your relations are still waiting.'

'Hell's bells, yes. I'll be in such trouble.' Lisa slipped down off the chair and grabbed her coat in such haste that the plastic hook came unstuck from the back of the door. 'Damn, damn, damn! The number of times I've replaced that wretched thing. Never mind, I'll see to it later. Where's my key? You'll lock the door when you leave, won't you?'

Flustered, she dropped her coat and Ashraf picked it up and with his usual grave courtesy held it out for her to slip her arms into the sleeves; being tall, he had to stoop, and Lisa struggled to force her hands into the arm-holes without losing too much dignity.

'Thanks. We'll be at the pizza place – and if Dr Greatorex turns up looking for me, I'll be back in an hour or so. Oh dear.'

The telephone had begun to ring again, and Ashraf smiled his perfect white-toothed smile at her.

'I'll say you left five minutes ago. Take care, Lisa – don't hurry too much.'

'Ashraf, what would I do without you?' She smiled back at him then straightened her shoulders, raised a fist and took a deep breath. 'Right. Onwards and upwards. See you later.'

She hastened down the long corridor, wincing as the soles of her shoes squeaked against the cork-tiled floor.

'There she is. Auntie Lisa!' Holly skipped across the room towards Lisa, holding out a gaudily-patterned carrier-bag. 'We've brought you a present. I said you liked fudge but Jack said you hated it. But I'm right, aren't I? Look!'

Lisa laughingly took the bag and looked inside. She wondered where Holly had got the idea that she liked chocolate fudge, and if Ashraf would eat it, but she put her arm round Holly's shoulder and gave her a squeeze. 'That was very clever of you. And aren't you looking pretty?'

'Mum said we're going to have pizza for lunch but I want chicken nuggets and chips.'

Suzie was sitting by the window, tapping her fingers on the

arm of her chair, her mouth a horizontal line of annoyance. She was wearing a rather formal dark-red jacket over navy trousers which contrasted with the youthfulness of her cropped and blonde-streaked hair. Jack was taking care to stand apart, pretending to read the equations and comments chalked on the blackboards, and it seemed to Lisa that his nine-year-old body was stiff with rejection. He's taller than me, she realised, and he'd probably rather die than be seen with me, poor boy.

'*There* you are! Did you get lost in your own department?'

'The lift got stuck.'

For a moment Suzie's eyes widened and it seemed she might be sympathetic, but then she must have seen that Lisa was joking. 'Oh for goodness' sake, Lisa.' She stood up briskly. 'Come on, Jack, we're going now. And you can stop moaning about how hungry you are.'

'Is there time for me to take you upstairs and show you the view from the penthouse? It's such a beautiful clear day that we'll probably even be able to see Wales.'

'I hardly think Wales has much to offer the children compared with pizza or chips, do you?'

Lisa sighed inwardly, she felt sure that Holly at least would have enjoyed seeing the Liver towers and the cathedrals, but she led the way towards the stairs.

As they reached the entrance hall there was a sudden explosion of voices and laughter and feet thumping on wooden boards.

'Wait a moment,' Lisa said. 'The lecture's just turning out,' and she grabbed Holly and pulled her back against the wall. The doors of the lecture theatre sucked inwards and a stream of students flowed out on the warm and fetid air, carrying rucksacks, purposeful kitbags and coloured cardboard files.

'Ouch!' Holly yelped as someone's bag swung against her head. The owner, turning round, caught sight of Lisa and winced with embarrassment.

'Sorry. Watch *out!*' He pushed his companion out of the

way and they both glanced back briefly as they drifted with the tide towards the exit.

'I sometimes wonder if I shouldn't wear a tall hat with a flag on top,' Lisa whispered to Holly.

'I'll make you one when I get home,' Holly whispered back and giggled.

'You'd think they'd have learned to watch where they were going by now,' Suzie said pointedly after the crowd had passed by.

'Term only started a couple of weeks ago. And anyway those were physics students, they only come here to use the lecture theatre. Our own students usually lower their horizons after a week or so. I think they gain a special proximity-sense.' She wanted to tell Suzie how she enjoyed the dance, the way the tall bodies swayed aside to let her pass, so that she sometimes felt she was walking through an animate tunnel of her own making. Or a curling wave, a surfer's 'tube'. 'And anyway, Jack, how are you?'

He nodded, without eye contact. 'Fine.'

Big trainers on his feet, hands in his jeans' pockets, he slouched along, several paces in front of them, so that Lisa had to call out directions to him a couple of times.

Suzie rolled her eyes in exasperation. 'That boy! They are so ungracious at that age and I suppose it can only get worse. Toby Simmons – you remember him? I bumped into him yesterday – he said it's the first twenty-one years that are the worst. Very amusing.'

'Jack doesn't want to walk with us because he says people stare,' Holly, who was holding Suzie's hand, obligingly explained. 'Ouch, don't! You're hurting my hand.'

'It's your mother's fault for being so attractive, that's why everybody looks at us. *So* embarrassing, isn't it?' Lisa felt the familiar coldness clutching at her stomach: Suzie was training her children well.

'Jack, look up to the right,' she called. He stopped and looked upwards then back at her with a shrug.

'Just beneath the roof, look. The water-spouts are lions' heads,' she explained.

'And shells.' Holly skipped towards her brother. 'I like the shells best.'

Jack shrugged again, one shoulder, even more dismissive. 'So?'

But he appeared slightly more impressed at the restaurant when the waiter hurried over to greet them. 'Hallo, Dr Wallace, how are you? We have saved a nice table for you and your family.' He led them to a table by the window and pulled out the chairs.

'Jack, why don't you sit here and you can see out of the window,' Lisa suggested, thinking that lunch might be less contentious if he had his back to the room. She sat opposite him, however, determined that he should eventually be forced to look at her, eye to eye.

'Grandad took us to a pub and let me have a drink of beer.' Holly began tracing the pictures on the table-mats with the point of her knife.

'I hope you didn't dance on the tables and sing.' Lisa raised her eyebrows at her sister.

'Ginger beer,' Suzie explained. 'He sent something for you too. It's still in the car so don't let me forget to give it to you. Some sort of gadget he's made.'

Suzie had been in Bakewell for a few days, visiting their parents, and Lisa was keen to hear news from home. Apparently the shop was not doing very well because the new supermarket sold ready-made bouquets more cheaply.

'Mum wanted me to bring you some carnations but I said I didn't think you liked them.'

'Why did you say that? Poor Mum. I would have loved to have some.'

'I thought you only went in for fancy things like single irises or orchids. Carnations are a bit down-market for you, aren't they?'

'Orchises or irids. Do you know why an orchid is so-called? It's because its root has the bulbous shape of a testicle. Hence "orchitis", for men with mumps. Jack, you must ensure that you get mumps while you're young, better to look like a hamster for a few days than an anguished jockey. And monorchic, as in the song about Hitler. In contrast to Göring who was microrchic and poor old anorchic Goebbels. Of course, the really interesting debate focuses on whether Hitler's monorchism was dextral or sinistral, or entirely mythical. No doubt Eva Braun could have elucidated if she'd still been around. Shall we get on and order? You've still got a long drive ahead of you to Bristol.'

Their waiter, thin-faced and with gelled dark hair, was standing at the back of the almost-empty room, as still and detached as a guardsman on palace sentry-duty. Lisa's mouth was dry and she felt as though her head was congested with hot blood, but she raised her hand to attract his attention, and he clicked his heels and saluted, then hurried over, beaming.

'Very clever, dear.' Suzie was quietly scathing. 'You amaze us all with your brilliance. Such a fund of cleverness stored within your head, I can't imagine where it all came from.'

'At least you didn't say "your pretty little head".'

'That wouldn't be quite accurate, would it?' Suzie had failed to hear the irony in Lisa's voice. 'Jack, put that thing away. Have you chosen what you want to eat? Holly?'

Jack, who was obviously old enough to have heard and understood the word 'testicle', had glanced quickly at Lisa and then flushed and hunched down over his hand-held computer game, but now he looked at his mother.

'Why do you and Auntie Lisa always argue? I hate it. I hate it when you're together. It's really embarrassing.'

'Sorry, Jack. It's a manifestation of sisterly love, really, isn't it, Suzanna? But you're quite right, it is embarrassing, and your mother and I should set a good example. You and Holly never argue, do you?'

'He's always arguing with me,' Holly said. 'I wish I had a sister instead.'

'Look, this poor man is waiting patiently,' Lisa smiled at the waiter, ' so let's tell him quickly what we want to eat, before he dies of boredom.'

The waiter flopped his hands and bent at the knees, pantomiming death.

Holly giggled. 'You *can't* die, we need some food.'

'If you die, we'll die too,' Jack added. 'We'll end up as starved corpses on the floor.'

Why do we do it? Lisa wondered while Suzie sorted out her children's orders. I am rotated on a drum and iteratively skewered by my sister; there is no escape until I can reach out for the correct tap and spray out a shield of words. But somehow I always find the wrong tap, a spray of volatile irritants instead of an emollient. I parade my knowledge with intent – of belittling her own intelligence.

Hurt and ashamed, Lisa watched Suzie covertly, admiring the taut clarity of her skin and the attractive manner in which she presented herself. But she would not permit herself to fall into that mind-set of believing that Suzie had all the advantages and she herself had none. Intellectual arrogance had its fragile benefits.

'Mum told me that local television had approached you about doing a cookery slot and you might become the Nigella of the South-West, Suzie. I'm sure you'll be really good. What an opportunity!'

'I haven't made up my mind yet. We're still discussing the details. I'm not sure I'd be organised enough.'

'Mummy dropped the spaghetti on the floor at Granny's. I helped her scrape it up and we washed it in hot water and put it back in the bowl.'

'Holly! You promised me you'd never tell.' Suzie burst out laughing and such a wave of warmth flowed from her that Lisa felt enveloped by it and laughed too.

Jack pressed his hands together, wrists touching, then opened and closed them quickly, making a slapping sound like a clapper board. 'Take fifty. Spaghetti sauce. Oops, there it goes again.' *Slap*. 'Take sixty-three, spaghetti sauce...'

'Hmm, I like the look of that gorgeous man staring in at us, he can come and join us any day. Oh, he's smiling at *me*, I'm thrilled. Shall I wave to him?'

Lisa turned and saw that Stefan was standing on the pavement, his hand cupped over his eyes as he peered in through the window. She beamed at him and waved, then beckoned to him to come in.

'That's Stefan. We live together,' she said and enjoyed seeing her sister's eyebrows shoot upwards.

Stefan pulled a chair across to their table and hung his tweed jacket over the back. He could be a model for one of those up-market brands of men's tailors, Lisa thought, with his floppy hair and tanned face. 'Clean-cut'. Like a diamond? No, that was too sharp.

'Stefan, this is my sister Suzanna, and my nephew Jack – and Holly. Suzie, this is Stefan Greatorex, he's a physicist.' She accentuated the e-acute in his first name as Stefan reached across to shake hands with Suzie and then, to their surprise, the children.

'Hi, Stefan. Nice to meet you. Where are you from?'

'I have been living in Brussels for many years. But I was brought up in Ruislip,' he said in his impeccable English accent, and smiled at Suzie as he sat down. 'Although I am afraid I don't feel that my roots are deeply embedded there.'

'Obviously not, if you can bear to come and live in Liverpool.'

'Do you want to order something to eat?' Lisa asked. 'There's not much in the fridge, I'll need to do some shopping if we're going to eat in tonight.'

'Lisa has a very spartan life-style as I'm sure you'll have noticed, Stefan. All those plain white walls and polished floors

– a complete contrast to the sort of clutter we grew up in, above the shop.'

'Minimalist, Suzie, is the word you want.'

'Houses with children are always a little more cluttered, it is the nature of the beast, isn't it?' Stefan grinned at Holly. 'Clothes and shoes everywhere, I'll bet. Is your room a mess, Holly? Does your mother manage to make you clear it up?'

Holly squirmed shyly and tried to spear a chicken nugget with her fork held left-handed, but the nugget shot off her plate at a tangent and was expertly caught by Stefan. 'Thanks, Holly. All those years of playing cricket at school had some point after all. Chicken–nugget fielder of the year, that's me. Shall I eat this now or keep it in case I get hungry later?'

Holly giggled and squirmed. '*No!* It's mine.'

'I have to play cricket at school,' Jack said. 'I hate it.'

'It sounds as though you have some experience of having children, Stefan?'

'Two lovely teenage daughters, although I have an uncomfortable feeling that distance lends enchantment. They live with their mother and her *partner,* her *nouvel amour,* in Brussels. And Lisa tells me you live near Bristol, so both you and she have moved a long way from your family home.'

'Suzanna is about to become a famous television personality. With her own cookery show.'

'I haven't decided definitely yet.'

Lisa was interested to see that Suzie blushed as she pushed rocket leaves onto her fork.

'More Love-in-the-mist than Saint Delia,' she added, but for Suzie's benefit, knowing that Stefan would not understand the allusion to the two contemporary female cooks.

Suzie ignored her and carried on eating while the waiter came to take Stefan's order for a coffee, then was finally able to ask him the question that had really been bothering her.

'So how did you and my sister come to meet?'

Stefan looked at Lisa and smiled warmly.

'You will not believe this, Suzanna, but we met in Amsterdam. We sat at the same café table in a sunlit cobbled square and began to talk, and not long afterwards we experienced one of those Aristotelian *eureka* moments, when we saw how our separate worlds could overlap. During the next few days Lisa persuaded me – I didn't require much persuading – to join her in Liverpool, so here I am. I am working with one of her colleagues, and we have applied for a grant for a continuing collaboration, so I hope to stay.'

'I can always support you, Stefan, in the short term at least,' Lisa said, smiling equally warmly. 'And there is plenty of room in my house, since it is so minimally filled. Even when you abandon your clothes all over the floor.'

'A wonderfully tolerant woman.' Stefan, still smiling, took his cup of coffee from the waiter. 'Thank you.'

Suzie lifted a long thin package out of the car-boot.

'This is what Dad sent. I've no idea what it is.'

Lisa felt it, trying to guess what the gadget could be.

'Ah. Leave the boot-lid open for a moment.' She tore off the brown paper wrapping, and pulled out a long metal rod, with a handle at one end and a broad flat blade at the other, curved over like a bent hoe and neatly covered with imitation suede. 'He was laughing at my plastic rake and said he'd make me something better. It's light, too, he must have made it from aluminium.'

She held the handle and lifted the rod, reaching up to hook the curved end over the edge of the raised boot that was too high for her to reach.

'Stand back a minute.' She pulled and the boot-lid was lowered smoothly, until she could reach it and bang it shut. 'Brilliant.'

Jack opened the boot again. 'Can I try, Auntie Lisa?' She passed it to him and he examined the gadget carefully. 'I like going in Grandad's workshop. Grandad's really clever.'

'What shall we call it, Jack?'

'Boot-lid-shutter,' Holly said.

'Captain Hook.' He gripped it against his side with his elbow and made growling noises as he walked stiff-legged towards Holly.

'Suzie.' Lisa walked round to the open door. Her sister was bent forward in the driving seat, stowing a packet of paper hankies in the glove compartment, but she straightened up and looked at Lisa. Eye-to-eye, Lisa thought. If only we could always see eye-to-eye. 'Suzie, I'm sorry that we—'

'I can't believe you managed to catch that good-looking man. It's... it's... It can't last, Lisa.'

There was naked disgust in her expression and her voice. She had been flirtatious at lunch and Lisa thought she had detected envy as well, but now, just when Lisa wanted to part with an attempt at apology or reconciliation, Suzie was clearly unable to leave without expressing her profound horror at a relationship that she perceived as unnatural. They stared at each other.

Lisa's first reaction had been to explain, 'It was a joke. He's not living *with* me. He's only living in my house until he has somewhere to stay.' But the revulsion behind Suzie's exclamation made her feel physically sick. Her stomach cramped and her hands were slick with cold. She hesitated, and Holly raced round from the back and dived in to press against her mother, to escape the waving hook.

'It's a gripper-gadget, a Holly-hooker, a pooper-scooper!'

'Jack! Stop that!'

'Here, Jack, give it to me. Into the car, now, and have a safe journey home.'

'"Bye, Auntie Lisa.' Holly waved as Jack climbed into the back.

The sisters, who naturally had several characteristics in common, recognised the crevasse that had opened up between them, and Lisa stepped back, feeling the icy haze that wafted around her ankles.

'I shall be expecting that hat for Christmas, Holly.'

'What?' Holly looked back blankly.

Lisa smiled and waved for the children's sake as Suzie drove away. But after the car had turned the corner and disappeared she stood in the same place, clutching Captain Hook tightly as though he were a comforting toy that would banish the whimpers of misery that washed deep inside her. She must not cry! But she was unable to stop the burning tears that welled up and spilled over, and she ducked her head quickly to search for a tissue in her bag.

'Here, let me take that for you, whatever it is. It looks terrifying.'

Stefan was suddenly beside her, and she did not dare look up. He had stopped at the mini-market to buy food for their dinner, and now he took the boot-grab from her and tucked it into one of the carrier-bags.

'Sorry. I need to blow my nose.' Still keeping her head down, Lisa surreptitiously wiped her eyes.

'No hurry. You must be feeling sad to see your sister driving away. I don't suppose you are able to meet up with her very often, are you?'

'No. And I'm afraid we will see even less of each other in future.'

'Is she moving even further away, then?'

Lisa straightened up but looked away across the street, pretending to be distracted by the loud hilarity of a group of students while she struggled to feel adult and detached. 'No. It's just that we don't—' Her throat was tight. 'We don't seem to... We don't see eye to eye. It's more a case of eye to stomach.' Her attempt at joking was useless and tears spurted from her eyes. 'We say such terrible things to each other. Oh God, Stefan, I'm sorry. This is so embarrassing. "Embarrassing", that's the Word of the Day. You'd better walk on and pretend you don't know me.'

He put his hand on her shoulder and steered her into the

boarded-up doorway of a shop, then brought out a handkerchief from his jacket pocket with a flick of his wrist and a slight bow.

'Allow me to present you with a perfectly ironed and folded, perfectly clean, mop. I will look the other way while you use it.'

'Stefan, you are the perfect gentleman.' She giggled weakly as she wiped her swollen face and wished for a sudden downpour of icy rain to hide the signs.

'I can imagine that you might have a difficult relationship since you and Suzanna are so very different,' Stefan observed casually, with his back to her.

'Very different? Talk about stating the bleeding obvious. A person would have to be blind not to notice the difference.' she exploded.

'What do you mean?' He looked down at her in genuine surprise, and then suddenly he blushed, the way he had blushed so many months ago in Amsterdam. 'Oh, I see. But I wasn't referring to your relative statures, Lisa, I was commenting on your individual characters. Please believe me, the physical differences between you didn't even come to mind when I said that, they were irrelevant, they weren't part of the equation.'

She looked at him with astonishment: he really had been thinking of her in terms of who she was, not how she looked. She wanted to hug him, and be hugged, comfortingly, in return, but the only people who had ever hugged her had been close family, and she wondered how it would feel.

'Thank you. What you just said more than compensates for Suzie's parting shot. I'll wash your handkerchief and then you can do the ironing. In fact, you can live with me for ever, if you like,' she added lightly.

But as they walked back to the department, Stefan told her that he had arranged to hire a car for the weekend and was planning to drive to Cumbria.

'I thought I'd try to see Ruth again, and having my own

transport will give me a few extra degrees of freedom,' he explained. 'And it will get me out of your way for a couple of days.'

FOURTEEN

The sheets snapped in the wind and Madeleine tethered them with an extra peg or two along the line. She saw that a blackbird was trapped inside the cage around the few remaining autumn raspberries and she hooked up the net at one end to free it.

'*Out!* Get out of there! There are still some elderberries around. The raspberries are mine, you ungrateful devil.'

With a racketing stream of swear words the bird flew out and over the wall, swerving upwards at the last minute to avoid a car that was coming up the lane.

Madeleine could see the top of the car and did not recognise the colour, so it was possibly someone looking for accommodation, despite the 'No Vacancies' sign down by the road. She walked around the side of the house into the yard and watched the dark green Volkswagen drive in, bumping through the pot-holes and stirring the dogs into a frenzy of barking and leaping in their pound. The windscreen reflected the racing clouds so it was not until the driver stepped out that she recognised him.

'Good morning, Stefan.' She could not remember his surname, but since he was a friend of Ruth's, first names would have to do.

'Mrs Tregwithen. How are you?' He smiled warmly. 'Is it all right if I park here – the car won't be reduced to a wrecker's cube by George's tractor racing around the corner? You've probably guessed that I'm here to see Ruth, although I don't see her van.' He looked around the yard.

'Is she expecting you? She was here earlier.'

'Well, yes. I phoned last night to say I'd be here by lunch-time.'

Madeleine looked at her watch: it was just past noon. 'She'll be back soon, then. And George's not here, it's his day for working at Henshaws', so he's of no account. Will you come in and have a cup of coffee while you're waiting?'

'That's really very kind, if you are sure I won't be in your way.'

Madeleine's mouth twitched at his politeness and she led the way in, pulling off her boots and waiting while he wiped his clean shoes on the door-mat with exaggerated care.

The kitchen was warm and humid in contrast to the early November cold and Stefan pulled off his jacket and hung it over the back of a chair. Madeleine, who normally did not bother too much about what she was wearing unless guests were staying, was relieved that she was wearing her smarter trousers and cardigan. She filled the kettle and put it on the hob and took green and white cups and saucers from the cupboard instead of the usual mugs. Stefan was still standing by the kitchen table and she gestured for him to sit down.

'Thank you. Lisa asked me to send her regards,' he said. 'And she wanted me to ask whether you stay open in the winter, because she would like to book a room and come and see you, before too long.'

'I never close,' Madeleine said. 'There's folks coming to this area to walk and climb, all year long. But tell her she's always very welcome, in any case.' She was touched that Lisa wanted to come back. 'And please thank her for her postcard. That was a kind thought.'

She brought the cups to the table and as Stefan shook his head at the proffered jug of milk, he said, 'She is a kind person, very thoughtful. And I'm becoming more hopeful that I can stay and work in Liverpool, in the short term at least. Which means I shall be able to get out into the Fells, a very welcome change from the Belgian flatlands, I can tell you.'

'And does that mean we shall be seeing a lot more of you up here?' Madeleine pushed her teaspoon round her saucer.

'That rather depends on Ruth, I think. I was hoping that if I came on my own this time we would have a better chance to get re-acquainted.'

He doesn't sound very hopeful, Madeleine thought. He's right not to.

'Mrs Tregwithen, I know I shouldn't ask, but you seem to know her well. Has she mentioned anything about me to you? I'm not sure if she is even very eager to see me, she can sound rather off-hand, and I find it rather difficult to know what she is really thinking. She seems so much more complicated than when we first knew each other.'

'And you're much simpler, are you?'

'*Touché*.' Stefan gave a little smile. 'Though she makes me *feel* like a simpleton.'

'She's had some difficulties. It's been hard for her. I think she maybe wants a quiet life – and love, or whatever you want to call it, isn't a quiet business, is it? But you'll have to ask her yourself.'

Stefan was silent and she drank her coffee.

'I was scared to come here this morning,' he finally said. 'Isn't that crazy, at my age. I set off from Liverpool far too early and arrived a couple of hours ago, so I drove around wondering what to do. I even debated whether to head back to the motorway and drive to Scotland, and hide away in one of those deep valleys off Glen Coe. But I finally decided to keep driving towards the sea, and I ended up by a shore with sand-dunes. It was like a different world, Madeleine. It's so clear and windy here on the farm, but driving northwards I could see a long band of fog creeping along the coast, and when I reached the Solway the air was completely still and there was zero visibility.'

'So you couldn't even see Scotland.'

'Not a thing. The sea must have been very calm because I

could scarcely hear the waves, and I certainly couldn't see them. It was like walking inside a moving cocoon of thick cotton-wool, with nothing to see but the turf and that whippy grey grass you find on dunes. And rabbit droppings. It was a very calming experience – a type of sensory deprivation, perhaps, with no distractions except looking where to put your feet.'

'And it gave you courage to come back here?'

'It would appear so.' He nodded ruefully.

'I went there with my husband, not long after we first moved here. There were little kids swimming, and I often thought I would go back on my own one day and try it myself. The sea's very shallow there. But of course I never did. Silly, really, it's not far to go.'

'No.'

They were each silent for a while.

'I brought Ruth a present,' Stefan said. 'It's a dead bird, some sort of owl.'

'Well. She'll like that.' Just what a girl needs, she didn't say.

'The way I came by it was rather sad. I was driving back along that narrow coast-road and I had to pull out to pass a stationary lorry. The driver was down in front of the cab looking at something in the road and for a moment I was afraid he'd hit someone, or a sheep, so I slowed down. He waved me to stop and he showed me this owl. Apparently it had flown right out in front of him and crashed into the windscreen. He was pretty upset about killing it, it's a fine bird.'

'If it came off the dunes it would be a short-eared owl. They hunt in the day-time.'

'Is that what it is? Anyway, I told him I had a friend who preserved birds – actually I said "stuffed" since Ruth wasn't there to get annoyed – and I'd give it to her. That cheered him up. But Ruth may curse me.'

Madeleine stood up and cleared away the cups.

'I'm fully booked tonight,' she said. 'But if she chucks you out and it's too late to drive home, there's a sofa here. And I dare say I can throw you a crust or two in the morning, when I feed the hens.'

She liked the way he laughed at that, but she felt anxious on his behalf. Then again, he was old enough to look after himself, he was a doctor of some sort so he must have a few bits of brain to rub together. Trouble was, brains often didn't enter into all this, did they? Like that new tup she'd bought, daft as a brush but balls on him the size of – well, balls. A rugby ball. She muttered the words under her breath, then looked up quickly to check that Stefan hadn't heard.

They both heard the van arrive. A door slammed and then with a perfunctory knock, Ruth strode in wearing short leather boots and a sort of poncho over her boiler suit. Her hair was loose and glinted like fine wire in the fluorescent light. Stefan jumped to his feet but neither of them seemed to know how to greet each other and there was an awkward stand-off.

'I had to get that polecat into the post before the post office closed,' Ruth said, partly to Madeleine. 'And there was such a bloody long queue.'

'Madeleine has been looking after me. And she assured me you would come back.'

'And why wouldn't I? I said I'd be here.' She was quick and spiky and Madeleine saw that she was very much on edge.

'Do you want a coffee, Ruth? Or are you two going somewhere for lunch?'

'I need to go up to the studio. Are you coming, Stefan?'

'Sure. Thanks, Madeleine. I may see you again, you never know.'

The poor lad was putting a brave face on it, sharing their little joke. Madeleine massaged the corner of her mouth with her thumb and forefinger as she nodded at him.

'Ruth, wait a minute. I have something in the car for you, and you would probably prefer to put it in your studio rather than take it home.'

Ruth felt as though her skin was sparking with irritation; she wondered if her hair was standing on end. She did not know whether she wanted to shriek at Stefan to get in the fucking car and leave her alone, or to fucking well forget about whatever was in the car and come up to the studio. She even considered running screaming up the stairs and locking the door. And then he held out a fucking dead bird, his face looking hurt and schoolboy-ish and expectant all at the same time.

'Right! That's all I want. A short-eared owl. Do you know they're protected? Where the fuck did you find it? Now I'll have to fill in forms and all the details, and get my fucking log-book up to date.'

'A lorry hit it, down by the coast. I thought you might enjoy it and be able to do something with it.'

Despite herself, she smoothed the feathers on its back and felt its skull to see where it was damaged. The head flopped: as she had guessed, the owl's neck was broken cleanly so the bird would make a good preparation.

'Well. It'll just have to go in the freezer and wait its turn. I'm way behind with commissions as it is. Thanks, though,' she added grudgingly. 'Come on up.'

The familiarly ancient smells of the stairs, the whiff of grey powdery wood and a memory of hay, were dispelled when she opened the studio door, displaced by the delicate acridity of solvents. She placed the owl's body on the workbench and pulled off her poncho; the heater had been left on so the room was still warm.

'You would prefer that I went away, wouldn't you?' Stefan had remained by the door.

The quiet resignation in his tone wrenched at her heart and drove away her anger. She had avoided eye contact from the moment when she had barged into Madeleine's kitchen; she had felt the psychological barrier as though it had been physical, forcing her eyes to slither away from focussing on his face.

But now, despite her confusion, she made herself look at him. He was pale, his face suddenly looked older and more haggard, and the skin beneath his eyes was baggy with tiredness. In the months since she had last seen him, she had sometimes thought of him as a threat, an intrusion, but he was none of those things, he was no more than a man hoping to re-create an illusion from his past.

'No, don't go. I've been in such a muddle.' She walked towards him with her hand held out, trying to re-create her own fantasies. To do so would be such a relief, an unburdening. 'I'm sorry. I had actually been hoping that you'd come back, and now I've messed things up. Not irreversibly, I hope.'

'You have been wanting me to come back?" He was astonished. 'You managed to keep the secret extremely well, Ruth, I would never have guessed.'

He took her hand and examined it, running his finger along the lines in her palm, then lifted it to his lips and kissed her knuckles. A small gesture, not even erotic, but it was sufficient.

She slipped her arms behind his shoulders and pulled him against her, kissing him hard. After a moment's open-eyed surprise Stefan responded, and as their tongues flickered and tasted each other, Ruth's need grew. She struggled to undo the buttons on her boiler-suit and pulled it open.

'That's a clever trick,' Stefan gasped as he squeezed her bare breasts, and pinched and pulled her nipples so that she groaned and writhed against him. She could feel the waves of heat building within her, she couldn't wait, and she pushed his hand down inside her knickers, thrusting against him. His fingers were barely inside her when she came, noisily and shudderingly, and she bent limply against him. He held her close, waiting, and she could feel that he was still hard and erect.

'Sorry, I couldn't hold on,' she whispered into his neck and pulled down her boiler suit, stepping out of it, trying to help him with his belt.

Messily, unaesthetically, they joined together, Stefan panting and moaning, Ruth's bare back juddering against the door so that it rattled rhythmically. But she exalted in it, excited by the discomfort, feeling herself on the threshold of deep orgasm. She used her fingers, helping them both and suddenly they were there, flying, before the inevitable fall.

Despite their mutual recognition of the incongruousness of flesh bared in a taxidermist's studio, there was little awkwardness between them. Stefan admitted to feeling slightly dazed, but was able to follow her later as they drove in convoy to her house. Glancing occasionally in the rear mirror to check that the green car was still behind her, Ruth wondered what he was thinking. A very clean and recently-registered Renault was parked outside her house, and she recognised it as belonging to the daughter of the old lady that lived next door, so she stuck her hand out of the window and waved at Stefan to park, then drove on to a gateway along the road.

He stood waiting quietly by the gate and then caught hold of her and kissed her very gently. Her carrier bag was oozing red juice and she held it away from her as she responded.

'What's that? Another dead and maimed creature?'

'In a manner of speaking, yes. Some steak for our lunch. Or dinner, if you would prefer.'

He looked at her intently. 'Did you say steak? You bought steak for us both? So you *had* been wanting me to come here, even to stay. Ruth, I am completely bewildered.'

'You're lucky. I almost decided to throw it to Madeleine's dogs instead.' Ruth laughed at his expression. 'Quick, let's get inside, it's cold out here.'

Especially when you're only wearing a boiler-suit, she thought, and cringed inwardly. As usual, when her acute sexual need had been assuaged, she felt ashamed of her fantasies and sartorial excesses.

Stefan followed her into the kitchen, silent and serious, apparently still pondering the significance of her revelation about forward planning.

'Do you want a drink?' she asked, wanting to break his silence.

He shrugged and gave a half-smile, eyebrows crumpling in a frown, then held out both his arms to her. 'No. No drink. Truthfully, I only want you. But you knew that.'

She could not ignore the waiting arms, and she let him hold her, rocking her slightly while he spoke into her hair. The warmth of his body crept through her thin clothes and soothed her, so that at first she did not fully understand the significance of what he was saying.

'Did you know that I have never stopped loving you? When you abandoned me for Jay – you see, I have not forgotten his name? – all those years ago I thought I'd never recover. I know that sounds melodramatic, but I sat in my room and was unable to eat or work, or do anything very much. It was as though my brain became dormant. It took me weeks to see sense and realise that I was wrecking my future if I didn't start working again, so then I immersed myself in maths and physics. A real nerd, no doubt about it. That didn't stop me trying to find you but you seemed to have vanished. I even phoned your parents but your mother, quite rightly of course, told me that she could not pass on any details, but that if I wrote to you at your home address she would forward it.'

'Did you write? I didn't receive anything.'

'I wrote you several letters but at least I had the sense to see they were full of self-pity and hardly likely to bring you back. So I tore them up.'

'But it was all right in the end, you met your wife.' Ruth leant away from him so that she could see his face. His groin pressed tightly against hers and she managed to restrain herself from pulling his buttocks towards her and rubbing herself against him.

'It's possible to marry someone without truly loving them. I always hoped she believed I loved her, but she saw through me in the end. Perhaps she always knew but, like me, accepted that we were compatible and would make good marriage partners. Until she was in a position to find someone more exciting.'

'That's an extremely cynical viewpoint, and I'm not sure I believe you.' She licked his ear-lobe. 'Will you come to bed with me? It'll be warmer and much more comfortable, and we can lie together and talk and talk. We can show each other that we're not in the least compatible and that we don't know each other at all.'

'What about the steaks?'

'Oh forget the fucking steaks!' But then she saw that he had been teasing her and was contrite.

They were awakened by farewell calls and the slamming of a car door. The bedroom was growing dark even though it was barely four o'clock, and Ruth's mouth was dry with the sour taste provided by an empty stomach. Stefan groaningly accepted her offer to fetch them glasses of water and rolled onto his back as she swung her legs out of bed.

On her way back from the kitchen she went into the sitting room and hunted through her music collection, finally choosing a CD of re-mixed hits from the late eighties, turning the volume up loud so that the bass throbbed throughout the house.

Stefan was sitting up in bed, the pillow propped vertically behind his back.

'We used to dance to this,' he grinned. 'You always were a very sexy dancer.'

'Get out of bed and dance with me now. Come on.' Ruth put the glasses of water on the bedside table. 'You don't need to get dressed.'

'No, I'm exhausted and I'm weak with hunger, you have worn me out. And in any case I feel vulnerable if my dangly bits are exposed while I'm jiggling about. But I've been staring at the clothes in your wardrobe – what an amazing collection. What's that silvery thing? You must look stunning if you wear that when you help with lambing.'

The wardrobe door was always open, Ruth had not given it a thought; she no longer noticed the untidy piles of discarded daytime clothes that lay on the carpet and the wooden chair. Her bedroom was always like this, it was merely the place where she slept and stored her clothes. She looked at the wardrobe and saw what Stefan saw: the crush of bright tops, imitation leopardskin, silver, scarlet sequins; the short skirts; and heaped at the bottom, a tangle of strappy shoes and leather boots.

'My clubbing clothes,' she said. 'A girl has to have some fun now and again.' The heavy beat of the music reverberated through the floor, and recklessly she dragged out a silver halter-neck, and a leather miniskirt and held them in front of her, fluffing up her hair. 'I'll dress for dinner. Make-up, strappy shoes, the lot.'

'You go clubbing? Where?' He was clearly amazed.

'We go to Carlisle. I go with some friends now and again, just for a laugh,' Ruth lied. 'I enjoy getting dressed up occasionally, to get out of jeans and boiler-suit.'

'Yes, I suppose so.'

He sounded very unconvinced and Ruth smiled inwardly as she climbed back into bed, her breasts swinging as she leant over and poked her tongue in his navel.

He giggled like a child. 'That tickles, stop! Why did you move here from Glasgow? It's pretty remote.'

'I needed a change. And don't forget that my mother's family came from the Borders, I have an aunt or two not far away. I was looking round for a place where I could rent a workshop cheaply, and I heard about the barn at Whitefoot Farm. Madeleine was just starting to diversify, they needed the extra income because her husband had organophosphate poisoning – from the sheep-dip – and they were thinking about selling off some of the farm...'

'But he died years ago, didn't he? I thought you had only been here a short time. Did you come here after leaving Jay?'

'Becoming the Grand Inquisitor, are you? No, since you ask, Jay and I split up before I started working at the museum. I stayed in Glasgow for a couple of years then I decided to get out of the city and to live in the country and be even more independent. Okay?'

'Uh-huh.' She could sense that there were many more questions that he wanted to ask so she distracted him with a well-placed hand.

'I'm going to take advantage of you every minute you're here,' she murmured vampishly. 'It's so much more comfortable in this bed than in the back of the van.'

FIFTEEN

George's pickup drove into the yard, sending muddy water sheeting towards Ruth. She jumped back, screeching.

'You did that on purpose, you devil!'

'Yup, nearly got ya.' As usual, he was grinning broadly. 'Filthy weather, couldn't get through down by the bridge, water's more'n a couple of feet deep on the road, so I had to come over the top. Are you going in?' He tilted his head towards the house.

'No, I've only just arrived, I was going to the workshop. Can't stop, I'm getting wet.' She shook her head and rain drops sprayed out to the side and trickled down her nose.

The kitchen door opened and Madeleine made a face at the weather and shouted, 'Come in out of the rain. You too, Ruth, there's a letter for you.'

'A letter? Here?' Ruth frowned and dodged the puddles as she followed George inside.

'Sit down while I put the kettle on. Here, Ruth,' she handed her the white envelope. 'You'll need to take the dogs and change the raddle on the tup's harness, George. He's red at the moment, so put in the blue. Will you be able to catch him with the dogs or do you want me to come too?'

'Aye, I'll catch him, no problem. There's a good number of red bums already on they Herdwick yows, he's a randy bugger.'

Ruth only half-heard their conversation as she examined the envelope with the Liverpool postmark and the hand-written address, the writing recognisable after all these years: 'Ms Ruth

Kowslowski, c/o Mrs M. Tregwithen, Whitefoot Farm.' She pulled out the letter and unfolded it, enough to read, '*My dear Ruth, I apologise for sending this care of Madeleine, but I realise that I do not know the postal address of your house – merely its geographical location and that it is "the one on the left".*'

A real letter, instead of an email, seemed unnecessarily portentous. She decided to read it in the privacy of the workshop and slipped it back inside the envelope.

Madeleine set a mug of coffee down in front of her, clearly trying to contain her curiosity.

'From Stefan Greatorex,' Ruth told her. 'He knows your address better than mine.'

'Nice bloke,' George observed. 'Not too bothered about things, like. You know she ran out of petrol when she was driving him around back in the summer? Lucky for them that yours truly came that way.'

'Of course Madeleine knows, I used her spare can, remember? You're such a knight in shining armour, George. Saint George saves the day.'

'Bet you wished it was the night.' He leered at her while dipping a custard cream in his coffee.

Ruth could not remember when she had last received a letter that was not a bill or related to work. Apprehensively she sat down at her workbench and pulled out the two hand-written pages. Stefan had left last Sunday morning in a mood that, because she did not know him well enough, was unreadable. She turned on the desk-light and angled it closer. His writing was neat and legible, almost like calligraphy in its stylishness, black and positive on the page.

My dear Ruth,
What a strange and wonderful day and night we had, what an extraordinary person you are. On Saturday afternoon as we lay and talked I began to feel as though the 'Ruth-shaped hole' that I have carried

around within me for so many years was being filled in at last.

But I have to be completely honest with you and tell you that the revelations that you made have disturbed me and thrown my feelings into turmoil. I told you that I love you, and I believe this still to be true, but it is tempered by the hopelessness of our situation, for you were (regrettably) honest in your expression of your feelings for me: that you do not love me. Your enhanced libido (to give your obvious need for and enjoyment of the sexual act its formal title) threatens to overwhelm my own feeble offerings, immensely desirable though you are. Perhaps because I now seek a relationship from a different perspective, from a different background of experience, and from my love for you – I find it difficult to conceive of merely acting as your 'partner in sex'.

You were right when you chided me that I did not know you. Your transformation at dinner, from the Ruth who dresses in such a way as to make herself inconspicuous, to the startlingly exposed and sexy version, thrilled but also, I have to admit, daunted me. Who was this powerful and voluble woman who was out to get her man? I did not know you and I cannot imagine knowing that Ruth, I am afraid I am too much of a coward and perhaps already too set in my ways.

After I left you I went walking in the fells, in the hope that height and clear air would offer me a different perspective. As I walked up the path, which was steep and uneven, I had a memory of the time when I used to backpack in rough country in Scotland (I must have passed through Glasgow several times during the period when you were living there – how close we were, all unknowing). Although I was only carrying the small rucksack last Sunday I suddenly remembered the feeling of a heavy pack, how it alters the centre of gravity, and tensions the muscles in the neck; how one must watch one's feet continuously and choose the optimum foothold. You must seek a rhythm, and then adjust your step-size so that the rhythm is not broken, placing your boot on a stone that is angled to give you thrust or, if you are descending, that will prevent your foot from slipping. You have to use the edges of your boots, digging in for purchase. Always there is the steady plod-plod-plod, the rhythm that takes over your mind and heart and that indirectly controls your breathing.

As I said, my rucksack was light, but I fell into that steady plodding and my perspective was very limited because I stared mainly at the ground ahead of me. When I finally reached the ridge and a suitable stone where I could sit and take a rest I was rewarded with a clear view of Derwentwater where small boats were sailing, and I could just make out cars on the road on the far side of the lake. Microscopic people going about their lives! I turned around to look towards the North and thought I could pick out 'your' valley, which seemed distant and enclosed.

Then I played a silly game – in the valley beneath me was an old mine, and above it a track that zig-zagged up to some higher adits on the hillside opposite to where I sat. The zigs and zags were sharp and acute-angled and I imagined you standing at the top, dead-centre. I decided the zigs tending left were negative and zags to the right were positive. If I climbed upwards (mentally) and reached you from the right, I was destined to stay with you; if from the negative, left side, I must leave you in peace.

Do you want to know the outcome? I 'arrived' at the top and found myself on the apex of the right-hand zag, about to 'claim' you from the right – and my immediate reaction was dismay, Ruth.

A silly little game, but it showed me how I had been deluding myself. I know you don't need me to disturb the life you have carved out for yourself. I realise that it was pointless and foolish of me to get back in touch. However, I do intend to stay in Liverpool should the grant be forthcoming, and if you should need me (as a friend) you have only to call.

Please, dear Ruth, take very great care.

Thank you again, my dear friend, for the insights into your life and I wish you the very best.

Yours,
Stefan

Ruth re-read parts of the letter then put it down on the table. I feel nothing, she thought. 'Daunted,' indeed! So stilted, so wordy. What a fucking bore. *Phoo!* She puffed out her breath, partly irritated, partly amused at this lengthy dismissal. But she was relieved, too. The twenty-four hours they had spent together had been good, and would probably keep her off the boil for another few weeks if she tried very hard.

It had been clear that her behaviour, and the hints she had dropped, had preyed on his mind; sex and love were partners in Stefan's mind. She reminded him that when they had been together back in their student days, they had spent most of their time fucking then too.

'But I loved you, Ruth. I love you now.'

'When I worked in the hospital I remember a couple of the nurses were discussing the daughter of one of their colleagues – the kid was only sixteen and pregnant, and she had a bad reputation for "sleeping around". Is that how you classify me, by the way? But one of the nurses said that there was a wide spectrum of sexual activity as in everything else, and some girls were not that interested while at the other end were girls whose hormones were very active or hyperactive. They needed sexual release most of the time, they couldn't help themselves. I thought at the time that it would make sense, biologically. I'm not way out at the top end by any means.'

He had seemed mollified and they had dropped the subject, and the conversation had gradually shifted to wider matters, politics, books, essays.

When Stefan left he had told her to 'take care'.

Take care, take care. Of course I take care. Never again will I be careless.

Ruth thumped the table and leapt to her feet, pacing backwards and forwards around the studio. She went back to the table and picked up the two sheets of paper, tore them up and stuffed them deep down into the swing-top bin.

'*You* should have taken care!' she told the harvest-mouse in the display case that the museum had sent her to restore. She poked at the litter of mouse pups in their tiny artificial nest. 'This is what happens when you're careless.'

SIXTEEN

Making Eyes:

Ruth Kowslowski's blog

White spheres lie on cotton-wool in the compartments of a flat wooden box, blue, brown or green circles, dark centres – pot-boilers, money-spinners – artificial human eyes. On a workbench there are small bottles, pin-boxes and wooden trays containing different body-parts: glass tentacles of different shapes and colours, sponge spicules, tiny shells. 'Mix 'n match' invertebrates amongst the powdered glass and pigments.

In 1860, Philip Henry Gosse's *Actinologia Britannica* was published, illustrated with engravings of coloured sea-anemones and corals. A few years later, an Englishman living in Dresden showed these pictures to glass-maker Leopold Blaschka. 'Marine creatures preserved in spirits look like grey rubber,' he said. 'Why not show their true colours by modelling them in glass?' Leopold accepted the challenge. He had already made glass orchids, so now he merged his art with science, modelling the exquisite and minute details of invertebrate animals, making them objects for the museum and scientific study rather than ornaments for the drawing-room. Later, he and his son Rudolf were to give up animals and Haeckelian embryos for a ten-year commission to make the Harvard glass flowers, but in those early days their business was not yet profitable, so they created jewellery, and glass eyes for cosmetic use by the blind.

We don't know where Frederik Ruysch obtained the glass eyes to fill the orbits of his embalmed and Death-defying Dutch babies in the 17th century but they obviously did the trick because the babies' winning looks won the heart of great Czar Peter.

The philosopher Jeremy Bentham, who died in 1832, probably had the foresight to choose his own glass eyes (but he clearly had not planned that his mummified head would be stored in the dark *inside* his torso).

Can we defy Death, and preserve and repair our ageing body-parts? Can the blind really be made to see again? Human eyes are such complicated balls of cells. William Paley had argued in his *Natural Theology* in 1802 that the eye, like a telescope, could only have been designed by a Maker. (But the Maker must have been having a visual migraine when he designed the mammalian retina, back-to-front.) Charles Darwin struggled to understand how these 'organs of extreme perfection' could have arisen from chance mutations alone. '*To suppose that the eye... could have been formed by natural selection seems, I freely confess, absurd in the highest degree,*' he wrote. It's almost enough to turn one into a Creationist or propose the intelligent mind and hand of a Designer. There is the implication that Evolution had foresight and saw its future goal. We know now that Evolution is a conservationist and throws very little away: 'You want an image-forming retina? There's a bit of photosensitive pigment kicking around somewhere. A bit of this and a little bit of that, let's try them in this order instead...' The ingredients are mixed in a different sequence, to a different recipe.

The ingredient *pax6* has never been allowed to rest, we need that gene as much as a flatworm does. In the embryo of a fly the product of *pax6* directs the development of the eye. Gosse examined an insect's eye under his microscope in the 1850s: 'How gorgeously beautiful are these two great hemispheres that almost compose the (dragonfly's) head, each shining with a soft satiny lustre of azure hue,' he wrote. 'You see an infinite number of hexagons, of the most accurate symmetry and regularity of arrangement.' Each of those 'hexagons' contains a lens, and a careful anatomist with a steady hand can prepare an insect's eye so as to look through it himself. Van Leeuwenhoek (who lived a mere fifty years from 1675-1725, but achieved so much) looked through his microscope fitted with the prepared eye of a honey bee at a church steeple ('which was 299 feet high, and 750 feet distant') and saw multiple inverted images of the steeple. That microscope is in the Boerhaave Museum in Leiden, displayed near a shockingly pink toe injected and embalmed by Albinus (its severed end hidden by a lacy 'cap'). It scarcely seems possible that van Leeuwenhoek could have seen and understood so much of the natural world through a handheld instrument that is barely two inches tall.

The surface of the fruitfly *Drosophila*'s eye resembles a small raspberry. If the *pax6* gene is injected into the embryonic cells that should form a *Drosophila* leg, the raspberry-like eye grows instead. Even more exciting and astonishing is that the raspberry will also grow if the *pax6* equivalent from a *mouse* is injected into the fly embryo! A mouse's eye is like ours, as different from a fly's eye as is a fly's wing from a bat's. And so it is with *pax6* from the squid which, like the octopus, is almost unbelievably related to creeping slugs and snails, and which has an eye that is superficially like a mammal's (this time, God designed the retina the right way round). Squids, jet-propelled and predatory, need their big eyes to see their prey – the Blaschkas' glass squid is translucent and delicate, with lustrous dark eyes.

The *pax6* gene in the living, growing animals has been conserved, and put to different uses. Biologists have identified it and its related ingredients, they even know something of the recipe from which a human eye is made, but they cannot reproduce it in a culture-dish, they cannot make eyes. Yet.

Biologists can 'make' different sorts of cells. Take a fertilised mouse or human egg and nurture it in a culture dish for several days so that its cells divide and divide again, to form a hollow blastocyst. Imagine a football with a pork-pie suspended inside it, and shrink it down in your imagination to the size of a pinhead and you have a six-day blastocyst, with the pork-pie the ball of embryonic stem cells. Stem cells, which each contain the complete book of recipes to form any other type of cell in the growing embryo; 'the secret of eternal life', a cellular equivalent of a perpetual motion machine, the magic ingredient that will allow us to repair ourselves for ever. Not quite, but stem cells have their uses.

Van Leeuwenhoek looked through his tiny microscope and watched red blood cells circulating in the blood-vessels of a tadpole's tail. He would have thought it almost unbelievable that stem cells from a blastocyst could be turned into red blood cells *in a culture dish*; or into nerve cells, or muscle cells. (He would have been even more disbelieving to see how frogs' eggs could be manipulated to produce clones). Scientists can persuade corneal stem cells to grow new pieces of cornea, they can even persuade embryonic stem cells to change into a kind of retinal cell. But they cannot yet grow an eye, and if they could, how would they rewire it to the brain? All those millions of wires bound together in a cable, each needing their own connections in the brain. The Designer made an unintelligent muddle with those wiring diagrams, too, crossing over the cable from the right eye's socket to the left brain, and *vice versa*.

William Hunter, FRS (1716-1783), anatomist, and man-midwife to Queen Charlotte and the gentry, dissected many corpses throughout his studies and demonstrations of anatomy. As President of the Royal Academy, he also stressed the links between science and art, and commissioned paintings and drawings of the three-dimensional structures that he dissected, as aids to surgery and deconstruction. Many of the contents of his London collection were transferred to Glasgow after his death. Upstairs in the Hunterian Museum, on a wooden shelf, are multiple rows of jars containing eyes. Intact, they stare at you while you stare at them and, because they are dissociated from their faces you cannot tell whether they stare in hatred or fear or even, perhaps, amusement. Why did Hunter collect so many? Was he working on a study of the anatomy and development of the eye?

But look at this. A woman sleeps sweetly, unaware that her body has vanished, leaving only her head with its soft pink lips and perfect teeth, nestling on a silken cloth. We need only see her head because *Organ of sight* shows the blood and nerve connections to the eye, as known in 1803. Clemente Susini's wax woman's eyes are closed, so we need not be afraid, but the eyes of Ana Maria Pacheco's sculpted heads engage you at once – stark white with dark irises and pupils, outlined by thin black lines, they look out at us slyly, laughingly, wryly, openly, in sadness and in pain, from their painted wooden faces. In *Dark Night of the Soul* (1999) the naked victim has his head covered by a cloth so that he may not see the archers aiming at him, or perhaps that we may not look into his eyes and see the terror in this so-called terrorist's soul, but the eyes of the carved watchers reveal their despair and make us weep. Elsewhere, thirteen heads stare out of a compartmentalised box (*Box of Heads,* 1983) and their white faces and gashed red mouths catch our glance one by one, and hold it. Individuals, their thoughts are almost visible and we are forced to wonder about them, for though disembodied they seem all too real. (It is not just their eyes, but also their teeth, that make them real, the porcelain teeth, with all the irregularities and imperfections of individual human mouths). The tiny boxed heads are as pale as bleached skulls.

In a tall wooden Cabinet in Museum Vrolik, Amsterdam, rows of skulls are supported by pegs on ebony stands. Hydrocephalus, microcephalus, bathrocephalus, they are all sizes, distorted, grinning toothily but without eyes. Shelves of skulls, a presentiment of the Killing Fields. Nearby is the Curator's 'favourite' specimen, a little foetus with a fuzz of pale red hair, his arms hanging gently in the preserving liquid as though he is merely resting. He is a little 'cyclops', whose genetic recipe made for him only one small central eye. He did not live to see the light of day, nor have the good fortune to enter the Country of the Blind.

Seventeen

March: and there is still light in the sky as Lisa drives home down the motorway, light that caresses the smooth outlines of the Howgill Fells but does not sink into the valleys through which Lisa swoops in her Peugeot, exulting in the uncrowded tarmac. She is tired but contented; the tiredness is physical and her hips and lower back ache, but she thinks of it as a 'good' ache, an ache won by exertion.

'Are you a walker, then?' Stefan had asked in astonishment. 'Why didn't I know that? I didn't even notice any boots lying around when I lived here. I suppose you will tell me now that you have been to Annapurna base-camp and I shall be horribly embarrassed at boasting about my rambles in the Alps.'

She joked that she kept her boots hidden, because they were blue with flashing lights in the heel, and he had only taken her seriously when she showed him her custom-made boots.

'You're amazing,' he had said.

'No, just over-compensating.'

Amazing: the warmth of his amazement fills her even now.

Her weekend has been amazing too, but now she speeds South, enjoying her freedom, subconsciously aware of and responding to the road. She hurries home to the gift that he has given her, and that will welcome her into her cool white room.

She sees it clearly, not as an abstract summative image, but in all its hand-stitched simplicity. In her mind she traces the edges of each diamond-that-is-not-a-diamond, immersing her senses in the richness of the velvet: deep red, blue that is bottomless in its profundity, and the green of emeralds caught by the sun. The black, the ace of diamonds, forces an extra dimension, so that blocky cubes cascade into the room, their left sides deeply shadowed.

Mentally she stands back from the *trompe l'oeil*, and blinks her internal eye (she catches herself closing her eyes as she drives and quickly returns to the reality of tail-lights, and white lines on the road). Seen in two dimensions, the shadowy aces resolve themselves as vertical rows of diamonds; but in three places, the perspective has been altered so that a black diamond lies as horizontal as a lid.

'Why did she do that?' she had whispered to Stefan, awestruck. 'Was she teasing us or were they genuine mistakes?'

'By the light of a flickering oil-lamp. The distraction of a baby wailing in its crib. No, she was a mathematician who had discovered the secret of the fifth dimension and stitched a paradox.'

'It's most unprofessional, but let me give you a hug,' she had said, and he had laughed gently and bent down and hugged her as she put her arms around his neck.

Sometimes subjects cycled in and out of one's life, entering without warning and remaining for a day or more, and then exiting again as though erased. This weekend dwarves and babies had pushed their way in, small but not the same, one group stalled by a malfunctioning gene, the other with genes that had yet to function.

Yesterday, coming off the motorway at a large roundabout, Lisa had seen banners draped along a fence on the far side of the road: 'Car boot sale, Saturday and Sunday! Smokers welcome. Dogs welcome. Cross-dressers welcome.' Delighted, she had circled the next roundabout and returned to drive slowly past. 'Residents of Appleby welcome. Lap-dancers welcome.' Chuckling, she had debated going in to see what was on offer for such an eclectic mix of customers, but the distant hills had a stronger pull, and she circled again and resumed her journey. As it contoured around the feet of Blencathra the road headed inexorably downwards into the bowl where the small town of Keswick nestled as though poured.

'Chamonix of the North-West.' Who had said that, perhaps mockingly? She could not remember, but narrow streets were further narrowed by climbing-gear that festooned doorways and spilled out of shops, and there was an air of concentrated enthusiasm for the Great Outdoors amongst the ambling pedestrians. Serious walkers would surely be out on the hills at this time, late morning, Lisa thought: those remaining at ground level were the dreamers and the unfit, and people who lived here, going about their normal lives in this town that was not, after all, a theme-park; people who paused only occasionally to remind themselves that their horizons were unusually high, an undulating rim of rock and heather. It would be good to dream, to drift like a somnambulist... But the main street was crammed with market stalls and she quickly became distracted by local fudge and mint-cake, which she bought for her research group, and a display of woven rough-wool rugs.

'It's Herdwick, love,' the woman said. 'That's its natural colour.'

Lisa remembered the grey sheep that Madeleine had shown her, the sheep with the kindly faces, and she imagined how this rug, with the variegated colours of lichen-mottled stone, would look in her own house. She pushed her fingers into the weave, feeling the strong wiry fibres; the woman pulled out a wider selection and spread them over the scarves and hats at the front of the stall, and Lisa dithered over the different shades.

The owner of the adjacent stall, which glittered with cheap brass and baubles, occasionally interrupted his patter to slurp from a mug of tea. His long bony nose dipped into the steam and after each gulp, he wiped it with his sleeve. He caught Lisa's eye and winked.

'I've been telling Beattie here to knit me a nose-bag,' he said. 'It gets that cold. But she won't do it, dunno why.'

'I keep telling you, Derek, I haven't got that much wool to spare. You'd need a flock of alpacas to cover that one!'

Lisa laughed with her while Derek continued, 'I thought I'd get one of those balaclava things with just my eyes showing but then that Bush declared war on all terrorists and I was scared he'd send in the cavalry to nuke me.' He passed a hand-mirror to a girl who was looking at some earrings. 'Here y'are, lass, use this mirror. "Mirror, mirror on the wall". This mirror never lies, we're all beautiful people here.'

'He likes it 'cos it makes his nose look small,' Beattie whispered loudly. 'Now, love, have you any preference?'

'As long as it's only me nose. Look at these necklaces now, did you ever see such workwomanship? All the way from the mountains of Tibet, these – *Blimey*! Any minute Snow White'll be coming round the corner too!'

Lisa looked round sharply at the change in his tone, half-knowing what she would see.

Two achondroplasics were browsing along the stalls. They could not have failed to hear Derek's loud joke and the woman had stopped to examine a display of smoked trout with great concentration. The man, perhaps her husband, had glanced up and had caught sight of Lisa.

There was that awkward moment, the half-smile, the indecision that Lisa experienced on the very rare occasions when she met another achon. The mirror-image that she had forgotten about, that she felt had nothing to do with her daily life; the transient exasperation and the silent question, 'Why should I greet you like a brother, sister?'.

'Here come your friends.' Derek was inexorable, but not unkind.

The small man's crumpled, ridged face collapsed even more into a toothy smile. 'No, hadn't you heard? Snow White's banged up in jail. We always suspected she was a paedophile, and she was lousy at housework too. Hi there.' He nodded at Lisa. 'How're you doing?'

'Fine.' Lisa smiled. Passing shoppers were looking at them covertly or even with the classic double-take.

'Nice rugs. Come and look at these, Sheila, one of these would do very nicely for Johnnie's flat. Johnnie's our son. This is my wife, Sheila. I'm Terry, by the way.' He held out his hand to Lisa. 'Pleased to meet you.'

'Hallo. I'm Lisa. They are attractive rugs, aren't they? They're made from the local Fell sheep.'

Beattie was looking at them in surprise. 'Don't you all know each other, then? I just assumed, well, that you were all together.'

'Bit of a coincidence, isn't it,' Derek agreed. 'Something of a rare breed, not often we see—'

'We're just like buses. You don't see any for ages then three come along at once, eh?'

Derek roared with laughter. 'That's good. You wouldn't like to come and help out here, would you – Terry, did you say? We'd make a good team, I reckon.'

'We're not that rare, you know. But I don't know where we all hide ourselves, do you, Lisa?'

Lisa realised, unhappily, that Terry had evangelical tendencies: he would always be ready to 'fight our corner'.

His wife had clearly heard it all before. 'Terry, they're busy and we need to go.'

'If you reckon that one of us is born in every 20,000 live births, that should be about thirty new children a year with our sort of restricted growth. Our son is like us, of course. We knew he would be, and we were happy about that, weren't we, Sheila?'

'Thirty – that's a lot,' Beattie agreed, uncertainly.

'But you don't see them, do you? And it's not just because we're so small and escape your notice. It's a mystery. But it just goes to show that you shouldn't be surprised to see a few of us at one time in normal circumstances.'

'I think I'll take this one, I like the mixture of colours.' Lisa raised her eyebrows at Beattie, who grimaced sympathetically.

Derek had been briefly distracted, helping two women choose a pair of candlesticks, but now he leant across the wooden bar that separated the stalls.

'Colour. What about colour then? You three are white, but where are the black and brown ones? Don't they have persons who are vertically challenged or whatever we're supposed to say too, or is it a culture thing? The wrong 'uns get left out on a hillside to die. Or get shut away.'

'Derek! You can't say things like that!' Beattie was shocked, but Terry laughed.

'In Brixton and Bradford? No, it's a valid point.'

Lisa suddenly wanted to be far away, preferably soaring in tandem with one of the paragliders who were circling beneath Skiddaw. Counting out the correct money, she grabbed her parcel from front of the stall. 'Sorry, I have to go.'

'Join us for a coffee, Lisa. Sheila and I would be glad of your company, wouldn't we, dear?'

For a moment the two women made eye contact. Eye to eye: the realisation was like a physical blow. Almost simultaneously Lisa understood that for Sheila and Terry this was unremarkable, routine. At home, in their kitchen, bathroom, sitting-room, at whatever time of day, they could see each other face to face and for them this was normality. Normal proportionate family life. And they had had a normal proportionate baby, who had now grown-up to be their size. Only outside their front door was the world a difficult and disproportionate place.

Lisa hesitated.

'He means well,' Sheila said softly. She could have been in her fifties; she wore a badly-fitting tweed coat and a knitted woollen hat from which grey curls escaped, but she stood within a shell of calm.

'Yes.' Struggling to hold the rolled-up rug, Lisa held out

her hand. 'But a friend is expecting me. Thank you.' When Sheila took her hand to shake it, Lisa suddenly leant forward and not quite knowing why, managed to kiss her on the cheek. 'Thanks. 'Bye, Terry. Enjoy your day.'

* * *

Ruth was uncertain. 'She's Stefan's friend. We didn't get on well last time.'

Madeleine stood at the bottom of the hayloft stairs. 'That was several months ago and she doesn't hold it against you. I asked her if I should invite you too and she said "yes".'

'But you both get on well together – I'd be superfluous.'

'Last time I took her for a drive around the farm and it was easier, there were things to look at. I'm not that good at conversation, Ruth, you know that. You're bright though, you'll think of things to talk about. Do come, we'll have a nice time all together.'

'She's a guest, why can't she eat dinner in the dining-room like everyone else?'

'That couple with the baby don't want dinner, and Lisa doesn't want to sit there on her own. She came because she wanted to see me, she said so, and I can't abandon her.'

'All right. If I must.' Ruth shook her head wryly. 'I'll expect a five-star meal though.'

It turned into one of those evenings where, for some indefinable reason, the atmosphere and individual moods and circumstances combine to produce a certain light-heartedness and easy conversation. Madeleine had made a steak and mushroom pie, with a perfect pastry crust that was decorated with a circle of tiny pastry roses; there were bowls of carrots and broccoli, and a mound of floury potatoes that seemed never to diminish. The hilarity scarcely decreased when there was a knock at the kitchen door.

The young woman spoke anxiously to Madeleine, saying that her husband had been vomiting.

'We stopped off in Glasgow and bought stuff for lunch. He had a mutton pie, he said at the time it tasted funny. I only had a cheese roll, thank goodness. What would the baby do if I was taken sick too?'

Madeleine followed her upstairs to see what was needed.

'Mutton pies!' Ruth laughed. 'Have you ever had one of them?'

Lisa shook her head.

'I had a real craze for them for a while when I lived in Glasgow. They're hot and peppery, and when you bite into them the fat pours out. The paperbag turns translucent with the grease. Disgusting. And there used to be something called an ashet pie, too, a slice of flat meat pie. Deep-fried.'

'Is it true you can get deep-fried pizza in Glasgow or is that a myth propagated by Edinburgh?'

'No, it was certainly true when I was there. Deep-fried Mars bars in batter too. How could I have forgotten?'

They both squealed in mock horror.

Madeleine came back into the kitchen and pretended to chide them. 'Listen to you! That poor young man's rolling around in agony and all you can do is laugh. I should think it was that mutton pie, all right. But he's getting rid of it fast. "Better out than in" and all that. Lucky there's a break in the lambing or I'd not be in here to keep an eye on him.'

'Sheep have a lot to answer for, it seems.'

'Yes, you could say that.' Ruth caught Madeleine's eye for a second.

Lisa continued, 'I met a killer sheep once, in a village in the West Highlands. It didn't have any fear of humans, it followed people around like a dog.'

'It'll have been bottle-fed, a pet lamb, they get like that. But not vicious, surely?'

'It definitely had the killer instinct. Apparently at first it came up to people when they were having their lunch by the lochside and then, because it was given the occasional sandwich crust, it started to equate all people with food, and would get really obstreperous if nothing was forthcoming. It came after me and I can tell you it was enormous, obese in fact. It wouldn't leave me alone, it kept coming after me with its head down – I was terrified! I had to get my thermos cup out and throw water in its face.'

'I wish I'd been able to see that. Perhaps if you'd given it a Mars bar instead...'

'Now there's an idea.'

The younger women, still laughing, looked at Madeleine in surprise.

'I was planning on ice-cream with home-made raspberry sauce for the sweet, but how about if we melted a couple of Mars bars for the sauce instead?' Her face, already pink from alcohol and the rain-forest climate, turned pinker.

In a few minutes Madeleine was hacking the bars into thick slices and Lisa was standing on a chair pulled up to the Aga and stirring the melting glossy mixture.

As Ruth burrowed in the freezer searching for the ice-cream, the thought hovered in her mind: three flawed females, but who is to say which of our flaws, external or internal, is the most punishing?

'It's like a witches' coven in here,' she commented elliptically.

'More like a play-group,' Madeleine retorted.

They were murmuring their appreciation of the pudding when the anxious young woman appeared again, very apologetically requesting a bucket and cloth. She was carrying her baby and was distraught.

'Why don't you leave the baby here while Madeleine helps you clean up?' Ruth suggested. 'What's she called? She'll be fine here with us.'

'Oh no, I couldn't do that, you're having your tea, I don't know whether she'd stay with you... she's called Amy, she's only eight months old.'

Ruth stood up and held out her arms. 'Let me try, it will

give you time to concentrate on your husband. And it's not as though you'll be far away if she hates being left with us. Hallo, Amy. Are you going to come to me?'

Reluctantly the woman handed over the child, and Ruth cradled the warm little body against her chest, stroking the soft hair of the head tucked beside her neck, feeling the child's soft skin against her own. 'There, little Amy.' She rocked her, swaying gently. 'Come and look at the pretty flowers. She'll be fine for a while, don't you worry about her.'

With an anxious smile Amy's mother followed Madeleine, and Ruth revelled in the feel and smell of the child as she wandered around the kitchen, showing her the early daffodils that Lisa had brought, and the lights and coloured objects.

'You're so good with her,' Lisa said, and Ruth knew she was surprised. 'Did you work in the maternity wing when you were at the hospital?'

'No. I think I must just like babies.' One of Amy's hands was tangled in Ruth's hair and the other was outstretched as she gurgled softly. 'Here, come and talk to Auntie Lisa.' Ruth bent down so that Lisa could reach out to the tiny fingers, which tightly fastened around her own.

'There is nothing so beautiful as a baby's hands, is there? So perfect and delicate, every bone in place. Do you know that you can tell whether a child will be left- or right-handed *in utero*? Ultra-sound scans show which thumb they prefer to suck.'

Amy's hand, its nails as pink as cowrie shells, gripped Lisa's stubby fingers. In Amsterdam's Museum Vrolik the tiny foetuses had perfect hands, Ruth remembered. They lay in their clear glass jars in front of bright, chrome-shaded lights, so that their skin was made translucent, and the silhouettes of their bones were as defined as an anatomical diagram.

Lisa takes the slip-road that will lead her back to Liverpool. She is tired now and has been listening to music to stay alert.

The complexity of Stefan's gift has eluded her again and the abstract image of pale spheres has returned to trouble her. The density of the traffic is increasing now, and she needs to concentrate fully on reaching home, but for the first time the 'home' image seems empty and resonant with echoes. She imagines Sheila and Terry, playing with a tiny, short-limbed baby who is sitting on a Herdwick rug.

Eighteen

Bob ran ahead, dodging legs and push-chairs. He was always full of purpose, intent on accomplishing some private business. He braked suddenly to snatch up a soggy chip and then hurried on again, a back leg tucked up for greater speed.

'Daft. Must've only got three-quarters of a brain – but he makes up for it with his smell. Worse than a midden in summer,' one of John's friends had said. But John insisted that the terrier had to be sharp to use three legs instead of four.

'Using four comes natural,' he said. 'You have to be able to think what you're doing if you want to use three.'

John loved the dog and it went everywhere with him, never at his heels – John with his two sticks was now too slow – but always nearby, keeping his master in his sights. Bad-tempered as well as odoriferous, the dog was obedient when he chose, and now he came at once to John's whistle.

'They don't allow dogs,' Madeleine said, as the three of them reached the café. 'They won't let him in.'

'They'll not notice you, lad, will they?' John said softly. 'Heel, now. Wait, Maddie, let these good ladies go in first and we'll follow right behind.'

At terrier-height the room was a forest of walking-sticks, shopping bags and legs, both wooden and alive, canopied by coats and table-cloths. Almost instantly, Bob was hidden beneath draped red gingham, and sniffing delicately at his master's shoes.

'Hallo, Madeleine. Morning, John – are you all right then?'

The subterfuge had been accomplished so quickly that Madeleine had not noticed that the adjacent table was occupied by friends but now, as she finished piling her mess of shopping-bags beside her chair, she saw that Elaine Nicholson was there with her daughter Abigail. Young Rick hung sideways off his chair and lifted the cloth by John's knees.

'What's its name?'

'*Ssssh*!' John tapped the little boy's arm with his shaking hand. 'It's a secret, mind. We don't want anyone to know or we'll all get thrown out.' He winked and Rick dropped the table-cloth quickly and hugged his elbows, his eyes bright with the shared knowledge.

'Rick, turn round and finish your Coke,' Abigail said sharply. Her black hair was piled loosely on top of her head and her cyclids were smudged with kohl; she looked sexy and as though her body pleased her, for her breasts were tautly outlined against her scoop-necked black pullover, and her neck and cleavage were tanned deep brown. Although she smiled at John, her brief glance at Madeleine was cold and hard.

Elaine, unaware of her daughter's antagonism, was already in full flow, leaning across and confidentially touching John's arm, her hands constantly on the move, weaving delicate patterns of explanation as she talked. Her posture was good, her hair (subtly dyed to hide the grey) well-cut, and her camel-coloured jacket was brightened by a handsome scarf.

Madeleine busied herself with the menu. 'A pot of tea for two and a bacon roll. I'll have a piece of shortbread.'

The schoolgirl waitress, white shirt flapping over an abbreviated version of a skirt, scribbled the order on her pad. Madeleine had been longing for a bacon roll, imagining its smell and texture, the soft warmth of it in her hand, but she no longer had the courage to eat it. Elaine would not eat a bacon roll, not in a genteel place such as this. Madeleine was so conscious of her own dreary clothes and ugliness (the word clattered in her mind, 'ugly, ugly, ugly'), that she fell into a profound silence as she automatically poured out milk and tea.

'Here's your grandad at last, Rickie.' Elaine stretched her neck, looking over their heads towards the door. 'What do you think his excuse will be this time?'

Madeleine felt the hair at the back of her neck prickle and she kept her head bowed as she pushed shortbread crumbs into a pile with her knife.

'Sorry I'm late. I bumped into old Gareth Richardson, and you know how he keeps you talking. Hallo, John, good to see you. Morning, Madeleine.'

Daniel, dapper in tweed jacket and twill trousers reached over Madeleine's shoulder to shake John's hand. He held the back of her chair and her cheek was scalded by his closeness.

John, head trembling, stretched out his palsied hand. 'Do... Donald. Haven't... haven't seen you for a long time.'

'Not since yesterday.' Daniel laughed. 'Watch your elbow now!'

But the jug of hot water tipped onto its side, its lid tumbling off the table. Steaming water momentarily pooled on the cloth then trickled over the edge. Bob yelped more in surprise than pain. He backed out of his hiding-place at high speed and the red-and-white gingham squirmed and rippled as he leapt onto John's lap.

As the waitress tipped her curtain of hair to one side to see what the commotion was about, the high voice of the manageress carried clearly across the crowded room.

'Excuse me. We don't allow dogs in here. Will you take it outside, please?' The 'please' was for emphasis, not politeness. Heads turned: a ring of faces showing curiosity, amusement, affront.

Madeleine pushed back her chair, careless of Daniel's proximity.

'I'll take him to the car. You stay there, John, and talk to Elaine.'

She grabbed Bob around his barrel-shaped belly and slapped his nose when he growled and tried to bite her.

'Can I help? Do you want me to bring your shopping, Maddie?' Daniel asked.

She looked directly at him. 'No thanks, Daniel. Elaine and Abigail have been waiting for you. I'll come back for John and the bags.'

The waitress held the door open for her, and whispered, 'Sorry. He was such a good little dog, too, I wasn't going to say anything myself.'

Madeleine smiled and whispered back. 'Thank you – that's kind.'

She held the terrier tightly as she carried him back to the Land Rover, squeezing him with her elbow while she unlocked the back door. She saw her reflection in the window and it seemed that there was a blankness where her face should be, and that the darkness was gathering about her. She made herself think of Danny, and light glimmered like ripples on black water.

When John was settled in the Land Rover, with his sticks tucked beside the seat, he insisted that Bob should sit in his usual place on his knee. He had become a little tearful in his weariness and Bob licked his master's chin and trampled a circle in his lap. John, stroking the animal's wiry hair, was somewhat restored.

'She's a nice woman, that Elaine, very well turned out. Daniel must be doing all right. Is the boy his son?'

'No, of course not, he's Abigail's son. Daniel's grandson. Rick and Abigail live with them on the farm.'

'Where's the boy's father then? In the Forces, is he?'

'They split up and Abigail had nowhere else to live, so she came back to the farm.'

'Tarty piece with her tits hanging out. Must be bored stiff on a farm. Can't see her helping Donald with the cows.'

Madeleine glanced sideways. John had never used words like 'tits' and 'tart' before.

'He's got a herd of pedigree Limousins, did you know that? These foreign cows are taking over, it's all the fault of that EU. Illegal immigrants all of them.' He laughed softly. 'Isn't that right, Bob lad? Illegal immigrants.'

'He's got foreign sheep too – did he tell you that?' Madeleine asked after a while. 'He's got a couple of Texel tups, and swears by them.'

'Ugly beggars, look like pigs.'

'They sometimes sit on their haunches like dogs, have you seen that?'

But he must have forgotten what they were talking about because he stared silently out of the side window, stroking Bob's head, over and over.

They were nearing home when she became conscious that he had been staring at her too.

'Perhaps you could get that thing seen to.' He spoke quite gently and his tone was so kind that she could not for a moment understand what he was referring to. 'I went into that beauty place and asked the young woman in there – very smart she was, with her painted face and fancy nails. She said there was a treatment that used a laser. You'd need to go to a hospital. They use it for tattoos.'

Madeleine was astonished. 'When did you go in there?'

'When you were in the Co-op.' He looked pleased with himself. 'Bob fancied a massage, didn't you, lad? They use lasers to remove tattoos, that's what she said.'

'Would you want me to? John?'

'You weren't like that when I married you. We did well smuggling this little beggar into the café, didn't we? They never noticed a thing the whole time we were there. You were a good lad, Bobbie, good as gold. We can take you out in polite society any time we want.'

'But—'

'I had a good crack with that chap Daniel, he's a nice fellow. I invited him to come over in a couple of days to look at the yows. You could do with a hand now and again, and he said he'd be happy to help.'

'But he came over often during the lambing, John. He was over yesterday, he brought you that notice about the scrapie tests.'

'Did he? Why are we parked here, Mad – aren't we going home?'

NINETEEN
What do you look like now? What will you look like then?
Ruth Kowslowski's blog

Louis van Bils sold his secret recipe for embalming bodies to the States of Brabant and the University of Louvain, in 1664.

For embalming bodies that are to be displayed in public
Take:
Two tin boxes, each 8 feet long, 2 feet 6 inches wide, 3 feet high and a wooden box that is caulked and has a lid.

Step One:
Into one tin box put:
60 pints of best rum
50 pints of Roman alum, finely ground
50 pints of pepper, finely ground
1 sack of salt finely ground
200 large glasses of best brandy of Nantes
100 large glasses of wine vinegar
— and mix all very quickly
Optional extras:
20 pounds of best myrrh, finely ground
20 pounds of best aloes, finely ground

Place the body, wound in a white linen sheet, on a wooden platform so that it is covered by at least two feet of the liquid. Close the box tightly for thirty days, although the mixture should be stirred at least three times during this period. When the mixture is stirred, remove and unwrap the body and wash it in fresh brandy, before re-wrapping and replacing.

Step Two:
In the second tin box, make up a mixture of rum, alum, pepper, salt, brandy and vinegar as in Step One.
Allow the body to dry then transfer it to this second box for <u>sixty days</u>, and turn and stir three times.

Step Three.
In the emptied and cleaned first tin box, place a mixture of pepper, brandy, wine vinegar, myrrh and aloes in the proportions of Step One. Mix and stir, and remove the clear liquid that comes to the surface

Also, make a mixture of finely ground
44 pounds of aloes
44 pounds of myrrh
20 pounds of foulli
20 pounds of cloves
20 pounds of cinnamon
20 pounds of nutmeg
plus ¼ pound ambergris
½ pound black balsam
¼ pound oil of cinnamon
— and apply this mixture several times to the exterior of the body, and allow to dry.

The body must lie in the third mixture for <u>sixty days</u>, being washed and rinsed with the clear liquid skimmed off previously. After the body has thoroughly dried, the ambergris mixture is applied again, and the body may be stored best in a tin box.

In 1669 de Bils tried to sell his recipe in the northern Netherlands, in Leiden and Amsterdam, with the help of Dr Tobias Andreae, 'Professor of Physick at Duysburgh on Rhyn', but they met considerable resistance from Dr Frederik Ruysch.

His own recipe was secret, after all, and would later be the envy of a Russian Czar.

These days embalming is a quicker, cheaper process, syringes attached to electric pumps, cheap ready-made preservatives, and suction tubes. Let's not bother with the details. Better to drink the rum and brandy with the funeral meats.

Regnier de Graaf, 17th-century Dutch anatomist and physician (and also a Fellow of the Royal Society in London) whose name lives on today in the Graafian follicles of the ovary, devised a syringe that Jan Swammerdam found very useful. By then, the European anatomists were all at it, shooting up warm coloured waxes or mercury or resins into blood vessels and lymphatics, and dissecting tissues or dissolving them away – corrosion casting – to follow the course of the now-visible vessels. (Some still do it today, with the modern techniques of injection and plastination. Anatomy can no longer keep a secret.)

William Hunter, surgeon, accomplished teacher and *accoucheur* to royalty, and his brother John, surgeon and anatomist, plus their assistants and their protegés – they were all busy injecting and dissecting, delving into the twists and anastomoses of the body's vessels, in chickens and alligators, rabbits and frogs, humans, dogs and leopards. For how could one perform corrective surgery on humans in the metaphorical dark? Comparative anatomy was a useful tool, for what might be indistinct in one species might be more clearly visible and understood in another.

De Graaf started with the proverbially fecund rabbit, William Hunter worked with women. In 1751 he procured the body of a woman in late pregnancy, and during the next twenty years he studied pregnancies at various stages. There are ten life-size plaster models of the gravid uterus in Glasgow University's Hunterian Museum, each uterus *in situ* in the abdomen, the mother's thighs sawn through to expose gigots of meat. No lacy caps disguise the stumps, this is anatomy for instruction, not moralisation. We don't know whether the real-life mothers were prostitutes nor do we care. The colours of the plaster casts are as fresh and bright as though uterus and foetus are alive, pink flesh, red and blue blood. The complex spatial puzzle, the three-dimensional fit between mother and child is made clear. 'The whole of them are exactly like nature herself, and almost as good as the fresh subject.'

Hunter employed artists like Jan van Rymsdyck to draw and paint pictures of the injected and dissected specimens at each stage. The texture of the life-size paintings in *The Anatomy of the Gravid Uterus* is almost the equal of Rachel Ruysch's skills, a window is reflected in the damp membrane around a life-size foetus rather than on the moist bloom of a Ruyschian grape. Or on the glass cornea of an artificial eye.

Amongst the many specimens in the Hunterian Museum is a glass receptacle containing one of William's injected placentas, a grey slab of tissue through which the silvery worms of mercury coil, anastomose and interdigitate. Who discovered what? John Hunter, too, had worked on the human uterus. Dispute arose between the brothers, and Benjamin Franklin again poured oil on their troubled waters. In Joshua Reynold's portrait of John, the glass jar standing close to Giant O'Brien's bony feet holds a section of placenta injected with red wax.

John, now Surgeon-General in the army, experimented on bringing dead bodies to life, or the near-dead, anyway, bodies rescued from near-drowning. By pumping warm air into their lungs, they were resuscitated and began to breathe again. Although he dissected and described the electric organs of the ray *Torpedo*, he did not try to use electricity to galvanise bodies to life. That was for Mary Shelley to imagine. But in 1818 James Jeffroy, Regius Professor of Anatomy at Glasgow, used bellows to blow air into the lungs of the dead murderer Matthew Clydesdale. The terminals of the newly-invented galvanic battery had already been connected to Clydesdale's body, and when the current was switched on, his eyes opened, his tongue protruded and his lips moved. Did Jeffroy believe the man had come back to life? He plunged a scalpel into the murderer's carotid artery, and the man 'fell dead on the floor'. Onlookers fainted!

Dr William Hunter and his colleague Dr William Cruikshank put the injection technique to a less honourable use. In 1775 they embalmed Mrs Mary van Butchell, aged thirty-six years – with the help of her dentist husband Martin.

Hunter's recipe was quick and simple: Mix 5 pints oil of turpentine, 1 pint Venice turpentine, 2 fluid ounces oil of lavender, and vermilion.

The solution was injected into Mary's blood vessels until all her skin took up the reddish colour, and the body was left to lie for a couple of hours to allow the solution to diffuse further through her tissues. Then her viscera were removed and washed in water, and injected and steeped in camphorated 'spirits of wine'. She was injected a second time, her viscera were replaced and the body cavities filled with camphor, nitre (potassium nitrate) and resin before being sewn up. The 'outlets' of her body were also filled with camphor and her skin was rubbed with oils of rosemary and lavender. Wearing a lace dress and with a rosy-pink complexion, Mary was laid on a bed of Plaster of Paris to absorb moisture and, it is said, was displayed in the window of Martin's house. It is also said that this bizarre display was (a) to drum up custom for Martin's dental practice and (b) because Martin could have access to Mary's money only while she was 'above ground'. Whatever version of the truth, the second Mrs van Butchell was unimpressed. Mary was sent to stay at Hunter's museum in Great Windmill Street.

Preservation for the after-life, preservation as an object of worship, preservation to 'make a point', icons and auto-icons, anatomical aids and anatomical art: we humans can rationalise almost anything that we do. Lenin, a modest man, did not have much say about the matter after his death, but Jeremy Bentham (died 1832) definitely wanted to hang around and be useful. It's a myth that he wanted to be displayed at University College London, for he wished to be useful as an anatomical specimen, and it's a myth that he was embalmed. He was a taxidermal preparation, dressed in his own clothes which Professor George Thane noted in 1898 'were stuffed with hay and tow around the skeleton, which had been macerated and skilfully articulated'. The head of the specimen is 'so perfect that it seems as if alive' – and is made of wax. Bentham's real head was mummified and dried, not unlike one of the shrunken heads in Oxford's Pitt Rivers Collection. Wrapped in a bituminous cloth, it was originally placed out of sight inside his torso.

The dead have so many secrets, so many different stories.

Frank Buckland did not mention the state of his hero John Hunter's body when he found the coffin in St Martin's vault but there are instances of bodies that fail to decay. Some of the 18th- and 19th-century bodies excavated from Christ Church crypt in Spitalfields in 1984 were preserved by saponification, their fatty tissue having converted into a stable brownish-white wax of saturated fatty acids and their salts. This adipocere characterises the famous 'Soap Lady' whom Joseph Leidy gave to Philadelphia's Mütter Museum in 1874. Perhaps the same had happened to Dante Gabriel Rossetti's wife, Elizabeth Siddall. It is said that she remained intact and beautiful when the impoverished drug-addicted poet sent Charles Augustus Howell to retrieve his poems from her coffin (though it's certainly a myth that her red-gold hair had continued to grow so as to fill the coffin).

Not so beautiful are the bog-bodies, nor are they as well preserved as the fatty 'bog-butter', 2000-year-old wrapped packages recently found buried in an Irish bog. But the torso of Lindow Man from a Cheshire bog and the bodies of Tollund and Grauballe Men from Denmark are a couple of thousand years old, and probably the victims of ritual killing. Tanned, shrunken but preserved by the anoxic acidity of peat, with teeth and hair intact, they can still reveal some secrets and Grauballe Man is the most revelatory of all.

Dissections are out of the question because these bodies are valuable archaeological specimens, but computerised tomography or CT scanning uses X-rays to generate 3D images so we can nevertheless look inside. Grauballe Man doesn't have a hard skeleton because the acid peat has dissolved the calcium, so his 'bones' are more like rubber. And his face has been re-modelled by the earlier conservators at the museum who, perhaps trying to 'walk like an Egyptian', padded the skin under his eyes with putty like a Pharaonic mummy. Sadly for Irish Cloneycavan Man, his face has been re-modelled too, but by the murder weapon. But he still has lovely red hair, slicked into a Tin-Tin quiff with Iron Age hair-gel, a mixture of vegetable oil and the resin of a French or Spanish pine.

No scalpel is needed now to look at bones and sinews, no syringe to find blood vessels and lymphatics. Sophisticated machines can look inside our living bodies, we can even watch our heart beat. We can watch our foetuses suck their thumbs. Twin CT-scanners, combined with positron emission tomography, PET, can create pictures of the insides of living bodies as they have never been seen before.

As for the preserved dead, we can analyse the DNA of their last meal. 'Ötzi', deep-frozen for 5000 years in an Ötztal glacier, ate ibex and red deer and vegetables before the arrow penetrated his shoulder.

Mis-quoting Papin, '*Through thy science... a dead person lives and teaches and, though speechless, still speaks*'. But the story, mis-remembered, can speak with many tongues.

TWENTY

'TWO PIECES OF THE JIGSAW PUZZLE'

That was the title that Stefan had proposed for the one-day conference on science and art. It stimulated considerable discussion, some of it laboriously witty or even ribald, in the tea-room but Stefan had held his ground, explaining that Maurits Escher had ended his lecture to the International Union of Crystallographers, in Cambridge in 1960, with the words '...science and art sometimes can touch one another, like two pieces of the jigsaw puzzle which is our human life'. Perhaps even more relevant, the physicist Roger Penrose had given Escher some identical wooden puzzle pieces a couple of years later and had challenged him to find how they could fill a plane. Escher solved the 'jigsaw puzzle' and Penrose later described the geometric characterisation of this uniquely tiled plane in mathematical terms. Now, the artist's complicated red, black and white design derived from this pattern was reproduced on the cover of the conference programme, and Stefan was well pleased. Escher had referred to his motifs as 'ghosts' but a biologist in the audience thought they were the freshwater planarian worms that looked equally as cross-eyed.

The conference had not been Stefan's idea but he had been manoeuvred into helping organise it by Adam Esterhazy, a colleague in the Physics department who was amused by the current fashion for re-creating 'Renaissance Man' from his (or even her) composite parts. Adam, politically-astute and with good connections, had found sponsors and several of the speakers, and delegates agreed over their cup of registration coffee that it promised to be an excellent day.

Stefan, despite his apprehensions about the smooth running of the event, always enjoyed giving illustrated lectures about Escher's drawings and the theory of 'regular division of the plane' that the artist, lacking mathematical training, had devised. These drawings, the patterns, the ideas, had been seized upon by mathematicians and crystallographers in the 1950s, and although they tended to talk of 'tiling' and 'tiling of the plane' instead of 'motif' and 'regular division of the plane', and used terms such as translation lattices and unit cells, the scientists had been excited by and had learnt much from the colour symmetry of the Dutchman's designs. Carolina MacGillivray, Professor of Crystallography at the University of Amsterdam at that time had even told her colleagues, 'Escher is crystallography!' and had sent her colleagues to the exhibition of his work at Rotterdam.

The interlocked fish and birds and lizards, the bats and shells and starfish, rigidly paved in two dimensions, but poised as though ready to leap upwards to freedom: which of the many designs should he choose? That was always Stefan's problem. Unlike the audience at the Amsterdam conference the previous Spring, these would be non-specialists, artists and writers and scientists of many genres and disciplines, who might only be acquainted with Escher's designs through postcards and pictures on arty calendars. So, when the inspiration struck him, he had actually laughed aloud.

He has been talking for several minutes and now he clicks on his next image. Red, white and blue squirrels fill the screen. They overlie pencil marks that show the underlying lattice of parallelograms, and small pencilled circles indicate where the motifs have been turned through 180 degrees. They are very fine squirrels, with their pointed foxy noses and upturned bushy tails.

'A crystallographer,' Stefan explains, 'would analyse this by looking for what is called a translation lattice. Let's take the points of the noses looking to the left, here – and here, and here. The translation lattice would then consist of all the points which are the tips of the squirrels' noses. We have to ignore the different colours of the squirrels to do this. You can generate the same lattice by choosing any point in the pattern – the midpoint of the back of the tail, say. The lattice is always the array of images of the chosen point. And while a single squirrel is equal in area to a parallelogram in Escher's terms, the crystallographer's "unit cell" contains two squirrels. The interesting point here is that though Escher and the scientists were intrigued by each other's results, they approached the problem from different directions – Escher starts with a blank sheet of paper and works out how to fill it with interlocking motifs. He looks for methods of creating periodic patterns. Crystallographers and mathematicians begin with a pattern and look for methods of logically analysing it. Escher draws a grid and decides to fill it nose to tail with squirrels. The mathematician sees a museum drawer packed tightly with squirrel skins, and analyses how the curator managed to pack them so tightly.'

At this point, Stefan stops to pour himself a glass of water from the bottle on the table next to the lectern. He glances at Ruth, who is sitting tautly at the end of the front row, and she raises her eyebrows. He then flips through a selection of slides to illustrate some simpler points, before showing a four-colour design of chubby fish, rotated around each other.

'Infinity. Patterns like this represented, according to Escher, fragments of infinity. The fish could continue on and on into space in this same arrangement. But, he says, "we are aware we cannot manufacture a plane that extends infinitely in all directions". Yet he wants to represent them in an infinite way. He solves the problem by carving this beechwood sphere so that when you turn it around in your hands – imagine yourself doing it – "fish after fish appears, continuing into infinity". Those are his own words. The same illusion applies to this netsuke carved in ivory by a Japanese craftsman to Escher's design. Where do the animals start and where do they stop? It is impossible to see. We think we can classify and enumerate what has been recorded so visibly – but we are deceived.'

Another drink, a pause, to make a natural break so the audience can digest the point he has made; he is well-practised, a professional speaker.

'And now finally, I'd like to show you the artist as pragmatist, with a photograph of a couple of pages of Escher's notebooks – written in Dutch, of course, so probably unintelligible to most of us here. But he is talking about the types of animal motifs that are suitable for designs on different surfaces, vertical or horizontal, and whether they should be seen in lateral or frontal view, or even from above, depending on their most characteristic outline. You have only to think of the side-view of a horse, or the outline of a lizard seen from above. The mammals, he writes, "are not conceivable without a supporting surface, unless they are viewed from above". Birds and fish, however, "gliding either in water or in the air, need in no case the suggestion of a supporting surface, because they are supported invisibly".

'These pictures illustrate his points perfectly... "Supported invisibly." And that seems to me to be a very appropriate place for me to finish, given the content of the next talk in this session.'

Ruth feels her heart beating fast and she wipes her palms surreptitiously on her trousers; she is sure her face is shiny with nervousness. What did Stefan just say? She has been unable to concentrate on the diary or notebook or whatever he has been showing, but he has mentioned something about 'supported invisibly' and the next talk. Hers. He gestures towards her, prematurely exposing her to public scrutiny. Her throat seems full of glue and she swallows hard, hearing neither the questions nor Stefan's answers.

Earlier she listened and watched with increasing fascination as Stefan revealed the elegance and wit of Escher's work. I think I called them 'anally-retentive graphics', she recalled with shame. Lisa had told her that Stefan's talk was knowledgeable and very polished, but Ruth still marvelled at this unsuspected aspect of Stefan's character, how he took the audience with him, guiding them easily through fragments of the abstruse maths, imbuing them with enthusiasm for the artistry, and showing them the warmth not only of the artist but also – and here Ruth was genuinely surprised – of himself. Her apprehension was set aside throughout Stefan's exposition: but now her turn to speak has arrived, and the nervousness returns with force. As Adam Esterhazy comes to the lectern to introduce her, she asks herself, yet again, how she could have allowed herself to be persuaded into this.

Standing, gathering up her notes, she glances at Lisa, who is sitting next to the aisle a few rows back. Lisa surreptitiously gives her a 'thumbs-up' sign and smiles. Dear Lisa. But it is her fault that Ruth is here, her invitation had been so persuasive.

'You're the expert, don't forget. You'll know more than anyone else there and they'll all be dying to learn about taxidermy. You can write, you already know how to communicate – when you can be bothered! So now do it aloud. But don't read your talk. Learn it if necessary, and look at the audience. Engage them. They'll love it.'

Last night, they had worked through the talk together, Lisa sitting in what she called her Little Chair, telling Ruth where to pause, where to emphasise or even repeat a certain point.

'It's rather impersonal,' she had said. 'Is there an amusing anecdote or a funny incident that you can throw in? Why you left nursing to become a taxidermist, for example. I bet there's a story there.'

'I have given my talk the title of "Putting the pieces back together" because that's what I do, I'm a taxidermist, and I fill empty spaces inside animals.'

185

Her mouth is dry and she takes a drink; her notes shake and she puts down the page and tries to imprison her hand in the pocket of the new, smart jacket, but the pocket barely has room for two fingers, so she grips the edge of the lectern instead.

'Before I became a taxidermist I was a nurse, of sorts, so I suppose you might think that I took to dealing with patients who were already dead because it was a less traumatic option. But actually it was because I was given a preparation of a fierce ginger tom-cat by a man whom I hardly knew. And seeing Dr Greatorex's slide of Escher's squirrel pattern a few minutes ago reminded me of something else about this rather strange old man – that once he came and sat next to me on a park-bench in Glasgow and composed a poem about a squirrel that we were watching. He asked me for words that described the flowing movements of the animal. I wondered later, after I discovered he was a taxidermist, if he tried to capture the squirrel in words because he knew he couldn't capture the animal and turn it into a prepared specimen. I was never able to ask him because not long after he gave me the ginger tom, he "flitted" as they say in Glasgow, apparently leaving a room full of stuffed cats and a few months' of unpaid rent.'

A murmur of laughter and interest: everyone likes stories, Lisa was right.

'But the real reason I mention this man is because he used to leave out food, meat mostly, for the neighbourhood cats, and – again this became clear with hindsight when I was able to re-interpret something I saw him do – he would occasionally lure one of the cats into his house. When I started learning my new trade at the museum I discovered that it wasn't necessary to keep the skeleton as the internal support for a mounted animal. I remembered treading on a small shoulder-blade on the steps up to the old man's house, and I suddenly saw its significance. And I do wonder now–' here she pauses and grins at the audience, suddenly beginning to relax and enjoy herself '–whether he used cat stew as bait!'

She allows the gasps and laughter to die down, and puts up a slide showing a fibreglass mannekin suitable for the torso of a cat, and explains that such solid shapes, made by the taxidermist using a variety of light strong materials including papier mâché and wood-wool, are used as the main form.

'In the seventeenth and eighteenth century, dry preparations of animals were literally "stuffed" – the skeleton was used as support for the tanned skin, which was stuffed with straw or horse-hair, with little reference to the underlying musculature. Nowadays we use the skeleton as a guide, and take photographs. We make drawings and measurements, to get as complete a record of the intact animal's shape and colour as possible – and then we make an armature of wood or wire to act as support for the mannekin. We keep and use the skulls because the shape of the eye-sockets and the jaws or beak is important. And finger- and toe-bones, sometimes even tails. Think of the bones in bats' and birds' wings.' She shows slides of their delicate framework.

'They are so integral to the function and the form of the animal. Having said that though, I should explain that we have to pick the brain out of the skull and every piece of muscle off the remaining bones or the animal would – to put it bluntly – begin to stink. And every piece of fat has to be taken off the inside of the skin as well. With some animals, domestic animals in particular, there can be a very thick layer of fat and removing it can be very time-consuming. Nearly two centimetres in a spaniel that I had to prepare!'

There are slides of prepared cats, dogs and rabbits, arranged in a variety of positions, as she talks.

'By the way, even if I don't know a dead animal's provenance, I can tell at least whether it's wild or not – for example if a stag is from the Highlands or is semi-domesticated from a Park – just by looking at the thickness of the subdermal fat.

'But if I pick the muscles – the "flesh" – away from the

fine bones, how do I build the limbs up again to make them look life-like? If you look at your biceps at this moment... feel them if you can't actually see them... and now bend and raise your arms to shoulder height... the biceps have changed dramatically in shape, haven't they? Perhaps with some of you more than others.'

There is an outbreak of flailing arms and muted hilarity.

'My point is that this is where art and science must interconnect in taxidermy. It's necessary to know something about the arrangement and thickness of the different muscles, and which of them bulge and how during a particular movement.

'You're probably familiar with drawings like these by da Vinci of the muscle blocks of the arms and legs – the art of anatomical science, you might call them. These solid models, though, in this slide... and this... and these... illustrate the muscles in three dimensions. They're what are called écorché preparations. They are plaster casts of flayed corpses – in other words, corpses from which the skin has been removed to show the arrangement of the underlying muscles. This painting by Zoffany shows the anatomist William Hunter giving one of his annual lectures to the Royal Academy of Arts in 1772. Hunter was insistent that artists needed to understand human anatomy, and used this plaster écorché of "Standing Man", probably a hanged Jewish thief, as an example.

'You probably know that the anatomists of that period got their hands on the bodies of people who had been hanged, and on other bodies too, but the so-called body-snatchers are a different topic which I'm not going to talk about further. One of the most extraordinary and beautiful écorchés is of "Smugglerius", we see him here, this very muscular smuggler whose corpse was taken from Tyburn Tree in 1775 and set by Hunter, before rigor mortis set in, to mimic the pose of a Roman statue called "The Dying Gaul".'

'Shock them!' Lisa had said.

Gaetano Zumbo's coloured wax head, skin intact on the left side, but the right side flayed and dissected to show nerves and muscles and salivary glands, raised a few mutters of disgust. But it was Citarelli's wax model of an écorché standing male, with its shadowed eye sockets, and mouth open as though in conversation, that had the greatest visual impact.

'He was made about a hundred and eighty years ago. We can believe he is alive, can't we? His colours are so real and fresh. But common sense tells us that a man whose skin was missing couldn't stand there looking so relaxed. Similar techniques were used with the corpses of animals, as you can see in these pictures by George Stubbs... This is really helpful for taxidermists, as we need to have this sort of information if we are going to prepare animals, and particularly mammals – birds with their feathers are more forgiving – in dynamic action. The muscles need less prominence in animals at rest.'

And so Ruth continues, showing photographs of animals mounted or suspended in active poses, where some knowledge of animal behaviour at the very least, informed the preparation. Once or twice she hesitates or loses her place, but even as she talks she is also conscious of being a detached observer, and is pleased with her performance.

The questions come fast and seemingly unendingly, such is the interest that has been raised.

'That old man you talked about at the beginning – why did he make cat preparations? Do many people want their pets preserved?'

'It's cheaper than cloning – and the animals become so much more obedient! I don't know the cat-man's reasons, as I said he flitted. And I live in a rural area where not many people ask me to do pets, so I can't speak generally, I'm afraid.'

A woman near the back asks (too quietly – she is requested to 'Speak up!'), 'Farmers and landowners in the eighteenth century commissioned artists like Stubbs and Weaver – there's that lovely painting of the Durham Ox – to paint portraits of their prize animals. Were any of these animals preserved by taxidermy after they reached the end of their usefulness or died? And have you ever had to make a preparation of that kind?'

Ruth thinks it was likely that preparations of prize stock could have been made, but has no definite examples. 'No, I haven't done any cows or pigs, though I once had to prepare a domesticated roe deer stag. And I had to help a taxidermist friend to skin thirty stags in a single weekend, for a wealthy Arab and his entourage in Dubai – it's a long story! I smelt of deer for a week and dreamt about skinning deer for several nights afterwards.'

'You've talked about taxidermy in relation to animals.' The young woman is dressed in black except for a rainbow scarf that is wound several times around her throat. 'And you've told us about plaster casts of flayed humans. We all know about embalmed humans, and the unpleasant eighteenth-century habit of displaying the skeletons of what were considered unusual specimens like Eskimos and giants. But you haven't mentioned dry preparations of humans. Without putting too fine a point on it, taxidermy preparations of humans. Did, or do, such things exist? And if not, why not?'

Heads turn to see what sort of human could be asking this question. Faces alive with prurient curiosity stare at Ruth, waiting to hear her answer.

It is the sort of question that she dreaded. She does not want to have to arrange the relevant details in a logical or succinct reply. She does not want to have to talk about such matters. She wants to say, 'I don't know' and leave the platform.

But Esterhazy looks at her, and says, 'Yes, you've time – but this had better be the last one so that we don't cut into our time for networking and lunch.'

'Foma,' she says, and cannot help sighing. 'Peter the Great brought Foma Ignatiev to his court as a living exhibit in 1722.

When Foma's novelty wore off he was put to work doing manual labour, though it isn't clear what work he could have done. He had what's known as the "lobster claw" deformity so his hands appeared to have only two opposable digits. He lived in the museum compound for fourteen years and when he died Peter had him stuffed and put on display. It's possible that his skin was tanned with bark extract then stuffed with straw around a wooden armature. There is also a report that the skin of the giant Nikolai, also known as Bourgeois, was stuffed, although other reports say it was his skeleton that was displayed in Peter's museum. Maybe both. His testes and heart were pickled and displayed. Perhaps there were specimens of other complete humans elsewhere. I don't know. They would have looked unnatural. Generally humans are embalmed.'

Lunch is a hubbub of noisy conversation and debate, voices rebounding from the cafeteria ceiling and mixing with the clatter of cutlery and china. Ruth is still humming with adrenalin, and astonished at how much she has enjoyed herself.

A man puts down his tray next to Ruth and says, 'The vegetarian option seems unusually popular today.'

He chats to her, questioning her in a practised manner that serves to show the breadth of his own knowledge. Unused to these tactics of the male academic, she now feels belittled and depressed. Stefan is nowhere in sight, but they have had no time to talk to each other so she is not sure whether they are still on friendly terms. Two tables distant, Lisa is deep in conversation with Chris the composer; she looks across to Ruth and mouths 'All right?', and Ruth nods resignedly.

Ruth had not mentioned that Foma was a dwarf although one report calls him 'a boy'. It is said that Bourgeois' mother was a dwarf. Could this be possible? Peter the Great collected dwarves too, and arranged marriages between them.

'Peter the Great arranged the marriage between the giant

Bourgeois and his very tall Finnish mistress who was pregnant,' Ruth tells the academic, knowing well that this has no bearing on what he has asked. 'He hoped thereby to breed giant offspring, and sell them to other kings and emperors who required tall soldiers for ceremonial purposes. Eugenics goes back a long way. Excuse me, I have to go.'

TWENTY-ONE

The music is spare and minimalist but strangely hypnotic. Ruth and Lisa soon lapse into silence, still recovering from the post-conference dinner. Lisa's back is aching so she lies on the sofa and Ruth has curled up in an armchair. Coloured velvet cubes tumble continuously off the wall and Ruth manages to ignore them by concentrating on the elaborate shadows in the plaster cornice.

'G380R' is dedicated to Lisa and was played in public today for the first time.

'A world premier,' Chris Fazackerly declared, to much applause. Chris is a composer of electronic music, and has long, wavy brown hair tied back in a ponytail. His face is pallid and his nose fleshy, but his short-sighted eyes are strikingly green. He has collaborated with a friend of Lisa's, Garry McIver, who works on the molecular biology of cells.

Chris and Garry performed as a duo, complementing each other. 'In the same way that a molecule of messenger RNA is complementary to a strand of the DNA helix,' Garry quipped, but not everyone understood the reference. They had written the script and practised it until word-perfect, because they had understood they should treat this as a performance.

While they talked, strange electronic music played almost inaudibly from several points around the lecture-theatre.

Garry is blond and extrovert, he wears jeans and a sweatshirt and gesticulates continuously, so that the listener's eyes are drawn to his hands rather than to his words. But a video looped continuously behind him, focussing attention; it showed achondroplasics of all ages in close-up and in action-shots; talking, sitting, dancing, walking, even climbing or abseiling; doing housework and shopping in supermarkets; ultrasound scans and newborn babies, bones and fluorescently-labelled cells. It was a celebration and for most of the audience, a revelation. Some of those sitting near Lisa tried not to look at her, others glanced at her and smiled, hoping to catch her eye. She looked straight ahead and wished the duo would finish their explanation and allow the music to take centre-stage.

Garry: 'Your genome is the recipe-book for *you*, your genes carry the instructions to make *you* and allow you to function from the moment of fertilisation of the egg to the day you die. The instructions are in the form of three-letter words, each made up of three of the four small molecules called 'bases', whose fancy names have the initials A,C,T or G. Each three-letter word codes for one of the twenty amino acids that are the building-blocks of proteins. A gene is a string of three-letter words so it is the recipe for a single protein. There are thousands of different proteins making our bodies, and we have about twenty-three thousand genes.'

Chris: 'The notes of a scale are the building-blocks of music. Each tune or composition has a different recipe for the order and arrangement of the notes. The building-blocks and the recipe may vary from country to country, and the age – think of Indian ragas compared with an Elgar concerto, or JS Bach as against Schoenberg.'

Garry: 'As humans, we have two sets of twenty-three chromosomes in each of our cells. Chromosome one is a different size and shape from Chromosome two, which is different from Chromosome four, and so on. Think of them as twenty-three chapters in a book, all of which are needed. Each chromosome chapter is a very long molecule of DNA, containing a string of genes. Each chromosome contains different genes, so each chromosome has a different set of three-letter words.'

Chris: 'Some of you here will be able to read music and play an instrument. Some of us read the music recipe perfectly and turn it into what the composer meant. But others read inaccurately and make mistakes. The music doesn't sound the way it should. It might be better, it might be worse, or perhaps the mistake is so small that no-one listening notices the difference.'

Garry: 'This can happen with the recipes for genes. The words in a gene might be read wrongly or, more fundamentally – and now I'll step away from Chris's music analogy – small changes may occur in the words of the recipe itself. They are read correctly, but the end-result, the protein that is made from the gene, is not quite what it should be. One of the ingredients, one of the amino acids, is wrong. This might not matter too much, or it might be beneficial – or, depending on the role of that protein in the development and functioning of the individual, it might have quite a marked effect.'

He pressed a button on the lectern and the video was replaced by a photograph of the characteristic shapes of the 'twenty-three pairs', each identified by a number or in the case of chromosome twenty-three, by 'XY'.

Garry: 'On Chromosome four is a gene with the initials FGFR3 – it is the recipe for a protein called fibroblast growth factor receptor three, to give it its proper name. In a few people just one of the three-letter words in that gene recipe gets slightly altered. One letter changes, that's all, and as a result, a different amino acid building block is chosen. And as a result of that *single change–*'he pauses briefly '– a *single change* in the amino acids of which it is formed, the FGFR3 protein is also altered just very slightly. The effect is dramatic, though – it becomes over-active during the child's growth and it stops cartilage turning into bone.'

Chris: 'Why do we call our piece of music G380R?'

Garry (pressing the button so that the video is restored): 'Going back to the amino acids, the building-blocks of proteins

– 'G' stands for the amino acid Glycine, and 'R' is short-hand for the amino acid Arginine. The effect of that change in a single letter in the recipe is that the amino acid Arginine is picked up and popped into the FGFR3 protein instead of Glycine.

And this is what causes achondroplasia.'

He turned and gestured at the video in case anyone had failed to see the connection.

Chris: 'The music of achondroplasia. Imagine those four letters ACTG represent four notes on the C Major scale. Each three-letter combination strung along the gene has a different characteristic sound. Imagine allotting other notes to represent the twenty amino acids. This is the basic recipe for my composition 'G380R'. The letters for the normal protein and its amino acids are the theme upon which the variations are based. You will hear a repetition of the four notes representing ACTG as the ground bass.'

He sang them, unaffectedly.

'Listen for them. I could tell you much more about the structure, but you are not musicologists. You can read the explanation in the conference proceedings. Now we just invite you to listen.'

Garry: 'We are very grateful indeed to the Restricted Growth Association for the massive amount of help they gave us in putting together the video. And we dedicate this composition, 'G380R' to our friend and colleague, Dr Lisa Wallace.'

At that point, the video stopped and instead there were three stills of Lisa, delivering a lecture in front of a large class of students, in close-up laughing, and wearing walking gear and sitting on a rock eating a sandwich.

Then the volume was turned up and 'G380R' was played from its beginning to its end.

'Do you like this music?' Lisa feels as though she is floating; the pain in her lower back has vanished from her consciousness. 'I'm struggling to comprehend its formlessness.'

Ruth brings her gaze down from the ceiling and tries to focus her eyes. 'The atonal qualities are too insistent, perhaps?' She splutters with laughter.

They both giggle and Ruth suddenly sits forward and holds up her hand.

'Listen carefully to the music, Lisa. Subjugate your mind. Tell me how you *feel*. Your body is supposed to respond to the music. It should be "recognising itself at a very deep level", remember.'

'Oh, that was the woman who composes "protein music". Poor Chris couldn't get a word in edgeways, could he? Ssssh, I'll let my body listen and tell you what it says.'

Lisa closes her eyes and crosses her hands on her breast and they are both silent in mock expectation.

'No. Nothing... Ah, yes, a voice, I can hear a voice. Yes, yes, I'm listening. Oh, my body is speaking to me... my body is saying that it needs... it recognises it is low on alcohol. Quick, pass the bottle.'

'"I want to go inside the chemistry and hear the frequencies",' Ruth pronounces in an indeterminate American drawl. 'The combinations of the tannins and ethanol are stunning.' She tosses her hair back over her shoulder theatrically but the effect is slightly spoilt because of the hair's wiry elasticity.

'And Chris... and Chris is trying to explain...'

Ruth makes spectacles of her thumbs and forefingers and holds them against her nose while trying to look earnest. 'We find that the frequency pattern "one over f" is found in the DNA sequences and we filter the data—'

'What Chris is trying to say is we map the physical properties—' Lisa gesticulates exaggeratedly like Garry, but gouts of laughter make her hands shake.

'You guys are referring to a sonic description of the visual structure, right?' An imaginary tendril of hair is hooked back by Ruth's little finger.

Lisa bends double, speechless.

'Oh stop it! My stomach hurts,' she manages to splutter, and Ruth falls backwards and pummels the arms of the chair. They are both hysterical and shrieking.

Groaning and wiping away tears of laughter, they become calmer and Lisa decides they should listen to Oscar Petersen's 'Night Train' instead.

Ruth seems to be contemplating the contents of her wine-glass, turning it to catch the light.

'What did you really think about Garry and Chris's presentation?' she asks after a while. 'You became the absolute focus of attention, didn't you? And you stayed really cool. But you don't make many concessions to being short, not here at home anyway, where I would have thought it wouldn't matter.'

'Why should being at home make a difference?'

'In terms of being less visible to other people. Just a few wooden platforms, lower light switches, various other aids – everything else seems to be much as in anybody else's house.' Ruth shrugs. 'That must make your life more difficult.'

'I have a specially low and comfortable bed. But I suppose the question you're not quite asking is how I felt about having "my condition" thrust upon me so publicly today, when I seem to be in denial about it otherwise. Is that it?'

'Yes. Sorry. It's none of my business, really. I hardly know you.'

'I think we're getting to know each other quite well. We weren't very impressed with each other at first, were we?' Lisa remembers her visit to Ruth's house and smiles wryly.

'Stefan was getting in the way. That Y chromosome makes a hell of a difference. In all kinds of ways.'

'It's the frequencies. The music of the spheres.'

After a beat Ruth shouts with laughter and slaps her hand on her knee, sending a spray of wine-drops from her glass. 'Damn!'

'I know I said this earlier, but your talk was excellent, you were a natural. But the question about stuffed humans bothered you, didn't it?'

Ruth is startled. 'Hey, I thought we were talking about you. But... Yes. I suppose I always wonder why someone wants details, wants that sort of information. Surely they must be able to visualise how you have to go about that type of preparation. I thought I made it clear that filling a skin has to be done very carefully because mistakes are so obvious.'

'Do you think it is gruesome, even voyeuristic?' Lisa frowns because she feels that Ruth is being evasive.

'I think it's heart-breaking. It's very, very sad that people like poor little Foma were kept as exhibits and when they died, probably of unhappiness, were *stuffed.* Embalming would have been more respectful. Lisa, don't you *see?*'

An image of a scarecrow, pale skin sewn with large stitches to keep the stuffing in, comes into Lisa's mind. The creature's face is pale too, and smooth and sad, an image of degradation and loneliness; it has the down-turned mouth of a clown.

Ruth sniffs. 'Shit. Getting maudlin. I've had too much to drink, and it's awfully late. I should go to bed.'

'Me too, I suppose, though my head feels as though it's still buzzing with ideas from dinner. Garry is unstoppable once he gets going about modern biology, and then he and Stefan got involved in a long discussion about salamanders, of all things.'

'Stefan seems well entrenched in the local scene – do you reckon he'll stay here?'

'He's certainly looking around very determinedly for further funding. And he's committed himself to a year's lease on that flat. Will it be awkward for you, having him around?'

Ruth is surprised. 'No, not at all. I'm not likely to bump into him in Cumbria, am I? He made it clear that he didn't want to pursue our relationship any further – and to tell you the truth, Lisa, I know it's awful but it was just a bit of fun for me. A diversion. I've moved on too. We had a good shag or two and that was it. Got it out of our systems. *Fini.'*

'Oh.'

'Though I suppose I might find the need to come to Liverpool now and again. There was this guy, Tony Luchini, in our party this evening, and we got on really well. I'm meeting up with him tomorrow. He's a stone-mason, he's got a room in one of those tenements.'

'I see.' Lisa raises her eyebrows. 'Fancy him, do you?'

'I'd say it was mutual.'

TWENTY-TWO

Sparrows were shouting noisily at each other on the floor of the feed-store, raising dust with the stiff agitation of their wings. Madeleine stood watching them but, like lovers quarrelling, they were too absorbed in their own small drama to worry about her scrutiny. The sound had stalled her, tweaking her memory, needling her to burrow through the layers to find the hidden clue. The words returned. 'A sparrow sauna.' And a picture: sparrows shouting in a steaming hedgerow, and the sly laughter of the sullen girl, laughing with her in a blackthorn winter. 'Mad!' John had called out to her, 'Maddie, Mad, mad-Maddie.' And the three of them — John, the doctor and the girl — had halted in the lane and had come to seek her where she had hidden in the thicket. She had hidden but the woman doctor had sensed her long before.

She remembered too how the woman had sensed her at the kitchen window, even though she had stepped back behind the curtain, and now, as she turned away from the suddenly-silent sparrows, it was as though a wave of empathy from the doctor rushed towards her across the years. Which was strange because she had barely spoken to the woman, who was not a medical doctor but a fluke-doctor. A woman who studied worms! What had been the result of that search for flukey snails? Had John discussed the findings and their significance with her after the doctor had left? Madeleine could not remember and for a moment she remained still, frowning, oblivious.

The collie backed away in front of her, watchful, his tail

waving tentatively as he waited for a command, but she strode to the house, toeing off her boots outside the kitchen door and ordering the dog to 'Stay!'

In the small room that was the farm office she pulled open a filing-cabinet and shuffled through the papers that remained from the Ayrshire days, letters from the land agent about the sale, statements from the mart, even old feed bills, with the smeared and gritty feel of age. Remnants of a previous life: she found a new hardness within herself and dumped each file in the waste-bin as she finished with it. The letter she had hoped to find was clipped to the back of a thin sheaf of veterinary bills and easily recognisable by the heading 'Department of Veterinary Pathology'. It was signed by Claudia McFie.

'Claudia.' Madeleine said the name out loud. The letter was concise, thanking Mr Tregwithen for his help and noting that he would see from the attached summaries that snails from the fields around Dodds Burn had a particularly high incidence of fluke infection, etcetera. Madeleine skipped the rest of the letter and glanced through the three attached pages, but she had no patience with the figures. She wasn't interested in the incidence of liverfluke in Ayrshire, she wanted Dr McFie. Decisively, she sat down at the wooden desk and dialled the number.

'Department of Veterinary Pathology, how can I help?'

'I'd like to speak to Dr McFie, please.'

'Dr McFie? I'm sorry, I don't think we have anyone of that name here, unless he's a visitor and isn't on the list yet. If you could tell me what he works on...?'

After some discussion in the background, Madeleine learnt that Claudia McFie had moved to Edinburgh eight years previously.

'She moved to a chair. I can give you the departmental secretary's number and you can phone and ask if you can speak to Professor McFie.'

The chair confused Madeleine, through its instantaneous and incongruous link with Lisa, about whom she had not thought for days, and she was momentarily distracted from the change in title. When the call was over she tried to imagine Claudia McFie and felt she might no longer be approachable.

'She's important and busy. She hasn't got time to waste in talking to me,' Madeleine reasoned to herself. 'A professor's a very different bunch of grapes from a doctor. Lisa's a doctor – with her Little Chair.' Her eyes glinted with her inward smile at the brief thought that a professor's Chair might be Big.

The idea of meeting the fluke-woman (as she preferred to think of her, for this endowed the Professor with reality) continued to nag at her over the next few weeks and to assume a growing importance for reasons she herself did not understand. Finally she made the telephone call. Professor McFie was apparently in a meeting, but Madeleine explained to the secretary that the Professor had carried out some research on fluke on her farm in Ayrshire 'a few years ago'. It had been fifteen or more years previously, but she was not going to admit that their acquaintance had been so far in the past, and she had no real expectation that her call would be returned. When Claudia McFie called back a couple of hours later, and made it clear that she remembered the Tregwithens and their farm, Madeleine was almost speechless.

'I farm in Cumbria now,' she managed to say. 'I wondered if you were interested in what's happened since foot-and-mouth. About fluke. I don't know if you're still interested in fluke, I...'

There was a short silence and then the scientist said, 'Mrs Tregwithen, this is so extraordinary. I don't believe in Signs, but–' Madeleine could almost see her lift her palm in amazement '–I've been mulling over an idea for a film about FMD for the past few weeks. I've been stupidly busy – there's a big departmental reorganisation going on – and I haven't had time to give it proper thought but you've just provided me with the impetus I need. I would love to come and see you and your farm and talk about this. May I do so?'

Her voice was warm and low, and Madeleine visualised her clearly, as she had looked all those years ago.

'Yes. Yes, come any time.'

'Let me look at my diary – Cumbria isn't so far.' Pages were being turned and then Madeleine heard her sigh, quickly and with exasperation. 'Which part of Cumbria?'

'North, North-West really.'

'This is ridiculous, I've almost no free time. But look... I know this isn't ideal, but I have to go to Manchester for an afternoon meeting on the fifteenth. I could drive down instead of using the train. Would there be any chance that we could meet up at a motorway service station, because I'm not sure I would have time to divert across to where you live. Would it be far for you to drive across – *do* you drive? Would Mr Tregwithen come across too?'

Madeleine was startled. Focussed on finding Professor McFie and still slightly bemused that she had found and was indeed speaking to her, she had somehow forgotten that it had been John who knew the woman.

'My husband's – my husband died. Quite a few years ago.'

After a short awkward pause, Professor McFie said, 'I'm so sorry. But you're clearly still in the farming business.' She was hesitant now, uncertain of Madeleine's role.

Madeleine replied robustly, 'Of course. I run the farm myself. And I'm free to meet you that day, I'll come across.'

She sat for a while, absently picking at the oak veneer that had lifted from the corner of the desk. The arrangement had been made, and with such ease as though pre-ordained, but she was no longer certain of its purpose. She noticed that the pink-flowered wall-paper was freckled with stains in the corner behind the desk and she stood up and prodded it, feeling the softness of rotten plaster behind.

* * *

A column of elderly women bustled and tottered into the ladies' toilet.

'He said twenty minutes, didn't he, Dot? Was it twenty minutes?'

'Aye, an' it'll take us that an' all to get our knickers down. Come on, then, Betty, in you go, lass, or we'll have wet oursel's. Eh, look at that one, Dot. Eadie had a thing like that on her face, didn't she?'

'Hers was smaller, though. She used to slather it with that pancake, d'you remember? Thought she was covering it but just turned it orange'.

'Heh, heh. Blackberries, look, this one's got a proper fruit bowl on her face. Heh, heh – oh, don't make me laugh, I'm needin' a wee that bad.'

They were staring at Madeleine in the mirror as though she were sequestered behind a sound-proofed glass partition.

A rubber ferrule poked Madeleine's ankle and she was tempted to kick it away, but imagined how the old woman would clatter onto her side like an overturned tripod. Instead, she shook the water off her hands so that droplets sprayed over the commentators and as she pushed past she leant down and whispered, 'I hope you pee your pants and have to sit in them all day.'

She was hot and a little breathless but still grinning at her unexpected childishness when she returned to the foyer.

'Mrs Tregwithen? Hallo. Goodness, something has amused you.' Claudia McFie was waiting by the flower-stand outside the shop. She held out her hand, smiling. 'It's good of you to drive all this way.'

She was shorter than Madeleine remembered and her hair was short too, thick and dark with pale streaks; the skin round her eyes looked tired but she had a fine straight nose. Madeleine suddenly doubted that this was the woman she had seen before, for surely she should be approaching fifty and this woman seemed too youthful.

'Sorry, I didn't recognise you for a moment,' she muttered. The blackberry-and-damson fruit-bowl on her own face was ageless.

'No, well, it's been a long time. I checked my records before I came and it's almost sixteen years.'

'It was icy cold,' Madeleine said.

'And you had lambs.'

They chose a table by the window. Madeleine smeared butter on a sultana scone and was impressed by the professor's rapid and competent attack on a flaky Danish pastry; the woman ate determinedly and silently, for which Madeleine was grateful because she could think of nothing to say.

'Ah, that's better. Breakfast was a long time ago. Now, tell me about your farm, and how you manage to run it on your own.' She wiped her mouth and fingers on a paper napkin and then took out a notebook from her briefcase. 'Let's start with your flock size and the kind of sheep you have.'

So Madeleine started to tell her some basic facts. At first Claudia's intense concentration and sharply-focussed questions made her shy and awkward and she knew she was repeating herself, but gradually she relaxed.

'Sorry, you'll have to explain that to me again,' Claudia interrupted at one point, with a short laugh. 'There's a lot I need to learn.'

'I rent out the barn, too, Professor,' Madeleine added after she had talked about the bed-and-breakfast business.

'Diversification, that's the name of the game now, isn't it? Do just call me Claudia, by the way. Who do you let it to, some sort of business?'

'A taxidermist. We had the hayloft converted as a studio. And there's space you could use too, I thought perhaps... a sort of laboratory.'

'Wait, wait. A taxidermist! That's intriguing and I'd like to come back to that in a minute. But I'm also intrigued by your suggestion of a laboratory. What did you have in mind?'

Madeleine wished she had not blurted that out; she should have explained her reasons first. She blushed, and felt sweat trickling down beneath her breasts.

'I was thinking about the liver fluke,' she said. 'When I spoke to you on the phone, I wondered – but no, you're interested in foot-and-mouth disease.'

'No, go on about the fluke, because it ties in with FMD.'

'I thought you might find it useful to have a farm as a sort of base, where you could come and look for snails, and compare, oh I don't know – you could do things and see if the snails with fluke changed, or something... You could use Whitefoot Farm as an extra laboratory, we could convert the old tack-room for your microscopes and things.' Her face felt red and shiny and she wiped her damp top lip with her napkin. 'Sorry, I'm not explaining it very well.'

'You are, you've obviously thought about it carefully, Madeleine. And of course your late husband suggested something similar on your Ayrshire farm, that we should take it over as a field station. I can certainly see the advantages of having a Cumbrian base, but we don't have the sort of money to do anything large-scale. But I've been looking at the effect of FMD on fluke populations, and I have a new PhD student starting soon. Let me think this through and get back to you – I can see some possibilities.' She nodded and made a note. 'I was so sorry to hear about your husband. You said you'd been running Whitefoot on your own for about ten years – so at least he didn't have to see the disaster that was foot-and-mouth. You were rather quiet about that, incidentally, in relation to your own farm.'

'My flock was culled out,' Madeleine said quietly. 'If John had been alive then, I think that might have killed him anyway. We failed in Ayrshire, and to have lost everything again...'

'But *you* didn't give up, Madeleine. You had the strength to

207

keep going and to rebuild the flock when it became possible again. That was very courageous.' Claudia's voice was sympathetic, her brisk efficiency suddenly put aside. Madeleine stared out of the window towards the car-park, wondering about courage. A woman was heaving an obese golden retriever into the boot of her car, her hands underneath its backside. Her head was tilted sharply backwards because the dog's tail was beating against her face.

'There was nothing else to do,' she said eventually and, for the first time, looked directly at Claudia. 'You said on the phone that you wanted to make a film about foot-and-mouth. But I think we've all had enough of that, there was too much unhappiness, too many died.'

'More than a million animals. It's almost impossible to comprehend.'

'But people too, Claudia. Friends. Nobody wants cameras poking in, it doesn't do any good.'

'You're worried that what I'm planning is merely an exercise in voyeurism, a tear-jerker. A hunt for the hardest-luck cases. No. I want to look at the FMD epidemic and the killing from the point of view of the environment. We all know that opinions are still divided about the efficacy and reliability of the epidemiological models, but the end result was that an enormous biomass of food animals was killed and removed from the food-chain. You as a farmer will have an idea of the resources of water, minerals, arable crops and grass, pharmaceuticals, that went into feeding those animals. And the energy resources in the form of fuel to bring feed to them, and to ferry animals around between fields and marts. And it was all halted. Just like that. A whole ecosystem wiped out. And then there's the effect of the animals' absence on the environment to consider – both good and bad. Increased genetic diversity as plants were able to set seed instead of being eaten—'

'The increase in bracken on the fells.'

'Yes!' Claudia tapped the table with her fingertips. 'Yes. You see what a fascinating experiment it was, if you'll forgive me the hard-hearted perspective for a moment. And the removal – for at least nine months if not a year – of a reservoir of parasites from the land *has* to have had a knock-on effect on the subsequent epidemiology of those parasites. The lack of faecal input, especially faeces containing anthelmintics that also act as insecticides, will have had an effect on the numbers and diversity of invertebrates, insects and worms especially. It's fascinating,' she said again.

'They've made a nature reserve over the burial pit. Families can go there and walk around on top of the thousands of corpses, to look at insects and flowers. Tree roots feeding on the dead animals. Each day tankers came in to take away the filthy liquid that oozed out. "Leachate", they called it! My sheep are in there too.' Madeleine shook her head. 'It was years ago. We're all trying to forget it. We've re-stocked. There are lambs in the fields again.'

Claudia's eyes were screwed up against the light as she stared out of the window at the sky, and she had caught her lower lip between her teeth, which made her look even younger. She was silent for a while, then asked, 'Why did you call me, Madeleine? What was the real reason – it wasn't to do with liver fluke in the aftermath of foot-and-mouth, was it?'

'I don't know why,' Madeleine admitted in a low voice. 'It was the sparrows reminded me of you.'

Claudia's eyes opened wide and she laughed out loud. 'Sparrows?'

'Oh no, I don't mean you're like a— No, no, the sparrow sauna. That girl that was with you at the farm, she said... I saw the sparrows in the barn and I remembered you, and I suddenly wanted— You seemed to understand. Oh, I'm sorry, this is daft.'

'You weren't very well, were you, when we first met? But

you're fine now, I can't believe how different you seem, so much more sure of yourself.'

Madeleine nodded.

'You know, your husband was so worried about you. And when he came to see me in Edinburgh, to ask if we would take over your Ayrshire farm as a field station, he wanted me to find out about places where you could stay and be looked after. I think he felt you would be safer and happier if you could be cared for properly. I gave him some names, and I think he went to look at one or two. Auchineden, perhaps – does that sound familiar?'

Madeleine, speechless with shock, finally managed to speak. 'John went to Edinburgh? To see you? *When*?'

Claudia looked at her in dismay. 'Mrs Tregwithen, I'm so sorry. I assumed you knew about that, otherwise I would never have mentioned it. I think he must have come over to see me at the time when you were selling the farm, it was a big upheaval for you both and I expect he was wanting—'

'No. *Na*'

The darkness hovered, the tempting, numbing blanking of the senses, and Madeleine concentrated on the bowl containing sachets of sauces and sugar. Salt and sweetener, salad cream and brown sauce: Lisa had found a supermarket where bottles of soy sauce were on the bottom shelf. It was lucky she didn't like tomato ketchup, she had told Madeleine, because it was always shelved too high. John had liked tomato ketchup, especially with shepherd's pie.

'You'll think about sending a student, then, will you?' she asked eventually. 'We could make some work-space for him.'

'Well, we use rather more than microscopes these days, but it might be possible to set up a project using Whitefoot as a field study-site. Come and visit us, Madeleine, if ever you're in Edinburgh. I'd be very happy to show you round if you'd like to see what we do.'

Madeleine sat in the Land Rover for a while. She did not think about Professor McFie. The thought that filled her skull with sodden blackness was that when John had disappeared for those two days, he had gone to Edinburgh not just to plead for the farm, but to see about putting her away. No, she said to herself. No, no, no. She was strong now, she could push back the dark curtains; but the silence of escape was seductive.

In a distant field, a green combine-harvester was cutting wheat, half-hidden by a moving cloud of dust. She watched a police car slowly tour the car-park; saw a man standing by the bonnet of a green Fiesta, eating a sandwich; noted a rook swaying on a spindly rowan branch. She saw the man burrowing behind the driver seat, and the rook hopping and sidling across the tarmac; saw the rook flapping away heavily, weighted by the half-eaten sandwich that had been left on the car roof.

'Bloody thief! Calculating bastard!' the man yelled, then, seeing Madeleine watching, pointed at the bird and roared with laughter. He shared the joke with her and she was saved.

She smiled broadly and waved.

'Calculating bastard.' It was a misrepresentation, but it would have to do.

Twenty-three

Golden light, leaf-rippled, on the bedroom wall; intertwined golden notes of dawn-wakened birds; happiness lying heavy like a gold silk eiderdown: Lisa felt golden herself, and precious, in the unreality that drifts before the coming day intrudes.

There was gold on the table by the window too and she slipped sideways out of bed, leaving the curving wave of bedclothes undisturbed, and padded across the uneven floor. Her toes curled against the ancient glossy wood, sensing its age, but the oak was a child in comparison to the fossil that glinted on the table-top.

The ammonite was barely a centimetre across, and its delicate ridges were picked out in gold, contrasting with the smooth darkness of the mudstone matrix in which it was embedded. A small nugget lay next to it, crystalline light sparking from its many facets, and Lisa touched it with her little finger, marvelling at its delicate precision. Pyrites, fool's gold; iron and sulphate ions, falling out of solution from an ancient sea, a gilded mask enriching an ammonite here, a bivalve shell there.

She had been scrambling over the sandstone blocks that lay at the foot of the cliff, whooping and flailing her arms as she slithered on green-slimed boulders and, prising apart delicate layers of shale and hardened mud, she had found her tiny golden ammonite. A fossil-collector who was splitting a pebble with his hammer had watched her anxiously and probably with disbelief, but then he had walked over to show her the large ammonite that had appeared, like a hatchling, from the cracked-open nodule that he held in his hand.

'Seen anything like this before, lass?' he asked. 'It's an ammonite, Hildoceras. After St Hilda.'

She had looked up at him and laughed. 'Why? What did the poor woman do to deserve that?'

'No, you've got it wrong, it were an honour,' he had grinned back. 'She founded Whitby abbey in the seventh century. The story is the land were infested with snakes and so she got down on her knees and prayed and prayed for the good Lord to get rid of them so the monks and nuns would be safe – you'd think monks and nuns all mixed up together would've got more to worry about than snakes, wouldn't you? Anyroad, the snakes wouldn't go away. So she got a bit more practical, like, and took a whip to them as well as a prayer, and chased them over the cliff. They lost their heads – some say she cut them off with the whip – and their bodies turned to stone.' He rubbed stone-dust off the the ammonite with his thumb.

'A coiled, headless snake. I like that.'

'They're not really snakes, of course,' he added quickly. 'They're more like the Nautilus. You probably don't know what that is, most people don't. It's a mollusc, same as slugs and snails.'

'Right. Thank you. Is this an ammonite too, then?'

Her new tutor had explained, rather grandly, what she had found.

Now she touched it again, the tiny shining serpent, and a strange tremor ran through her inside as its image became confused in her mind with golden apples and thin white figures, a hand holding out a half-eaten apple, offering a bite.

'What are you doing?'

She jumped slightly, having been unaware that Stefan was awake. She kept her back to him, covered her naked breasts with an arm and, almost, her pubic area with a hand, the automatic classical posture of defence.

'Thinking about fig-leaves.'

'Don't.' Stefan sounded sleepy and warm. 'Don't hide.

Will you turn around, Lisa, and let me look at you? I want to understand you in the daylight.'

'"In the cold light of morn." Like those vodka adverts.'

'I rather think they implied the dawning of regret, which is not the case, for me any rate. Please – come back to bed.'

She tried to walk unselfconsciously, her arms by her sides, seeing how Stefan's eyes examined her body, seeking understanding; she was unresentful because she understood precisely what he meant. He wriggled across the bed towards her, reaching out and smoothing her hair away from her shoulders and the back of her neck and he pressed his face against her breasts. The tremor inside her became a shudder of desire and she climbed back into the bed.

The small hotel was on the outskirts of Robin Hood's Bay and at that time of year, early September, the other couples down at breakfast were elderly and silent, hinting at long marriages and unspoken, because already known, sentences. The clientele was probably always similar because the little town had long passed its hey-day. Stefan and Lisa exchanged complicit grins and said little; Lisa didn't want to attract attention although she could be fairly certain what would be passing through the other patrons' minds.

Stefan was over-considerate in his awkwardness, and soon Lisa was hedged in behind the marmalade- and butter-dishes, the sugar-bowl and jug, as he ensured that everything was within reach.

'Araucaria,' he said suddenly. 'I've been trying to remember the name. Monkey-puzzle trees. Araucaria.'

'Because of the jet.'

Stefan nodded and leant backwards so he could extract the piece of fossil wood, black as a beetle's wing, from his pocket.

'You were so lucky to find it. That geologist said that people hardly ever found any these days, even at Whitby.'

'I was going to give it to Annette until he said that, but now I'm rather tempted to keep it myself. When the girls were small, they were fascinated by monkey-puzzle trees, we used to look out for them and count them on car journeys. I don't know why.' He shook his head and smiled. 'One of those strange family traditions that become established. Like trainspotting. You will be impressed to learn that my sister and I were trainspotters for a while. We lived quite close to a station and we used to go along with our little notebooks and stand at the end of the platform and fastidiously write down the names of the diesel engines that came through.'

'Trainspotters?' Lisa spluttered out loud. 'Oh, what a hideous mistake I've made!'

The corners of Stefan's mouth turned down in mock apology, and his expression was so warm and amused that her breath caught and for a moment she was dizzy.

'Sorry. I suppose that signals the end of our beautiful relationship? We've hit the buffers, come to the end of the track?'

'Definitely. All change!' She recovered, and glanced round the room, and the inquisitive faces turned away to examine toast and marmalade and the *Telegraph*.

'What about your family – did you have some special traditions too?'

Lisa thought for a while, staring blankly at the mantelpiece, above which a sun-burst clock resonated with heavy electronic ticks.

'Suzy and I used to pull certain plants to pieces,' she said eventually. 'No, really, it's not as bad as it sounds. Silver birch, for example – you know the way the bark curls? We used to pull off the discoloured strips to see the pure white underneath, more pinkish-silver, in fact. We had competitions to see who could pull off the largest piece. And then there were those orange flowers called Escholzias that grew in borders in the park – the buds look like wizards' hats, and if you pull off the

215

hat very carefully, you see the petals furled inside. Oh, and wild bindweed, you know the one with a conical white flower, that grows on fences? You pick the flower and wrap the stalk around the base in a loop, then jerk it upwards.' She demonstrated with an imaginary plant. 'And you have to shout "Whoops! Granny JUMP out of bed!" at the same time as the flower-head shoots off into the air.'

A woman with short white hair and a wrinkled, weathered face, sitting on her own with a paperback propped open against the teapot, leant over towards their table. 'Sorry to butt in, couldn't help hearing. I did that too. Granny in her white nightdress. Suppose those sorts of games would be frowned on now, damaging the ecosystem, reducing biodiversity, all that sort of thing. Not green. Probably get fined, not even allowed to collect a few cowslip seeds these days.'

'Sheer vandalism!' Stefan was delighted. 'I'm surrounded by vandals. At breakfast-time too.'

'We used to make dolls out of wild poppies. You don't really see those so much these days, do you, those fields that were scarlet all over?' Now the woman with the faded red hair that was swept up into a roll at the back of her head joined in. 'We turned the petals down and tied the stalk around like a belt, and the middle bit of the poppy was the doll's head. Your saying about the bindweed stalk reminded me of it. Goodness, I don't think I've thought of that in years.'

She giggled shyly and wiped her mouth with a crumpled pink paper-napkin. 'Do you remember the poppies, Harry?'

Her husband had a bulbous nose and florid face and he cleared his throat noisily and portentously.

'Well, I dunno about all these flowers, but talking of trains – hearing you talking about diesels there,' he nodded in Stefan's direction. 'I'm talking now of the old steam-trains, mind, what you might call proper trains. When I was a lad we'd go down to the signal box and the signalman'd let us come up and help him pull the levers for the points. Only a little branch-line, mind, we couldn't do no damage. And I'll tell you another thing, though the wife here won't be pleased.' He looked very pleased, himself. 'There was an iron bridge over the line, we'd go up there and we'd try to pee down the engine's funnel when it went underneath.'

'*Harry!*'

'Took some doing, trying to aim when that cloud of smoke came rushing at you.' He spluttered with laughter, coughing.

His wife was horrified but Lisa and Stefan joined in the laughter, and suddenly the general reticence was swept away and conversation broke out amongst the half-dozen tables. The young man with the old face who had been ferrying in the plates of bacon and beans and racks of toast, appeared at the doorway of the dining-room and stopped in exaggerated surprise.

'Eh, what's woken you all up, then?' he exclaimed. 'Sounds like a bingo 'all in 'ere. 'Ave you been disturbing the peace, then, Mr Todd?'

'I was telling them about—'

'No, Harry. Just eat your toast. Don't encourage him,' his wife said to the waiter. 'Can we have some more hot water for the tea?'

'Anyway, it wasn't me, it was all the fault of the young lady there, making us remember the nonsense we got up to.'

'Oh aye.' The waiter grinned and stopped to pick up Stefan's plate. 'Are you 'ere on 'oliday then? You'd better 'ang about if you can get this lot talking. It's like a morgue in 'ere, usually.' He could not quite manage to look at Lisa, and she handed him her empty cereal bowl.

'We had to go to York on business,' she told him, 'and we thought we'd stay on a day or two and see the area. Can you recommend anything we ought to see?'

'What sort of business is that, then?' He directed the question at Stefan.

'We were at the university. My... friend had to give a seminar.'

We're mathematicians, so we were visiting the maths department.'

'Are you now? Sums and all that. A right pair o' clever-clogs, aren't you?' The young man was clearly taken aback.

'So you'd better not make any mistakes with our bill.'

He looked at Lisa sharply then, but when he saw she was joking, he managed a feeble smile as he piled the empty toast rack on top of the plates.

'Oh aye. Well I never. Takes all sorts, doesn't it?'

'"My friend". That was so embarrassing, I suddenly didn't know what to say. "Friend!" And the way I hesitated, that made it so much worse.'

They had loaded the bags into the boot and were sitting in Stefan's car, a black Volkswagen Golf with alloy wheels, second-hand but still a young man's car. A 'boy-racer's car', Lisa had teased him, but neither of them was in a mood for teasing now. The implications of what had happened to them in the past twenty-four hours, especially at this hotel, had a sobering effect.

'I could hardly say "my lover", could I? And "partners" implies a longer history than, than...'

'Than currently pertains. The brief history of our time.'

'Yes.'

Lisa no longer felt buoyed up with excitement: she was tired and she hurt.

'Don't look now but that waiter, or whatever he is, is watching us from the bay window, cheeky bugger. Are you ready, Lisa, shall we go? We won't see any of them again, anyway.'

She remembered the sheet on the bed, and was relieved. Does post-coital *tristesse* have the same causal root as post-natal depression, she wondered, imagining the hormone concentration plummeting in her blood.

A thin orange cat streaked out of a gateway ahead and a

cyclist, his bottom taut and shiny in purple lycra, swerved. Stefan braked hard and the road atlas skidded off Lisa's legs and landed beneath the dashboard. When he leant across, stretching down to reach it, Lisa's earlier sense of unreality returned as she looked down at his tilted face, dark lashes, faint trace of stubble on his jawbone, at the back of his hand, his square neat thumbnail. He gave her the atlas and touched her cheek with the back of his hand.

'Lisa.'

She pressed his hand against her face and exhaled sharply. 'Stefan.'

She was so full of uncertainty that she felt like a child, and suddenly she longed to curl up in Little Chair. She wanted to go home, she wanted Stefan to come too, so that they could be together in a familiar and safe place to talk this through, because the fear creeping inside her like nausea was threatening to overwhelm her. It was growing out through her skin, snarling her in a spiny thicket, stabbing her with questions.

She replaced his hand on the wheel and when he glanced at her, there was uncertainty lurking behind the tiredness in his eyes.

There were too many words and images entangled in her head and all she could say was, 'I'm so happy that we were friends *first*. If we didn't have that, that firm foundation of friendship, I'd be even more frightened.'

It was late morning when they reached the abbey. They had both been uncharacteristically untalkative throughout the journey, as though the normal topics – work, other academics, the department they had visited the day before yesterday, the countryside through which they now passed – were all too trivial. Or perhaps our brains have been deadened, Lisa wondered. Didn't the endorphin levels increase dramatically after penetrative sex? She was sure she had read that somewhere. The opium of the masses: but then she

219

remembered that the original quotation referred to religion and was therefore distinctly inappropriate in this setting. She would have liked to explain the joke to Stefan, but felt that even mentioning 'sex' in a general context would somehow cheapen their new relationship.

The ruined buildings of the abbey compound divided and compartmentalised the lush valley site, so that the other visitors were only intermittently visible. Lemon light smeared the lower sky beneath the high grey clouds and cast indeterminate shadows.

Stefan had wandered away from the main abbey building and had found a quiet corner amongst the low uneven walls that marked out the rooms where monks had slept and fed and washed clothes.

'Our very own refectory,' he said, as he pointed out two flat stones for seats, and started to pull the picnic lunch out of his rucksack.

The previous day, they had met up after Lisa's talk and had wandered around York. They had bought the food in a small delicatessen which smelt of cheese and roasting coffee, and where the shelves were crammed with tins and jars: slender bottles of glistening red chillies in olive-oil; flat hexagons of pressed figs; quails' eggs, chestnut purée, fat green olives, gingham-topped jars of pickled peaches, and waxy packets of black bread. Mounds of cold meats, sausages, intact or sliced, wheels and spheres and slabs of cheese, red and white and speckled with blue mould or alien seeds were laid out in the purring chilled display unit, and Lisa and Stefan had dithered and argued about what to buy. Eventually he had insisted Lisa should try jägerwurst, the thin sausage with a square cross-section, partly because it reminded him of walking trips in the Alps, but mainly because he thought that their shape would appeal to her.

'They can be stacked together so as to eliminate spaces, like bricks.'

At that moment Lisa had reached up to investigate the contents of a shallow wicker basket but unfortunately, the basket had been full of slippery foil-covered chocolates which now poured down the front of the cabinet and over her arms like an avalanche.

'Swept off my feet by love!' Lisa had exclaimed, gathering up a handful of the multi-coloured hearts.

Stefan had grabbed a purple one. 'Wearing my heart on my sleeve.'

'Hearty apologies. Oops, that one's got a soft centre. Sorry, I'd better buy it.'

They had collected up the chocolates and Stefan had replaced the basket, apologising to the white-coated woman who was trying to maintain a severe expression. 'You must be heartily sick of careless customers like us.'

She could not help but relent.

'It's enough to melt anybody's heart,' she said awkwardly, and then smiled shyly.

As they left the shop, still laughing, Stefan had put his hand on Lisa's shoulder. The contact was like a jolt and Lisa had felt her core become very still.

He kept his hand there as they walked along the street, and people had glanced at them curiously and moved aside on the pavement so that it had seemed to Lisa that she was walking through a narrow gorge.

'Are you steering me?' she had asked after a few moments, trying to resist the unexpected urge to lay her cheek against his hand. He had looked down at her and his expression was so serious that her whole body seemed to clench inside.

That had been the beginning.

'It was so corny. Chocolate hearts!' They had laughed about it last night. 'We must never tell anyone about the hearts.'

Now, Stefan pulls something out of his rucksack and falls down on one knee, presenting the object to her with head bowed.

'Madam, a token of my heart-felt appreciation'.

The tube of love-hearts, striped with sickly pastel colours, provokes a splutter of laughter from Lisa, and she puts her arms round Stefan's neck and hugs him.

'Stefan, what are we going to do?' She glances round, fearful that someone might have seen them.

'We are going to eat our lunch and immerse ourselves in the peacefulness of our surroundings. We're on holiday until tomorrow so we can talk of nothing, or of cabbages and kings.'

The act of sharing food, cutting slices of cheese and sausage with Stefan's Swiss army knife, spreading butter on broken-open rolls, confers its own kind of tranquillity. Their conversation becomes lighter and intermittent, and after a while they sit in a silence that Lisa finds 'companionable'.

Time stretches so that the pauses between a thrush's iterations of its song become longer and longer, and her breathing slows. She drifts into sleep, propped against the ruined wall, and when she wakes Stefan has tidied away the remains of their lunch and is standing, stretching to ease his back.

'Did you sleep well? You looked very relaxed. I was just thinking about walls.'

'Walls like these?' She pats the one behind her, grey stones set in mortar.

'They were the trigger, if you like, because I was thinking about their divisive effect in separating people from each other and from their environment. Separating the lives of the privileged religious from the lives of the underprivileged and un-saved poor. But that led me to puzzling about drystone walls.' He holds out his hand and pulls her to her feet.

'How they divide territory and therefore people, including their animals?'

'Yes, that was how I rationalised them at first. There are some extraordinary walls that go straight up mountain-sides, in Cumbria and in the Scottish Highlands too. On the top of

Sgurr na Ciche in Knoydart – a bosomy mountain, 'ciche' means breast, like 'pap'; Jura and GlenCoe have paps too. The Gaels must have had breast-fixations when they named their hills... sorry, I'm losing track. On top of Sgurr na Ciche there's a high wall, and you come across it so abruptly that you think you must be imagining it, and that it is really a natural rock-formation rather than a human artefact. Why is there a wall in the middle of nowhere? Who built it and for what strange purpose? And it's the same in Cumbria but on a lesser scale – walls that have been erected through scree and boulder-fields, straight from the valley-floor to the peak, or they march along the tops of ridges. Apparently it takes a day to construct a metre of drystone wall, and that's probably on the flat.'

'Presumably the walls you're talking about were built as boundary markers. Unless it was a punishment, like being sent to white-wash coal – the landowner or laird or whoever sends the awkward squad away up the hill.'

'Could be. "Stay there until you've used up all the stone." But then I started thinking about the walls from the opposite point of view, in terms of symbols of unity, uniting people within and between neighbouring families, even uniting the people with the landscape. Wall-building isn't usually solitary work, there would have been several men involved, whether father and sons, or two neighbouring farmers. Or men from nearby who hired out as labourers. A wall was the result of communal activity so it meant people came together to work and to chat. Have a "crack".'

'And they sat down on the stones to rest and eat their dinner.' Lisa nods, trying to picture the scene. 'And – and, it unites them in that extra dimension of time too,' she adds, warming to the idea. 'Some of those walls must be at least a hundred years old, probably even two hundred, and they need to be repaired as the years go by. So sons become fathers, and then their sons help. Perhaps.'

'Perhaps. Or the sons bugger off to the big town to earn

their fortune. But your little ammonite reminds me that the time-line stretches back through geological time, too, uniting the period when it was a warm undersea-scape with the present upland landscape.'

They have been walking slowly, dawdling as they talk, towards the perpendicular ruins of the presbytery, and now they enter the vast shell of the ruined nave. Smooth pillars splay their flutings like spread fingers, and the space echoes with perspective and pale shadows.

'Imagine what it must have been like when the windows were intact – triple beams of light, symbolic of the Holy Trinity, anointing the rows of the faithful.' Lisa stares up at the three tiers of pointed arches.

'"If God is for me, who can be against me". Do you know, Lisa, that line from The Messiah almost made me a convert? What a comfort that statement would be, wouldn't it, if one could accept it as the absolute truth? We need fear nobody, ever.'

'The price you would pay to have your heavenly bodyguard would be the everlasting requirement to be good. But then again, you *are* good, Stefan. You're almost unbelievably good to me,' she adds, awkward because she does not know how to tell him what she feels.

He halts and speaks earnestly, emphatically. 'I'm not being *good* to you. This isn't all about me doing you a favour. I don't want you to feel grateful, as though—'

'No. That's not what I meant. It's just that this happened so suddenly, one minute we were friends – think back to when you shared my flat, and you saw me pottering about in my dressing gown and cleaning my teeth, and we sat and ate breakfast together. And now, in the past twenty-four hours, less in fact, you've seen me pottering about, admittedly without a dressing gown, and cleaning my teeth, and we've eaten breakfast together – but our relationship is about as different as it could possibly be. My behaviour is much the same as before, but my body, my mind, my feelings are overwhelmed by you. All I can think about is you, and I'm terrified, actually.'

'Please don't be terrified.' Stefan squats down beside her and grasps her hand.

'Not of you. Of *them*.' She nods towards the small cluster of people who are slowly approaching. 'And all our friends and colleagues. Of Ruth – you mentioned Cumbria. Even your ex-wife. They'll all ask, "*Why her?*" I ask myself, "Why me?". It doesn't make sense, Stefan.' Tears are streaming down her face, and she feels in her jacket pocket for a tissue.

'I've got one here. I carry them especially for you.' He produces a perfectly folded white cotton handkerchief.

'Of course, you're the Handkerchief Monitor. Don't you dare wipe my nose.' Lisa tries to laugh through her tears. 'You'd better wipe your own eyes, anyway. What a silly pair we are.'

The group of people is closer now, and the smartly-dressed woman who is obviously their guide is explaining the height and structure of the now-absent roof.

'Imagine how the choir's voices would soar and echo,' she enthuses, pointing upwards and spiralling her arm. 'Imagine the colours. Imagine the sounds. Magnificent! It would have been magnificent.'

'Let's move,' Lisa whispers. 'I'm beginning to feel dwarfed by all this magnificence.'

Stefan's expression lifts and smooths in fond amusement. 'I can't believe that you just asked, "Why me?"'

TWENTY-FOUR

Ruth learnt two items of news that Thursday, both of which she knew would interest Madeleine. She learnt the first when she and Abi had a lunchtime drink in a pub in town, and she learnt the second, which was disturbing and entirely unexpected, when she telephoned Tony Luchini shortly afterwards.

Abi had darted out of the newsagent's shop and called to Ruth. Wind was gusting down the street, trapping leaves and scraps of paper in swirling funnels by doorways and corners, but Abi, bare-legged and high-heeled, seemed oblivious to the cold in her black sweater embroidered with shiny pink flowers and her short black skirt. Her nail-varnish matched the flowers exactly, Ruth noted appreciatively.

'Come and have a drink, pet, you look as though you could do with a rest from those bags. I'm meeting someone for a drink at The White Tup but I'm early and he's always late and I hate sitting on my own.'

'Ladies who lunch, why not? Hey, wait for me then, Abi.' Ruth tried to keep up with the clicking heels, and when Abi turned and raised a perfectly-plucked crescentic eyebrow, explained, 'I can't keep up with you, these bags are heavy, I always buy too many veg.'

'Too healthy, that's your trouble, Ruth – forget about the spuds, all you need is crisps.' She pushed open the door of the pub and swept up to the bar. 'Oh look who's here, then. Phoo, you've been at the mart, boy, haven't you? Anyone could smell you a mile off.'

George nodded lugubriously. 'Hi Abi, hi Ruth. And I'll

not be going there no more, I'm packing it in. You're in time to join the celebration – next round's on Tim here. Get the ladies a drink, Tim.' His ruddy, good-natured face was slack and his neck sunk between his shoulders like a sullen tortoise.

'What's all this?' Ruth dropped her bags by an empty table. 'I thought you were going to take some yows across for Madeleine next week. No, I'll get them, Tim, I'm not going to celebrate with him until I know what he's talking about.'

Tim, an older man whom Ruth only knew by sight, shrugged. 'Usual story. The lad wants to gang off till the big city and mek his fortune, reckons he's had enough of dykin' and cultivatin' and runnin' around at ever'uns beck an' call.'

'Feeling sorry for himself, is he? Got a sore head? Don't be soft, lad, you'll surely be better sticking to the contracting,' Abi said. 'There's that shortage of labour you'll always be needed – and it's not like you're trying to run your own farm and losing money every time you open the curtains. Look at what happened to us – without my mam's tea-room and what I bring in, we'd've had to sell up long ago. But you're your own man, boy.'

'Getting my balls shaken on the tractor all day, what sort of a life's that, then? Go out for a beer and the women say I stink.' He hunched morosely on the bar.

'You sound like Eeyore, George,' Ruth said unfeelingly, but Abi was more sympathetic.

She gripped his arm. 'We're all struggling, boy, you know that. There's hardly a farm in Cumbria that isn't struggling. But we can't give in. Though Christ knows as soon as Rick's away I wouldn't mind chucking it in and going to live in Manchester.'

'What'd you do there, Abi? Work in Asda?' George lifted his empty glass and peered ostentatiously into its emptiness.

'You're a cheeky bugger. I'd join a modelling agency. They need women with mature figures–' she pushed her chest forward and waggled her shoulders '–instead of those scrawny little size zeros or whatever you see everywhere.'

'You're not really going to give up, are you, George?' Ruth asked as she handed Abi her vodka and tonic. 'We need you, Abi's right. And what would you do instead, anyway?'

'I'll train as a plumber or a brickie, or I'll win the lottery.'

'Well, if you win the lottery don't forget your friends. Come on, Ruth, let's go and sit over there and leave him to cry into his glass. He's just having a bad day, aren't you, lad? Things'll look better tomorrow.' Abi ruffled his hair and laughed. 'Bad hair day, too.'

Ruth envied her the easy way she treated George, and the smirk and grunt with which he responded.

'Do you really think he'll pack it in?' she asked Abi as they sat down on the cushioned bench by the window.

Abi crossed her legs, and sighed. 'You couldn't blame him if he did. There's nothing for him here. He lives with his mam and dad, there's no bus and you've seen what an old wreck his van is. The big event in the village is the travelling library and the weekly grocer's van. How d'you get away from that?'

'Marry a girl who's better-off and lives somewhere else?'

'Yeah, right. And how does he find one of those? Not by riding round on a tractor and going to the mart.'

'But he's not stupid. There must be clubs or meetings he can go to.' Ruth shrugged helplessly. 'I don't know, there must be something.'

'Young Farmers' meets? They're all kids. And have you seen the sort of people who go to the clubs and societies round here? They're all pensioners, white-haired and snooty, offcomers most of them. There's no place for the local twenty-somethings, poor loves. Who gives a fuck about them, when it comes down to it, Ruthie? Nobody in the towns and cities gives a shit about what's happening in the country. Anyway, don't get me started – or I'll end up crying into my booze and getting panda eyes.'

Ruth frowned and pushed the edge of a beer-mat against a spill, watching the brown liquid crawl into the fibres. 'People do care, but for the wrong reasons – there's always an outcry whenever changes are planned.'

'It's just a fucking theme park. Lake Disneyland. Disney mountains, Disney sheep, just so's the tourists and offcomers can say "Oh how pretty." Never mind that farmers are trying to make a living from it.'

'Madeleine makes a bit extra living off the tourists,' Ruth said mildly.

'Ruth, pet, I came here to have a drink and a chat, not fight about all this stuff. Forget it. But talking of Mrs Tregwithen – she's still managing okay, isn't she?'

'She may not manage that well if George goes.'

'She's a tough woman, you've got to admire her. I reckon she's better off without her old man, too. Was he still around when you arrived? He was a mean old bastard – to her, anyway.'

'John? Well, he could be a bit short with her...' Ruth had never been certain what she felt about John. He was already suffering from the neurological effects of the poisoning when she first rented the studio, and she had watched his decline with pity and discomfort. Rarely had she seen him and Madeleine together, but sometimes she had heard his peremptory tone or withering sarcasm, and she had cringed inwardly for her friend.

'*Short!*' Abi put her glass down with a thump and leaned forward so quickly that her dangling ear-rings hit her cheeks. 'He was outrageous. I'll never forget, Ruth, one time when me and mam were having a coffee in Brewsters' and they both came in. It must've been eight, ten years ago or more, 'cos mam was still at the school. He was ill then, of course. But you should've seen them, Ruth. They sat down next to us and he was encouraging Rick to feed his stinking little terrier with cake, and she sat there silent as a mouse, poor thing, eating her beans on toast or whatever while he carried on at her like nobody's business, giving her a hard time because she'd forgotten to buy the dog's favourite biscuits. We were waiting for dad, and my mam was fretting because he was late but I knew he was off buying her birthday present so I kept making excuses for him. Anyway, when he turned up there wasn't a spare seat so do you know what John Tregwithen did? Right out loud, so everyone could hear, he said, "Mad–" he called her Mad, isn't that awful? "–Mad, give Daniel your seat and take the shopping back to the car. You can drive over and pick me up here".'

'No! Surely he wouldn't have spoken to her like that, not in public?'

Ruth was startled, but also distracted by Abi's impressive cleavage which was now displayed to full effect on the table. From the corner of her eye she sensed that George and Tim were impressed too. 'You'd better keep your voice down, Abi, George can hear.'

Abi flashed a glance towards the bar. 'Mind your own business, you two. This is girls' talk.' Then she lowered her voice. 'Yes he did, I swear. He just ordered her to go.'

'And did she?'

'Yeah. Poor cow. Gathered up her bags, offered my dad her seat, and left.' Abi leant back against the window-ledge, ending her story abruptly for full effect.

'That's terrible. But perhaps he behaved like that because he was ill. I remember that dog, Bob he was called. He really missed John, he just lay around and pined, and then he just sort of faded away. Madeleine said that she tried to act as though she was fond of him, but she reckoned the dog knew it was just pretence.'

'Dogs get like their masters, or the other way round. The old man was nice enough to Rick, so maybe it was just his wife that wound him up. You never know what goes on in other people's marriages, do you? Dad used to go over to help at Whitefoot now and again when John was really ill, but he never said much about what went on over there.'

'Yes. I remember seeing him around now and again. How are things with your Rick these days, anyway? I saw him in the distance a few weeks back, he's grown into a big lad.'

'Yeah. He keeps going on how he wants to leave school at the end of the year, but he's hanging in there and doing his GCSEs.' She leant forward again and whispered: 'That drugs business, it gave us all a shock, I can tell you, the stupid lad. Trouble is, I keep worrying what he'll get up to next – as we were saying earlier, there's not much to keep them occupied and then they get into trouble.'

'What happened about the cannabis fuss, then? I didn't hear the outcome.'

'They decided he wasn't dealing and let him off. He was bloody lucky, but don't ever say I said so, and it made our lives hell for months. Mam says she still feels sick whenever she thinks about it. Hey, you admiring my boobies, Ruth? If I hadn't seen you tarting round the clubs I'd think you were a dyke!'

'They're a bit "in yer face", Abi, when you sit like that. I'm just jealous, really.' Ruth raised her eyebrows.

'Aye, you could do with a bit more up-front yourself, though you don't seem to have much trouble pulling. How is your lust-life these days, anyway – still keeping in practice?'

'Abi, you really are shameless. But I'm seeing someone I met in Liverpool several months back, he's a stone-mason.'

'Oooh, they have such horny hands.' Abi squirmed her buttocks on her seat suggestively and raised her eyebrows.

'Enough, enough! I have to go.'

'Oh come on, Ruthie, you can't leave me, my bloke hasn't arrived yet.'

'You can persuade George that he's a valued and respected member of the community, while you wait–' and she added more loudly for George's benefit '–and that we all need him and love him.'

On the way home she parked the van in a gateway at the top of a hill, one of the few places where she knew there was a signal, to call Tony on her cellphone. What he told her was so upsetting that she drove to Whitefoot Farm instead.

Madeleine was struggling with one of the bolts on a wheel of the sheep-trailer; the tyre was very flat. When Beth saw Ruth she came wriggling towards her, then lay down on her back, so that the tip of her wagging tail tickled her bare pink belly.

'That bitch is completely useless, I don't know why I keep her.' Madeleine glanced up briefly and carried on hitting the hub with a heavy spanner. Ruth bent down to rub the dog's silky muzzle, and Beth crossed her front paws over her chest and rolled her eyes at Madeleine with a triumphant wolfish grin.

'You look as though you're struggling.'

'The bolt's rusted on. And it's George's day to be helping over at Dawsons, I could have done with a bit of brawn about the place though I hate to admit it.'

'We may all have to do without him unless we can persuade him otherwise. I just saw him in The Tup and he was crying into his beer and talking of giving it all up to become a plumber or some such.'

'No! He can't do that.' Madeleine was aghast, and Ruth hurried to reassure her.

'We can talk him out of it, I'm sure. He was just feeling sorry for himself and Abi telling him he stank of pee from the mart probably didn't help.'

'Abi! He was never there with that girl, was he? She'd better not get her claws into the lad, he's an innocent compared with her.'

'Christ, Madeleine, of course they weren't together. And don't be such a bigot. I went for a drink with her because she was meeting her bloke and didn't want to wait on her own,' Ruth snapped in irritation. 'And anyway, I thought you'd be glad to hear that Ricky – your dear old friend *Danny*'s grandson – is finally in the clear.'

'What do you mean?'

'The police said he wasn't dealing and he was just a naughty boy.'

'After all this time... Elaine will be glad.'

'And Abi was telling me some story from years ago about you all being in Brewsters and John sneaking in that terrier. Actually she said "stinking terrier".'

'Abigail seems to be uncommonly fixated on smells.' Madeleine was acerbic. 'You obviously had a fascinating conversation. Brewsters', yes. Poor old Bob – I think I had to take him back to the Land Rover.' She stood up, rubbing her back and frowning. 'Drinking with Abi doesn't seem to have improved your mood.'

'It wasn't Abi, or the beer. There's something else. I just spoke to Tony and he told me...' Ruth paused for a second, she was still too astonished by the news. 'He told me that Lisa and Stefan are seeing each other. They're an item, a couple. They'd been keeping it fairly secret, apparently, but Tony found out from one of Lisa's friends.' From Chris, the musician and composer.

'Goodness.'

Madeleine looked briefly at Ruth then gazed across the yard. 'Goodness me.'

'*Goodness*? Is that all you can say?' Ruth thumped the side of the trailer with her fist. 'Where's the *goodness* in that? It's horrible, it's incongruous. It's like a – a wolfhound and a peke. Or a steeple-chaser and a shetland pony. How could they do that?' She was becoming incoherent with fury. 'It's beyond belief. And they were supposed to be my friends, for fuck's sake.'

'You needn't swear. You surprise me, Ruth, I hadn't thought of you as intolerant. I don't think it's any of our business, anyway, and I'm sure the effect on you is the last thing that crossed their minds.'

Madeleine's tone was chilly, and Ruth realised that she had said far more than was appropriate.

'Sorry. It's just so unexpected.'

'These things often are. I have to go in now, I need to phone Dawsons to catch George – though from what you've said he's in no fit state either.'

Dropping the spanner with a clang so that the dog leapt up and cringed, she flapped her arm brusquely at the animal. 'Get on Beth, get away into the kennel.'

'I'll be up in the workshop, then,' Ruth muttered. 'I've got to work on that woodpecker.'

That wooden-fucking-pecker. She ran up the stairs and then, in the solitude of the long low room, slumped in her chair and put her head on the worktable. She felt nauseous with anger and incomprehension. How could Stefan have done this? That was all she could think about. She kept seeing his thoughtful expression, that seemed so familiar, and the way his face went slack and momentarily lined after he had exploded inside her; she could remember the feel of the warm, smooth hollow behind his clavicle where she burrowed her nose to tickle him and made him shout with laughter, and the strong tautness of his bare thighs; his muscled buttocks, hill-walker's buttocks, hard beneath her gripping hands; and his fingers inside her, stroking her silky wetness. The memory was too strong, she wanted him *now*. She lay back and slipped her hand inside her jeans, pretending her fingers were his until the heat grew unstoppable, and her body arched and she moaned and gasped.

Several minutes later, tidying herself, she remembered Abi's remark about Tony's horny hands. Now, tension released, she could think about Stefan without passion. Stefan, with his well-chosen clothes and well-polished shoes – her mother would have referred to him as 'well brought-up' or 'nicely-mannered'. She had often wondered whether his carefulness of others' feelings arose from genuine kindness or from uncertainty about himself. The trouble with Stefan was that he had no spark. But he would be kind to Lisa and she would appreciate that.

No! She did not want to think about Lisa in the context of Stefan, but she was sure their relationship must be platonic, how could it be anything else? She felt ashamed of herself, sullied, in that she had, yet again, reduced everything to sex. To fucking. De-fused and dull, she stood aimlessly by the table. The woodpecker, still frozen and wrapped in polythene, could wait.

But gradually, an idea began to grow and she sat down and started to jot down some notes: matryoschki with their stylised features; pregnant sharks; an Elizabethan dinner...

'Where do you get all the information?' Madeleine had once asked in amazement, as she skipped through a print-out lying on Ruth's work-table. 'How do you find out about these things?'

Ruth scarcely knew, herself. 'My mind's a bit of a rag-bag, I suppose, full of snippets and remnants of things I hear or read. I reach in and guddle around a bit to see what's there. Some of the specialist stuff I researched in libraries. And it's easy enough these days to find out more, with the internet, and a few phone calls.'

Now, as she scribbled down links and interconnections and ideas that might even lead to dead-ends, she shrugged off the memory that Stefan had been good at this game too.

'*These things often are.*' Unexpected. But perhaps the pairing of Lisa and Stefan was not so unexpected, for they were similar in so many ways. It was only the comparison of their physical appearances that made them seem unfit, Madeleine thought. Her eyes crinkled as she remembered Lisa, standing on the chair against the Aga and stirring melting Mars bars.

The plastic container of washing-up liquid was almost empty and the plosive squelch when she squeezed it onto her oily hands sounded like the pink obstetric gel at lambing time, plopping gloopily from the bottle. That noise, the mention of the incident at Brewsters café, her own acknowledgment of the unexpected; all these brought Danny so forcibly into her mind that she could almost feel his presence in her kitchen.

Daniel had been able to recall details, he had remembered minutiae. They had sat in his four-by-four and he had told her what John had said.

'There you were, sitting at adjacent tables. All of you like a group of statues in the middle of the January Sales. You were staring into your tea-cup as though you wanted to drown yourself, poor old John was fidgeting and fussing with that stinking terrier. Abi had a face like thunder, the Lord knows why. Rick – what was he doing? Oh yes, pulling a bun to pieces and throwing bits to the dog. And Elaine was nattering away, life and soul of the party, as though nothing in the world was wrong and you were all hanging on every word. She gave me a bollocking of course for being late, but I couldn't help that, there was a queue at the feed-store. Anyway, there was a chair next to John, so of course that was where I sat. I can tell you I was nearly gassed by the fumes from that dog, I can't understand why they let him bring it in.

'Well, John and I got talking about this National Scrapie Plan and the business of testing for genes. It's a crazy scheme, ask any sheep-farmer, why do we need to get rid of scrapie from the national flock? It's not as though it's ever done anybody any harm, there's no evidence of people getting anything like mad cow disease from sheep. If we cull out the susceptible ones – *susceptible*, mind, which isn't at all the same as saying they've *got* the disease – Lord knows what we'll end up with in the ones that are left. Those genes have been there for centuries, there must be some point to them. It's like the Nazis and their eugenics – "we don't like that lot, so out they go". Kill 'em and burn 'em. These government people should ask the farmers, we're the ones that know about breeding, we're— Sorry, Maddie love. Hobby horse, eh?

'Anyway, you were sitting there eating like you were having tea with the Queen, and John and I were chatting about this and that – and I was thinking that there was nothing much wrong with his brain, we're all a bit forgetful now and then. It was his co-ordination that'd gone, poor old chap. And we were getting on all right even though you and Elaine were not joining in – I don't count Abi and Rick – when suddenly he leaned really close and he said, "Why are you always hanging round my wife? I see you sneaking round the place. I know when you're out there in the barn, with your arms around her and your leg over her too, I've no doubt." Madeleine, I was so shocked I couldn't think of anything to say. "You leave my wife alone," he said. "She's learning to manage without me. She's a strong woman, in more ways than you think. We don't need you," he said. Poor old bugger. What could I say?'

Where was the truth? Madeleine asked the African violet on the window-sill. She was no longer sure. The vile Bob had been dead for many years but he would have lied in any case, had he been able. She often found herself wondering about truth: it seemed that everyone had a different story to fit the same event, each person put so much energy into remembering the past in a certain way, for reasons that might be hidden even from themselves. She wiped her eyes and discovered that there was still detergent on her fingers. She should phone Dawsons because she needed George to sort that ruddy trailer wheel.

TWENTY-FIVE

There was an old lady who swallowed a fly:
Ruth Kowslowski's blog

There are many ways of killing flies, but the extreme solution of swallowing a spider is certain to cause discomfort.

Spiders – the non-bird-eating species – have evolved a variety of web-designs for snaring their prey. Much as a sea-trout swims into a net fixed across a stream, so might a fly be caught, and held tightly by minute globules of glue. After a quick paralysing bite, the spider packages up the helpless creature in a silk winding-sheet. The sundew plant uses sticky globules too but its treatment is less aesthetic, the edges of its scarlet-fringed leaf curl over the insect, imprisoning it so that it stops wriggling and dies, and gradually, very gradually, its body is digested. All that remains on the web or in the sticky leaf is an empty husk, the insect's scarcely recognisable, undigested exoskeleton.

Entomologists and butterfly collectors need their dead insects to be whole and unharmed. Gaseous carbon dioxide, freezing, fumes of chloroform or nail polish remover, or pickling in alcohol or formalin, the methods all have their advantages and drawbacks. To make a Killing Jar: place a layer of ten finely-chopped laurel leaves in the bottom of a honey-jar and screw the lid on tightly, to capture the marzipan fumes of hydrogen cyanide.

Unlock and fold back the polished wooden bar on its bright hinges and slide out the shallow drawers of the specimen cabinet, one by one. Look at the hundreds of beetles, thousands of green-eyed flies, their dry bodies pinned onto cork, with tiny labels giving the name and place and date. The 'Type Specimen', the acknowledged example of its kind, and dozens of variants with minute mutations and alterations. It's like stamp-collecting, you must check the number of perforations, the graded colours of the patterns. But the modern collector does not merely tick the box but prefers to ask 'how?' and 'why?'. The modern taxonomist deals in molecules not just in external signs, and seeks the remnants of genes in mummified or pickled corpses, or from the blood-meals of mosquitoes preserved in the sticky exudations of trees.

The Dutch anatomist and botanist Frederik Ruysch was a collector of insects as well as foetuses and curious natural objects. Insects symbolised the transiency of life on Earth: the beautiful butterfly bursts forth from its papery brown pupa-case but lives for a few short weeks (unless it has the wit, or inbuilt programming, to hibernate). Adult Ephemeroptera, the mayflies, live for a single day, escaping one medium into another, from water to air, to fly and mate. Brief encounter, brief lives!

Ruysch's moralistic and allegorical tableaux on the theme of death now exist only as engravings (drawn 'from life' by Huyberts) in the large leather-bound volumes of his *Thesauri Anatomici*, his *Omnia Opera*. Insects, bones and anatomical curiosities share the stage. The skeletons of foetuses stand or lie in different postures, amongst pebbles and kidney stones and taxidermal preparations of birds and other animals, arranged artistically on ornate wooden stands. In a tableau depicted in Thesaurus VIII, dried blood vessels project upwards as a forest of branches, a skeletal arm waves a scroll of paper, and two foetuses weep into lacy handkerchieves of dried mesenteric tissue. Well might they weep, for the hollow rock beneath them is a dried injected uterus, cut and opened like the door of the Tomb to show the dead embryo inside. *'Ah Fate, ah bitter fate!* sings a foetal skeleton in a different tableau, as it accompanies itself on a malformed bone 'violin' with a dried artery for a bow. Its grinning companion encircles itself with a snake of injected sheep gut, the vase-like form of an inflated testis adds artistry and elegance, and in the foreground a prostrate tiny skeleton holds an adult mayfly.

Her father's collections provided a handy source of specimens for Rachel Ruysch. Moths and butterflies, grass-hoppers and flies rest amongst the richly-coloured, richly-textured flowers in her still-life paintings. A lizard, a frog, snails with striped shells – the invertebrate creatures have such depth and colour as to seem alive, halting briefly for a single moment in time. No other artist could capture the texture of velvety petals and reflections on the damp bloom on grapes so well as Rachel Ruysch. She became famous, her works were much sought-after, and in 1708, aged forty-four years old, she was appointed Court Painter to the Elector Palatine of the Jülich-Berg duchy, Johann Wilhelm. She and her husband Juraien Pool stayed at the court in Düsseldorf until the Elector died. In her *Arrangement of flowers by a tree-trunk*, in Glasgow's Kelvingrove Museum, six different butterflies and moths fly amongst the flowers, one drifting down to alight on a pure white trumpet of convolvulus, another fluttering vainly between the flat jaws of a lizard. But these insects, unlike her father's specimens, are not moralising statements for they exemplify reality, their details have been observed and recorded, and are offered to us in all their glorious detail.

In 1697, Peter the Great, aged twenty-five years old, worked in an Amsterdam shipyard and attended Frederick Ruysch's anatomy lectures. Peter enjoyed carving and joinery, he liked to work in wood and stone and human flesh, he even fancied himself as a bit of a dentist and a surgeon. His portrait was painted in Amsterdam by Jan Weenix, who later painted twelve large murals for the Elector Palatine. Perhaps Rachel sometimes stopped by to watch and advise: 'Put a deer-fly or two on that stag's skin.'

The portrait painter Godfried Schalken overlapped with Weenix in Dusseldorf in 1703 although not with Rachel Ruysch, but he had already painted her portrait in Amsterdam. In her late thirties she still has the same long straight nose but now she also has a double chin and lace at her bosom.

In 1699, a year after Peter left Amsterdam, boasting that he had bought his new boots with the proceeds of his work, Sybille Merian visited Frederik Ruysch's house to study his insect collection. She wanted to learn about insects, their metamorphoses and lives, and that same year she took her youngest daughter Dorothea and went abroad, to Surinam. She saw how caterpillars pupated into chrysalids from which a moth or butterfly crawled out, damp and crumpled, and spread its wings. She watched insects, she collected them, she wanted them alive as well as dead, and she painted their life-cycles and their food-plants. The details were as scientifically exact as the glass insects and flowers of the Blaschkas' series on insect pollination. The colours glowed.

Thirty years previously the Leiden anatomist, Jan Swammerdam, famously dissected a preserved caterpillar for Cosimo de Medici. Swammerdam, according to the naturalist Boerhaave, wanted to preserve parts of the dissected body in constant readiness for anatomical demonstrations, freeing him 'from the difficulty of obtaining fresh subjects, and the disagreeable necessity of inspecting such as were already putrified'. He, like all the other Leiden experimenters in embalming, used oil of turpentine (at that time, the distilled resin of the terebinthe tree, *Pistacia*): take a tin vessel large enough to hold the corpse or dissected organ, and place a grid in it two fingers' width above the bottom; pour in oil of turpentine to three fingers' width, place the corpse inside and cover the vessel tightly with a lid. An embryo requires two months, a spleen ten days, a liver one month.

Swammerdam preserved the body of a month-old child, and a whole lamb.

The oil of turpentine converted the body fats of insects into a harder limey substance which could be washed away, leaving fibrous tissue intact. Inside the dissected caterpillar de Medici saw the wings of the future butterfly, and saw too that metamorphosis was an unfolding of parts already present rather than an alchemical change. Swammerdam turned down de Medici's offer of 12,000 guilders for his insect collection.

Sybille Merian is portrayed with a *Nautilus* shell and holding a box of butterflies and moths on pins. She died in Amsterdam at the age of seventy and that same year, 1717, Peter the Great returned to Amsterdam and bought not only most of Frederik Ruysch's great collection of tableaux, 'Naturalia', embalmed babies and decorated foetuses, for 30,000 guilders, but also the late Sybille's *Metamorphosis Insectorum Surinamensis* and part of her insect collection. He also acquired Dorothea, persuading her to use her skills to design the decorations around his new collection in the Kunstkammer. Her husband, Georg Gsell, went too, and when the giant footman Bourgeois died in 1724, Georg painted him – posthumously – so that his fleshly appearance was preserved in a portrait before he was boiled.

Rachel Ruysch was long-lived like her father, and painted her last still-life at eighty-three years old, in 1749, less than a year before she died. In one of her paintings a caterpillar hangs by a thread. In Merian's drawings from Surinam, caterpillars munch holes in leaves, spin silk around themselves to form protective cocoons, or their skin hardens and changes shape to form a pupal case or chrysalis. Inside the pupa, as Swammerdam had seen, organs and appendages shrink or grow, change shape, wings sprout, and antennae.

But now we know that parasitic wasps may lay their eggs in living caterpillars, eggs which hatch into larvae that devour the caterpillar's tissues from inside, the wasp larvae growing, moulting, themselves changing shape until they burst out, leaving an empty husk behind them. Did Merian and her daughter observe this metamorphosis of aliens, this apparent transmutation of species? The caterpillar as host, the food-provider, the life-support system, the container for a new life-form.

Thus it is with some modern matryoshki, variants of the wooden nested Russian dolls. The traditional dolls with rosy cheeks and peasant scarves, one inside another, date from the late 1800s, long after Peter the Great practised his own wood-turning skills. The mother figure is a symbol of birth and renewal, the handing on of the lineage and the mitochondrial genes. But modern versions of the matryoshka escape the human form, so that a cow contains a sheep, which contains a pig, a chicken and, of course, an egg. The outer form hides its inner secret wherein one species generates another.

The recipe for an Elizabethan dinner does this too, but in reverse, for it symbolises death rather than birth. It omits the mammals and sticks with our feathered friends. 'Take a boned swan, stuffed with a boned goose, stuffed with a boned capon, stuffed with a boned muscovy, followed by a boned pheasant, then a partridge, a woodcock and a dove, stuffed with a boned snipe, a boned sparrow and a dozen lark's tongues.'

As for that old lady who swallowed a fly, she took in the whole range from mammals to invertebrates:

There was an old lady who swallowed a cow.
I don't know how she swallowed a cow!
She swallowed the cow to catch the sheep...
She swallowed the sheep to catch the dog...
She swallowed the dog to catch the cat...
She swallowed the cat to catch the bird...
She swallowed the bird to catch the spider
That wriggled and jiggled and wiggled inside her.
She swallowed the spider to catch the fly.
But I dunno why she swallowed that fly
Perhaps she'll die.

And as for the old lady who swallowed a horse, what did you expect? *'She's dead, of course.'*

In a museum a large glass vessel contains the formalin-preserved stomach of a horse, the stomach wall distended and inflamed by the larvae of hundreds of parasitic bot-flies.

TWENTY-SIX

The traffic heading out towards the Mersey shore was heavier than usual.

'They cannot all be going to Arne's do, surely?'

'I gather that Arne's not one to hide his light under a bushel. What is a bushel, anyway?'

'You'll have to ask your farming friends in the North.' Stefan changed gear and braked as the traffic light turned to amber. 'Though it all sounds like a primitive fire-hazard to me. Talking of corn, I was thinking – as one does! – about crops and crop circles last night and wondering how the other shapes such as squares and triangles are made. Circles are easy, but how do you ensure a triangle remains equilateral without having an alien spaceship overhead to say "left a bit for ten paces" or "ten antenna lengths", or however aliens measure units?'

'Is that why you were flinging your arms around in bed? Measuring cubits?'

'No, they're unquantifiably small.'

'A bit too small to compute?'

'Oh, clever-clogs.' He looked across at her and grinned. 'That was what the waiter at Robin Hood's Bay called us, wasn't it?'

Red and amber, then the traffic light turned to green. A shopping trolley followed by a blue baby-buggy hurtled across the junction. The green-and-white flags that the lads were holding were whipped horizontal by their speed and two Sainsbury's carrier-bags tied to the trolley with string were ineffectual drogues.

'*Fuuuuck*!' The lads careered on down the hill, yelling jubilantly, and were gone. Stefan and Lisa stared after them, wordlessly.

The rutted and muddy carpark amongst the dunes was already occupied by a dozen cars and a minibus. Sheets of sand blew in shallow rippling waves along the shore and the sullen brown swell of the sea imitated the louring sky. A sand-blasted Highland terrier plodded miserably behind its owner. Near the bottom of the shore a group of people clustered around a large silvery object; Lisa and Stefan set off towards them but were much diverted by following a young woman who was tottering and tripping through the soft sand in high-heeled black shoes. Unaware that anyone else was close, she was swearing grimly to herself about the stupid fucking sand but then, as Lisa caught up with her, she clapped her hand to her mouth.

'Bollocks! *Bother*, I mean. Sorry, I didnae know there was anyone there, I was concentrating that hard. And look at you, you knew to wear proper shoes. I wish I'd brought my boots,' she wailed. 'I jist didnae *think*.'

Her lipstick was bright red, her hair black and shiny, and her black suit was clearly business-dress, to show she was a person not to be trifled with. But now, out of her normal environment, she was in considerable disarray.

'You could just head up to the hotel and forget about the launch,' Lisa suggested.

'I have tae be there with Arne, I'm doing the PR,' the girl said. 'I'm gonnae hand out press releases for the journos that turn up on spec. Oh, I hate the sodding seashore!' A tangle of black, dried wrack had snagged her heel and she bent down and pulled off her shoe and threw it across the sand. 'Here, lend me your arm.' She grabbed Stefan's arm as she pulled off the other shoe and threw it after the other. 'Wa-hay! Freedom!'

Lisa and Stefan burst out laughing, as she hopped about, still hanging on to Stefan's arm, giggling and gasping. 'Ayeee. I'll no' be goin' anywhere, the sodding sand's that cold.'

'Stefan's got spare walking-socks back in the car, you could wear them like slippers.'

'They're red,' Stefan added. 'They're really cool.'

'It's an arty event, you can get away with anything.'

The girl looked at her cold bare feet consideringly and then suddenly grinned. 'Yeah! Go for it. Why not?'

She wriggled her toes into the sand as Stefan ran back towards the car.

'Shame, though. I fancied him carrying me. Gorgeous hunk, isn't he? I'm Catriona, by the way.'

'Hi Catriona, I'm Lisa.'

'Hey, you know what? The three of us could hold hands and dance aboot and they'll think we're a Happening, like in the sixties or whenever. You know what I mean?'

'Indeed, yes,' Lisa murmured.

Chris, the composer, was already part of the group on the lower shore and, seeing Lisa, he waved enthusiastically and rushed up to meet her, beaming. His pony-tail twisted and shimmied round his shoulders in the wind.

'Pretty fancy boots,' he said to Catriona, when he was introduced. 'I hear they go down big in Finland.' Then, to Lisa and Stefan, 'Do you want me to introduce you to Arne–' he dropped his voice '–otherwise known as The Artist formerly known as Arnold?'

Arne, however, busy with wire cables, gave them only a cursory glance. 'Hi. Trina, where the fuck've you been? Give that woman over there the press release, would you, she hasn't a fucking clue what's going on, fuck knows why these morons don't do their homework.'

'Ooops. Artistic temperament by the bucket-load round here,' Chris whispered. 'Let's go and have a look at the monster, shall we?'

The Octocalliope was not, however, a single octopus but eight, conjoined. The creatures' large black eyes peeped out disconcertingly from the tangled mass of silver sacs and twisted, intertwined tentacles. The whole construction was roped onto a light wooden pallet, which was itself attached to several buoyancy bags.

Stefan walked around the artwork, rubbing his chin. 'It reminds me of something,'

'A stringy blob of chewing-gum?' Chris peered with slitted eyes then took off his glasses and rubbed them with the hem of his denim jacket.

'But look at the craftsmanship – these suckers, for instance,' Lisa was admiring the double rows along each tentacle. 'It must have taken him ages to make them. And what are the bodies made of?'

'Your friend Red Sox gave me a press release... something about silk. Yes, here, look. "Spider silk" Does that mean cobwebs? "Spider silk is so strong that if the threads were twisted into a cable ten centimetres thick, it could carry a jumbo jet." Well, wow.'

'This thing is made of cobwebs, then? How did Arne collect so many and weave them together. That must be wrong.'

'Wow, again. Listen to this. "The spider silk was produced by genetically-modified goats. The protein was purified from their milk and spun into threads, which were woven to make the strong and flexible material from which the body of each octopus in the Octocalliope has been created." Created. I approve. None of your coarse manufacturing nonsense here.'

'And then he's sprayed them with a thin layer of this silver material so that they keep their shape but still remain flexible. Very clever. It'll be interesting to see what shape they take up when they're set afloat,' Lisa said. 'What a shame we can't get a seagull's eye view.'

'Let's grab a drink while we're waiting for the tide,' Chris suggested, and they walked over to where a folding-table had been set up with rows of plastic cups containing wine or fruit juice; two black bin-bags were taped to the front corners.

'We had a fancy tablecloth,' one of the girls pouring out the drinks explained. 'But it took off like a kite. You'd better put your empty cups in there or they'll end up on the Isle of Man.'

Already about sixty people were wandering around the artwork and camera flashes winked here and there. There was a sudden buzz as a small group of people were seen coming down from the dunes; they were clearly of significance because they appeared to be accompanied by bodyguards.

'Hey, it's Ringo. Arne invited him but he almost never comes to anything. What a coup.'

'Nah, he's too tall for Ringo. It's Macca.'

But the new arrivals turned out to be merely some city dignitaries, and everyone turned away again, to watch the more impressive spectacle of the octopi being lifted onto a trailer attached to a small caterpillar tractor. The tide had been coming in quietly and inexorably, its leading edge fringed with brown foam, and now the tractor trundled down towards the advancing water then turned and reversed the trailer into the waves. Arne's acolytes and technicians, several dressed in wetsuits, clustered round and manoeuvred the artwork off the trailer. Lisa, having found a better vantage point near the upper strandline, watched as it wallowed and glinted in the grey light.

'Arne is going to make a pronouncement, we'd better get closer,' Stefan said. 'Oh, look – there's Ruth and her man. Of course they'd be here too, we should have expected that.'

'Where?' Lisa was ashamed that her immediate instinct was to scurry away.

'They're down there talking to the divers, she's standing next to the chap with the flashy yellow top. You can see her red hair.'

'Oh Stef.' She took hold of his hand. 'I really dread meeting her. It's silly, I know, but...'

'Yes.' He squeezed her hand then leant over to hug her. 'We'll be all right. You're not on your own, you know. We're—'

'—in this together. Yes.' *Whatever 'this' is*, she wondered as she kissed him. 'Come on then. Let's go and hear what Arne's got to say.'

Arne was apparently explaining that a concrete plinth, three metres square and one metre thick, had previously been buried deep beneath the sand beyond low water mark. The plinth had metal loops embedded in its surface and the divers were now going to swim out towing the Octocalliope, then dive down and anchor the hawsers to the plinth. Every stage was being recorded on video and this was part of the artwork too.

'It's a synergy between the installation and performance art, that evokes and conceptualises the interaction between living organisms and Gaia, the emergence of biotic life-forms from the uterine warmth and nourishment of the primaeval sea.'

Chris, who had wandered over to join them again, nodded solemnly and then sang softly and tunefully, 'O hear us when we cry to Thee for those in peril on the sea.'

For indeed the octopi were now fully afloat and wallowing on the swell. The divers raised their hands and, accompanied by a black rubber safety boat, the symbol of symbiosis was towed towards its anchoring place. The watchers cheered, Arne stood at the water's edge with his arms raised in blessing and cameras flashed to capture the moment and perhaps also Catriona who, still wearing Stefan's socks and with a never-empty cup of wine seemingly welded to her hand, was kicking lumps of brown scum into the wind.

Sunlight poured through a hole in the clouds, picking out the distant cranes and warehouses, and the sea's response was cheerfully blue. The octopi bobbed harmoniously in a tangle of translucent silver bubbles.

'Hey, Tony!' Chris shouted. 'Over here, man.'

Lisa had seen Ruth a few times during the summer when

she had come over to Liverpool to visit Tony; she had seen Ruth and Tony together too, and today, as previously, she thought they were overtly intimate. Tony, wearing his usual faded blue smock and tattered jeans, waved, and pushed Ruth forward with his other hand, which seemed to be down inside the back of her jeans. She laughed and wriggled and leant towards him to whisper in his ear, and he took her hand instead.

Lisa thought: Stefan and I could never do that – even if we wanted to.

Ruth thought: I wonder if he holds her hand in public? They look really awkward standing there together. But then Stefan leant towards Lisa and said something, and their mutual smiles lit their faces as he rested his hand on the back of her neck.

'They look happy,' Tony murmured. 'You'd better pack your prejudices away in your back pocket, Babe Ruth. Not that there's much room in there, O gorgeous-buttocked-one.' He tried to force their linked hands into the tight rear pocket of her jeans.

Ruth saw that Stefan had noticed and for a perverse moment she tried to recall how his hands had gripped her bare buttocks as he had pulled her against him. Was Stefan remembering too? She looked at his crotch, she couldn't help herself, although she knew he would see where she was looking. 'Is that a gun in your pocket?' The famous question echoed in her mind and she caught Stefan's eye, but his expression was impossible to read.

Chris knuckled Tony's shoulder, Tony and Stefan shook hands; Lisa and Tony greeted each other like old friends. Hanging back, alone and adrift, Ruth stared around at all the people chatting and drinking and waiting on the windy beach.

'Ruth?' Lisa touched her arm. She was hesitant and uncertain, and Ruth looked at her bleakly

'Hi, Lisa.'

'How are things with you? And Madeleine?'

Ruth knew she was being rude but she could not stop herself, she could not bear to speak to Lisa at that moment.

'Ach, I can't stand this sand any more, it's getting in my eyes and ears.' She rubbed her face irritably and scrubbed her fingers in her hair. 'Come on, Tony, let's go and wait in the dunes out of the wind. Assuming there's still something to wait for.'

'The great climax,' Chris assured her. 'Is it anchored yet, can anyone see?'

Thankfully, Ruth stepped away from Lisa, lifting her chin, pretending to seek a better viewpoint.

Indeed it seemed that the Octocalliope was safely moored at last, for it was bobbing in one place, the boat circling it like a neurotic sheepdog. A diver surfaced, head questing like a seal, and then the other re-appeared and raised his hand. The boat lifted on a crescent of spray as it roared towards them and the boatmen heaved them aboard.

Arne waved for everyone to gather round and raised the megaphone.

'In approximately half an hour, when the cables are pulled taut by the rising waters and the lower part of the installation is pulled beneath the sea, the Octocalliope will begin to sing, to celebrate and acknowledge the life with which the waters have endowed them.'

He handed the megaphone to a young woman elegantly swathed in a peacock-blue pashmina. Her rich, well-modulated voice effortlessly imparted information.

'While we await this special moment that we are privileged to share with Arne, you are all invited to walk up to the dunes, where we have arranged an enclosure with chairs and tables, and where you're all welcome to sit in comfort and eat the complimentary food provided by Lancashire Luxuries, with the very generous support of the de Savignac Trust. And if you would like to find out more about this art scheme and our excellent sponsors, Catriona can give you the press release with more information. Catriona – can you make yourself visible, please. Wave your arm so we can all identify you. Catriona?'

A whoop, and the waving in the air of what might once have been a red sock, indicated Catriona's continuing presence.

'Free food. They know about penniless artists. Come on, let's beat the rush.' Tony grabbed Ruth's hand. 'Run! Run like the wind! Or do I have to carry you now?'

She squeezed his hand. 'You'd better carry me while you can. No, no – I didn't mean it. Put me down!'

'Save us a place in the queue,' Stefan called as Chris hurried off too.

Tony's heavy work-boots had left huge corrugated prints in the sand. 'They protect my wee tootsies,' he had once explained to Lisa. 'Think of the damage a half-ton of sandstone could do. Aaaargh!' And he had hopped about on one leg holding his other foot in his hand.

'Tony was friendly enough just now but Ruth doesn't want to talk to me,' Lisa said, as she and Stefan followed.

'The situation is a little difficult for her–'

'And for you too?'

'–but she will resolve it, eventually, in her mind. Tony is a sensible chap under all that banter and he obviously really cares for her. I hope Ruth realises that. I hardly recognised him, incidentally – surely he had dreadlocks before?'

'Yes. But he cut them off because he said they got clogged with masonry dust, and when he got wet it turned to cement. He's going to be working on a church in Dumfries soon, apparently, so that's not too far from where Ruth lives. Stef?'

'Mmm?'

'We don't have to go and join them if you'd prefer not to. I know I shouldn't ask but I can't help it, but are you still bothered by Ruth? Do you still want to be with her?'

'Lisa.' He stopped walking and looked at the ground, pushing a broken shell with his toe, and she was so horribly certain what he was going to say that she felt sick.

She persevered. 'She's so sexy, or so switched on by sex, that... well, you know... we...' She did not have the courage to say what she really meant.

'Lisa, you have to realise that I was hankering after an idealised version of a long-gone version of Ruth. And to be absolutely honest, this version terrifies me.' He grimaced. 'She'd have exhausted me in a week.'

His reply was so unexpected that Lisa started to giggle with relief.

Lancashire Luxuries proved to be two fast-food vans, one offering organic pork rolls and the other a vegetarian option. Ruth and Tony were already seated at a plastic table, biting into enormous buns from which meat dangled, but Chris was nearly at the front of the veggie queue, so Stefan and Lisa decided that the choice had been made for them.

As they carried their food over towards Ruth's table, the woman with the blue pashmina hurried over. 'Stefan! Stefan Greatorex. I've been longing to catch up with you again, I *so* enjoyed your exposition of Escher's work.' She clutched his arm and her voice purred; she was probably in her mid-thirties but had the charm and confidence of someone older.

Stefan transferred the paper napkin and veggie burger to his free hand. 'Oh good. I'm delighted. You were at the—?'

'Siobhan Davies-Brown. I'm arts director for the Paternoster Society and as you know we sponsor a great deal of cross-disciplinary work. Let me give you my card now, but I would love you to join us after you've finished your food. I'm going to be meeting with—' She smiled vaguely at Chris and gently steered Stefan a few paces away, dropping her voice so she could not be overheard. She touched his elbow delicately. 'Do come, you're absolutely the person I need,' she added more loudly.

Stefan looked back at Lisa. 'It sounds fascinating, Siobhan. But let me introduce you to my partner, Lisa Wallace – Lisa is very interested in pattern-formation too, in several dimensions in fact. Siobhan wants to explore ideas for a project in the dockside area,' he explained to Lisa.

'Ah, so you're the artist in the partnership, are you?' Siobhan asked Lisa.

'I'm a mathematician, though my work approaches more closely to theoretical physics these days.' Lisa smiled, suddenly very happy.

'Siobhan has kindly asked us to join her later, Lisa, but I was about to explain that we have to get home as soon as the fat octopi finish singing. We have to collect my daughter tomorrow.'

The arts director became temporarily speechless and, well-bred and charming though she was, could scarcely disguise her thoughts.

'Yes, we've got an early start, I'm afraid,' Lisa added. 'But it sounds like a project that would be just up Stefan's street.'

'Do give me a call at work, Siobhan. I haven't got a card on me, but just call the physics department and they'll find me.'

Chris, hovering nearby in obvious enjoyment of the situation, added, 'Why don't you come and join us at our table instead, Siobhan? We're quite an eclectic mix of artists here. A weird bunch, even. You can choose amongst a taxidermist, a stone-mason, a video-artist and a couple of mathematicians who like to pretend they know about patterns.'

'Thank you. But I'd better hurry back to see how Arne is getting on – the Octocalliope should be tuning up any minute. Do keep in touch, Stefan.' With a nod and a vague smile, she glided elegantly away.

'Nice one, Stefan,' Tony clapped softly and approvingly.

'What a bloody woman.' Stefan, who almost never swore, shook his head in disbelief. 'Are you all right, Lisa?'

'Very much so.' She climbed up onto the chair. 'Though I think I've lost my appetite for this bun.'

Ruth reached across the table and took her hand. 'You

255

were great,' she said softly. 'I'm sorry I've been so... you know.'
She shrugged. 'I keep forgetting what you have to put up
with, every day. And my being stupid about you and Stefan
doesn't help, does it?'

'Ah well. I get used to it and try not to let it bother me.
Thanks, though. And I'm sorry for your sake that it just had
to be Stefan,' she whispered. 'That hasn't helped either, has it?'

'Is Stefan's daughter really coming to stay?'

'With him. Yes. Though it's not true that I'm going with
Stef to collect her tomorrow – I'll see her when I get back
next weekend. I'm really nervous about meeting her, to be
honest.'

'I can imagine.' Ruth chewed her lip and Lisa frowned as
they exchanged looks.

'What on Earth is *that?*' Tony stood up quickly. 'Listen!'

A strange wheezing, wailing sound could be heard.
Everyone hurried to the edge of the dunes and looked towards
the sea. In the distance a waving mass of silver tentacles rose
and fell, rose and fell, as the gentle swell wafted underneath,
and Ringo's song was carried in snatches on the wind.

'...in an octopus's garden in the shade... we would sing and
dance around... I'd like to be under the sea...'

Amid whistles and cheers, the watchers joined in: 'We would
be so happy you and me, No-one there to tell us what to do,
I'd like to be under the sea, In an octopus' garden – with you.'

Arne was to be seen capering like a cartoon figure by the
sea.

TWENTY-SEVEN

The green tea was cold and smelt of compost, and Lisa pushed the mug aside. The October evening was chilly and she was glad of the small amount of warmth from the light that hung low over the kitchen table where she was working.

She was working through the text of her talk and had been searching for the most logical way of presenting the research. Time for an image, for the few people in the audience who might struggle with visualising this abstract concept. Pulling the laptop towards her again, she selected the relevant diffraction pattern from a file and inserted it into the slide, then checked back through the written version that would be published in the book of conference papers. Why had she included Dirac combs? It was the usual problem: she had had to submit the paper three months ago, and since then her group's research had shifted in a new direction.

She saved the file of powerpoint slides and sat back, surprised to see that it was already dark outside. She ought to eat; she ought to pack; but she did not want to break off now and lose the productive line of thought that she was following. Putting the talk together had sparked a new line of enquiry in her mind and its shape was slowly clarifying. She sat quietly, allowing it to grow, and then grabbed the paper and her pen. As she worked, that rare thrill – of knowing that she was making a leap forward, that intuitive leap for which she would subsequently need to find the proof – seized her. She knew the idea was good and she would be able to talk it through at the conference with... She wondered who would be the most useful person. Kees! Kees would of course be there. She smiled at the thought of drinking wine and beer with Kees; he thrived on discussing the more philosophical implications of 'order'.

The telephone rang and she jumped, reminded sharply that Stefan had not yet called to tell her about Annette's arrival. But it was Ruth, asking if she could come over and see her.

'I know it's late, but I wanted to see you before I go back to Cumbria. I won't stay long.' She seemed to be trying to suppress some excitement and this had the effect of making her sound girlish.

'I have to go to Berlin tomorrow and I haven't even eaten yet, let alone packed.' Lisa was torn, but there was still so much to prepare for her trip away.

'Lisa, please. Tell you what, why don't I pick up a pizza on my way over? And a bottle of something. I'll even help you pack, you can't have got a very big suitcase.' Her giggle was infectious.

'All right. But don't worry about bringing food.'

By the time Ruth rang the doorbell, Lisa had organised her papers and books and packed them into her rucksack. She had prepared and eaten a sandwich, finishing off now-pungent Brie with some salad, and had closed the curtains and put on the lights in the sitting-room.

Ruth flourished the bottle wrapped in tissue-paper – 'It's chilled already' – and followed Lisa into the kitchen. 'And thanks, Lisa – I know you're up to your ears with things to do.'

Lisa stepped up onto the wooden platform to take down wine glasses from the cupboard. 'Actually I'm so relieved that you wanted to come over. I was afraid that we might'nt have had the courage to remain friends – you know, that we'd just make polite chit-chat and a few comforting noises when we met now and again, and that you and I would have no more proper conversations, or fun, like we did at Madeleine's and after the sci-art conference.'

'Courage. Yes. That probably is the right word. I was a bit confused that day, Lisa, and I'm sorry I was so spiky. But anyway, that's all in the past now – I want you to hear my news.'

She pulled the half-bottle out of its wrapping. 'Celebration time.'

'Champagne! This news must be good.' Lisa waited as Ruth carefully untwisted the wires. The bottle opened with a quiet hiss and Ruth poured the pale fizzing liquid into the glasses.

'Very professionally done. Right, tell me quickly.'

'I'm pregnant! My doctor confirmed it today, I phoned him from Tony's.'

'Oh Ruth, congratulations! Cheers.' They clinked glasses. 'How exciting – you *are* excited, aren't you? And Tony, too?'

'He's thrilled. I can't believe how happy he is, he's been going round grinning and keeps coming up to rub my tummy. He's longing to see the first scan.'

'That was quick,' Lisa ventured.

'Perhaps a little quicker than we intended.' She was diffident, slightly embarrassed. 'But we'd been talking about moving in together and this pushed us into making the final decision about where to live. It has implications.'

'It certainly has. Bring the bottle and let's go through to the sitting-room and talk in comfort.'

Ruth was wearing a silky jacket, a swirling pattern of green and blue and gold, over a long brown dress made of some soft stretchy material. Her hair was caught up into a chignon at the back of her head. Unself-consciously, she unzipped her boots and then curled up in the big easy chair with her feet tucked beneath her.

'You look fantastic,' Lisa said, thinking that she had never seen Ruth look so smart. She was surprised that she felt a little prickle of jealousy. 'Pregnancy suits you.'

'Early days yet, I'm barely six weeks gone. I had a business meeting this afternoon so I had to get dressed up – I'll tell you all about that in a minute.'

'So, where are the three of you going to live?'

'You know Tony's going to be working in Dumfries for a while? And he's been talking on and off about trying to find a studio so he can get back to sculpturing, as well as contract masonry work—'

'So Cumbria and Whitefoot are the obvious choice.' Lisa laughed.

'Right! Wouldn't it be perfect, Lisa? My house is big enough, there's the spare bedroom for... for the baby. And I'm going to ask Madeleine if she would rent out part of the ground-floor of the barn to Tony.'

'I imagine she could do with the extra income.'

'Did she tell you about an idea she'd had for using part of the barn as a laboratory? She had a meeting earlier this summer with a professor from Edinburgh University, quite a high-powered woman, Madeleine said, who wanted to do some sort of field survey on a farm.'

'No, it must be a couple of months since I last spoke to her.'

'Well, anyway, she told me she'd decided against it because John – you know, her husband – had had the same idea when they farmed in Scotland. She can be a bit vague on occasions, so I didn't fully understand. She was quite strange about it, actually, something had obviously upset her.'

'Odd. But you think she'll be amenable to Tony using the space?'

'He could even help her, when he's around. George's still talking of leaving to join the plumbers' army, and Madeleine could employ Tony to do some of the heavier work. He's strong enough.'

'So all you need to do now is ask her. It all sounds perfect.' Lisa raised her glass in salute. 'I'm so happy for you. And you must look after yourself. At your age you'll have the indignity of being classified as an "elderly primagravida".'

'I'm not a primagrav, this'll be my—' Ruth inhaled sharply and her eyes widened.

Lisa stared at her, then pushed herself off the sofa to get the bottle from the table. As she passed the wall-hanging she reached up and stroked the nap of a velvet cube.

'Do you want a top-up or are you going to give up alcohol?'

Ruth held out her half-full glass, avoiding Lisa's eyes. 'I didn't give up last time, but perhaps I should have. I lost the baby. It was when I lived in Glasgow. That's why I moved to Cumbria, to get away.'

'How old was—'

'I don't want to discuss it, Lisa.'

'No. Of course not. I'll forget you ever had to mention it and I won't say a word to anyone.'

'Please don't. But I have told Tony, in case you're wondering, because I didn't want him to find out by accident. He's been great. He's such a good bloke. I can't believe my luck, really. After all the others...' Ruth wiped her eyes with a finger, and then looked at Lisa. 'I mean, Stefan's a good bloke too, but...'

'Not your type,' Lisa agreed. 'I know. Listen, talking of Stefan, I need to call him to see how his daughter's settling in. I won't have time in the morning.'

'You said you won't be meeting her until the weekend, after you get back from Berlin?'

'That's right. It'll give Annette time to get used to being with Stefan and for him to prepare the ground, as it were. I almost wish I didn't have to meet her but she's part of his life so I can't pretend that she and Sabine don't exist. I'm sure, too, that their mother's very attractive in that elegant and understated way.'

'Appearances aren't everything.'

'Try telling that to a teenager.'

'She'll love you, Lisa. Just be your usual self.'

But as she watched Lisa walk out of the sitting-room with her awkward, clumping gait, Ruth recognised her own hypocrisy. She uncurled herself from the chair and wandered restlessly around the room, picking up books, stroking a small soapstone sculpture of a seal, touching the petal of a pale pink orchid and discovering that it was a perfect non-living replica. Its detailed accuracy surprised her for a moment: it could not possibly be a Blaschka, but she wondered if Lisa was familiar with the glassmaker's exquisite flowers.

She could hear the murmur of Lisa's voice, and occasional laughter, as she talked to Stefan. An elegant Belgian mother, two lovely daughters; enough to make anybody feel insecure.

'The flight was late, but they've had a busy day and they've just been out for dinner,' Lisa said, as she returned. 'Anyway, you were going to tell me the reason why you're looking so smart.'

'I was indeed. And that's thanks to Tony too.' Ruth continued wandering around the room. 'He'd been talking to someone on the Arts Forum about my anthropomorphic preparations and their references to the work of Plouquet and so on, and this person became very excited about the idea. So I had a meeting with some of their movers and shakers this afternoon, and they want to fund an annotated exhibition of my work. There's a photographer, Maurice Platov, who's made some beautiful black-and-white studies of craftspeople at work, and they want to involve him too. If he agrees, he'll come to Whitefoot and we'll work together. The more I think about it, the more excited I am. It could give me the breakthrough that I need, credibility and exposure in a much wider context.'

'That's so exciting. You're going to be so busy!'

'Typical, isn't it? All the exciting things happen at once. This glass orchid's extraordinary, Lisa, it has all the perfection of a Blaschka.' She walked back to her chair and pushed her discarded boots out of the way before sitting down again. 'And another thing – a company of puppeteers got in touch with me. They're working on ideas for a new show that they're going to tour, and they want a hamster or perhaps a rat as a workable puppet, not a model but a prepared specimen whose limbs will move. And they've asked if I could do that for them.'

'Could you?' Lisa wrinkled her nose. 'Won't children think it's rather gruesome?'

'The play's for adults, although it's possible they'd be more of a problem. Children like gruesome things, but adults might complain that it's demeaning to animals. And where did I get the hamster anyway? And so on. You can imagine the questions that might arise. It's a risk – but it's worth thinking about, and it's a very prestigious company, their puppets are famous as works of art, not just as dramatis personae.'

Lisa sat in Little Chair for a while after Ruth had left, trying to make some sense of the thoughts and images that were churning round her head. One recurring image was the pale spheres. She knew that image, she had rationalised it before, but it now seemed to be linked to puppets or their faces; she explored it further and found that it was, after all, linked with dolls, those large china dolls with pale faces and staring eyes that were in the box in Ruth's spare bedroom. Now it made sense because that was the room that would become the baby's nursery, and the image represented the baby's face. Ruth and Tony would make a good couple. She smiled to herself, and then focussed her attention minutely on the new idea that she wished to discuss in Berlin.

Later, as she picked up the glasses and the empty bottle, she remembered Ruth's comment about the glass orchid. She searched through a pile of coloured cardboard wallets, and opened the green one that held several print-outs. 'Making eyes': the Blaschkas made glass animals and the famous glass flowers. They had also, early in their careers, made glass eyes. Lisa skimmed through the rest of the article and then sat for a while longer in Little Chair.

263

Twenty-eight

March 18th 2001. Madeleine receives the phone call from the Ministry that she has been expecting and dreading. Whitefoot's flock is to be culled, a contiguous cull because it lies within three kilometres of a farm where foot-and-mouth disease has been confirmed. For each infected farm, there are three or four others that must be culled out.

The lad who speaks to her on the telephone is dispassionate, he doesn't know her, he's merely doing his job. Mrs Tregwithen owns the farm next to Low End, so her animals must be killed.

His office is in Carlisle, he's probably not long out of school and is looking forward to the end of the week to go drinking with his mates. The valuer and the vet will visit her farm this evening, he says, to estimate the value of her sheep – the hoggs, the ewes in lamb, the tups, all her flock. The slaughterers will come tomorrow.

She has to fetch the sheep in, to collect them together in the in-bye land. She calls George on his mobile.

'I can't come, boss,' he says. 'I'm "dirty". I was wanted over at Sowerbys' yesterday and I've got to wait forty-eight hours before I'm officially clean.'

'But my sheep will be killed anyway,' she says. 'You can't infect them now. What does a few hours matter?'

'It's bloody stupid, aye. A month ago we had to wait seven days, then they said five'd do. Now they're that short of help they need us all the time.'

'George.' She cannot bring herself to plead but she needs his companionship, she needs a familiar face.

'Aye,' George says softly, and she senses that he's nodding. 'I'll come.'

Ruth is staying away, despite the mats and footbaths of disinfectant, because she doesn't want to risk carrying the virus onto Whitefoot land. She and Madeleine have discussed this, and although it is the safest solution it is also inconvenient because she has had to set up a temporary workshop in her kitchen. She never seems to have the right materials to hand. But it surely cannot be for much longer, surely the disease will soon be contained.

George and Madeleine stand in the yard and listen to the roaring of the sheep, as they mill around in indignation and fright.

'Will you stay?' Madeleine asks, knowing she is being unreasonable.

But when the valuer walks into the yard, she recognises him as David, an auctioneer from the mart, a man she trusts and likes.

She touches George's shoulder, an unusual gesture for her. 'No, go along home, lad. You need a break.' In fact, she longs to throw her arms around him, and hug him, to weep against his shoulder.

David looks grey and drawn. 'Madeleine. George.'

George nods, then lifts a hand in farewell. 'Aye, I'll be off then. See you, Madeleine.'

What more is there to say?

As they move amongst the sheep, Madeleine tells David what he needs to know about their background, and he takes notes as he goes, filling in columns, counting. The Herdwick hoggs, still black-fleeced, are in particularly good condition, fine sturdy little animals, and he compliments her and gives them a good price. She'll receive financial compensation, money to help her re-stock; that is why David is here.

'But where will I get more Herdwicks, David? Will there

be any left to buy?' She feels empty, completely devoid of hope.

David, normally a robust, smiling man, known for his wit and persuasiveness in coaxing higher prices out of buyers at the mart, is flat-voiced with tiredness.

'Robinsons down in Borrowdale have got it now. If it's in the fell sheep, that's the end. You can't contain it. They're setting up a Herdwick sperm bank – but how do you replace a hefted flock? How do you ever replace the generations that know their home heaf?'

'Robinsons!' She is shocked that the disease has crept so far amongst the fells, to strike at the best, and most-prized flocks.

'Aye, and Mark and...' He stops writing and looks away, swallowing hard. 'Mark and Dorrie Platt. They were culled out as dangerous contacts. Three hundred and forty sheep. And when the results of the test came back, not a single sheep had tested positive. They lost stock that had been in that family for two generations. Dorrie brought some of her dad's ewes over from the old farm when they moved across. She said those animals were like family themselves.'

Madeleine is silent: there's nothing to say. She knows and admires Dorrie, a small blonde woman who is tough and uncompromising, daughter and grand-daughter of hill-sheep farmers.

David refuses the offer of a cup of tea. 'Thanks, no, Madeleine. I've scarcely seen my wife and children for four nights in a row.'

'You look like you could do with a good night's sleep.'

'That too. I wish.'

He grips her hand with both of his, and she can see that he is on the verge of tears again as he turns and walks away.

March 19th. The vet comes early next morning and she sets to work taking samples from the sheep. The slaughter team arrives soon after and takes control, herding the sheep into the pens.

They move through with their bolt guns, laughing and joking amongst themselves, shouting to each other as they work. Thud. A ewe falls to her knees. Thud. Another keels over, legs twitching. Every one of the breeding ewes, each with one or two lambs inside her.

Madeleine picks out some of the sheep she knows: a good mother; a bad influence; an old ewe with a uterus as cavernous as an aircraft hanger, inside which a third lamb has been known to hide – an old ewe with a kind white face.

'Treat her with respect. Why don't they treat her with respect?' Tears trickle down her cheeks.

The vet is a young woman who speaks with a Welsh accent. 'It's the only way they're able to cope, Mrs Tregwithen,' she says. 'Jeff – he's the team-leader – told me he's already had to kill twelve thousand healthy sheep.'

She takes Madeleine's hand and holds it tightly, and they watch as the bodies are carried out and piled in neat straight lines.

Later, when the team has left, she comes and sits in the kitchen, exhausted and traumatised. She cannot speak in sentences.

'At the old motel,' she says. 'Drafted us in from all over the country. Can't sleep. Vets are supposed to save lives, not take them.'

She tells of a milking-parlour. 'Empty – except for an old armchair covered with a blanket. Robbie Stebbings and his pedigree Holsteins. No-one came to collect the cows' corpses for nine days. Virus everywhere. When the wagons came Robbie had to move them himself. Bodies falling apart as he scooped them with the tractor. Legs, and guts falling out of rotted skin. His little boy's stopped talking.' She cannot stop. 'And ewes down by the river, further west. Some had lambed. Dead lambs. A ewe with feet and head hanging out of her backside. No-one would go near to help. No farmer with cows'll go near. Mrs Tregwithen. Will no-one listen? Why doesn't Blair come and see?'

She cannot stop, her speech is slurring, but she has to keep talking.

'And on the salt-marshes, we had to chase the sheep ourselves, and two stuck in the mud and we couldn't reach them before the tide came in. No fences. No dog.'

'Why don't you stay and have something to eat?' Madeleine breaks in, even though she would now rather be on her own. 'Go upstairs and have a hot bath, Bron, before you set off again. Get the smell of sheep off your skin. You need a break.'

'Have to get your tests sent off. Too much paperwork.' Bron's mobile rings. 'I'll be there in half an hour,' is all she says, and she is already picking up her bag.

Madeleine goes out to the field to look: a long dyke of grey and white bodies already stiffening, like stones.

She is quite alone.

The three Suffolks are incongruously large, their size exaggerated by the corpses of the lambs that lie beside them.

Danny keeps Suffolks and he persuaded her to try them; he sold her the ewes for a good price. She liked their haughty black faces and their floppy black ears, and the way they strode around stiff-legged, looking down with queenly disdain at the shorter-legged fell-sheep.

'You should rear pure-breds,' Danny said. 'Bring them over to me, Maddie lass, and we'll put them to my tup.' Had he winked at her? No, that had been in her imagination as had, surely, so much else. Danny would not have winked.

She kneels down next to the stocky black-faced lambs, their eyes glazed and dull, and she strokes a soft ear and a gentle muzzle that only a few hours ago was tugging its mother's teat for milk.

In the distance, two lorries grind up a hill with loud gear-changes, but here in the afternoon there is nothing but silence.

She thinks of them as Danny's lambs. The small dead Suffolk lies on her lap. It is cold and stiff, but she cannot bear to let it go.

She sits by the little dog's grave, that is marked by a rough lump of sandstone and set amongst the bare trunks of the birches, and she is numbed and her mind is empty.

The wagons come, and George returns with his tractor and the scoop. Madeleine hides in the office, with the local radio station turned up loud, and she jumps when Ruth shouts her name from the kitchen.

'I couldn't let you be here alone. I saw the wagons, I had to reverse all the way back along the track to let one by. I've got my sleeping-bag, I'll stay in the studio, I don't—'

'Oh Ruth!'

And then she is clutching at Ruth and she cannot stop the grief that wails out from deep within her. 'Oh Ruth. What am I to do? They're all dead. My lovely sheep.'

The words gasp and judder out of her, and Ruth puts her arms around her, and rocks her wordlessly, like a child, until she has quietened and can breathe again.

Ruth brings mugs of tea, and the brandy from the sideboard, and Madeleine turns off the radio because the news is now too personal.

'What am I going to do, how will I fill the days?' she eventually asks, rubbing at her sleeve that is damp with tears.

'Knitting? Take up watercolours?' Ruth tries to lighten the mood.

'I hear that felting's all the rage.' Madeleine attempts to smile and takes a gulp of tea. 'Perhaps you'd better teach me to stuff animals instead.'

March 19th. Just after seven in the morning Danny telephones; Ruth is asleep in one of the guest rooms but Madeleine, out

269

of habit, is up. She assumes he has called to find out how she is faring after the cull.

'Six of the Lims have got it,' he says straightaway. 'And the old cow, old Jayne. She can't stand any more, her feet hurt so much. You should see her, Maddie – she looks to me to help her, she calls to me when she sees me. And I've let her down.'

He goes quiet, she can hear him breathing deeply, and she knows he's struggling.

'When's the vet coming?' she asks, to give him time.

'There's stuff coming out of her nose, her gums are bleeding. I'd put her out of her misery right now if I had the means. Soon. "Soon", that's what they said. "As soon as he can get there". Maddie, it breaks my heart.'

Jayne. Daniel had named the young heifer after Jayne Mansfield, 'because she had a big tit'. When he told Madeleine the reason she had been disconcerted, because she had not imagined Daniel to be 'like that'. But that had been many years ago.

And now old Jayne is in distress, and Danny's beasts are ill and suffering. All of his one hundred and fifty-strong herd of dairy cows will soon be dead.

'The army are coming so at least they'll take them away quick. After.'

'Yes.' She cannot tell him about Robbie Stebbings. 'And the ewes'll go too?'

Danny lets out land to a fell farmer for winter grazing for in-lamb ewes.

'They have to, now. Jimmie was going for a voluntary cull anyway, to save my cows.'

Neither of them speak for a while. Words are no use.

'I'm sorry, Danny. I don't know what else to say.' She wants to say, 'I love you', but that would be inappropriate.

'No, Maddie lass. There's nothing left to say, and you've been through it too. But it's the end, Maddie.'

March 21st. The samples taken from Whitefoot's sheep show that two had been infected with foot-and-mouth disease. Whitefoot must be treated as an infected farm, and its name is posted on the website and listed amongst the lengthening tally on the radio. Daniel and Elaine Nicholson's farm too. All over Cumbria, farmers are hearing how the disease is creeping closer to them.

Friday April 13th, Good Friday. All through the north-west of the county, uninfected sheep are herded into lorries and taken away to be slaughtered. None will rise again.

June 21st, Midsummer. Daniel Nicholson owns neither a bolt-gun nor a shot-gun, but he finally finds a way to take a life. He hangs himself from a beam in the milking parlour.

Twenty-nine

Madeleine was looking vaguely at Lisa's feet.

'What's wrong?' Lisa asked. 'Are my shoes on back to front?'

'It's the "Start-rite" shoe advert. That's what they remind me of. You know the one – the long straight road and the two children setting off down it, holding hands?'

Lisa shook her head. 'Sweet. I've never even heard of Start-rite, though it sounds like a useful aid package for freezing winter mornings.'

'Before your time, I expect. But the shoes were just like that, the same red.'

'Well, I'm just an old-fashioned girl. With an old fashioned mind, or whatever the song says.'

Madeleine surprised her by singing the words, rather croakily. '"An old-fashioned house with an old-fashioned fence, and an old-fashioned mee-lyon-naire".' And then she pressed her palm against her chin and left cheek with her characteristic head-down gesture. 'Goodness,' she muttered.

'What an unsuspected talent,' Lisa said, 'and a millionaire or two would be a help, however old-fashioned, I imagine. Think Imelda Marcos' shoes.'

They had driven up the lane to look at the ewes because Madeleine had wanted to check that the tup was doing his business. An ugly brute with fat haunches, he was standing to the rear of a ewe, head stretched forward and lips curled as he sniffed the air. As they watched, his penis was extended, long and thin and curved. The ewe turned to look at him, not moving away, and at once he was up onto her, front feet scrabbling at her flanks. He jerked vigorously, and was done, pulling out and falling back on all fours. The ewe's backside was coloured blue, matching the tup's chest and chin.

'Oh, I hardly know where to look! Voyeurism isn't my line. Or blue movies.'

'Scarlet women, next week,' Madeleine said with a flash of humour. 'Come Monday, he'll get different-coloured raddle in his harness. That way we know when the ewes've been tupped. Gives us an idea when they'll lamb.'

'When will that be?'

'Nearly five months' time, or thereabouts – April.'

'Ruth won't be able to help you with lambing this time, then. Her baby's due in May, isn't it?'

'Ruth has to keep well away! I've told her she's not to come near the ewes, it's too dangerous. Especially after everything else that's happened.'

Lisa was startled at the sharp vehemence of Madeleine's tone.

'Why? What do you mean?'

'Abortus. Pregnant women can catch it. You can lose the baby.' She was flustered, even upset.

'Oh. Ruth told me about...' Lisa stopped. Perhaps Madeleine did not know that Ruth had already lost her first baby, several years ago.

Madeleine looked at her strangely, as though trying to guess what she had been about to say. After a moment she changed the subject abruptly and without finesse.

'George – you remember George? – George's packing in the contract work. He's signed on for a plumbing course come January. I could do with that millionaire's cash to hire some new help, right enough. Tell you the truth, Lisa, I've been worrying away at what to do with the farm, and I've decided I'll let out the land next year. I can't go on with all this uncertainty.'

'You'd give up farming? But you'd stay in the area, wouldn't you? You wouldn't want to move away entirely.'

'I don't know. I decide one thing one day, then the opposite the next. Usually in the small hours when I'm lying awake and everything looks hopeless.' She managed a smile and Lisa smiled back in sympathy.

'It's a big decision to make.'

'Well, I need this lot to get in lamb, and then we'll see...'

She helped Lisa up into the Land Rover, and climbed in the other side.

'Sheep have a lot to answer for, don't they?'

'What do you mean?'

'Well, this abortus that you told me about and—' Lisa had been going to mention sheep dip, but stopped herself in time. 'And twin lamb disease, and all those late nights lambing.'

Madeleine gave her that same strange look as before, then turned on the ignition and swung the Land Rover back into the lane.

A silver-grey estate car was already parked in the yard, its boot-lid raised. There was a wire dog-cage in the boot and a young girl wearing a purple anorak was curled up next to it, talking to the unseen occupant.

'Louisa Mason. Arrived yesterday. Her mum's vegetarian so I told her I don't do dinners at this time of year. She won't let the child have a boiled egg for breakfast.'

'What a shame. Stefan enjoyed his eggs and soldiers.' Lisa's insides lurched at the thought of Stefan, and she glanced at Madeleine. 'No, don't ask now. I'll tell you all about it later.' But perhaps not all.

The caged dog must suddenly have become aware of them because it hurled itself at the wire, a small brown creature yipping squeakily and ecstatically.

Louisa shrieked and put her hands over her ears, then scrambled out of the boot.

'He's just a puppy,' she explained when Lisa and Madeleine came over. 'He's a Patterdale.'

'That sounds very important,' Lisa said.

'Would you like to see him?'

'Don't let him loose in the yard, now. We don't want him chasing the hens,' Madeleine said sternly, carrying on walking towards the kitchen door.

'No, I won't. Keep still!' She reached into the cage and grabbed the puppy around his middle.

The fat little terrier squirmed and wriggled and tried to lick her face as she held him out towards Lisa.

'What's his name?' She gingerly patted his wet nose.

'Mr Jimmy Melcho,' Louisa said proudly.

'Mr Jimmy Melcho! What a wonderful name. Why did you call him that?'

'Because he's small.' She looked at Lisa, then put her hand over her mouth and giggled.

'Oh, of course.' Lisa laughed. 'That makes perfect sense. And how old is Mr Jimmy Melcho?'

'Eight. We're the same number – he's eight months and I'm eight years.'

'I have a niece called Holly who's almost the same age as you.'

Louisa held the puppy tightly against her chest to stop him escaping, and stood up straight.

'Is she bigger than you? I am, aren't I? If she's bigger than you, does she look after you?'

Lisa frowned consideringly and looked at Louisa, who was thin and tall, and whose face was level with her own. 'I don't think I see her often enough for her to look after me.'

'I could look after you if you like. If you're staying here I could look after you. We're going out for dinner tonight to a place that's called the Pear and... and... some other fruit. It's vegetarian. But I could look after you at breakfast.'

'Well, that's very kind, although I'm not sure I need looking after because I'm quite old.'

'How old are you?'

'Thirty-three – years, not months.'

'Oh.' Louisa's face twisted as she chewed her lip, then she went back to the car and pushed the terrier back into his cage.

'I'd like to come and see Mr Melcho in the morning, though. Thank you for introducing us.'

'It's all right.' Louisa climbed back into the boot, and gave a little wave, but she looked rather disappointed.

Lisa stood close to the Aga, feeling its radiant heat against her body and face. A plastic freezer-box, labelled 'beef cass' stood on the worktop nearby, gathering frost on its surface: dinner for non-vegetarians.

'I'm on the computer, but I'll be through in a minute,' Madeleine called from the office. 'Put the kettle on, Lisa, and we'll have a cup of tea.'

There wasn't a stool so Lisa lifted a chair across to the sink and filled the kettle from the tap, then reached up to unhook the mugs that were hanging by their handles. By the time Madeleine returned to the kitchen the teapot with its knitted cosy, the jug of milk, and the mugs were waiting on the kitchen table. Lisa noticed how the unforgiving fluorescent light accentuated the wrinkles in Madeleine's face, bleaching her skin so that the purple growth sat even more darkly beside her mouth.

'I was checking back through the bookings diary,' Madeleine said, as she sat down and began to pour the tea. 'Last time you came to stay was March – and on your own. That was before you and Stefan got together, wasn't it? Ruth told me about the two of you, two or three months back. I think she was a bit peeved then, to tell the truth, but she's very happy now. Not that it's her business, anyway, as I said to her then. He's a nice lad, that Tony, more sensible than he looks too, just what she needs, especially with the baby coming.'

Her approach was from such an unexpected direction that

Lisa remained silent as she took the mug of tea. Twin threads of steam spiralled upwards, intertwined, and then swayed apart.

'Dear me, sorry Lisa, that sounds awful. I didn't mean that Stefan isn't nice and sensible too, that's not what I meant at all.'

'No, I know. It's just that... well, perhaps Stefan was a little too kind and reliable.' Lisa felt her eyes filling with tears, and she looked down at the table and blinked to clear them. 'We're not together any more.'

'That didn't last long, then!'

Lisa gave a little snort of amusement at Madeleine's forthright exclamation, and then wiped her face with her sleeve.

'No. And thanks for your no-nonsense approach. But we had a lovely time while we were together.' She sighed. 'We had a lot of fun, we're on the same wavelength about so many things. But in the end, it just didn't feel right, Madeleine. We split up about ten days ago, an "amicable separation", as they say. But I decided I'd come away for a day or two – to take a bit of time to clear my head, and get a different perspective on Life with a capital L. And where better place to come? Even at this time of year.'

'So you're "just good friends" now, are you, like all those so-called "celebrities" when they split up,' Madeleine said drily.

'Something of the sort.' Lisa took a sip of the strong tea.

'I imagine that's easier said than done, if you live in the same place. And you work together.' She was unusually persistent.

'We manage. And his project grant runs out in four months. At the end of March he'll have to go back to Belgium.'

'He told me about his daughters. Teenagers. One of them didn't like the mother's new man.'

'Did he tell you that? That's the older one, Sabine. The younger one, Annette, was over staying with him two or three weeks ago. I met her after I got back from Berlin.'

'That would've been difficult for you, then. Was that why the trouble started between the two of you?'

Lisa suddenly felt exasperated. 'No, Madeleine, it wasn't. It was nothing to do with Annette. As a matter of fact she and I got on surprisingly well, because she enjoyed having a female ally against her father. Sometimes Stef can be rather serious and we both enjoyed teasing him. And she didn't treat me like an aberration of her father's, either,' she added sharply.

Madeleine's mouth turned down and she made a face, but Lisa slipped down from her chair and took her half-empty mug to the sink. 'Sorry, but I need to go and make a phone call. Let me know if there's anything I can do to help for dinner.'

Her room was the one that Stefan had had when they had stayed here last year. He hadn't spent much time occupying it that night; but in the end Ruth had been an aberration, too. Lisa climbed onto the bed and lay down and closed her eyes.

When she had returned from Berlin she had been so disturbed and unhappy that she had been unable to sleep or even to think clearly. As her first lover, Stefan was perfect. She had so much to thank him for: he was considerate; he was intelligent, and gentle with her mind and her body. Once or twice she had thought she even loved him, and that perhaps he loved her too because why else would he want to get together with her? But they had never spoken those words, it always seemed too soon.

She would have liked to be able to reach out to him now, on the bed beside her, and say 'I'm sorry.' She wondered if he felt that she had used him, for he had given her a present whose value could not be measured. He had given her the certainty that others were able to treat her as a sentient being – and then she had left him. But that was being overly dramatic and self-centred. She tried, yet again, to recall every word and nuance of that evening at his flat, and she was certain that there had been a hint of relief when, after the tears and talking, he had finally hugged her and said goodbye. If Stefan had been the one who had brought their relationship to an end, that would have been so very much worse for them both.

Now, she was tired with the mental strain and anxiety and she pulled the bed cover over herself and turned onto her side. There was a faint sickly-sweet smell from the chest of drawers, where she had shut away the bowl of pot pourri, but she buried her nose in the pillow and fell asleep in seconds.

Lisa drank two glasses of red wine at dinner with her beef casserole and baked potato. She felt slightly, but with pleasure, that she was no longer quite in control. Mr Jimmy Melcho lay dozing and muttering in a cardboard box in front of the Aga, because Madeleine had told Mrs Mason that the dog would freeze to death if he was left outside the restaurant in the car. The sky was crystalline with blue-gold stars.

They had moved to the small sitting-room which was for Madeleine's own use, and Lisa sat slumped at one end of the sofa with the blue and grey rug over her legs, fiddling absently with its fringe, plaiting and twisting the threads.

Madeleine knelt by the fireplace. 'What are you doing for Christmas?' She placed kindling and pieces of coal on top of the crumpled newspaper. 'There's only four weeks to go. You said you had family in the Dales, I recall.'

'I don't know, I haven't thought about it yet. I usually go across to Bakewell to see my parents, but they're going to my sister's in Bristol this year. Suzanna and I don't get on very well, and anyway she's got two children so there'll be a full house.'

'Ruth and Tony are coming here for Christmas dinner. If you and Ruth are friends again, you could come too. I close for Christmas, so there'll be plenty of room for you to stay over.' She stood up, grunting a little, dusting her hands together, and picked up the coal-scuttle.

Lisa's benevolence and optimism now extended to the entire population of the world. 'What a wonderful idea. Yes, I'd love to come. Thank you! I'd give you a big kiss if I could get out of this sofa.' She gestured helplessly from her cocoon and laughed as Madeleine blushed.

'You know, I was thinking about Suzie earlier, because Louisa is the same age as my niece Holly. And I've just remembered that Suzie met Stefan ages ago in Liverpool and flirted outrageously with him. Outrageous. Of course, she's very good-looking. Sex goddess – no, no, I mean kitchen goddess. She cooks. But Maddie – Madeleine. This is the funny part. Stef was living with me – well, not living with me, but staying in my flat. And we pretended that he was my boyfriend, just to tease her. She was so jealous, it was extra... extraordinarily funny. And then later she never even knew that Stef and I *were* a couple, really and truly a couple. So now she won't even need to know that we're not.'

'Not sure I follow all that, Lisa, so I'll take your word for it.'

'Yes. It is a very difficult concept.'

'You sit there and keep an eye on the fire and I'm going to make some coffee, you look as though you need some. And I need to check on that wretched little pup. He's probably widdled in the box.'

Lisa snickered. 'Yes, a Mr Jimmy Melcho would widdle. What would Louisa have called the puppy if he were a Great Dane, I wonder? Was your husband tall, Madeleine?'

Madeleine stopped in the doorway, startled. Smoke puffed out of the fireplace and curled up and over the lip of the mantlepiece.

'He was... he was about the same as me. Why? What's that got to do with the dog?'

Lisa was puzzled and thought for a moment, but she could no longer follow her own train of thought. 'I'm not sure. I've forgotten.' Then, unconsciously succumbing to the logic, because this was what she had really needed to explain, she said, 'I went to a party in the physics department with Stefan. And I could tell that when the students saw that Stefan was with me some of them were thinking "Surely he could do better than that!" Especially some of the female postgrads.'

'And so you decided to finish with him because of what other people might or might not have thought?' Madeleine came back into the room and sat on the arm of the sofa. 'I always thought you had more sense, Lisa.'

'No. At least, that wasn't the main reason. But that was part of the reason why we weren't right.'

'Even if you're daft enough to worry what others think, I can't see it would have helped if he'd been ugly. And since you asked about John, I didn't have this thing when we first met,' she added with asperity. 'Or at least, not the way it is now. And I had a friend – a friend who said it was what was inside a person that mattered. He didn't care about how the thing looked. But he's dead now anyway so he never had to worry how we looked together. I'm going to see to that blasted pup.'

She stood up abruptly and stomped out of the room.

Lisa sat very still and watched how the flames rooted themselves in redness on the coals. They flickered and wavered, and sometimes one would lift and vanish altogether.

After a while she stood up and put the fireguard in front of the fire and left the room. She could hear Madeleine muttering and clattering dishes in the kitchen, but she pulled herself up the stairs by the bannister and fumbled along the corridor to the bathroom. When she came out again, she went into her bedroom and turned on her cellphone. The signal was weak, but sufficient after a few moments to ring out with the four beeps for 'message received'.

The message was from Kees. '*I miss you. Come to Montpellier with me for Christmas. K.*'

She sat down on the wicker chair. Her hands were shaking so she gripped them tightly together, fingers interlocked. In Berlin – no, her brain was too hazy with alcohol to think clearly about Berlin and too much had happened since then for her to sort out the images. But Kees had told her about the Pont du Gard near Montpellier, a Roman aqueduct, three tiers of arches, that crossed a gorge. He had walked across it with his parents when he was small. You can walk inside it if you are not too tall because it is like a very long box with holes in the lid, he had said, or you can walk along the top and jump over the holes.

The pattern that his words conjured now was a strange repetitive image of verticals and rounded arches, which both confused and excited her. Where would she and Kees walk? She picked up the phone and, with complete certainty, typed in '*Yes. L*' and sent the message back.

Mr Jimmy Melcho had jumped up when Madeleine had come into the kitchen, and the cardboard box had fallen onto its side. He ran to Madeleine, but his paws skidded on the lino so that he slipped and fell on his chin. She picked him up and tucked him under her arm while she set the box and the old towel within it to rights.

'Why did I say that to Lisa?' she asked him. 'What possessed me to even think that? Must've been because she mentioned John. I don't know, pup with a daft name... I don't know what's real any more at all. Come on, back into your box.'

But the little terrier had heard a car outside and he jumped out of her grasp and attempted to scamper, like a cyclist with wheel-spin, towards the door.

Thirty

'What're you thinking about, Ruthie? You've been sitting there for ages.' Tony, who was proving to be surprisingly domesticated, pushed in through the back door with an armful of underclothes and work-shirts. 'It's been raining.'

Ruth, sitting on a stool beside the cluttered worktop, was staring out of the window. Scarcely conscious of what she had been seeing – winter-sepia vegetation, rusting roof on the now-empty hen-house, streaks of rain against the glass and Tony reaching up to un-peg dangling clothes – she was thinking about the boy growing within her. She was not imagining him as he was now, a foetus of about four months, a comma with appendages and digits, but rather she was trying to imagine him in the future.

'I was thinking about little boys. Do you remember that wee boy along the road, with the bull – I hope our boy grows up like that.' Strange how 'our boy' made him so much more human than 'our son'.

'No chance of that unless I'm not his dad – he had dark hair.' Tony cleared a space near the kettle and dumped the pile of damp clothes.

'He was so funny and so confident. Completely unselfconscious.'

'That's what I like about living here. Where else would a wee lad dare to talk to two strangers in a car? Unless he was going to demand money with menaces.'

An old white pick-up with dogs in the back had been driving slowly along the road, herding a small group of cows and calves and a large brown bull. Sometimes the leading cows stopped to snatch a mouthful or two from the hedges (so much more desirable than the monotony of grass) and the driver hooted and waved his arm out of the window to hurry them along. Ruth and Tony had crawled slowly behind in the van, laughing at the bull's massive, wobbling flanks as he hurried to keep ahead of the nosing truck.

It was late July: the lush hedges and verges held the dark and dusty green of summer; white trumpets of convolvulus shone amongst tall grasses and swathes of goose-grass; blue vetch wrapped its feathery leaves around the stalks of yellowing meadowsweet. Ruth had grabbed at a dry head of cow-parsley and its flat oval seeds had sprayed through the window and onto her lap. The pick-up stopped before an open gate and several of the beasts, followed by the bull, turned into the field and immediately started to graze, but three cows continued trotting briskly up the road in search of greener grass. At once the dogs leapt out of the back and a small boy, perhaps nine or ten years old, jumped out of the passenger side. He stood in the centre of the road and held up his hand, an unmistakeable 'Stop!', and Tony waved and turned off the engine. Meanwhile the pick-up careered along the verge attempting to get ahead of the now-galloping cows and turn them back.

The boy came over to the van, pointing at his chest and beaming.

'*Phwooah*. Lucky the bull's gaan in. Or he'd've bin after me and I'd've bin—'

He held his arms out in front of him like a diver, facing the van as though to launch himself through the window.

'Yeah, right – the red on your pullover. Lucky we were here or you wouldn't have stood a chance,' Tony agreed.

The pick-up and the dogs had succeeded in turning the runaways around and they were now heading back down the road.

'I'll get out and help you make sure the cows go in,' Ruth

offered. She left the door open to extend the barrier, and stood next to the boy. The youthful brown smoothness of his face and the way his eyes seemed lit up with uncomplicated happiness made her want to hug him.

'That's my granda. And the brown dog, see, she's mine but she stays with granda on the farm. Uh-oh. The bull's lookin' at us.'

But the bull was more interested in the return of his wayward wives, who had halted by the gate to stare suspiciously at the humans. Ruth waved her arms and the cows slowly plodded into the field. Flies followed them.

The boy took a green rubber ball out of his pocket. 'See this – if he comes after us I'll thraw it and get 'im in the knackers.' His grin was so wide that Ruth laughed aloud.

'And what would your granda say then, if the bull couldn't make any more calves?'

'He might tell my nana not to give me any tea.' And his comic parody of dismay as he had run to shut the gate had set Ruth laughing again.

'You were so taken with that lad that I bet you were pregnant already. That must have been the morning after the night when you woke me at least ten times for another shag – or was it twenty? I gave up counting. All I know is that I couldn't walk in the morning.' Tony put his arms around her from behind, stroking her stomach and then gently squeezing her breasts. 'I want you to grow a big stomach like Ron Mueck's pregnant woman sculpture and huge breasts like a Freudian nude.'

'You're such a hypochondriac, you were quite capable of walking.' Ruth rubbed her face against his sandy stubble and held his hands against her breasts.

'And nipples like the teats on a baby's bottle,' he continued, his hand inside her pullover.

'Stop, Lisa'll be here any moment.'

'Elastic waist-bands are a serial shagger's dream.'

Clutching at each other, they hurried into the sitting-room and fell onto the sofa. In less than a minute, it was over and they lay twined together, panting and laughing.

Tony pushed spirals of red hair away from his face. 'I love you, Ruthie.'

'I love you too,' she said and yet again she felt surprise that this was true. 'I feel content – and complete. It's a very good feeling, and it's because of you. And because of him inside me, as well.'

Tony kissed her taut stomach. 'I can hardly wait to feel him moving. That must feel weird.'

'The other one didn't ever do that,' Ruth said quietly. 'So I can't imagine what it will be like. It's a weird idea, too, that an independent being – a male even – is growing inside me and will kick and hiccup and move around, and make his presence felt. There's something almost monstrous about the idea, isn't there? And yet of course we accept it because we're mammals and that's the way we do things. We don't bud off babies from our arms or legs.'

'We blokes feel left out. Men should make nests and women should lay eggs and then we could take turns sitting on them. Perfect excuse for lads to sit in front of the telly for hours with a few cans o' lager. No football, though, or we might get too excited and leap around. Ooops – sorry, love. Sorry about the scrambled eggs.'

'Shut up, Tony.' Ruth closed her eyes with an exaggerated sigh, and pushed his head away. 'Pull your jeans up or you'll fall over.'

'Shit! Listen, there's a car.'

They hurriedly tidied themselves and Ruth had reached the front door while Lisa was still walking down the path.

'I see the house next door's for sale.' Lisa pointed at the sign that was just visible above the thick tangle of honeysuckle stems, and then shook her arm as water-droplets spattered onto her sleeve and hair.

'We're going to buy it and knock through so we can house our ten children.' Tony grasped Ruth's buttocks as he spoke over her shoulder, so that she giggled and then felt juvenile and foolish.

'Ten! Shouldn't you be living in a shoe? But you're looking fantastic despite that number, Ruth. And you've hacked back some of the jungle, too.'

A pile of twigs and brown, slimy leaves was heaped against the front wall.

'Tony did that – he said it was man's work. He's becoming so conventional.'

'We're turning the garden into a pram park. We've got stretch-prams on order, complete with chauffeur.'

Ruth bent to hug Lisa. 'Potential paternity's addled his brains. It's great to see you, Lisa. Come on in and get warm.'

'Potential? Whadda ya mean, potential? I thought you said he'd already got my nose.' Tony led the way to the kitchen.

'Potential as in not counting unhatched chicks.' Ruth's voice was sharp, but she turned to smile at Lisa. 'He thinks evolution's got it wrong and that humans should lay eggs.'

'Like a duckbilled platypus. That's such an improbable animal that it has to be the archetypical example of unintelligent design.'

'The first time someone saw a dead one they probably looked for the seams to see where the taxidermist had cobbled it together from spare parts,' Ruth agreed, then shivered. 'It's so cold in this kitchen, I hate November. Tony's going to make some soup to warm us up, aren't you, sweetheart?'

'Nothing like a bowl of steaming broth to warm the cockles. Tell us what the heart's cockles are, Ruthie – you're supposed to know about this stuff. Hey – stuffed hearts! Did you ever eat stuffed lamb's heart? My mum was a great one for the nasty bits. "A thousand and one things to do with offal" was her favourite cookbook.' He busied himself opening cupboards and drawers, pulling out a pan and knives while Ruth filled the kettle.

'Madeleine once told me that nothing was wasted after a lamb was butchered, except the skin. Kidneys, sweetbreads, tripe, and the men of the house were supposed to eat the testicles for the obvious folkloric reasons. They even boiled the sheep's head, though that might have been for the dogs.'

'Do we have any pig-meat in the form of bacon?' Tony was already dicing carrots, and Ruth opened the fridge to look and handed him the opened packet.

'Shall I peel the potatoes for you?' Lisa was amused by the sudden flurry of activity.

'Nope. Ruth'll do the spuds, it will do her good to get some exercise. And you can snip the bacon, Lisa. Cut it into pretty patterns and then put it back together again in twenty-six dimensions, or whatever it is you do.'

'Five is enough. Have you got some scissors?'

'Here – shall I put the plate on the stool? And tell us about Berlin. I haven't seen you since the night before you left, and you were working on a new hypothesis before I interrupted you. Did you get some useful feedback?'

'Yes indeed. The conference was good beyond all expectations,' Lisa said gravely, and stopped snipping at the bacon rasher that was draped over her left palm. 'I met up with an old friend too. He was very helpful.'

At the change in her voice, the hint of repressed information, Ruth turned off the tap.

'Go on, then. Tell us about him. What he's called, where he's from.'

Lisa took a deep breath and was clearly trying to remain cool and disinterested. 'He's a Dutch cosmologist, Kees van Damm. We met about eighteen months ago in Amsterdam, at the same conference where I first met Stefan, in fact, because he looks at patterns too – at the distribution of matter in the universe. Oh, but you know of him, Ruth! He was the one who sent the list of anatomical names from the Surgeon's Guild.'

'Foreheads and hooves. Of course I remember, he—'

'So he was helpful, was he, Lisa?' Tony interrupted. '"A worthy helpmeet". There you are – meat. It all comes back to hearts again, by the sound of it, wouldn't you agree, Ruthie? Since she's already told you on the phone that Stefan's not in possession of that any more.'

'Tony! Forgive him, Lisa, he's so insensitive. Here, take these potatoes and do something with them.' Chopped onions were already hissing gently in melted butter in the pan. 'What does a cosmologist do apart from contemplate the cosmos?'

'Kees of the Cosmos, supergalactic hero.' Tony was muttering to himself and yelped as Ruth prodded his side, only slightly playfully. 'Okay, okay. I'll get the soup on the go, and then I'll go too. I have to go to church,' he explained to Lisa, and put his hands together in prayer and closed his eyes.

'Do you really?' Lisa glanced at her watch: just after eleven o'clock on a Sunday morning. She looked at him consideringly, as though she had learnt something new and profound about his character.

'I have to go to St Egbert's, because the font needs repairing. It needs replacing entirely, but Christ alone knows if they've got the money for that. And anyway I'm overloaded with work for this Dumfries job at the moment. The church is locked during the week and only opens for a service every other Sunday – and that's today. Grab an apple and a hunk of bread and come with me, if you want. There's an ancient yew in the church-yard, king of the pagans.'

'The branches have curved down and rooted to form a circle of baby yews. I love the idea that because they're clones of the parent, the old tree makes its bid for immortality. But we're going to stay here, aren't we, Lisa? Girl talk.'

Lisa nodded and handed Tony the plate of bacon snips. 'In one of the parallel universes, these bacon rashers still exist intact.'

'A sort of bacon heaven. "We shall all be made whole again".'

'You seem to be on very familiar terms with religion.'

'It's because I do so much work in buildings that are heaving with iconography and symbology, most of which are meaningless to your modern God-ignorant population, formerly including myself.'

'He read the Bible, "from cover to cover", as they say,' Ruth explained, stroking Tony's neck. 'He's one of your self-educated peasants who's dragged himself up by his bootlaces.'

'And naturally I read the King James' version. Accompanied by the Lonely Planet Guide to the Old Testament because otherwise how would I remember where Mount Ararat was, or who was Aesop, and Rebecca, and the wee chap in the Moses basket, and how Abraham begat X and X begat Anthony who took Ruth to himself and begat eighteen children.'

'I am impressed,' Lisa said. 'On both counts. And irrespective of your beliefs, I hope you'll baptise your own chip off the old block at St Egbert's, assuming you'll have finished the font in time.'

'Good thought. Though of course I had already thought of it myself, and I'm laying in a crate of Dumfries Highland and Island malts to fill the font.' Tony kissed Ruth passionately on the mouth, kissed Lisa on the top of her head, and spun out of the door, arms flailing. 'I'm off to bother God. See yous, as Ruth tells me they say in Glasgie. Don't forget to add the stock to the pot.'

The front door slammed and Ruth sat down on the stool and wiped her pink, damp face with her upper arm. 'Phew!'

'He *is* rather different from Stefan,' Lisa said drily. 'Much more your type.'

'And since you've now mentioned Stefan – twice – I'm surprised how calm you seem about breaking off with him. You said it was a mutual decision but that's usually what the half who's been given the push says.'

'That doesn't mean that it doesn't hurt.' Lisa, without any

attempt at melodrama, put her hand to her heart. 'But I already told Madeleine all about it and I don't think I can bear to explain everything again. We can still work together, which is a relief. With Kees, though, life seems so very normal and relaxed, and importantly, I don't feel uncomfortable on his behalf. He's unusual, he isn't beautiful or well-dressed, he has curly brown hair that's a bit of a mess, he wears jeans and rather scruffy jackets. He grows his own weed in his backyard, and plays the clarinet. He's bright, he's difficult. And he misses me and has asked me to spend Christmas with him in France. Where he's been working on blobs, walls and filaments – how matter is distributed in the universe.' She gave a little gasping laugh and put her hand back to her heart, again unself – consciously. 'My heart is racing just thinking about him. I'm ashamed of myself.'

Ruth leapt up. 'Shit, the vegetables are burning. We forgot the stock.' She seized the pan and began scraping it with a wooden spoon which was asymmetric with frequent use. 'Oh damn! I'm so pleased for you. You're much too unusual to have stayed with Stefan, you need a mad-man.' She stopped and looked at Lisa, laughing. 'That was meant to be a compliment, by the way. I was telling Tony earlier that I felt complete with him. It's such an unexpected feeling, I realise how much it had been lacking before. It sounds as though you and Kees could be the same.'

She gave Lisa a questioning look and Lisa nodded slowly. 'I hope so, although it's too soon yet to tell. We'll have to see what happens after we get to know each other better next month. Anyway, how are things with you, and is all well with the baby?'

Ruth took a deep breath and crossed her fingers. 'So far so good. I feel really good too. We've had the results of the tests and the scans, and he seems to be doing what's expected and has the right number of fingers and toes, and so on.' She smiled.

'What tests did you have?'

'For Down's syndrome – trisomy 21, they can check for an extra chromosome. And a blood test to check for spina bifida ...' She poured hot water from the kettle into the pan and added a handful of red lentils.

Lisa tucked her hands inside the sleeves of her pink fleece pullover, and walked over to the back door. 'What would you have done if the baby had had Down's?'

'I would have had an abortion.' The familiar feeling of sick dread was in Ruth's stomach, but she said quietly, 'How could we have looked after a Down's child, especially living out here?'

'Arguably you, being self-employed, would have been more able to look after the child than a woman who had a nine-to-five job. But no, it's a horrendously difficult decision, and these decisions are increasingly being forced upon parents – in the developed world. You know, I'm so grateful, Ruth, that my parents had no way of knowing that they were about to have a child with the mutation that ensured she would be a dwarf. What advice would they have received? And would I be here now?'

'Foetal scans are producing more and more information. And I read that there're nearly a hundred genetic tests now, particularly for families with a history of genetic disease...'

'Pre-implantation genetic diagnosis after in vitro fertilisation is becoming simpler and increasingly commonplace. Coupled with "informed consent"! In the States some clinics even let parents choose the baby's sex.'

'Better than leaving it out on a hillside to die.'

Lisa exhaled quickly. 'Suppose there's a simple prenatal or PGD test for achondroplasia, and an embryo or foetus tests positive. If the parents decide to "discard" the achondroplasic embryo or terminate the pregnancy, that implies to me that my own life is considered not worth living. That – taking the argument to extremes – that people with my disability should be put down. Culled. If that becomes the norm, I shall be one of a dying breed, achondroplasics will become extinct and our nasty genes will be exterminated from the human gene-pool. Apart from the occasional mutation.' She drew a horizontal line in the condensation on the window and cut it off with a vertical bar, then wiped a clear patch with the side of her hand so that she could see out into the garden. 'I've decided that I don't ever want to get pregnant.'

'But—' Ruth's voice rose in surprise. 'Why not? You must be the epitome of a successful and happy achon, you can pass on your knowledge and expertise, as it were.' She stopped. 'Sorry, I've made an assumption here, haven't I? That your child would also be an achon. But I don't know whether Kees – I'm assuming that you're thinking in terms of Kees as your partner – is tall or short or of normal height.'

'He's "of average stature", which is the politically-correct way of referring to people of your height rather than mine. Although mathematically-speaking, we should be using the term "mean", which has unfortunate connotations. You've also made the assumption, based on a sample size of one, that being an achon seems to be merely a matter of inconvenience. And, as you say, you've assumed that my child would also have the same mutation and be small. Not necessarily – and imagine yourself giving birth to the size equivalent of a seven kilo baby!'

'But you would have a Caesarian.'

Lisa closed her eyes briefly and rubbed her forehead. 'It isn't simple, Ruth, though I know you know that. You probably think my decision is a coward's way out, but you can be sure that I've thought about this a great deal over the years. All achondroplasics have to weigh the pros and cons and make their own decisions, in fact anyone with a heritable genetic disability, whatever its severity, and who is capable of rational thought, has to do the same.'

'Doesn't love come into this anywhere, Lisa? You're being too analytical.' Ruth walked agitatedly around the kitchen, still holding the spoon. 'You've always said how much your parents loved you. You would love your own child, and your love would be irrational, and almost overpowering.' She grabbed Lisa's hand and held it, but Lisa shook her head and she let go.

'But you see, I think any relationship I have will always be very fragile because of the outside pressures, and from what I've seen of friends' and my sister's marriages, having children changes the internal dynamics quite dramatically too. If I have a child, whether or not he or she is achondroplasic, one of us will be different from the other two in the family.'

Ruth tried to find calmness by stirring the soup: the precise forms of the lentils were becoming furry-edged. 'Lisa, you are so used to having to show the world that you're a competent, independent individual – but you'll not be on your own if you and Kees, or whoever, get together. You can help each other, there'll be two of you to make the decision.'

'To plan to have a baby.' Lisa suddenly grinned. 'I seem to remember you said something about you and Tony being taken by surprise.'

Ruth started to shake: she had tried so hard to obliterate that from her memory. 'This is so different. We wanted a baby, it didn't, doesn't matter when.' Her teeth were chattering and she ground them hard together, and then thumped the worktop with her fist. 'Oh god, oh god, oh god.'

Lisa was staring at her, shocked. 'I'm so sorry. How could I have forgotten. Even though... even though...' Her face was so white that Ruth, despite her own great distress, feared that she might faint.

'Even though what? What are you trying to say, Lisa?'

'The baby you lost, did you embalm it? I read the pieces on your blog, about Ruysch's babies and Peter the Great, and I... I wondered... Is she upstairs amongst the dolls?'

What?' Ruth could not take this in. She sat down on the stool again, and clutched her hair with both hands. She felt fear, and then anger. She felt sick. She scarcely knew where to start in refuting this terrifying edifice of suppositions.

'No, is the quickest answer. No to everything. Lisa, where did all this come from? How long have you been worrying about this?' She shook her head, still feeling nauseous, but trying to imagine what Lisa must be feeling.

'Ruth, I'm sorry. Please forget it.'

'How could I possibly forget what you've asked? If I embalmed *my baby*! You've asked what happened to my baby, the one I told you about in Liverpool. And it's nothing like you think. She wasn't even a baby – she died when she was about the same age as this boy inside me now. I went to hospital and she was taken away from me. She had hydrocephalus, so it was a relief but so unbelievably horrible that I try never to remember it. She wouldn't have survived even if she'd reached full term... Even if I had been allowed to take her away... Oh god, Lisa, how could you even imagine that! She would not have looked like a *china doll*. A fucking china doll. Lisa, you can see that, can't you?'

Lisa grasped Ruth's hands now. 'Don't go on. Please. Don't.'

But now Ruth could see her way through the maze. She felt curiously lighter, and her mood was suddenly swinging towards laughter.

'The dolls! Weren't they ghastly? But they've gone. They belonged to old Fann who lived next door, she'd asked me to re-paint their eyes and touch up their faces so she could give them to her grand-daughter, but I never got around to it so they just sat there in the spare bedroom.'

'What did you do with them after she died?'

'I tried to give them back to Fann's daughter when she was clearing up the house, but she didn't want them either, so we sent them packing, with their shiny, characterless little faces, off to the auction. Fann's daughter said I should keep the money and put it towards a cot for a real live baby.' She shook Lisa's hands, feeling the firm stubbiness of her fingers. 'Silly Lisa.'

'Oh, Ruth. I am such a fool.' Colour was coming back into Lisa's cheeks, and she let go of Ruth. 'Your articles, and some strange pictures that kept recurring in my mind... they united to create this fantastic scenario.'

'Fantasies. Stop. I'm exhausted with all this talk of babies.' She hugged Lisa and stood up. 'Let's eat, just listen to my stomach groaning. I read that a foetus hears sounds at about fifteen weeks and that its world is really noisy – the poor lad in there will be deafened.'

She started ladling soup into earthenware bowls. 'There are spoons in the drawer by the sink. We'll go through to the sitting-room, it's warmer. And let's forget about all this and lighten up. I'll tell you about the puppeteers I'm dealing with.'

'I'll tell you about Mr Jimmy Melcho.'

After Lisa had left, Ruth went upstairs to the baby's bedroom. The room had been considerably cleared in the past two weeks: the clothes and books had been given to charity shops or thrown away and the wooden box with the glass lid had been emptied. George was supposed to be coming around to help Tony carry the box and the mattress and metal bed-frame downstairs to the van, so that they could be taken to a second-hand store. Brightly-coloured curtains, still in their packaging, and an unopened tin of primrose emulsion paint stood on the chest of drawers. Ruth leant against the door-frame, visualising what Lisa had seen. Tears lurked, and she was tired and her legs ached, but she went into the room and looked down at the heap of animals in the corner.

Furry toys were piled next to specimens, a large pink teddy-bear that she had won at some club or other and a knitted elephant that had come with the dolls, shoulder-to-shoulder with a black-eared Suffolk lamb and a small golden monkey. She stirred them gently with her foot, and picked up a small white bootee and several blue and white beads that had lain hidden amongst the balls of dust and hair. The teddy-bear was ugly and cumbersome, too big for a baby's toy, and the monkey's fur had come away in patches on his back.

'You'll all have to go,' she said.

She thought of the little grave on the mound beneath the birches and tears spilled down her cheeks.

She picked up the lamb, the symbol of Madeleine's enduring guilt, and rubbed his nose. 'Especially you, poor little Larry the Lamb. It's time to move on. There's not going to be room in the inn for any of you.'

Thirty-one

The cold air scoured her lungs and drew tears that trickled down cheeks that felt like cardboard, but Madeleine's heart lifted as she watched her ewes. They jostled round the metal feeder where newly-opened silage steamed in the freezing air; they looked fit and sturdy but soon they would no longer be her responsibility. She would get them scanned in the new year to see how many lambs they carried, and she would sell them in-lamb. Sheep had been part of her life for thirty years, but she would do no more lambing, there would be no more anxiety or long hours or bottle-feeding, no more vet's bills or forms to fill in, no further need to treat fluke or scouring or foot-rot. Whitefoot's land would be auctioned off for grazing.

Water lay in the fields like frozen milk, and the distant fell was stark in black and white, its contours and gullies dazzling between dark crags. Her footsteps crackled on a frozen puddle and left faint imprints in the thin powdering of snow. A sudden gust of icy wind rattled the bare branches of the alders, and she pushed her clenched hands deep into the pockets of her ancient quilted jacket as she stopped by the two small graves. Snow had caked along the windward side of the sandstone rock, but the new, unmarked mound was smooth and almost hidden. She stayed for a while despite the cold, frowning, lips pursed, and then walked back to the edge of the field and looked towards the North-West, towards the boundary, invisible from here, between Whitefoot and the adjoining farm.

A couple who had previously farmed in Oxfordshire owned it now: Elaine Nicholson had sold up and had bought a modern bungalow on a new estate in the nearby town. Her house was near the school and Rick, to everyone's surprise, had stayed on to get his A levels and was living part-time with his gran; Abigail had moved out some time ago to live with her new man.

Even now, Madeleine could not stop herself looking towards the farm that had been Daniel's and projecting her thoughts towards where she imagined he would be; her silent communication had become a habit over the years. In the beginning she had hoped that he would sense that she needed him, and her thoughts had seemed to her like arrows, one of which would surely strike him when he crossed the yard or was letting the cows out of the milking-parlour, pricking him like a tattoo-artist's needle with the simple message 'meet me at the moorland gate'. There had been times, too, when the blackness had hovered, shimmering at the edges of her senses, and she had called to him for help: one time an arrow must have struck for he had arrived with the hour and – this still surprised her – he had brought her a wild white violet that he had found amongst the primroses in a dyke.

'For luck and good fortune,' he had said, and she had touched it against her face.

He was still there, she was sure, spreading like an invisible mist through every corner of the farm. She could not forget him, she would probably never stop puzzling about the collection of ill-matched parts that was his character. Nor would she ever be able to unravel the confusing memories of their relationship, for she no longer knew what had been real or what she had imagined, or the truth of what had happened when the grey cloud briefly claimed her.

The single event that she would always remember with the greatest clarity was that meeting by the gate on March 18th 2001 – the date was unforgettable – when the news that her sheep, her apparently uninfected sheep, were to be culled. She should not have called him, he should not have come. They had taken precautions, she wore clean clothes and her boots were scrubbed with disinfectant, but the subsequent terrible events had been her fault. It must have been her fault. He had kept his cattle close to his farmhouse, well away from any sheep.

Despite everything that had been written about transmission of the disease, by wind or smoke or on the tyres of the contractors' lorries – it must have been her fault. Even the short time that had elapsed between their meeting and the diagnosis in Danny's cows – the contamination must have been her fault.

Danny's suicide had been her fault. She had been unable to stop blaming herself for years.

Today, as she again faced that north-west boundary where the ghost of Daniel Nicholson still hovered, buffeted by the wind that hinted at more snow, she spoke aloud: 'I have to stop blaming myself sometime, Daniel. I'm no longer going to worry about what you knew or what you thought, or to ask you "Why?" Christmas is here, Danny – let this be the end. Let us be at peace. The ghosts are laid.'

Feeling a little self-conscious, she kissed the palm of her hand and blew the kiss into the sky. She tucked her chilled hand back into her pocket and hunched her neck into the collar of her coat, then picked her way back across the field, stamping her heel onto a plate of ice, her eyes glimmering with enjoyment at the splintering crunch.

There was a wood-burning stove, its metal feet resting on cold floor tiles that were suitable for a Mediterranean summer. The living-room of the apartment was hazy and scented with wood-smoke, and an opened bottle of red Languedoc wine was warming near the fire. They had agreed to have a simple Christmas and not to buy each other presents.

'I don't yet know what you like,' Kees said. 'A present must be something that is perfect and not to be discarded. Next year we will be sure.'

Lisa had already observed that he travelled light, with few clothes or unnecessary possessions.

Yesterday morning, despite the cold, she and Kees had sat outside a café and drunk coffee and schnapps. They had sat side by side, facing the square, and Kees had put his arm around her shoulders.

'If we lived here we could learn to ski,' Kees had said, and they had laughed and become excited, planning how they could both work here at the university. Kees was already collaborating with a team in Astrophysics and Lisa's expertise would be relevant to the Mathematical Physics department.

A black cat had approached them cautiously on delicately-lifted feet and Kees had bent down, holding out his hand to encourage it. It had sniffed at his fingers, its whiskers stiff and white, and had then leapt lightly onto his lap, and had at once curled up with its tail around itself, as though this was its normal place to rest.

Lisa had stroked its soft head and it had stared at her consideringly then closed its eyes. Its sides had vibrated as it purred.

'We could have a cat,' she had said, surprising herself, and suddenly that was what she had wanted more than anything, to live with Kees and share a cat.

'Better to have cats than babies,' he had said, and she had known this was a critical moment.

'Yes. Altogether much simpler. You can't leave babies with the neighbours when you go ski-ing.' She had kept her voice light as she looked at him, her eyes almost level with his, and he had nodded.

Now, she lay on the pale sofa, her head resting against his side, feeling the heat from the open doors of the stove. Kees, bare-armed in tee-shirt and bare-foot, hunched forward staring into the screen of his laptop on the low table in front of him. They had been talking about their research, sparking new ideas, talking fast, in bursts punctuated with pauses for thought.

Sometimes Kees had not been able to find the English words and they had hunted, trying for synonyms in English and French and German.

Lisa swung herself upright. 'This is such a perfect Christmas Day. And I'd better call my family to wish them happy Christmas. I want to tell my mother about the lavender fields, she'd like that. They'll have finished lunch by now, and my niece and nephew will be playing with whatever new gadgets they've got, Dad'll be snoozing—'

'"Snoozing"?'

'Half-asleep. And Mum will probably be helping Suzanna clear away the plates. They'll have Christmas cake and a cup of tea and probably a brandy in an hour or two. There'll be a film, like "Wallace and Gromit" on television...'

Kees looked at her. 'I think perhaps you do miss it though?'

She frowned, a little sadly. 'This is the first time I haven't been with any of them at Christmas, and talking about it made me miss them – just for a moment. But in reality, Suzie and I would have made each other unhappy.'

'Perhaps if you belong to me and not your parents, she will be happier?'

She saw that he was quite serious and she hoped she understood what he was asking, indirectly, because it was so very important to get the answer right. 'Belong?'

'Do you think you would be able to belong to me or would that be too hard for a very independent person like yourself?'

'I think you must belong to me, too. It must be equal on both sides.'

'We will be very equal. We will share.'

'I think we'd better have two cats, then.'

'They must be the same sex. No babies!'

Tony had made coloured paper-chains and fixed them around the kitchen and the dining-room, where they hung in loops or were draped where they had come unstuck and fallen.

Madeleine opened the Aga door and she and Ruth together lifted out the heavy tray that brimmed with hot fat: the goose shone brown and crisp on top of its rack. Ruth held the bird back with a fork while Madeleine tilted the tray and tipped excess fat into a bowl.

The pudding-bowl bumped in its saucepan of simmering water, potatoes and parsnips were roasting, carrots and sprouts were prepared ready for last-minute cooking in the steamer.

'Shall I shake the bottle first?' Tony asked and the two women shrieked 'No!' together, as he twisted the wires on the bottle of champagne. He poured three glasses and handed them round.

'Happy Christmas, everyone! And thank you, Madeleine.' He and Ruth kissed each other and hugged Madeleine.

'Madeleine, I've left your present outside – will you come out and see it now, before it gets dark? It's in the yard, you don't have to go far.'

'What on earth can it be? Is it alive?' Madeleine chuckled with anticipation.

'You know Tony, anything is possible.'

The dogs in the pound whined, and rattled the wire-netting with their paws, wanting to join in the activity.

Tony was wearing a headband with two tinsel stars shimmering on wobbly stalks, and he posed by the sandstone mounting block, against which a shiny indeterminate object was propped. As Madeleine approached he swept aside the foil sack to reveal a stone cross about two feet high: unmistakeably a gravestone.

'Oh!' She stopped, fearful, and looked at Ruth, but Ruth was smiling. 'It's okay, he doesn't know a thing,' she whispered, then said aloud, 'You have to come and read what he's written on it.'

The stone was dark Blencathra slate, polished so that it gleamed in the grey light of late afternoon. At the centre of the cross, Tony had engraved the name 'Bob'.

'I thought it'd look better than that old lump of sandstone,' he said. 'And I gather the old dog was a bit of a favourite. I'll take it across to the grave and put it up for you tomorrow.'

Madeleine ran her finger across the letters, feeling their clean sharp edges. She began to laugh. She laughed so hard that tears streamed from her eyes and she had to hold onto Tony's shoulder. He stared at her, bewildered, and she gripped him tightly so that he winced. 'It's the best present you could have given me. If you knew how I hated that stinking little dog... May he now rest in peace!'

In the distance the telephone was ringing. Ruth rushed inside to get it and as Tony and Madeleine noisily re-entered the brightly-coloured steamy kitchen, she was shouting, 'Who?... Oh, *Lisa*! Hallo... yes... happy Christmas. Yes... you sound very merry too...'

THIRTY-TWO
March came in like a lion, went out like a lamb:
Ruth Kowslowski

"Pray, George, have you got five guineas? Because if you have, and will lend it to me, you shall go halves."

"Halves in what?" (asked George Nicol of the Strand, bookseller to King George III – perhaps anticipating something good to eat or drink).

John Hunter, FRS, replied, "Why, halves in a magnificent tiger which is now dying in Castle Street."

Is half a tiger better than half a leopard? John Hunter had two live leopards in his menagerie at his Earl's Court house and when dogs attacked them, Hunter ran into the yard, "laid hold of them and carried them back to their den". When he later thought about "the risk of his own situation, he was so much agitated that he was in danger of fainting". Yet he was happy to "wrestle in play" the "beautiful small bull" that Queen Charlotte gave him in return for the gift of twenty-eight prepared animal specimens for the Royal Observatory at Kew.

Unusual animals and humans came to him from all around the globe. A tapir, a llama, a black swan and a giant kangaroo, and the 'stuffed skin' of a fine male giraffe, the first of its kind to be seen in England, were in his museum. The Giant O'Brien, and the skeleton of "Mr Jeffs, aged 39" were Hunter's, too. The "corpse of a fine Sierra Leone Cat, the inside of which is at your service" was a present, ready for macerating in the Earl's Court copper kettles, from Sir Joseph Banks.

Civet cats and servals, tigers, leopards and a lion's skull – but Hunter didn't have a winged cat. Of the two or three taxidermal specimens, one had been exhibited live in a circus in the nineteenth century and there are reports of winged cats well before and since. Some are merely ungroomed cats with wings of matted hair, some have an unusual mutation that makes their skin hang in flaps, others are fakes. The skeleton of one winged cat has two bony protrusions from its shoulders, but is most likely the survivor of conjoined kittens, Siamese twins not Siamese cats.

Cats, unlike dogs, are not Man's best friend, but are still kept as pets and companion animals. Mummified cats have been found in Egyptian tombs, preserved and wrapped and buried with their owners. Pet dogs, too, dunked in resin and oil before being wrapped in linen bandages. Dead cats, embalmed, were presented to the Egyptian goddess Bastet and the gods and goddesses received offerings of embalmed falcons, baboons, lizards, beetles and fish. Rams and bulls, the Apis bulls of Memphis, were entombed in sarcophagi. Imagine the number of humans who were employed to enable visitors to buy godly protection, a society of embalmers, stone-cutters, craftsmen of many kinds, and surely farmers, hunters and zoo-keepers, too. An estimated 1.5 million mummified ibises were sealed in pottery jars! A kind of genocide, a massive slaughter of the transiently living in favour of the eternal after-life.

Unlike an Egyptian ibis, Rosalie Chichester's pet blue-headed parrot was allowed to live for more than 46 years. Polly flew around the rooms at Arlington Court in Devon, and was immortalised standing on but not nailed to a perch in a water-colour painted by her mistress (or perhaps his, it's not easy to sex a parrot). Pythons know that "the Norwegian Blue parrot prefers kippin' on its back." The kippin' ex-parrot, deceased, and not embalmed, was buried in 1919 beneath a granite slab in the garden.

The final resting-place of Theo, Rachel Ruysch's pet dog, is no longer known, perhaps he was dumped in a seventeenth-century precursor of a skip. The black-and-white spaniel died at the age of twelve, in 1690. Unfortunately, Rachel was not yet married to Juraien Pool, else he might have offered to paint Theo's post-humous portrait. Rachel would have liked to keep her dead pet as a *memento mori,* but her father was not going to waste his good Nantes brandy and spices on a dog, so she took the taxidermal option. If Theo couldn't be embalmed, he would be skinned. The maid could forget the family washing for a day or two, and Theo's body would be macerated in the copper; his soft furry skin would then be wrapped around his skeleton and padded out with straw.

Anna Ruysch, aged twenty-four, was bored with still-life paintings, and had been practising painting woodland scenes with the help of some animals – lizards, frogs and snails – borrowed from "Schnuffelaer" van Shrieck's vivarium. She painted a sylvan backdrop for Theo's stiffly-posed and static body. This was probably the earliest example of a painted diorama. When the young Peter the Great came to live in Amsterdam in 1697, he was greatly taken with the display and on his return in 1717 he asked Dr Ruysch if he might see it again, and purchase it for St Petersburg. But sadly, mites and other insects had played havoc with poor old Theo's skin, and he had long since been thrown away.

Some of the earliest dioramas were created by the American William T Hornaday. In 1879 he "returned from a collecting trip to the East Indies, having in mind numerous designs for groups of mammals", and out of this grew his preparations of orang-utans, fighting, feeding, playing, and "arranged as to represent an actual section of the top of a Bornean forest", complete with trees and vegetation. The Buffalo Group followed, with a backdrop of sky and hilly ranges, and the museum revolution towards the use of "habitat groups" was in place. Carl Ethan Akely, a self-taught taxidermist, was nearly killed by a charging bull elephant in 1909, and killed a leopard with his bare hands. As a taxidermist, and subsequently conservationist, working for the Chicago Museum, he visited Africa several times. In 1921 he went to Rwanda to collect gorillas and from then onwards fought for their protection and established a gorilla reserve. He died of fever there in 1926 and is buried at the site featured in his famous mountain gorilla diorama. The gorillas now face extinction and soon will live on only in zoos, and in memories as taxidermal specimens in museums.

A British diorama that embodied a memorial to 2001 showed an apocalyptic landscape of black smoke and vermilion flames. The taxidermal specimen in front of it was a small, black-headed Suffolk lamb, his head and body turned to face the smouldering pyre.

A few years later, when the Suffolk and Herdwick and Swaledale tups returned and grew in all their splendour to re-populate the land, the time of mourning had passed. Larry the Lamb was wrapped in linen bandages and dedicated to the ram-headed god Amun, with a prayer that pestilence would never again fall upon the land. Or something like that, anyway.

And he was buried next to Bob, the representative on earth of the jackal-headed god, Anubis, who presides over the embalming of the dead.

Bibliography

(This is just a selection – for additional information see the relevant pages on www.annlingard.com)

Taxidermy, embalming, body preservation and anatomical models:

S.T. Asma, 2001. *Drama in diorama*, in *Stuffed animals and pickled heads: the culture and evolution of natural history museums*. Oxford University Press.

Harold J. Cook, 2007. *Matters of Exchange: Commerce, Medicine and Science, in the Dutch Golden Age*. Yale University Press, Newhaven, pp. 271-276.

J. Dobson, 1953. Some early 18th century experiments in embalming. *Journal of History of Medicine and Allied Science* 8, 431-441

M. Kemp and M. Wallace, 2000. *Spectacular bodies: the art and science of the human body from Leonardo to now*. Catalogue of the exhibition at the Hayward Gallery, London, 2000-2001. Hayward Gallery Publishing.

G. Worden, 2002. *Mûtter Museum of the College of Physicians of Philadelphia*. Blast Books, New York.

The Ruysch family

J.V. Hansen, 1996. Resurrecting Death: anatomical art in the cabinet of Dr Frederik Ruysch. *Art Bulletin*, 78, 663-679

A.M. Luyendijk-Elshout, 1970. Death Enlightened. *JAMA*, 212, 121-126

R. Wolff Purcell & S.J. Gould, 1992. *A Dutch Treat: Peter the Great and Frederik Ruysch*, in *Finders, Keepers: eight collectors*. Hutchinson, London.

Frederik Ruysch, 1737. *Opera Omni* (the *Thesauri Anatomici*) (held in the Bodleian Library, Oxford)

John and William Hunter
J. Bailey, 1893. *Catalogue of the collection of Hunterian relics exhibited at the Royal College of Surgeons of England on Wednesday July 5th 1893*. Taylor & Francis, London.

W.F. Bynum & R. Porter, (eds) 1985. *William Hunter and the 18th century medical world*. Cambridge University Press.

A.T. Marchall & J.A.E. Burton, 1962. *Glasgow Royal Infirmary's catalogue of the pathological preparations of William Hunter*. Glasgow University Press.

J.F. Palmer, 1835. *The works of John Hunter*. Longman *et al*, London.

Other
A. Day, 2004. *To bid them farewell: a foot-and-mouth diary*. Hayloft Press, UK

M. Senechal, 1990. *Crystalline symmetries*. Adam Hilger

D. Schattscheider, 1990. *M.C. Escher, Visions of Symmetry*. WH Freeman, New York.